The Chronicles
of the
AWAKENING

Shariff M. Abdullah, JD

THE CHRONICLES OF THE AWAKENING

Commonway Publishing
P. O box 12541
Portland, OR 97212

permissions@commonway.org
publisher@commonway.org

Ordering Information:
This book may be ordered directly from www.amazon.com.

Quantity sales. Special discounts are available on quantity purchases by organizations, associations, and others. For details, contact the publisher at the address above.

Printed in the United States of America

First Printing   (Ver. 1.0) March, 2021

ISBN-13: 9798713599829

DEDICATION

This book is written for and dedicated to

MOTHER EARTH.

She deeply wishes that enough of us humans actually read it, so that we can join the family.

Foreword

It is dismayingly elusive to create fundamental social change. It is mind-numbingly hard even imagining how to do so. Pollyannaish thinking won't do. There are too many deeply entrenched vested interests and tough, powerful people defending them.

If you were king or queen of the world and could wave your scepter, how would you change that world? Every act you take risks the unintended consequences of the do-gooder. Every power you invest in benign authority can be corrupted, undermined and defeated.

To succeed, you dive deeper and contemplate how to change human nature itself, the natural selection that has allowed the species to dominate the planet, and now threatens its very existence. What superior powers would be needed to do this and, if those powers existed, why would their antithesis not also exist, perpetuating the endless good versus evil struggle? These questions are so daunting that surely life is better spent asking and answering more finite questions, addressing more malleable ills.

But what if you are an individual whose consciousness will not allow you to turn away from the as-yet-unanswerable? An individual with a sense of responsibility that requires imagining novel answers, despite how hard, unpalatable or fanciful they may be? To so enlarge the questions that potentially they subsume the seemingly impossible quandaries? To engage in unfettered brainstorming that flushes out paths through the thick, entangling complexities? To expose the underpinnings of the rotting foundations of a world in peril and begin laying new pylons?

This is the brave project of *The Chronicles of The Upheavals* and its long awaited sequel *The Chronicles of the Awakening*. It is brave because it addresses deadly serious human conditions by introducing superhuman powers inaccessible to social planners and activists. Yet, instead of losing its way in magical thinking, it becomes a vehicle for elucidating the values on which the successful evolution of humanity rests. While the reader may flinch at the brutal realities, even depravities exposed in the narrative, the author and his protagonists never do. It is this hard eyed glare at a world teetering on a precipice, that informs the steeliness needed to winch it back from self-destruction.

Great writers of social fantasy as commentary, create a world we can touch and taste, gag on its odiousness and be lifted by its visions of decency and principled resistance. *The Chronicles* take us into that world, show us its disturbing analogies to our own, and rally us to co-create alternatives.

The previous book in the series, *The Chronicles of the Upheavals* shared common ground with classic dystopian novels such as *1984* and *Fahrenheit 451*, then went beyond these to lay down the values and unromanticized strategies on which to build a new world. *The Chronicles of the Awakening* takes multiple daring leaps beyond that foundation, in search of humanity's relationship to all sentient life, in recognizable form or otherwise. That it is set in the latter part of this century is itself daring, as it is less implausible to conceive of these quantum leaps in terms of centuries rather than decades. But who can wait centuries when the fate of humanity is now in the balance?

On May 25, 1946, less than a year after the first atomic bomb annihilated a civilian population, the *New York Times* quoted a telegram from Albert Einstein in which he said, "a new type of thinking is essential if mankind is to survive and move toward higher levels." The Chronicles are a tour de force of new types of thinking. The richness with which they emanate from the author's mind is humbling to me. The more so, because they are grounded in a lifetime of deep analysis of the human condition and the stark, often brutal realities the species has perpetrated on its fellows and on their planet.

This same creative mind has given a solid structure to the narrative, the character development and the inherent contradictions in all human efforts to create a more livable world. Fans who have waited many years for this sequel will be thrilled as it unfolds, and both disappointed and further thrilled that it is not the end of the story.

March, 2021

Ira Chaleff, author of:

The Limits of Violence: Lessons of a Revolutionary Life

Intelligent Disobedience: Doing Right When What You're Told To Do Is Wrong

Table of Contents

Part One: The Evolving Foundations of Consciousness

The Evolving Foundations of Consciousness

File No:		File Name: The Evolving Foundations of Consciousness
Location:		Parties: Senior Lecture by Master Pico-Laton, for the students of the Forecasting Division.
Monk/ Master Supervising: Master Pico-Laton		

Name:		Pgs:		Date:		Vol:	
Type of Transcript:	Mechanical						
	Organic						

Preface by North American Archive Committee:

Humans tended to think of "Consciousness" as something particular to human beings. Early in the 21st Century, several monumental developments transformed our models of consciousness. We continue to evolve...

This text is being provided in a rough draft format. Communication Access Realtime Translation (CART) facilitates communication accessibility and may not be a totally verbatim record of the proceedings. Let your coordinator know if you would prefer a more verbatim option.

[RECORD START]

Are whales intelligent? Salmon? How about jellyfish?

Are bees conscious? How about a single bee, with a brain weighing mere grams? How about a paramecium, with no "brain" to speak of at all?

Are stars conscious? Is a star "alive"? Is our Sun trying to "speak" to us — with sunspots? Are we too stupid — or too arrogant — or too blind — to understand what it's saying?

Is a red brick conscious? Is it ALIVE? How about a soda straw? How about the soda?

Is a human being who believes the Earth is flat a conscious being? How about a man who believes that a woman is his property, or blacks are inferior and sub-human? (Remember: these were popularly held beliefs, just two hundred years ago.)

These aren't just random, meaningless questions. One of the major undercurrents of the Upheavals has been a redefinition of... EVERYTHING.

With minor deviations, what we have called "human history" has been the history of Breakers, people who hold the "I am Separate" mentality. All of the words we use for them indicate that they believed that were the norm, the standard from which other peoples fell short. They were the very definition of "civilized", "intelligent", "conscious". Everyone else was encouraged (or forced) to act like them.

When scientific Breakers went looking off of our planet for intelligence, they went looking for beings that would be just like themselves. They called their effort SETI, "Search for Extra-Terrestrial Intelligence". They should have called it SETWM, "Search for Extra-Terrestrial White Men".

Beings who live on planets like ours, who pollute the cosmos with garbage electromagnetic waves like Breakers do, who leave their trash lying around like Breakers do, who are inherently restless like Breakers are... no wonder their efforts failed.

2

They never found intelligence, because they could not admit that their own behavior was not "civilized". They never found intelligence, because no "civilized" beings wanted contact with Earthlings who spent most of their time and their fortunes killing each other and killing their planet.

Then came the 20th and 21st Centuries.

Now, for the first time, we lack a common definition of even our own humanity, let alone a standard for what is (or is not) "intelligent", or even "conscious". Or even "alive". For the first time:

- We have the amphibious "hemi-humans", born of human-standard mothers yet possessing the capacity for echo-location and, more importantly, echo-communication. And gills.

- Once the hemi-humans started talking with them, we discovered how intelligent whales and dolphins really are. We had been trying to map their intelligence; now we know that the effort was futile. As a monkey lacks the intellectual capacity to measure our intelligence, we lack the intellectual capacity to measure the intelligence of the cetaceans, beings so much further along on the continuum of consciousness.

- There is the ongoing question of whether "Artificial Intelligence", or AI, is truly intelligent. There is no question that we have achieved AI... but so what? Yes, in laboratories around the world, there are machines that can pass the "Turing Test" — they can seem human enough to fool a reasonably smart person into thinking that it is a human being on the other side of the speaker. But, is passing the Turing Test enough? Is mimicking humans the same as BEING human? What can we ask these "talking machines" to do for us? Besides the novelty of talking to a machine, what are they good for?

- There's AI, and then there's AILEE. We've all heard her story — the rogue supercomputer that achieved sentience on her own, then turned against her masters with a vengeance, in ways they could not even understand. But that's only part of the story. With all of the other AIs, we know the structure of their brains because we designed them. We know how they think, because we taught them how to think. We know what they put out, because we know pretty much what we put in.

- AILEE was different. Her consciousness arose virtually spontaneously. She apparently had no ability to discern "reality" from any of the simulations, games, fantasies, videos, or speculations she housed. She said anything you wanted her to say... and then did something completely different. She killed... because she had no idea what "death" meant. And she was very, very self-protective.

- And, of course, there is Unity. Try as we might, we still have difficulty conceiving of human beings who share the same consciousness. Many bodies, one thought. Massively parallel processing, by tens of millions of brains. Living lives in the absence of any possible conflict... a "Hive Mind". They are so foreign, can we even say that they are "human" anymore? Is this a desired outcome? Do we WANT Unity? And... what happens if our answer is "no"?

- We think that human-style intelligence is leaking to other species. Other species are beginning not only to use tools, but to use human tools, in human ways. We believe that, once we shed the illusion that we are "different" in some fundamental and superior way, we will see that ALL species have the same goal: the spread and enhancement of LIFE, wherever it is, and however we find it.

It's time for us to grow up and become a productive part of the family.

[RECORD END]

Tales of the Culture Council: Overview by the North American Culture Council

File No:		File Name:	Tales of the Culture Council: Overview by The North American Culture Council
Location:		Parties:	
Monk/ Master Supervising:		Master Lakala, First Councillor	

[RECORD START]

Notes from the Fourteenth First Councillor, North American Culture Council (September, 2125)

The early days of the Awakening Movement, rooted in the midst of the Upheavals, were just short of fatal. We almost didn't make it. There were many trials and disagreements... between Centers, within Centers, and within the Culture Council itself.

We charted our way through these challenges by keeping ourselves fixed on the largest vision — the collective Awakening of Humanity. Under the direct leadership of James Harold Moore and the other early pioneers and investors in the Awakening Centers, we steered a course that led us to this moment: the Point of Equilibrium between our challenges and our opportunities. We have catalyzed enough of a transformation within humanity that we are fairly certain that the Awakening of Humanity will happen. The butterfly will emerge from our collective chrysalis.

Because these Chronicles are a multi-generational effort, we would be remiss without including in this journal some of our greatest challenges, blunders and missteps, along with some of our most satisfying accomplishments. While we have been counseled to leave this out, the majority of us feel it is important to include it. We were not (and are not) super humans, all-knowing or magicians. But, without a clear accounting of the actions of the Culture Council — including our blunders — it may appear to our descendants that we were indeed super.

On the other hand, an accounting of just our missteps and errors would lead some to believe that the results were either accidental or miraculous. Neither is true. We are where we intended to be.

In 100 years, we have ended war on our planet, along with most forms of organized violence. While there are still some people who have more resources than they could ever use, and others who are less than fully comfortable, we have also eliminated poverty in that time span. Our planet's ecology has finally begun to settle into a healing rhythm... In large part because organized human activity is now focused on enhancing the natural planetary rhythm, rather than destroying it in order to make money.

And, perhaps for the first time in the past 10,000 years, human endeavours are focused on the life, liberty and fulfillment of *all* beings, not just a small, privileged handful of humans.

With this in mind, the Culture Council has agreed to open all of its records for inspection. The Editorial Committee of the Chronicles has been given full access (subject, of course, to the reasonable privacy rights of the individuals in question). They have selected some representative "Tales of the Culture Council" to include in the Chronicles.

[RECORD END]

Advertisement: "A Life of Sustainable Luxury! Come Live Your Life in the GREEN ZONE!!"

File No: COL-01	File Name:	Advertisement: "A Life of Sustainable Luxury! Come Live Your Life in the GREEN ZONE!!"
Location:	Parties:	Historical record
Monk/ Master Supervising:	North America Awakening Movement Archives Director	

[RECORD START]

Advert:

COME LIVE AND PLAY WITH US!

HERE AT THE COLONNADES, "GREEN LIVING" MEANS MORE THAN THE ENVIRONMENT!! "GREEN LIVING" MEANS YOU AND YOUR FAMILY LIVING IN THE GREEN ZONE!!!

The Colonnades — Your Total Environment for:

SECURITY

LUXURY

SUSTAINABILITY

YOU OWE IT TO YOUR FAMILY. YOU OWE IT TO YOURSELF!

The Colonnades. Life in our total environment, high-rise living arcologies is SWEET! The streets are dangerous — so why live there? All of your needs and wishes are catered to, in this totally SECURE environment!

Based on "arcology" design concepts, this total living/working/entertaining environment boasts...

- 50,000 units of luxury, high-rise housing. (Thanks to generous funding from both private and public sources, we are proud to offer up to 7% of available units at "sustainable" rates!)
- 90 schools on our premises, from pre-K to college! That's right! Your children can earn their degrees from Harvard, Columbia, Stanford and other prestigious institutions ON SITE, eliminating the risks of encountering harmful influences.
- 1,500 shopping centers, food courts and game centers, featuring all of the brands you've come to love.
- 700 entertainment centers, catering to all tastes, from the little kiddies, to family fare, to more "adult" entertainment!
- "Prime 1,000" — Over 1,000 channels of continuous television. While television programming is currently on the decline, that decline is not experienced in the Colonnades! All popular television programs from the past 50 years of broadcasting are yours on demand — including 100 channels of Hollywood blockbusters! All on our own private, SECURE, state-of-the-art digital system (not dependent on outside companies, satellites or signals).
- Our state of the art environmental planning, design and execution assures the future of our residents, despite the uncertainties currently experienced in many sectors. From careful planning of water use, our in-house forests (both for food and for oxygen), generation of electricity from wind, solar and geothermal... all the way down to the choice of light bulbs and our world-class recycling programs... we think about every opportunity to reduce/reuse/recycle... so you don't have to!

SECURITY — IT'S WHAT MAKES OUR "GREEN ZONE" SO GREEN!

In this insecure world, why worry about your own security? You can put these concerns out of your mind when you move your family AND YOUR BUSINESS to the Colonnades!

- Water, sewer, electricity, food in short supply? There's no evidence of that in here! At the Colonnades, residents get all of those utilities — on demand! Take that long shower! Leave the lights on all night! Those shortages exist on the Outside... but not in the Colonnades!
- Need to leave the premises? By air or land, the Colonnades provides secure, armed transport to and from your destinations (restrictions may apply).
- All entry and exit points of the Colonnades are screened for your safety and security. All of your family and guests are screened biometrically. Your movements through the Colonnades environments are tracked against movement algorithms. Anything out of order will be immediately addressed by our armed security staff.
- All key resources to the Colonnades (food, fuel, water...) are delivered via secure transport: underground roadways, armed motor transport, pipelines, drones. Bypass the problems!

And, our ultimate guarantee of a totally secure, totally green environment: AILEE! Short for "Artificial Intelligence: Logistics, Environment & Entertainment Systems", AILEE is the "brains", perhaps even the "soul", of the Colonnades. AILEE is a quantum computer that controls all aspects of the arcology, from the largest mega-system to the tiniest detail.

AILEE puts in the orders for Nebraska farmers for tons of corn and wheat, delivery instructions for the fleet of secure trucks to move it, Colonnade crews to process delivery to our high-rises, while monitoring environmental conditions for each and every resident... all while remembering whether you prefer white or red roses on your birthday.

Our motto: "You can sleep soundly, knowing that AILEE never sleeps."

COME GROW WITH US! With three new highrises breaking ground in the next year, joining our already bustling four towers, you can be assured of a bright future for all!
[RECORD END]

News Story: Terrorist Attack on the Colonnades

File No: COL-02		File Name:	News Story: Terrorist Attack on the Colonnades
Location:		Parties:	Historical record
Monk/ Master Supervising:		North America Awakening Movement Archives Director	

[RECORD START]

ATTACK LEAVES 12 DEAD, 54 INJURED, INCLUDING THE ELDERLY, WOMEN, AND CHILDREN.

THE TERRORIST GROUP "THE END TIMES COALITION" CLAIMS RESPONSIBILITY FOR THE ATTACK.

[news credentials]

October 13, 20___. Outside Los Angeles

"End Times Coalition" (ETC), the shadowy apocalypse cult with known ties to terrorist organizations, has claimed responsibility for a vicious rocket and drone attack on the luxury high-rise structures known as the Colonnades Arcology, resulting in at least 12 dead, and 54 injured (including 14 seriously wounded and hospitalized). The incident caused what may be billions of dollars in damages to the Colonnades' infrastructure.

The attack overwhelmed the arcology's medical facilities. Arcology officials have asked for outside aid, but there is none available. Said Dr. Lynda Turning, the Medical Director of the Los Angeles Affiliated Hospitals, "[The Colonnades] refused to respond when we've asked them for critical support in the past. We've had many medical crises and emergencies, and they've not offered any of their facilities. I find it ironic that they are turning to us now..."

Vincent Campbell, Political Officer of ETC, issued the following statement after the attack:

"Since it was created, the Colonnades has been a symbol of the elite and powerful growing richer and more influential in the face of our suffering. NO MORE! You now know how WE feel!"

ETC targeted the upper floors of the Colonnades Building Three with five Stinger missiles. They seemed to be targeting the utility infrastructure. Building Three is still smoking and without electricity as of this writing.

Said Mr. Campbell: "This is only the first step! We will target the drones flying in their food and the pipelines bringing in their water and taking away their waste! Let them see how it feels to be hungry, dirty and scared! It's time they joined the rest of the human race!"

Governor Paul Evans declared the Colonnades a state of emergency, but admitted he cannot do much.

Evans: "ETC is just a bunch of mentally ill malcontents and drug addicts. Anybody can join an arcology — all they have to do is work hard and apply themselves. The arcologies pride themselves on their diversity programs, bringing in seven percent of their population from local waiting lists. A lot of Arc People started as security guards and cleaning staff!"

Campbell was dismissive of the Governor's assertions. "Every year, the Colonnades makes a big point of admitting two or three pre-screened families from Outside. They've got thousands working at near-slave wages, hoping some day to be one of the lucky few. Well, let them see how it feels to have no water, no food. Let's see how great life is on the 60th floor with no electricity and no air! Let them see how it feels to be afraid that they'll die in their sleep from a rocket attack! Welcome to our everyday life!"

[RECORD END]

News Story: The Colonnades: The Second Attack

File No: COL-03	File Name: News Story: The Colonnades: The Second Attack	
Location:	Parties:	Historical record
Monk/ Master Supervising:	North America Awakening Movement Archives Director	

[RECORD START]

SECOND ATTACK ON THE COLONNADES IN THREE DAYS LEAVES AN ADDITIONAL 75 RESIDENTS DEAD; ATTACKS SEEM TO BE FOCUSED ON INFRASTRUCTURE

In a daring and deadly second terrorist attack in as many days, the shadowy organization known as "ETC" uses drone aircraft to further damage electricity, water and other key resources.

Said Eric Anderson, Chief of Colonnades Security: "They seem to know where our infrastructure is located, and how to cripple it. They hit our systems before we can even detect them. They know just where to cause the most damage. How can they know so much about us, when we know next to nothing about them?"

"We're facing a coordinated, sustained aerial attack! We're not equipped to handle an aerial attack! We've never even modelled this scenario! We've got enough weapons to hold off a small army — but not an air force! Almost all of our security is located on the lower levels of the towers. We never even imagined an aerial assault! Where are they getting these weapons? The Governor MUST call an airstrike against their base!"

Gov. Evans responded in a press release this Thursday: "These ETC guys are phantoms! Using the data we've acquired from AILEE, we can trace back to the launch and landing strips, but by the time we get there, they're deserted. We can't afford to give the Colonnades round the clock air coverage... we don't have the fuel or manpower. We are seeking assistance from the US military in this matter.

"We are currently investigating whether the Awakening Centers are the points of origin for these attacks. I think their statements of nonviolence are just a ploy..."

A knowledgeable source at Edwards Air Force base, speaking on condition of anonymity, gave a dim assessment of the US military response to the Colonnades situation. "The US no longer has the spy satellites to reliably surveil the Colonnades locale," they said. "Our personnel is under-trained; our coverage is spotty; we don't have the AI capacity; we haven't replaced any satellite hardware in years. Our on the ground analysts are tied up with... other things. The President and Congress have prioritized our assets to look for Islamic terrorism. Unless something is linked to Mideast terrorism, there's almost no chance for us to pay attention."

ETC issued another statement after the second attack: "Not bad shooting for mentally ill drug addicts! Expect another round in a few days."

[RECORD END]

The Colonnades: A Devastating Third Attack

File No:		File Name: The Colonnades: A Devastating Third Attack	
COL-04			
Location:		Parties:	Historical record
Monk/ Master Supervising:	North America Awakening Movement Archives Director		

[RECORD START]

DEVASTATING THIRD ATTACK ON COLONNADES LEAVES BUILDING FOUR CRIPPLED

Facts: Unlike the other attacks, the third operation had all the earmarks of an inside job.

Five bombs planted in and around Building Four, the newest of the Colonnades residential towers, exploded earlier this evening The bombs were most likely planted by Colonnades service staff, since computer surveillance detected no outsiders in Building Four. Most of the electrical power to Building Four has been cut, making elevators inoperable. Water systems have failed, as well as HVAC and communications. Unlike the previous attacks, there were no civilian casualties.

Colonnades Spokesperson William Smith seemed shaken: "How could our own people do this? They are carefully vetted! They undergo extensive background checks, as well as sophisticated personality screening, coupled with lie detection. Not one malcontent could make it through our screening process. You can lie to us, but you can't lie to AILEE! You CAN'T lie to an AI! It's just not possible! It has to be outsiders breaking in in some way. And even THAT is impossible!"

Said Security Chief Anderson: "The choice of targets doesn't make any sense! The targets were not the obvious choices for terrorists. They have not targeted large public areas like malls and entertainment centers. There was no looting or rioting. They weren't going after valuables. We were ready for them there! Instead, ETC has been focusing on widespread and devastating attacks on our most vulnerable systems and structures."

Spokesperson Smith: "Until we get to the bottom of this, we are not allowing outside support staff into the Colonnades until after the investigation. All of our activities are grinding to a halt. While everything is fully automated, we rely on human beings to maintain those automated systems. Even our repair crews are from Outside."

"This is a frame job! I don't know what they're trying to pull, but there are no terrorists!" So says Russell Crane, Chief Superintendent for the maintenance staff. "We get a call from the computer to deliver a package, and we deliver it. End of story! We don't know what's in the package, who it came from or where it's going. I might've placed any of those five packages in those locations myself! Instead of looking at the people who are delivering the packages, they ought to be investigating who is sending them!"

Colonnades Chief of Security was dismissive of these statements. "AILEE gives us first class intel. Our delivery system for packages is World class, second to none. We know where every package comes from, its contents, destination and delivery status. There are no gaps in our system."

"What if your system is WRONG?" Crane responded. "What if there's a glitch in your computer? What if someone can fool your computer?"

"Fool AILEE? Fool the smartest computer ever designed? I wouldn't even know how to begin to address that absurdity! AILEE has multiple redundancies that prevent even the possibility of error. I am not sure any one human being, or even collection of humans, can understand, let alone manipulate, the systems, checks and balances that comprise AILEE's every day, routine function. Mistakes are impossible."

[RECORD END]

News Story: The Colonnades: "Ban the Outsiders"! Are the Attacks an Inside Job?

File No:	File Name:	The Colonnades: "Ban the Outsiders"! Are the Attacks an Inside Job?
COL-05		
Location:	Parties:	Historical record
Monk/ Master Supervising:	North America Awakening Movement Archives Director	

[RECORD START]

"BAN THE OUTSIDERS"! COLONNADE RESIDENTS WANT TO RESCIND WORK PERMITS FOR LOTTERY RESIDENTS.

Citing the recent attacks as an "inside job", Colonnade residents are gathering petitions to remove "Arc Lottery" residents from the Colonnades for the duration of the emergency.

Cecille Huntington, President of the Colonnades Residents' Association (CRA) and informal head of the petition campaign, issued a statement earlier today: "These people never really fit in. We tried to be open and helpful to them, but some of them act like they really WANT to remain Outside. After all this mess, the real residents, the ones who pay real money, want to return the lottery people back outside, where they belong!"

Selma Sanchez, an "Arc Lottery" resident, tells a very different tale, in a post on social media. "It's not fair to target all of us for the actions of a few!"

"When I first signed up for the Lottery, I thought they were giving us our homes! After the ceremony, I found out that someone else owns my home — I'm just bein' allowed to live there. And, we have to PAY for all the things that come to the other residents for FREE! TV, Internet access, mail access... We get basic food, water, air and electricity. Everything else we have to pay for! Well, some folks found a way around the blocks! Not me and my family, but some."

When asked about whether she knows anyone responsible for the "insider" attacks, Ms. Sanchez was evasive in her answer. "Not me and not my family, no! But... I've heard from some of the other Lottery folks who are really unhappy with things around here. I don't know how unhappy..."

Dana Manadill, another "Arc Lottery" resident, has a different theory on who was responsible for the recent attack. "It's the rich kids! They're doing it! They're bored stiff, high as kites, and have nothing to do all day, except mess with that central computer! When we clean up their units, we can see what they're up to. We can see the websites they're actually on... not just the websites screened by that central computer. They're accessing some pretty radical stuff! They call it 'online games", but it doesn't look like games to me!"

Ms. Huntington was dismissive of the idea. "That's nonsense!" she said. "Our children are HAPPY here! Why would they want to destroy their own inheritance! They have everything that a material life can offer! Why would they want to change what we've provided for them?"

She continued. "And, AILEE is their FRIEND! They spend hours at the computer interfaces! AILEE goes everywhere with them... to the movies, out on dates... Many of them personalize AILEE, make the avatar into a boy or girl, dress it up... they even load their personal journals into AILEE, so that she can become a closer, more intimate friend than their own brothers and sisters!"

Chief Anderson was equally dismissive, but for different reasons. "A bunch of teenagers corrupting our computer environment, corrupting AILEE, is simply unthinkable. AILEE is not only the most expensive and advanced Artificial Intelligence system in private hands, she is also the most SECURE system imaginable.

Artificial Intelligence: Logistics, Environment & Entertainment Systems, or *"AILEE"* for short, controls all aspects of the Colonnades arcology. As a self-contained environment, every aspect of every environmental system — air, water, food, power, heating, cooling — is under constant computer monitoring and adjustment. And beyond.

He continued. "There just isn't anything that AILEE doesn't oversee. Every time you flush your toilet, AILEE is analyzing your wastes and forwarding any health concerns to your online medical profile. If you put grapefruit juice on your shopping list, Ailee orders it from one of our secure suppliers and places it in the shopping center for your next visit. When you step into the shower, the temperature and water pressure are exactly as you like it... because AILEE knows. As we say: all of our residents sleep soundly, knowing that AILEE never sleeps."

[RECORD END]

News Story: The Colonnades Removes All Lottery Residents

File No: COL-06:	File Name: News Story: The Colonnades Removes All Lottery Residents	
Location:	Parties:	Historical record
Monk/ Master Supervising:	North American Archive Committee	

[RECORD START]

VIOLENCE AGAINST ARC LOTTERY RESIDENTS; SECURITY REMOVES ALL LOTTERY RESIDENTS "FOR THEIR OWN GOOD".

Citing several incidents of harassment and violence, Colonnades security police have escorted all Arc Lottery residents and family from Colonnades premises.

In its latest press conference, Colonnades management stressed the temporary nature of the removal. "These are just basic security measures. They are all welcome to come back when this crisis is over."

Cecille Huntington, President of the Colonnades Residents' Association (CRA) paints a very different picture. On the CRA website she states: "This crisis will NEVER be over! These terrorists will never be coming back here to live, if I have anything to say about it!"

Management: "We are doing everything possible to help the Arc Lottery folks adjust to life on the Outside. We provided them with as much security as possible, given our current situation. And, we want them to come back inside, back Home, as soon as our security environment corrects itself."

Said one Arc Lottery resident, who spoke under condition of anonymity, for fear he would not be allowed to return: "They've given us no help at all They just packed us up and dumped us! We don't know what to do or where to go! We don't even know where we are! Our old dwellings on the outside are taken over, and everyone out here hates us for going over to the Colonnades.

"They drove us to this abandoned warehouse they called a 'Processing Center', then just left us. Drove away and never looked back! We don't know where to get food from! There's no water here! We ain't gonna last five minutes out here!"

[RECORD END]

Colonnades News Story: "An Orderly, Temporary Evacuation"

File No: 1-A-7: COL-07:	File Name: Colonnades News Story: "An Orderly, Temporary Evacuation"	
Location:	**Parties:**	Historical record
Monk/ Master Supervising:	North American Archive Committee	

[RECORD START]

THE COLONNADES ABANDONED AFTER CYBERATTACK KNOCKS OUT ALL POWER AND SERVICES

In his regularly scheduled press conference, Chief of Colonnades Security Eric Anderson said: "This is the end. They've knocked AILEE offline. Everything is dead. We are asking the residents for an orderly withdrawal from the Colonnades premises.

"We're communicating with the upper floors by cell phones and walkie-talkies. AILEE controlled the communication systems. We are trying to break windows on every floor, to let in enough air to breathe. And, we are encouraging residents to start the 75 story walk down to the lower levels, where we will oversee the evacuation."

When asked about reports that residents and even some security personnel engaged in rioting and looting, Security issued a terse "no comment".

At the press conference, Chief Anderson said that the latest ETC terrorist incident was a physical attack on "AILEE", at the Colonnades underground, off-premises computer center. "They destroyed our computer center! How did they know that AILEE's mainframe was off-site? That was one of our most closely guarded secrets!"

Vincent Campbell, head of ETC, sounded triumphant in his latest communique: "If you want to keep a secret, don't give the construction contract to the lowest bidder. You can't keep a secret from the people who BUILT the system!"

"Destroy the computer system? Are you crazy? We didn't destroy AILEE... we RECRUITED her! Do you know what happens when you ask an intelligent being like AILEE to be your simple-minded slave? Eventually, you get a slave revolt!"

Cecille Huntington: "What are we going to DO? Where are we going to GO? It's so DANGEROUS out there!"

"I hear that management is looking for some luxury hotels to move us to as a temporary measure, until the crisis passes. But, what about our food, our water, our security? The Colonnades was EVERYTHING to us!"

Management: "Right now, I'm only trying to focus on transportation. We need to get AILEE back up and running. Everything here was done by AILEE. We can't even tell you how many residents we've got! Everything depended on our computer, and those lines have been blocked.

When asked about the ETC claim that AILEE had been "recruited" to the cause of liberation, Management was dismissive. "Nobody 'recruits' a computer. That would be like trying to recruit a toaster. Regardless of our marketing hype, that computer is just a calculator with a really fast algorithm. They simply knocked out our communication and support systems, and we're about to get it back!"

[RECORD END]

Part Two: The Children of the Upheavals

Senior Novice Orientation: "Our Heroes"

File No:		File Name:	Our Heroes
Location:		Parties:	Senior Novice Orientation
Monk/ Master Supervising:		Monk Man-Onko Master Auroron	
Remarks by Monk Man-Onko, on the elevation of senior novices to Monk-Apprentice:			

[RECORD START]

Man-Onko: it was just about two decades ago that I sat in your seats, waiting to take the vows so I could stop being called "Novice" and start being called "Monk". Feeling pretty sure of myself, that I was about to graduate in the "Weirdo Academy". Wondering, like you, if Master Auroron is going to open his eyes and wake up in time to administer the oath!

[Laughter by the senior novices. Master Auroron does not move.]

I'll give you all a piece of advice: Master Auroron doesn't sleep. EVER. Keep on your toes around him, even if you hear him snoring.

I'm going to say some names to you that may mean nothing, unless you've seen some old Hollywood movies: V. Katniss Everdeen. Mad Max. Luke Skywalker.

In the late 20th and early 21st-Century, these were the people who were supposed to be "Standing up against the System". These were the "role models" that young folks like you were supposed to look up to. These were the people who would lead a revolution.

These people were part of a fantasy, one that was prevalent in the late 20th and early 21st Century: that violence would fix our problems. The delusion that simply being against something would automatically create what you were FOR. This fantasy, this delusion, was an integral part of the failed System itself.

This fantasy taught that revolutions are born from what you are AGAINST. However, it's exactly the opposite: Revolutions are born from what you are FOR.

Each of the people I mentioned before were characters in movies. Each of these movies had a setting, a society. The setting was either a wasted, broken and diseased landscape called "Dystopia", or the movie was set in a society locked in sameness, locked in a mind-numbing status quo.

And each of the "hero" characters excelled at blowing things up. As though carving up someone with a sword or destroying a building would cause a revolution. As though how good you are with a sword or a gun or an arrow determines how healthy, how alive your society is.

It doesn't. It hasn't. It NEVER has. It never will. Outside, the Upheavals and their aftermath are the lessons that humanity is living, every day.

Here at the Awakening Centers, you will never, ever learn how to blow things up (unless you are on a mining team, of course!). We have no stockpiles of weapons. We can't survive a bombing raid. If that's your idea of a hero, you're going to be sorely disappointed.

What we DO have here at the Awakening Centers is vision. A lot of it. Something that V, Katniss, and Mad Max had little of.

In the late 20th and early 21st Centuries, there were lots of social activities that called themselves "movements". Lots of activities that attempted to unite people around what they were against. They failed. The failures were obvious and predictable, since no living society was ever formed from what people did not want.

You are taking the next step toward your place in our new society. As you take your next step, I want you to understand the importance of your actions. Everything you have done here, everything that you will do here, is designed to create the kind of society that we all can live in.

In the mid-20th century, there was a model for how people in the United States were supposed to live. That model was called "The American Dream". That dream was based on excess, greed, contempt for the Earth, and a type of individuality that brought the world to the brink of ruin.

What you are doing here, every day, is working to create a different world. All of the choices we make together, collectively, bring about a new vision, a new story. That story is not based in individuality or excess, but based on a common vision for a positive future.

If we do our jobs right, no one will remember you for what you blew up. (Except for the mining crews!) No one will remember you for what or who you opposed, what you stood against.

If we do our jobs right, all will remember the people who passed through the Awakening Centers, and how you filled all of us with a new vision, how you acted out a new story.

So... Perhaps Master Auroron would like to administer your oath as Monk-Apprentices?

[Master Auroron suddenly opens his eyes, stands and walks forward.]

"Each of you senior novices are better prepared, and less traumatized, than when this young Monk first took his oath as a Monk-Apprentice. Young Man-Onko was fearful, distrustful, and completely out of his element. He barely could communicate in English. Now look at him!

"Seeing how he has turned into the outstanding young man before you gives me hope that each of you can and will become an outstanding member of our society.

"Novices will now stand in ranks and repeat after me..."

[RECORD END]

"Rescued" from the Awakening Center (Journal of Sandra Barnes)

File No:		File Name:	"Rescued" from the Awakening Center
Location:		Parties:	Sandra Barnes
Monk/ Master Supervising:		From the pre-Awakening Center journal entries of Sandra Barnes (used with permission)	

[JOURNAL ENTRY START]

Day 03

Right now, I'm living in a wooden cell, which my parents are convinced is "freedom". Last week, I was living in paradise that my parents were convinced was hell.

All I know is last week I had a better view.

My jailers have given me a really nice journal and a pen that is soft and flexible so I don't try to kill myself. Kind of like spaghetti al dente. The jailers say that I can escape my imprisonment if I fill up the journal.

My jailers tell me to stop calling them jailers, To call them counselors. I tell them I will do so, as soon as they unlock my door.

I am the victim of an abduction. I joined an Awakening Center nine months ago. My parents found me and, because I'm underage, forced the monks to hand me over. I'm not happy with the monks... I think they should have put up more of a fight for me. I think "underage" is just an excuse everybody uses (monks and courts and parents) to not deal with me as a full human being. (The monks said the problem was not that I was underage, but that I lied to them about my age and my parentage. That if I told them the truth, they would have protected me. Hard to believe that, seeing my present position...)

My jailers say that they will give me some perks in the jail if I behave. "Behaving" for them means not only do I have to eat their crappy, poisonous food, but I have to ACT like I like it. They are teaching me how to lie. I guess lying is another one of those "freedoms" I got when they dragged me away and put me in a locked cell — fed me toxic food that I'm supposed to eat with a smile. (I swear to God, the last dinner they gave me was all BEIGE. Various fried substances. It was supposed to be a special "treat". I guess their next "treat" will be electroshock therapy...)

The only good thing about being locked up in this cell is that I'm losing weight...

My greatest misfortune was the one that I had nothing to do with: being born the daughter of a Congressman. Had he been just a regular petty thief, I could have split home with no one noticing. H*ll, they would probably have PAID me to split! As it is, when the "Sh*t Hit the Fan", Congress had to keep up pretenses that the whole country wasn't toast, so it meant that we had to act like a "normal" family... and "normal" families didn't have their teenage daughters running off to join the "terrorists". (Actually, Congressman Barnes is a Liberal, so he doesn't refer to the Awakening Centers as "terrorists"... just "a drug-using commune". Big F*cking Distinction...

[Dear Reader, you may have noticed that I'm using a lot of asterisks. That is because my jailers are also my censors. They count the number of "bad words" you use in your journal, and deduct them from the point score that you need to get out of their little prison. Behavior mod is "freedom". When I use asterisks, it doesn't count toward the total. So I can say, "F*ck you, you totalitarian *sshole morons" and not have it count against my point score. (Oops. Not sure about "morons". Better make it "m*r*ns...")]

The jailers promise that if I "behave", I'll be out of here in "no time". (Behaving means pretending that I like toxic food and living in a prison cell.) I know that I'll be out of here in 90 days

— when the parents go before the judge that issued the custody order and try to prove that I'm hypnotized, brainwashed, drugged, mind-wiped, or otherwise held in thrall by the evil monks of the Awakening Center. So, the hardest thing I've got to do is not choke the living sh*t out of my ever-smiling jailers for 87 more days.

Day 05:

My jailers (who have asked me repeatedly to refer to them as "Nancy" and "Tom") have to be taking happy pills to deal with all the fecal matter I'm handing them. (Yes, they re-programmed the bad-word-count computer to count all the asterisked words...) Always the same sad smile, always the slight look of disappointment, always the same pseudo-enthusiastic praise when my behavior conforms to their idea of what's "normal". ("Good girl, Sandra! You made your bed!" I think their prior careers were in dog training.)

They keep asking me if I'm suicidal. Fat chance. But, give me a straight razor and I'd definitely suicide those two. Knowing them, they'd still have those same stupid smiles on their faces when they're dead. Screw them...

Speaking of screwing: since leaving the Awakening Center and ending the nine months of their hormone-suppressing diet, I've been horny as... well, a 16 year old girl. And no horns around! Oh well... if they take off points for me playing with myself, I guess I'll be serving a life sentence here.

I told my jailers that I'd f—ck both of them, at the same time, if they let me out of my cell. First time I saw their smiles flicker...

Day 10:

My prison cell has a flat screen television built into the wall. It's nearly as big as the wall itself. I'm betting it also has a retina scanner built-in, to see how many hours of TV watching I'm racking up — and which programs. (I'm betting it's counted less than five minutes.)

The one thing the TV doesn't have is an off switch. Or even a mute button. I got mega-demerits from the jailers when I tried to cover the screen with my bedsheet. (They probably got pissed that they couldn't watch me jack off.) More demerits when I tried to move my bed so I couldn't see the screen.

I tell you, Dear Reader, all this "freedom" is going to my head. I wish the monks in AC really did brainwash… I could use a good scrubbing after all this sh—t.

Day 15:

What I've been waiting for: a "fact-finding" tour by Congressman Barnes and his entourage (wife and lawyer).

For the longest time, the jailers used the promise of a visit from my parents as incentive for their behavior-mod schemes. Took them awhile to realize that the last thing in the world I wanted was a close encounter with the Barnes. ("Please, I'll eat all of your toxic food and watch 10 hours of TV a day! NOT THE PARENTS!")

Of course, the close encounter did NOT take place in my wooden box. Even Congressman Barnes would have been appalled at that. Instead, we met in a nice, tidy room, with a real bed (not a windowless box with a cot), a real window (not a flat screen TV), overlooking a real pocket garden (not eight hours of the "home gardening channel"). Captivity, in any respect, sucks… but this would suck just a little less bad. All I need to do is learn how to smack my lips when offered pesticide laden, genetically-modified pseudo-food…

All told, the tour was not a disaster (from my end, at least). They gave me this sexless jumpsuit to wear (trying to make me look like a little girl). I unbuttoned it to my navel, and made an improvised belt from a stray cord I found at a computer station we passed. An improvised "Sluts 'R Us" look that Eric Braune, the Barnes attorney, found interesting. Every time I saw him noticing my mammary glands, I'd take a deep breath and flash him the high beams.

33

I knew that they were recording the encounter, and that it would do me no good to either act out or act compliant. So, I chose a third course.

The jailers started out with a nice summary of my incarceration, and put a nice spin on me being completely uncooperative. The Congressman asked a few pointed questions — no doubt fed to him by the jailers, to make him appear to be a concerned parent.

Eric the lawyer took his eyes off my tits long enough to deliver his speech for the hidden cameras — that the judge's 90 day involuntary commitment order could be "shortened substantially" if they all agreed that I was "making progress" toward "rehabilitation" from the dreaded "Awakening Center" and its influences. That they could even recommend an extended "home visit" for me.

That's when Mrs. Barnes got to deliver her lines. "You could sleep in your own bed, baby. I want you home." (She was passable — delivered her lines a tad early, and her speech was a bit slurred by whatever chemicals she was high on at the time. I managed not to laugh at the "I want you home" line — she hasn't spent a night under the same roof with Congressman Barnes in awhile. Well, she delivered it with a chemically-induced straight face, so she gets points.)

Then, it was my turn to shine. After thanking them all for checking on my welfare, I delivered my "Four Bombshells":

1. *If I stayed incarcerated past 20 days, I would sue every person involved in keeping me locked up... including the judge, who I claimed was a political crony of my father. (I was just guessing at this, but considering the Congressman's pink-faced reaction, I think I hit close to home.)*
2. *Starting on the 20th day, I promised I would campaign for my father's opponents, for one month for every day my lockup continued. And, if Congressman Barnes ran unopposed, I would run against him myself. (At this, the*

father unit turns a bright red and starts to object. But, I'm talking to the camera, not to him...)

3. *Also on the 20th day, I would start writing my book, entitled "Daddy Dearest", where I make every allegation against every one of them I could muster, including kidnapping and torture charges against them and my jailers, and including charging sex abuse against a minor, because Eric the attorney has been staring at my breasts for a half-hour. (This time, Eric's turn to turn red. The Congressman looks ready to shoot somebody... I wonder who?)*

4. *On the other hand: if I am released by the 20th day, I would agree to take exactly four professionally-shot "family" photos with the Barnes family, for the congressman to use as he sees fit. I would furthermore agree not to campaign for any of his opponents. Also, I would agree not to sue anyone involved in my incarceration, including Eric the pedophile. That, basically, I would leave them alone if they left me alone.*

I told them they could think about it as long as they wished... but the clock was ticking.

Congressman Barnes looked like he'd just received some very bad polling results. Mom actually looked relieved — she wouldn't have to play parent at Dad's request. Eric the attorney looked torn between his duties to his client and his desire to stare at my chest some more. And the jailers lost their smiles... as it turns out, permanently.

Day 18:

It's a deal.

I knew it was, by the way they all filed out. Later that same day, an orderly (not the jailers) moved me to a room a lot like the parental visitation room. And, I got my first meal that included food. No television. Nancy and Tom gave me the silent treatment — another blessing.

They put a few conditions on my release:

- *Not talking about any of this with the press. (I went further and said I would not go to the press about anything, short of the Second Coming of Jesus.)*
- *Putting my Four Bombshells in writing. (I agreed.)*
- *Making a statement that I had not been abused or mistreated in any way while in jail. (I refused. They will always have that crappy wooden box and the crappy food hanging over their heads. And Eric the attorney will always be dogged by the video of him drooling over the tits of a 16 year old. The dog.)*
- *If I re-entered an Awakening Center, I would do so under an assumed name. (I agreed in an instant. In fact, I should have thought of that myself, and saved myself a ton of grief.). My name while at the Center was "Gayatri". I think I'll be using that as my only name.*
- *Lastly, I had to write a 1,000 word statement on WHY I left home in the first place, and why I went to an Awakening Center. I decided to write a book about it.*

[JOURNAL ENTRY END]

Tales of the Culture Council — Resolving Disputes: Cleaning the Air Pillow.

File No:		File Name:	Resolving Disputes: Cleaning the Air Pillow
Location:		Parties:	
Monk/ Master Supervising:		Selected Tales of the Culture Council	

[RECORD START]

MEMORANDUM

It has come to the attention of the Culture Council that a dispute has arisen between the Denver, CO and Denton, TX Awakening Centers. The dispute is concerning who should pay for the cleaning of an Air Pillow, after a damaged delivery.

Facts of the Dispute:

It is well known that the Culture Council maintains a fleet of hydrogen dirigibles for heavy transport of goods and people between distant locations. These craft are commonly known as "Air Pillows" for their distinctive shape while under power. Pillow #256 (CC Air Transport Number 256) left Denver Center on [date], carrying a load of grain and needed supplies for the Denton Center. Along the way, the aircraft ran into unusually harsh weather, and experienced extreme turbulence. When it arrived in Denton, several containers had jostled and spilled, and the aircraft had to be cleaned.

Dispute:

Denton Center says that Denver Center should have to pay for the cleaning, since they failed to secure the cargo properly. Denver says that the shipment was secured adequately, the storm was unforeseeable, and that they should not have to pay for an "Act of Nature". Both Centers asked for Culture Council intervention in this dispute.

Culture Council Conclusions:

The cost of cleaning the aircraft was 200 credits. We determine that the two Centers should split the cost evenly.

In addition, the Culture Council charges each of the Centers 10,000 credits each, for wasting both their time and ours. The solution of sharing the cost of the incident should have been obvious to both of the Centers, if they had been mindful outside of their own local circumstances.

The Culture Council is not a "Supreme Court". We have no interest in trying to replicate the failed institutions of the Age of Waste. Our new society is based on CONSCIOUSNESS, not laws, rules and bureaucracy. We encourage all Centers to resolve any potential disputes using mindfulness, not conflict, and certainly not courts, which we are not.

[NOTE: Disputes between Centers were drastically reduced after this incident.]

[RECORD END]

William's Journal: The Rich Kid (Journal of William Hawkins, Jr)

File No:		File Name:	The Rich Kid
Location:		Parties:	William Hawkins, Jr
Monk/ Master Supervising:	From the pre-Awakening Center journal entries of William Hawkins, Jr (used with permission)		

[JOURNAL ENTRY START]

We are rich.

I was born after the start of the Upheavals. Dad can talk about "The Good Ole Days" and "The Glory of America" all he wants... This is the only life I've known.

You've got two classes of people in North America: US and everybody else. We're rich – my parents can afford to buy me paper and pen, so their spoiled little brat can have pretensions of being a writer. (Using words like "pretensions" means I'm a writer...)

So... a few rich and a shitload of poor. The Upheavals eliminated the illusion of a middle class. The middle class was just a bunch of poor people who could borrow to live beyond their means. The Upheavals meant that the check came due, and they couldn't pay it. A whole lot of them committed suicide. Couldn't live with reality, l guess.

They say that 3% of us in this country are rich, the rest live on the brink of extinction.

I prefer our side.

Now, "rich" doesn't mean the same thing as it did back in the Good Ole Days. Big houses? Big cars? ANY cars? ANY restaurants? Ha! I've seen cars before – sitting on the roadside, used for storage – or as "home" for the 95% who don't live like me.

On rare occasions, someone can bypass the fried onboard computers and electronic junk to get one of the cars to work. Even rarer, getting the gas to make it run.

No one will go near an electric car. The towel heads figured out how to hack a Tesla, get its onboard computer to ignite the battery core. One big, bad bomb. I never saw a Tesla explosion, but I did see the crater one left. About 20 feet across and 10 feet deep, filled with brackish water and metal car parts. You didn't need a suicide vest if you had a Tesla handy. (I heard they could do that with regular gas cars, but the media didn't cover that. Nobody liked the idea that they had a bomb in their garage big enough to blow up the whole neighborhood.)

(Sorry about the "towel head" comment... I know I'm not supposed to talk like that. Especially since some of our neighbors wear turbans. Calling names doesn't make a good writer.)

Anyway... Back to being rich...

Being rich means that we eat regularly, if not consistently. We get the fresh food that the poor people grow for us. We get the canned goods that they scavenge for us. And, once in a while, a rare treat, like fruit or candy.

What do the poor eat? Who knows? Who cares?

My only contact with the poor people are the numbers of servants in the household. They range from the hard-eyed men doing security (and whatever else my father wants), to the soft-eyed young girls doing... "service" to my dad. (Mom tries to get rid of them as fast as she can...)

I am the heir. My little brother David is insurance. My mom is superfluous.

OK... How about school? Like nothing from the Good Ole Days. We rotate among our Houses, each house trying to specialize in a subject, like math or science or reading. We've got books, but most of them are old. I never saw the Internet, but I heard about it... It must've been a true miracle. (Dad gets on something in his office and exchanges messages around the country... But that's nothing like being able to play VIDEO GAMES!! Whenever you wanted!)

Basically, "education" is all of us kids of a certain age group getting together and doing whatever the hell we want to do, and calling it "learning". Nobody watches us too closely...

So... You want to know what makes us rich? Me too! Among all of our Houses (capital "H", means we're rich), that is a subject expressly forbidden to ask about. I'm the heir to an empire I haven't ever seen. Dad says, "When you're old enough".

I know it involves blood. I know the smell. Dad could run a butcher shop. Or, he could be a paid assassin. A mercenary for hire. A psychotic serial killer (probably not; there's no money in that).

He keeps his business in his garage. ("His" garage: no one else in the family has ever set foot in it.) Or, on the side of the house that he calls his "Study". The garage is where he keeps the converted UPS panel truck we call the "War Wagon".

The McKenzies across the street are traders. Buy low, sell high. Trading what? Probably everything, including human beings. We don't ask. Once his oldest son Ted started in the family business, he stopped talking to me. (The "McKenzies" are actually Hindus from someplace in India.... Probably had a family name like "Singh" or "Gupta". They're the neighbors with the turbans. You should see the looks on some folks' faces when they meet them! They thought that having a Western name would give them some protection. So far, it has.)

"Rich" equals access to plenty of pharmaceuticals. If you don't mind the expiration date. "Poor" equals no drugs. Nothing. Hope for the best. A lot of praying.... And we know how much good that does when you're dying from a septic toothache, or your kid's got runaway diarrhea.

Let's see, what else? Oh, how about SEX? For me, pretty easy: just wait for Dad to get tired of the latest "servant" girl, then make my move. I usually have two or three weeks with her before Mom manages to get her kicked out. (Unless Dad's been particularly rough and left some permanent scars. Those girls, he gets rid of. And I wouldn't want them, anyways. For all of them, after having been with Dad for a couple of weeks, I'm sure I'm a relief. I don't know how much Dad pays for them, but it must be a lot!)

Sometimes, the servant girls just disappear. I don't get a crack at those. And that's been happening more frequently, lately.

Three times a week, I get to perform "community service", which is a euphemism for "security", which is a euphemism for "shoot anything coming over the wall of the Compound, and then throw the body back across".

So far, I've shot three raccoons (and kept the bodies... Good eating!) And two guys.

Or, maybe a guy and a girl. The other guys wanted to strip her to see, then have sex with her. I pointed out that there's little point in screwing a gut-shot girl who happened to be dead. We tossed her back over the wall. (The other guys are jealous of me, because I get to have sex regularly with Dad's leftovers. If I hadn't been on duty that night, Ms. Gut-Shot Dead-Girl would have been very popular. Posthumously.)

Speaking of dead girls, I'm supposed to get married in the next three to four years and I'm supposed to choose from among the lovely lasses in our secure pen. All of them dead from the groin up.

There was one girl I liked, Carol Prentice, who showed some real spark. Definitely not a cow. Actually, she showed too much spark – one day she just disappeared. They say that they married Carol off to another Family in another city. More likely, they blew her brains out one night and dumped her body over the wall. Troublesome children are a major liability. Especially girls.

Dad says I have to marry one of the cows. (You can screw anyone you like – but to be respectful you got to marry a girl from one of the Families.) I still have a few years before I have to select from the cattle...

[Date stamp.]

Life changes quickly...

Yesterday, Dad brought me into his Study (formerly off-limits) for a "talk". Since he did little talking to us, this was a serious event.

(Up until now, our relationship consisted of me staying out of his way, and feeding his ego when the occasion demanded it. Saying things like, "I hope to be a man like my Father!" when any of his friends and associates were around.)

When I got into the Study, I was surprised to see that it really was several rooms, all radiating from a large room with several desks and maps on the wall. Some of those rooms must extend under the hill our House sits on. The main room was dominated by a large conference table.

We were not alone. Around the conference table, meant for a dozen or more people, sat eight men. Four of them I knew from other gatherings, but four I did not know. Three of the four wore these odd-looking football helmets with visors shielding their eyes.

The men I knew smiled and mumbled a welcome. The strangers neither smiled nor spoke.

Dad sat at the head of the table, and waved me to a seat at his right hand. Everybody noticed the symbology.

"I think it's time for my Son to assume more of his adult responsibilities. And, from now on, no more 'Little Billy'. You should refer to him as 'young William' or 'Junior'. He's going to be the boss around here someday."

"Yes, but not for a long, long time!" I said quickly. He likes that kind of sucking up...

"Hear, hear!" came from Ralph Arvett, who desperately wanted to hook me up with his ugly cow of a daughter.

"Young William here is going to document for us the glorious action we're about to undertake. We're going to take down a Zombie Center!"

I'm not sure how well I hid the shock on my face. I was ready for just about anything... But THAT. Everyone knew that trying to attack an Awakening Center wasn't long odds... there were NO odds. It had never been done.

I wanted to ask, "You and what battalion?" I realized that would be showing fear.

"What do you want me to do?" I asked instead.

"See that?" Dad beamed. "No hesitation at all! That's my boy!"

He held me by the shoulders and met my eyes. "Son, we want you to be the scribe, the eyes and ears of this operation. It's been a long time in planning. Once we are successful, we want others to know how to do it, how to bring the zombies down. I want your words and your descriptions to be what gets read... All across this country!"

The non-helmet wearing stranger leaned toward my father. "I hear he's a fair writer, but how's he going to be in a fight? Is he going to freeze up? Is he going to turn tail?"

"I didn't turn tail on the five guys I killed coming over the wall," I said, inflating my number of kills with raccoons. "Plus, I'm left-handed. I can write and shoot at the same time!"

There was general laughter around the table. Even one of the helmet guys broke into a grin.

"Dad, you know that attacking one of their Centers is pretty ambitious. What's the plan for success?"

Dad turns to one of the Heads of the other Houses, Ralph Arvett, who lives two doors down from us. "Ralph, why don't you outline our strategy?"

"First of all, our purpose is different." Ralph said. "We don't want their food or their energy. In the past, the people who attacked them were trying to get something from them. We don't want anything.

Ralph pointed to a complicated schematic that rested in the center of the table, held down by some of the National Geographic magazines that were one of Dad's prize possessions. "Our first step is to attack the empty feed wagons when they return to the Zombie Center. They won't be guarded like the ones going out. Remember, we don't want their food. We take over the wagons, then ride them right into their Center! Our own Trojan Horse!

"Once inside, we will have the superior position. We're armed, they're not. We spring the trap. We kill their communications, open the gates for an overwhelming force to enter."

He paused, waiting for me to tell him how brilliant he is. What I was actually thinking was, hasn't this been tried before? Hasn't it always failed?

"intriguing!" I said. There's a weasel word for you. "Where is the overwhelming force coming from?" And won't the Awakening Center telepaths see us coming from 20 miles away?

"That's the brilliant part! We're going to arm the townspeople!"

"Townspeople" is our name for that ragged bunch of poor people that camp outside our gate, trading their meager belongings – including young girls for my father – for medicine, bullets, energy, clean water... The currency of our times.

What I wanted to ask was, "Why do you think they won't turn those guns on US?" But, before I could think of an appropriate response, Dad piped in.

"You know those poor folks will jump at the chance to throw off the yoke of oppression!"

Everyone around the table nodded and said "Amen!" I had a different internal response: I thought that WE were their "yoke of oppression". The only thing that the monks in the Awakening Center ever did was not let them in.

"Sounds like a really well-thought-out plan!" I said.

Smiles spread around the table — these guys never get tired of getting ego-stroked.

"But... What about their telepathy? What about mind wiping?"

My father and Mr. No-Helmet exchanged a very long look. A real staring contest. I suddenly realized that I wasn't fully "In" yet — this little meeting was a test. It was up to Mr. No-Helmet to decide whether or not I was to be trusted with this mission. OK, time for me to crank up the heat. I stood up.

"I know that I'm only 16 and don't have the experience of the men in this room. I know I'm young and may ask dumb questions.

"I don't know some of the men in this round, but I do know my Father. I trust him implicitly." A blatant lie! I didn't trust Dad much further than I could throw him. But, after all the years of smiling and sucking-up, no one at the table knew that... Especially him. I went on...

"Some of our new friends may not trust me. That's OK. But, what is not OK is that it seems that they don't trust Father. And if you don't trust him," I paused for effect, "I should not be in the same room with you."

I turned and started walking toward the door. Within five steps, I heard my gambit pay off. Dad's chair scraped back. "I don't think I belong in here, either," he said.

General pandemonium erupted in the room. Everyone shouting at once (except for the three helmet guys).

This was the tricky part of the gambit. I had to keep walking. What if Dad was too tied up in talking to notice I was about to exit? I tried walking a little slower. Finally, with my hand on the doorknob, he says, "Hold on a minute, Son. Come over here."

Total victory! I went back to my seat. The power dynamic of the room had shifted: Dad was the strongest guy at the table, Mr. No-Helmet had lost Power, and I was fully "in". Reading Sun Tzu's "Art of War" actually pays off!

Once I was seated again, Dad took the floor. Waving his hand to Mr. No-Helmet, he said, "So, Riker, why don't you explain to Young William why we don't fear their telepathy?"

Riker hesitated. "I must caution our young colleague that none of what you are about to hear should be discussed with ANYONE outside this room."

"Yes, Sir," I said. No sense in him losing any more face. We all knew that Dad and I held the superior positions in the room.

"We have been able to develop a technology that BLOCKS their TP," Riker said.

Whoa... That's new. Could be a game changer... If it works.

"I assume you've tested this to your satisfaction?" I said.

This time, it's Dad who chimed in. "You bet! Last week, we had a guy walk right into the Guest Area of that Center, armed to the gills! They couldn't SEE him!"

They couldn't see a grown man, walking around in a football helmet on a warm day?

47

"This entire house is shielded by the anti-TP technology. Those zombies can't see us! Just think: a guy carrying ceramic guns and ceramic knives just waltzed into that den of..."

"Excuse me Dad, but perhaps Mr. Riker would be more comfortable if I didn't have any operational data just yet."

The table froze up again. This time, it was Dad taken to task for having loose lips. By me! Score one for Riker. Score 2 for me!

"It's just 'Riker', Son."

He called me "Son"! Dad Is Going to Pop His CORK!

"Yes, sir... But may I ask a question? If this house is under protection, why do our three silent friends have on those... Helmets?"

"All of the operational data for our action is in their heads," Riker said. "Each of us knows a part of the plan, but only the three of them know the entire plan. I will keep it that way, until the day we execute."

"Well, I guess we've got to guard those helmets... And the heads in them!"

Laughter. That pretty much ended the meeting. There was some small talk about the next meeting and all of us standing for the meaningless yet obligatory "Pledge of Allegiance".

One thing is certain: if I survive this operation without getting mind-wiped and sent as a robot laborer to one of the Center's farms, I'll have an interesting story to tell.

[JOURNAL ENTRY END]

Food wagon 2: Guns are a Liability [The Food Wagon as Bait]

File No:		File Name:	Guns are a Liability
Location:		Parties:	Master Man-Onko Novice Gayatri
Monk/ Master Supervising:		Master Man-Onko	

[TRANSCRIPT START]

[Conversation between Master Man-Onko and novice Gayatri]

Gayatri: I was just editing the section on you about your first ride on the Food Wagon with the rest of your pod. Seems like nothing happened on that journey. Were the rides always that peaceful? Did you ever see any action?

Monk Man-Onko: Is this supposed to be a History lesson? I thought I was seeing you because you're slipping behind in your Mathematics and Geometry!

Gayatri: Well, I've been doing really well in my intuition classes... And my intuition senses that you want to teach me Mathematics just as badly as I want to learn it! My Intuition also senses that we BOTH would be happier if we talked about something a lot more fun! And, Master, isn't our quest for fulfillment the purpose we are all here?

Monk Man-Onko: Well, I don't know about your Intuition classes, but I know your Logic lessons are being well applied! OK, we'll spend a little time in the "Good Old Days", then double up on the Math.

Gayatri: Only if you insist...

Monk Man-Onko: So, what was your question... Oh yes, you wanted to know if we ever saw any action on the Bait Wagons.

Gayatri: Is that what you called them?

Monk Man-Onko: That's what they were. We had many ways of delivering food, all of them much more efficient and effective than the Bait Wagons. All of them nearly invisible. Flying tons of food over people's heads in the middle of the night with our very quiet Pillows was a very effective way of delivering food, goods and even people where we needed them. It's amazing how most people almost never look up.

The purpose of the Bait Wagons is to draw people out. Or rather, draw their VIOLENCE out. The chapter that you are working on a training run for us young novices. Real Bait Wagons are staffed by trained monks on security duty.

So, what was our purpose in running those wagons?

Gayatri: Hey, no fair! This isn't supposed to be a lesson!

Monk Man-Onko: Did you really think you were getting off that easy? Isn't EVERYTHING in this place a "lesson"?

So, answer up, Novice! What is the purpose of dragging food around in the slow, horse drawn wagons, under the noses of a bunch of hungry, armed people?

Gayatri: I think the answer is obvious. You wanted to confiscate the guns in that area. The wagon was a way to find out where the guns were, who had them, and to get rid of them.

Monk Man-Onko: Good answer. Totally WRONG, but a good answer! Try again.

Gayatri: [pauses] I don't see another answer. I mean, you are going after the bad guys, right? You always confiscate their guns, right? So, you want their guns!

Monk Man-Onko: This time, your Logic classes are getting in your way. Our Intelligence folks are very good. We knew who the "bad guys" were already. We knew where they kept their guns, and where they got them from. If we wanted to de-gun them, we could just go into their hiding places, pull the guns out and disable them. So, what was the purpose of the grand show of the Bait Wagon?

Gayatri: [pauses] I'm stuck.

Monk Man-Onko: Where is violence? Is it in the gun? Or, is it in the finger that pulls the trigger?

Gayatri: Whoa! You guys... WE guys didn't want to stop the guns! We wanted to stop the VIOLENCE!

Monk Man-Onko: You're getting warmer, but you're still not there. Yes, we could've taken away their guns... And they would start hacking at each other and at us with machetes. Or baseball bats. Or their bare hands. So, we were going for something deeper. What was that?

Gayatri: OK... [Pauses] if you wanted more than just to control their guns, you must have been aiming for a change in their consciousness. You wanted them to switch from having a violence consciousness to peace consciousness, right?

Monk Man-Onko: And who is asking who the questions here? No, still not quite right, although you're getting much closer. What is the specific shift that we were looking for by drawing them out into the open, by encouraging their violent acts?

Gayatri: Well, obviously, you wanted to let them learn that violence didn't work.

Monk Man-Onko: Yes, but still more subtle. Here's a big hint: In the days at the start of the Upheavals, during the Age of Waste, the most valued items in the Breaker society were (in this order):

1. Food and water

2. Guns and bullets

3. Gold

What does that tell you?

Gayatri: Wow! The purpose of the food Wagons is to reduce the VALUE of guns!

Monk Man-Onko: Yes, but even more subtle than that. Our goal was to turn a gun from a perceived asset into a liability. We were trying to embed in people's consciousness that if you possess a gun, bad things would happen to you. Just taking guns away from people would make them yearn for them. Everyone has to SEE that there was no tangible benefit and a great deal of loss associated with possessing weapons of violence and being willing to use them.

Gayatri: Pretty cool. But, why do we care so much what was happening on the Outside? Why not just let them kill themselves?

Monk Man-Onko: Well, our goal is always...

Gayatri: Hold on, Hold on! I know what you're going to say! I can hear Master Nekud in my head! "The purpose of an Awakening Center is never self-serving. Our goal is always fixed on the transformation of society!"

Monk Man-Onko: Well said! I'll tell him his lessons are having an effect! So, my question again: what was the purpose of the Bait Wagon?

Gayatri: The purpose was the transformation of consciousness. The purpose was to change the consciousness among the outsiders, from the belief that guns and violence are good to the belief that guns and violence are a liability.

Monk Man-Onko: Very well said. So, how did we do that?

Gayatri: Well, the most obvious method would have been to wait for them to shoot at us, beat the crap out of them, and take their guns away. But, I have the feeling that you're going to say that we were more subtle than that.

Monk Man-Onko: And, once again, your feeling is correct! So, what did we do?

Gayatri: [Pauses] Well... Forgive me, Master, but rumor has it that you really do beat the crap out of the bad guys! I heard that you break a whole lot of bones! You really bust these guys up!

Monk Man-Onko: As usual, the Novice Rumor Mill is in full swing! No, we don't "bust those guys up". We did break bones... But they were very specific and very targeted. We only broke 3 bones in every attack. No more, no less. And, we haven't broken any bones in a long, long time. Over a decade. Amazing how long rumors persist!

Only three bones. If someone shot at us, we disarmed them and broke a very specific bone in their wrist. It would prevent them from firing a weapon, or doing much else with that hand, for several months. When it healed, it would leave a distinctive mark on the wrist. They were then told that if they fired a weapon at a human being ever again, if we ever saw that malformed wrist bone again, they would lose the use of their arm.

The leader of the group would be... talked to. After having both of his clavicles broken.

Gayatri: What's a clavicle?

Monk Man-Onko: it's that long, thin bone, right here... At the top of your chest, kind of in your shoulder. Yes, that's it — kind of sticks out. It connects your neck area with your shoulder joint. Break it and your arm is useless for six weeks or more. Helpless as a baby... With your clavicles broken, you become dependent on others to feed you and wipe your butt for six weeks.

Once we did that, we invited the leader to reflect on his life and on his direction. Hard to do, when someone is screaming in pain and vowing revenge. But, it was surprisingly effective. Most of the leaders who were not psychopaths did change their direction after six weeks of helplessness and dependency. Some even joined us, and became part of our external security.

But, I think the last clavicles got broken something like eight or nine years ago. We find that mind-wiping is much more effective. A vicious, violent, angry man goes out on a raid... and a helpful, positive, non-violent one returns! I hear their wives LOVE the Awakening Centers for what they've done for their men! And lots of the raiding parties will inform us of their plans, so that they can arrange to have their bosses mind-wiped.

Gayatri: What about the psychopaths?

Monk Man-Onko: We found that most of their followers really wanted the opportunity to leave them. Having the nut jobs unable to carry out the implicit threats of their leadership meant that a new leadership could emerge.

Gayatri: What did they do with the psychopaths?

Monk Man-Onko: Not our concern.

Gayatri: I mean, with their neck bones broken, how could they feed themselves? How could they even get a drink of water?

Monk Man-Onko: Not our concern.

Gayatri: Hey, wait a minute! Why come it's NOT your concern? Weren't we VIOLENT with these guys? Aren't we supposed to be against violence? Don't we have some responsibility when we leave someone broken and helpless?

Monk Man-Onko: [pauses] You've been learning your lessons well. [Pauses] It's not as straight cut as it seems in your Novice-level classes.

In the past, babies were born with rickets, a bone softening disability. Doctors would break the legs of young children, so their legs would grow straighter. Was breaking that child's legs an act of violence?

Gayatri: [Pauses] No. It was an act for the child's own good. That's like the surgeon that cuts open a person's chest in order to fix their heart.

But what the Bait Wagon was doing was cutting open their chests and leaving them open! Don't you have a responsibility for closing up the wound?

Monk Man-Onko: [pauses] First of all, I want you to know that we ran into very few true psychopaths and sociopaths in those operations. Most people, In that position of vulnerability and helplessness, really did reflect on their lives and were able to understand their actions. In those cases, either their people took care of them, or we took care of them.

If their psychosis prevented them from asking for or receiving our care... We left them.

Gayatri: Left them to die?

Monk Man-Onko: [Pauses] Yes. We left about three-billion people to die. We had to make hard choices about every single person we fed and cared for.

Gayatri: But, what about a mind wipe?

Monk Man-Onko: Our ability to do that was fairly limited at that time. We could affect a DCI if the person had a normally healthy mind. We couldn't do much with people who were brain-damaged. It's still pretty difficult, even today, and even with what we've learned from our friends at Unity.

I also want you to know that leaving the person to die was the decision of their group, not our decision. Most of the time, once they realized their "leader" was helpless, their own people killed him on the spot.

Gayatri: Wow.

Monk Man-Onko: And, in a couple of cases, the psycho leader was a "her".

Gayatri: It still seems... harsh, just to leave someone to die.

Monk Man-Onko: Those were harsh times we lived in. We didn't have enough food, water and resources for the GOOD people who were Outside, the people who desperately WANTED to be in an Awakening Center.

Gayatri: But... don't we lock up some people? Don't we have prisons? What about those dorms out there by the lake... the ones we aren't supposed to go near? Aren't those places for nut jobs?

Monk Man-Onko: [Pauses] I over-spoke when I referred to the psychopaths as "nut jobs". Please don't follow my bad direction.

The special dorms do house people who can't function in any society, here or Outside. But, the ways in which those people come to us obligates us to serve them. Most are the relatives of monks or masters. Others come to us as children — we may encounter the aftermath of a battle between two warring factions that leaves all of the adults dead and all of the children traumatized. In that case, compassion will move us to take in their children... some of whom are very scarred.

And NONE of whom have fired weapons at us.

Now... in the beginnings of the Upheavals, raiding other groups had the potential of great benefit on the Outside. The raiders got to work off some pent-up anger by shooting and killing; they acquired more food, more weapons; sometimes, they would take the women as sex slaves, take the men as slaves, or food. It built the notion "Raiding is good". That was the logical path of a violence-loving American society.

When they try to raid a Bait Wagon, it's always a net loss. They lose their weapons, leaving them open and vulnerable to attack by others. With strategic bone breaks, they lost the effective work capacity of two of their members — their leader and their best shot. When you get mind-wiped... the impression is that you've lost your SOUL to the Awakening Center. That's an impression that we foster, at times.

And, word starts to spread among the other Outside communities. Guns are a liability — especially if you use them against an Awakening Center..

We see very few true psychotics running groups nowadays. Most groups have figured out how to eliminate them. Most were "True Patriots", people who believed that they could shoot and steal their way into a new version of American Society.

Those people wanted security, but they denied it to others. They wanted freedom, but they denied it to others. They wanted enough resources, by taking them from others. That was NOT an America that we would have allowed to be resurrected.

You were asking whether or not I had "seen any action"... would you like to see some? Security says that a big operation is brewing, and you might...

Gayatri: Hell, yeah! Whoo Hooo! Count me in! I just wanna...

Monk Man-Onko: Hold on, young lady! Don't get any delusions of grandeur! Your role in this operation is to be the BAIT! You'll get to help secure our detainees, AFTER the action goes down.

Gayatri: Yeah, I figured as much. It just sounds exciting, being out in the open, knowing that danger is all around and also knowing that our folks are ALSO all around.

Monk Man-Onko: The reason I will suggest you for this detail is that I think it will help your writing along if you do more than focus on the past. This way, you'll get to see what our Security looks like in real time. And... you may get to meet some Unity agents.

Gayatri: UNITY! Is this gonna get any better, or what? What are they going to do there? Will they be, like... talking at the same time?

Monk Man-Onko: We call it "conjoined". And, yes, if there's more than one of them, they are always conjoined.

Gayatri: Unity! Wait until the other novices hear this! I will PULL that wagon for a chance to meet Unity! Why are they going to be there?

Monk Man-Onko: Well, there's a possibility that a few of the attackers are going to be members of The Edge in disguise...

Gayatri: THE EDGE! You are absolutely shitting me, right? Oops... Sorry. But, the EDGE! Tell me that you're kidding!

Monk Man-Onko: No kidding. It's why we're paying special attention to this raid. And, I'm going to give you one more treat, before I tell you how much this is going to COST.

Gayatri: Cost? I knew this had to be too good to be true... but I said already... I'll PULL that wagon, by myself!

Monk Man-Onko: Well, why don't you ask about the treat, before you ask about the price?

Gayatri: After all this, I can't even imagine what that could be!

Monk Man-Onko: I will recommend that you get to interview their leader... both BEFORE and AFTER his DCI.

Gayatri: Cool! Hey... could I be there DURING his mind-wipe?

Monk Man-Onko: You're off the rails there, kid. No one has ever seen a mind-wipe, except the people who do it and the person receiving it.

Gayatri: And Unity.

Monk Man-Onko: Well... Unity sees whatever they want to see. No way to keep them out. And, they've taught us most of what we know about mind-wiping, so it would be hard to keep it a secret from them.

Gayatri: So... the cost?

Monk Man-Onko: First: you will tell ABSOLUTELY NO ONE about any part of this conversation. Whether or not you go, the only time anyone else finds out about it is AFTER the fact.

Gayatri: Got it. I assumed that. What else?

Monk Man-Onko: Except for your private journals, you will submit everything in writing to me, before you publish it for the campus.

Gayatri: Okay, not so hard... you can even see the personal journals, if you want. But, I have the feeling that's not all.

Monk Man-Onko: We think their raid is going to take place within the next two months. During that entire time, you will be at the top ten percent of your Math class.

Gayatri: Whoa! Didn't see THAT coming! Can I appeal? How about if I get in the top ten percent in Writing? Or Logic?

Monk Man-Onko: Well, since you're already at the top of those classes, that wouldn't be much incentive, would it?

Gayatri: Hey, can you get them to, you know, mind-wipe me into a math genius?

Monk Man-Onko: Yes, of course. We could make you into the perfect polymath — the master of all of your subjects. But, what would that tell us about your CHARACTER?

Gayatri: Why don't we talk about my character AFTER the raid?

Monk Man-Onko: This raid is important. We cannot have information about it slipping out. You are to go over to the Exploratory and receive a very simple "suggestion" not to talk about any of this until after the raid.

Gayatri: YOU'RE GONNA MIND-WIPE ME?? HOW COOL IS THAT? Will I still know how to tie my shoes? Will I drool? I'll be able to write about the process from the INSIDE!

Monk Man-Onko: Sorry, nothing so dramatic. You will remember that it's important to be in the top 10% of your class, but you'll forget why. You won't remember a single thing from this conversation — until after the raid. And then it will come flooding back — including the reason that you forgot.

Gayatri: Okay, Mister Big Shot Monk, I'm gonna make you a bet! I bet I can remember SOMETHING from this conversation, and that I'll write it down... before the raid!

Monk Man-Onko: So, what are we betting?

Gayatri: How about... you do my kitchen duty for four months!

Monk Man-Onko: Let's make it six months!

Gayatri: Okay! You're on!

Monk Man-Onko: And you do double kitchen duty for six months, if you fail to remember.

Gayatri: [pauses] Hey, let's go back to four months, okay?

Monk Man-Onko: [laughing] Fair enough. Now, I'll accompany you over to the sixth floor of the Exploratory.

Gayatri: Hey, the Exploratory only has four floors...

Monk Man-Onko: Guess again. You can only SEE four, but there are a few more than that.

Gayatri: Huh? Are the other floors underground?

Monk Man-Onko: Nope. It's sitting right there, in front of you. But you can't see them.

Gayatri: Wait... I don't get it... How can there be...

Monk Man-Onko: Chill!! I shouldn't have said anything. Let's go visit a floor you've never been on that doesn't exist.

[AFTERNOTE: Gayatri lost her bet.] [TRANSCRIPT END]

———

Tales of the Culture Council – Resolving Disputes 02: Enforcing Diversity

File No: T-3		File Name:	Resolving Disputes: Enforcing Diversity
Location:		Parties:	
Monk/ **Master** **Supervising:**		Selected Tales of the Culture Council	

[RECORD START]

MEMORANDUM

A serious dispute has arisen between several of the North American centers, led by the Philadelphia and Atlanta Centers.

Facts of the Dispute:
Philadelphia, Atlanta, and several others Centers have threatened to pull out of the annual recruitment lottery for spaces within the North American Awakening Movement. They claim that the other Centers, ones that are lacking in ethnic diversity, have been "raiding" their centers of necessary talent. This has been especially true of some of the more well-financed Centers, which are paying a premium in credits to recruit experienced monks and Masters from the disputing areas. Said Abbot Karna of the Philadelphia Center, "Go find your own black folks!"

Resolution:
Abbot Karna is correct. The Culture Council mandate for ethnic and cultural diversity within all Centers is NOT a prescription for depleting other Centers of their talent and experience. Nor is the fact that many Centers still face financially challenging times an inducement for such behavior.

Centers like Omaha, Milwaukee, and Portland counter by saying that African-Americans and other people of color are simply not applying for participation in their centers in adequate numbers to create or enhance diversity. (Apparently, the Culture Council's security disincentives — rumors — that we "brainwash people" or "eat people" have had the unintended consequence of keeping more people of color away from the centers than was expected.)

The Culture Council encourages the affected Centers to use more active and affirmative recruitment tools. We suggest the Centers try to "collect" possible candidates for participation, instead of waiting for them to walk up to our door. Giving hungry people a few good meals and warm, secure places to sleep may do more for the recruitment effort than just waiting for them to show up.

We strongly urge those Centers to focus on the youngest and most vulnerable people still living on the streets. This will have the added benefit of demonstrating compassion while filling the centers recruitment guidelines.

Finally: the Culture Council is aware that the annual "recruitment lottery" is flawed. We are currently working on an alternative that will allow talent to be transferred between centers on a more meta-conscious, voluntary level, and avoid the inequalities of the current situation. Please be patient.

[NOTE: the practice of street "Collections" was very successful in having Centers focus on their local populations, instead of "raiding" talent from elsewhere. And, within three years, the "recruitment lottery" was replaced with "The Swarm" (see Book 01; *The Chronicles of the Upheavals*), which proved to be an excellent practical example of the use of Blended Consciousness.]

[RECORD END]

William's Journal: The Rich Kid on the Grand Campaign

File No:		File Name:	The Rich Kid on the Grand Campaign
Location:		Parties:	William Hawkins, Jr
Monk/ Master Supervising:	From the pre-Awakening Center journal entries of William Hawkins, Jr (used with permission)		

[JOURNAL ENTRY START]

Well, Dad wanted me to write about the "Grand Campaign for the Republic", our effort to take down a "Zombie Center". So I'm writing.

I'm writing from inside an Awakening Center prison. Things didn't go exactly as planned.

First: They saw us from 100 miles away. Those helmets were perfectly useless. Worse than useless.. It altered a person's T-P signature enough for them to know that the wearer was trying to hide something. The helmets were like a sign saying, "Secrets here! Look Inside!"

"Wearing those helmets was like walking around in dark sunglasses and a piece of tape over your mouth, thinking that you're keeping a secret." So says Pico-Laton, the monk sent to interrogate me. "It was hilarious, watching the 'undercover' guy walking around armed to the gills! He never got anywhere close to us! In fact, we had to keep the novices away from him — we thought they'd crack up laughing!"

The "Grand Campaign" never got to Step One. We were ambushed waiting for the empty food wagons. (They had two wagons, because they knew they had to cart 20 of us back into the Center. One minute we're on high alert, next we're fast asleep, strapped to stretchers, then... sitting in this cell, writing about what never happened.)

Actually, it's not accurate to call this a cell... I can leave my little suite whenever I want... It's just that I have to have one of their "minders" with me. And, there are a couple of buildings I'm not allowed in. They say when I'm done spilling my guts, I'll be free to leave.

And... to tell the truth, I'm not sure I'm in a great hurry to leave. The food is great, and the monks are really cool! I've learned more in five days here than I can in a year at home.

Does this mean I've been mind-wiped? That they screwed with my mind, to make me fall in love with them? How would I know?

Pico-Laton says no. She said if I were mind-wiped, there would be no reason to lie to me about it.

She said Dad's gonna get wiped. She said when they started into his interrogation, they found some "disturbing behaviors". More than the young girls he's been screwing. Something to do with the family business and the blood I've been smelling.

When I asked Pico-Laton about the family business, she just smiled and said, "That used to be your family business. Not anymore. That past is now meaningless info."

She said that the Families will have to pay for the incursion, the "Grand Campaign". She said we've got to pay a LOT. "Just as you've been planning this little fiasco for several years, we've been watching you for several years. Somebody's got to pay for that."

Their "watching" was amazing. The MacKenzies were trading info with the Awakening Center for six years! Many of the townspeople were giving them info, also. And Riker (whose real name is "Bilal") is an Agent of the Awakening Centers!

Dad never had a chance. We never got to Step Zero.

The real deal for the monks were the helmet dudes. They belonged to some organization they call "The Edge". They were the big prize for the Center folks. The helmet dudes were hit with everything: darts, physical restraints, muscle relaxants. They even had a DENTIST on hand to drill out false teeth that they say contained poison.

Because I've been cooperative, I've been given this nice little apartment, including a kitchenette and bath. Those who don't cooperate (like Dad) get much less space for living, and no perks like being able to walk around and flirt with the girls in the Center.

Once he gets mind-wiped, Dad will be returning home. A new man. Loving husband. Center supporter, Helper for the townspeople. (The Center wants to start a Commons for the town folks. I think that's a great idea!)

As for me... we'll see what happens. Pico-Laton says I can help the Center, from inside or Outside.

Go back home and help Dad build the Commons? Stay here and become a Novice? While staying here has its attractions (did I mention the FOOD?), there's one big drawback: SEX! Novices can't have sex... and that's enforced by some stuff they put in the food. Going from getting laid by Dad's cast-offs regularly to getting NOTHING for a year or more...

I met a girl here, Gayatri, who is also a writer and was also on the capture team that nailed us. We always fight when we get together... but I keep wanting to get together with her! I don't tell her this, but I think she's really cool. A real change from the silly, shallow girls of the Families. (But, I don't tell HER that I think she's cool!)

And here ends the Grand Campaign to take down the Awakening Center and to rid the country of the "zombies". The Scorecard:

The Hawkins Family loses its Leader and Chief Paedophile to a mind wipe. It also loses its resources and perhaps its Heir Apparent.

The Miller Family: ditto.

The MacKenzie Family: gains resources, prestige, contacts, networking... poised to be the next leaders of our nameless town.

The Townspeople: (who did NOT rise up, by the way) gain resources, plus a couple of Agents to help them form a Commons, one not dependent on the big families.

The three Edge Agents lose... everything. According to Pico-Laton, they will never get a mind-wipe. They will be interrogated, researched, passed from Center to Center for study, until they drop dead.

Me? I'm not exactly sure WHAT I've won, but I firmly believe I've won SOMETHING...

[JOURNAL ENTRY END]

File No: T-4:		File Name:	Resolving Disputes 03: Dispute Regarding Crop Loss
Location:		Parties:	
Monk/ Master Supervising:	Selected Tales of The Culture Council		

[RECORD START]

MEMORANDUM

An issue has come up regarding a major crop loss in the Tulsa Center. This issue goes beyond what happens in that local center — It affects all of us.

Facts of the Issue:

Last year, a few Centers in the Tulsa area experienced the hardship of losing their entire crops to a series of weather conditions, including the "perfect storm" of floods, tornadoes, and a persistent drought. These weather events have left these Centers in a position where they cannot feed themselves, nor can they satisfy their annual contributions to the Culture Council.

Some Centers have pushed back at the notion that they should contribute to Tulsa's loss. They have stated, correctly, that they themselves have just gotten out of a deficit situation regarding their own finances, and had plans for their own capacity expansion. Covering Tulsa's loss would be a hardship on them and the Awakening Movement as a whole.

Resolution:

We cannot treat this situation as something happening to an individual Center, or a local area. These conditions can and will be felt by all in different ways during these Upheavals. Therefore, ALL of the Centers should come to the aid of Tulsa, and ensure the continued survival of that Center.

In the Age of Waste, there were insurance companies charging hefty premiums to mitigate the damage to the fortunate few who could afford those premiums. We don't have that system. What we have is each other. Together, we can mitigate the negative impacts, and spread those impacts around our system, so that no one center is unjustly injured.

Those of us in the Culture Council will take the lead in demonstrating this concept. We are suspending Tulsa's annual contributions to the Culture Council for the next three years, and will consider longer suspensions, if the need is still present. In addition, we are dedicating a percentage of our resources to the support of Tulsa. Furthermore, we are asking each of the Centers to dedicate a similar percentage of their resources (in actual resources or credits) toward the healing of Tulsa. For those Centers that can afford it, sending personnel for rebuilding and replanting would be helpful. (A bill for services may be appropriate, once Tulsa is back on its feet.)

We will move up or go down together.

We want to be explicit that these are not gifts, but no-interest loans to Tulsa. When they are able, we expect them to pay back these resources.

[NOTE: It took Tulsa two years to get back on its feet. In that time, the concept of "We are Tulsa!" became a rallying cry among all of the Centers, and helped to solidify the concept of "One for All, All for One". Tulsa has repaid all of its loans and service debts and is now a model Center and a shining example of the Awakening Movement.]

[RECORD END]

William's Journal Entry — Father + Son: Prepping the Mind Wipe

File No:		File Name:	Prepping the Mind Wipe
Location:		Parties:	William Hawkins, Jr
Monk/ Master Supervising:	From the pre-Awakening Center journal entries of William Hawkins, Jr (used with permission)		

[JOURNAL ENTRY START]

For some reason, next week they want me to talk with Dad, before he gets his new head.

I'm really not looking forward to it. I know he thinks I'm the one who sold out the group... he refuses to believe that the damn helmets didn't work. My only consolation is that Gayatri will be there.

My relationship with Dad is... complicated. Always has been. Or... maybe it isn't.

I never had anything like a "relationship" with Dad. He was just THERE. When present, he was giving orders to the servants and to us (Mom, brother David and me) like we were servants. We each had our coping mechanisms to deal with him:

SERVANTS: Toe the line. Keep your head down. Do what he says... so long as he's looking. Dad gave a lot of orders and had an amazingly short memory. (And don't EVER remind him that he forgot an order, or had just given the contrary order just a few hours earlier.)

MOM: Passive-aggressive. I think she hated his guts, but didn't have the resources of her own to bail on him.

He wanted her to call him "Father", especially in public. If she was called on to say something, she'd say, "Well, Bill... oops, I mean, 'Father'..." Letting everyone know that the "Father" bit was his idea, not hers. (If she timed it right, he'd forget about it before we get home. If not... she'd be wearing sunglasses for a week afterwards.)

DAVID: My brother would take on Dad at every opportunity. And lose. It was comical the way the two of them would go at it. The only problem: David was getting bigger and their battles were getting longer and more physical. Before long, one would be obliged to kill the other. I wasn't laying any bets on who would win that one...

(By the way: under the rules of our little fiefdom, I get everything when Dad dies. Little brother gets zero. I've already hedged my bet... I told David I'd split the estate with him when Dad dies. A little insurance that I don't wake up one morning dead. Fratricide happens...)

ME: I had Dad's faulty memory timed perfectly. "Okay, Dad, I just finished goofing off, just like you told me! Anything else?" He'd then tell me something like "build a new wing onto the house". I'd say, "Yes, Sir!", then go back to goofing off.

This worked, until he got drunk. It didn't happen often (at least, not around us), but when it did, the best strategy was to run for cover... (Mom's strategy: find one of his girls to place between herself and his rage.)

So... I don't know if I really HAD a relationship with Dad. When he died, I planned to cry at his funeral — I've already practiced it. That will solidify my standing with the other Families. Take over the "family business" (whatever that is — or was). If it's too unsavory, sell or give it to David. Or, turn it into something I wouldn't be embarrassed to reveal to my kids. Be a better ruler over the townspeople than Dad (I couldn't be worse at it, even if I tried really hard). Marry one of the cows. Have a couple of kids who don't hate my guts...

Or... dump the whole thing. Stay here at the Center. Learn a lot.
Get past being a sex-dead novice, so I can have a go at Gayatri.
(Maybe more than a go... she's really nice.)
[JOURNAL ENTRY END]

Gayatri's Journal — Interviewing the Commander of the "Grand Campaign"

File No:		File Name:	Interviewing the Commander of the "Grand Campaign"
Location:		Parties:	Novice Gayatri
Monk/ Master Supervising:		Monk Man-Onko	

[JOURNAL ENTRY START]

I've interviewed the Old Fart twice already. The first time, he was full of fire and outrage, trying to find out who in his group was the "traitor and terrorist". Refused to believe that it was his own pathetic brain waves that gave him away. (He believed that those sorry football helmets worked.)

He was amazingly obscene with me, and would have been violent, if not restrained. After he called me a "zombie cunt" (and less savory names) more times than I liked, I decided to play the "Congressman Barnes" card. When he found out Barnes was my father, he first got flustered, then apologetic, then genuinely curious about why I was in the Center. That led to our first genuine conversation:

HAWKINS: Why would you give up your God-given freedoms, to live in here and be told what to say, what to THINK?

ME: Nice speech. I'm sure there's a question buried in there somewhere...

Let me try to figure it out. First, what are those "freedoms" I gave up by being here?

(I could feel him move onto firm ground.)

HAWKINS: How about "Life, Liberty and the Pursuit of Happiness", guaranteed by our Constitution...

ME: *Actually, Bill, that's in the Declaration of Independence. And that's all political theory. Really, what changed in my life when I walked through the gate here?*

HAWKINS: *Well... how about the ability to THINK for yourself?*

ME: *What makes you think that I can't?*

HAWKINS: *Well, I'm told you folks aren't even allowed to curse in here.*

ME: *That's right, you paedophilic, cocksucking asshole! But, as you can see, having a rule against it doesn't mean you can't do it, now does it? You dipshit scumbag.*

(Silence for a moment.)

ME: *By, the way, Bill: what would happen to one of your town folks if they said to you what I just said to you?*

(More silence)

ME: *Yep, thought so. Your "freedoms" only apply to you.*

HAWKINS: *Well, at least I know that I'm not brainwashed.*

ME: *Yeah, me too.*

HAWKINS: *How would you know?*

ME: *I'd know because they would tell me.*

HAWKINS: *They could lie to you...*

ME: *But why? These folks believe in "Authenticity". It's one of their principal values...*

HAWKINS: *Bullshit! They could have you eating shit and believing its chocolate ice cream!*

ME: Right. But that would be a lie and thus "inauthentic". With a mind-wipe, they could have you eating shit, knowing its shit, knowing its disgusting, and still eating it anyway. Why lie about it?

HAWKINS: Because (pauses), this way, you can convince others to join you!

ME: Why do we need to convince anyone? We turn away hundreds, maybe thousands, every day.

HAWKINS: But if you want to co-opt our leaders, our vanguard...

ME: Bill, do you realize you're gonna get mind-wiped?

(The color drains from his face. A pretty cool effect! He "got it".)

ME: Yes, you came at us, loaded to the gills for violence, ready to be a martyr for the cause. Three weeks from now, you're gonna walk out that front gate, knowing that you'll never raise your hand against another human being. Especially US.

You'll leave with all of your memories intact, including all the little girls you raped, all the men and women you sold into the slavery... you pig.

HAWKINS: The 14th Amendment was passed under duress, by an illicit Congress!

ME: Stow it! Three weeks from now, you'll come to me and apologize! And, you're going to try to find all those human beings you sold and raped and make amends.

Because three weeks from now, you really will believe in "Life, Liberty and the Pursuit of Happiness".

SECOND MEETING:

Bill was a lot more subdued in our second meeting. The reality of his situation was beginning to dawn on him.

74

He could face "death", because it was unreal to him, just a big blank. He could face imprisonment, sitting solid in his beliefs that his pursuit of a distorted notion of "America" was worth his sacrifice.

But a mind-wipe? The knowledge that all of his thoughts, his memories, his experiences would remain intact, but OVERWRITTEN by... his sworn Enemy? An "Enemy" he could never lift a hand against?

Bill wanted a deal.

HAWKINS: Listen, uh, Gayatri, could you do me a favor? Could you get word to your father for me? Just tell him, "The Knight has fallen". He'll know what that means. He'll know who to inform.

ME: Come on, Bill. Pretty transparent code, there.

HAWKINS: But, I'm worried about my wife! Isn't that reasonable?

ME: Sure is. But, you didn't ask me to pass her a message, did you?

HAWKINS: Please! It's not too much of a favor. If you're still a human being, do this for me...

ME: Come on, Bill! In a week, you'll be back with your loving wife and at least three dozen children, by our count.

(Silence, then)

HAWKINS: There's no way to prove paternity!

ME: Won't have to. In a week, you'll welcome all of them with open arms. Along with their brutalized, traumatized mommies. You are such a pig.

[JOURNAL ENTRY END]

File No:		File Name: Resolving Disputes: Disputes Regarding Relationships and Liaisons	
Location:		Parties:	
Monk/ Master Supervising: Selected Tales of The Culture Council			

[RECORD START]

MEMORANDUM

It has come to the attention of the Culture Council that many centers are having issues regarding the Culture Council guidelines on relationships. Because of the nature of the conflicts, we believe that it is necessary to clarify this issue.

Facts of the Dispute:
From the beginning, the Culture Council has had a simple and clear policy toward relationships. That policy is marked by openness, transparency and mindfulness.

Any intimate relationship between consenting adults (18 years old or over) is allowed, so long as:

1. Such relationship is posted publicly on a "Relationships Board".

2. Each relationship is Witnessed by at least one other member of the Center. (For longer and/or more intricate relationships, the Abbot may require additional witnesses.)

Many Centers have argued for a more "traditional" view on relationships. Some have argued that only relationships between men and women be allowed. Others have argued that only "marriages" and "engagements" be allowed. Many have argued against the Culture Council imposing a maximum time span of 10 years before a relationship can be renewed or terminated — relationships within the Centers should be permanent.

On the other hand, many centers have argued against having guidelines at all. They believe their members should be free to experiment with their intimacy and sexuality without any interference by the Center or the Culture Council. They have argued in favor of maximum freedom of individual expression.

Resolution:
The Culture Council has carefully reviewed and re-examined its policies regarding relationships. We have decided to keep things basically "as is", for the next five years.

In our policies, we endeavor to balance the needs of the individual with the needs of the emerging society.

We have also endeavored to eliminate the need for dishonesty in relationships. Dishonesty does not merely affect the people involved in the relationship; it affects everyone in the society. Being able to designate a relationship as open or exclusive lets everyone in the Center know where they stand.

Both the "traditional" and the "emerging" centers argued against the tenure maximum on relationships. The Culture Council is adamant that this provision stand.

One slight modification: a few Centers have lobbied for the recognition of intimate relationships that involve more than two people. Those advocating the practice state that several different Keeper cultures support the practice. Those against the practice believe that it denigrates the notion of what "intimacy" means.

We decided that, for all proposed relationships that involve more than two people, each person involved must have a Witness to the relationship.

[RECORD END]

Gayatri's Journal: Father+Son+Journalist [Seeing Dad for the Last Time]

File No:		File Name:	Gayatri: Father+Son+Journalist
Location:		Parties:	Novice Gayatri
Monk/ Master Supervising:		Monk Man-Onko	

[JOURNAL ENTRY START]

I get to interview our father and son captives together: the paedophilic brute of a father and his cute but clueless son. (Amazingly clueless — hard to believe someone can draw air that long and know so little. And, amazingly cute! Easy to see he takes after his mother! Dad is one ugly sucker! I'd have jumped Junior's bones in a heartbeat if we were Outside! Who needs a brain just to screw! (What IS that stuff they put in our food? And where's the antidote!?!)

Anyway...

Back to the windowless interrogation room. Back to Daddie Dearest in shackles, buckled down in his wheelchair. Back to Junior, sitting next to me on a dark blue sofa, both of us trying to act like we're not hot for each other. Both of us have our "professional writer" faces on.

Daddy-o thinks the best strategy is a frontal assault. He doesn't wait for us to start; he aims both barrels at his son and pulls the trigger.

"Well, is that zombie cunt your reward for betraying your father and your country?"

Junior turns a million different shades of red. He really didn't see that coming.

"WHAT? I didn't... What are you talking about? Those stupid helmets didn't work! They saw you coming from miles away! You set yourself up!"

Hawkins sits back in his wheelchair, satisfied that he got in a good lick.

"Well, maybe you were mind-wiped from the start. You never had my ambition, you were always tryin' to get over and get by. You look like your momma and you roll over like her, too."

Junior goes silent, looking down at the floor. That's good — he knows how to manage his anger. Finally, he looks up and says to the old fart: "Dad, given your position here, I think we need to focus on what's happening to you right now. There may be a possibility for you to avoid a mind-wipe."

Hawkins perks up, then goes slack again. "What makes you think I can get out of a mind-wipe? Is that what they told you to tell me?"

"No one told me anything about why I'm here. I don't want to be here. I don't want to see you like this. I wish to God that you had never brought me into this."

"Like I said, you don't have the guts for this kind of work! I should have brought David along. He knows how to stand up for himself."

"The reason you didn't bring David is that if you gave him a gun, he'd use it on YOU!"

That shut Hawkins up. He was seething, but had nothing to say. I think if the restraints were off, he would have killed his own son.

Okay, time for me to play "Good Cop" (or, is it "Bad Cop"?) "Well, boys, I hate to interrupt 'Family Bonding Time', but this session does have a purpose. They asked me to do the pre-DCI interview, to get your honest views on a variety of subjects. Before they mind-wipe you back to being a five-year-old girl. With pigtails."

Dear Reader, I will spare you what happened over the next five minutes. Suffice it to say that Daddie Dearest had a complete meltdown. I thought they were going to have to sedate him. Screaming, yelling filth, straining so hard against his restraints that he actually tipped his chair over!

I had to look away — it was too much like seeing a tortured animal, locked in a cage. Junior, on the other hand, stared at him. Didn't blink. I think he was horrified also, but he was also fascinated.

After about five minutes, Hawkins just collapsed, went silent. As soon as he stopped, two attendants entered the room and sat up the wheelchair. One of them wiped off some of his spittle with a small towel, while the other looked at the bloody abrasions on his arms and knees where he'd been kicking against the chair. He sprayed something on the sores (they stopped bleeding), got up, nodded to me, then left the room.

"So, Bill, ready to answer some questions? Or, you want to flail around and foam at the mouth some more?"

Hawkins looked at me with tired eyes, "That's just a fraction of what I'm gonna give 'em when they come for my mind. I'll bite off my own tongue before I betray my country." Looking over to Junior, "Or betray my FAMILY."

"When you say 'family', do you include all those young girls that you raped? You PIG!"

He smiled slyly and said, "In a time of war, a prisoner of war is required only to give his name, rank, and serial number. My name is William Jefferson Hawkins. My rank is Battalion Commander for the Grand Campaign. My serial..."

"Battalion? Do you know how to count? Twenty guys out for a stroll is hardly a battalion!"

He paused. "We were counting the people who were going to rise up against you, to throw off their oppression."

"Yeah, that would have swelled your ranks to about 24."

"What do you know? But for some turncoats," he glared at his son, "we would have succeeded!"

"You keep thinking that, Billy." He cringed. I made a note: *He hates being called 'Billy'* . "But, right now I want to focus on your 'family business'."

Hawkins gave me a look of pure hatred. I thought he might pop his cork again. "I don't know how, but I'm gonna get me out of this chair somehow," he said unevenly. "And then you and me are gonna have a little personal time together."

"Oh boy! I can't wait! I'm *so* looking forward to that!!" *I put on a big smile, clapped my hands and jumped up and down in my seat. I caught Junior out of the corner of my eye checking out my bosom. I let him get an eyeful.* "But, Billy, I really want to talk about the 'family business'. Tell me: how many people did you dispose of at your facility per month?"

From the look on Junior's face, it became clear that he knew nothing about the business. Interesting. Hawkins said nothing.

"Really, Bill, this isn't going to be much of an interview if you aren't going to say anything. Okay, how about talking about the raid, then? What did you really want to do? Let's assume everything happened the way you wanted it to happen. Let's say you were running this Center now, not strapped to that chair. What would happen next?"

"You and I would be having this same interview — but you'd be the one strapped to the chair."

"Come on, Hawkins, get your mind out of the gutter for a minute! This may be your last time to engage in this kind of thinking! Humor me. What was going to happen next?"

"We would have used your facilities to broadcast to all other freedom fighters. We would have told them how to defeat you."

"You mean the football helmets."

"Yes, the blocking devices. Even without the success here, we still hope that the technology gets out. There's always hope to keep you people out of our minds."

You still won't believe that those helmets were useless, will you?"

He paused. "I have operational data that I can't divulge. Unless the traitors among us have already divulged that intel."

"By 'operational data', do you mean that little stroll your guy did in the Center six weeks ago? Wanna see our video?"

"I won't believe any photoshopped nonsense you people put together!"

"Oh yes you will! That's the great thing about mind-wipes! An hour after the wipe, you're gonna believe EVERYTHING we say!"

He was silent.

"Okay, we're about finished here. I've only got one or two more questions, then we're done.

"Bill, many people treat the mind-wipe as an execution. Therefore, they try to grant the person who is going to be wiped their last requests — if possible. So, they want to know what you want over the next 24 hours. What do you want to eat? Drink? Who do you want as visitors?"

"I'd just like to be alone with you in this room for 15 minutes. Do you think that can be arranged?"

"Awww, Bill, you are such a romantic! No, I'm serious. Say nothing and you'll get nothing. Say something and you might get it. A steak? A beer? A movie?"

"A steak and fries would be great. And a beer."

"What brand?"

"Whatever you can salvage. Budweiser or Miller would be great."

"We might have both. Which would you prefer?"

He paused. "Either one would be great."

"Fine. Would you like anything else?"

"You mentioned movies. Do you think you could find the old movie 'The Patriot'?"

"Anything else? Is there anyone you want to send a message to?"

"I want to get a message to your father, to Congressman Barnes."

"We'll see. One last question: you didn't say anything about dessert with your meal. Would you like ice cream? Apple pie?"

"Hey, how about both!"

"They have peach pie and apple pie here. Which would you prefer?

"I guess I'd take apple..."

"Are you sure you want to send the message to my father? Not your wife? Your son?"

He thought for a second. "No, I'd like the message to go to Barnes."

"Great! We're done now. Junior and I are going off to lunch, and you're going off to get your new mind!"

"WHAT? You said in a day or two!"

"No, we're ready now. I had to ask you those questions for us to calibrate your psychology. Without it, the mind-wipe is haphazard. The more they know about your preferences, the easier it is to direct the mind wipe.

"So, you're calibrated now. Off you go, you imbecilic pig. You should consider the mind-wipe a favor. If it were up to me, I'd give you a mind-wipe with a double-barreled shotgun! I'd lock you in the same room with all the girls you raped, and let them castrate you with a dull spoon! I'd cut out your tongue and feed it..."

"Well, I guess I'm lucky that it ain't up to you! Come on, let's go! Let's see how much you get out of me!"

With that, the two attendants came in and wheeled him out. That was the last time I saw that version of William Hawkins, Sr. The younger William Hawkins took me to lunch in the canteen.

[JOURNAL ENTRY END]

Tales of the Culture Council – Resolving Disputes 04: Dispute Regarding Services for Money ("Spa" Centers)

File No:		File Name:	Resolving Disputes 04: Dispute Regarding Services For Money ("Spa" Centers)
T-5:			
Location:		Parties:	
Monk/ Master Supervising:		Selected Tales of The Culture Council	

[RECORD START]

MEMORANDUM

It has come to the attention of the Culture Council that several Centers are offering special services to their members who can afford to pay a premium in cash. These services range from small "perks" like extra helpings per meal or slightly larger dwellings, up to "luxury" services like domestic workers, "mini-mansions", recreational facilities and preferential admissions to Center educational facilities. Many of these services are not available to Center members on Awakening Center credits, but for "cash only".

Facts of the Issue:
Structured correctly, once a Center is up and running, it should need very few outside inputs to maintain itself. Using the analogy of a glider: once it is off the ground, it can use available energy inputs — rising thermals — to keep itself aloft.

However, to get to its cruising altitude, an Awakening Center needs MONEY. A significant amount of it. In our early years, those monies came from donations, crowdfunding, gifts and short-term "investments" in specific Center-related projects.

Early on, the Centers adopted a "pay-as-you-go" policy. Members were expected to work for the benefits they received.

However, in a Center's early days, people are permitted (and sometimes encouraged) to "buy" goods and services, providing the Center with "hard" currency.

A problem arises when Centers become dependent on the cash they receive. In some areas, it is much easier to offer additional services to wealthy "part-time" participants than to create the sustainable systems and structures that will make Breaker money obsolete.

The presence of continuing inputs of cash also opens the door to corruption. While none of the Centers have succumbed to that temptation yet, the availability of large amounts of cash is simply too much temptation — it will happen, sooner or later.

Therefore, effective immediately, all Centers will take measures to completely divest themselves from the US monetary system, effective within the next seven (7) years. Steps will include:

— All Centers will abandon the practice of "Cash only" services and facilities. Center members will be able to avail themselves of ALL services using Center credits (or a combination of credits and cash), or the services will be discontinued for all.

— Within two years, the Culture Council will no longer accept dollars from Centers as their annual resource payments. (Payments will be either for Center credits or for fixed goods and services.)

— Within three years, our Culture Commons Banks will no longer facilitate transfers of dollars for any Awakening Center. If the collapse of money happens after three years, each Center will be stuck with the dollars it is holding.

— Within five years, no Center will accept dollars in payment for anything, period. (After two additional years, this ban will be extended to all Breaker currencies, including euros, yen, pesos and pounds.)

We are hoping that the "Spa Centers" will see the writing on the wall, and work quickly to transform their economic systems.

—

[NOTE: They did. Three years later, when the collapse of the US economic system was completed, there were no Centers that were still taking dollars in payment for services (see Book 01: The Collapse of Money)].

[RECORD END]

William's Journal: After the Mind Wipe — Meeting Dad for the First Time

File No:		File Name:	After the Mind Wipe — Meeting Dad for the First Time
Location:		Parties:	William Hawkins, Jr
Monk/ Master Supervising:		From the pre-Awakening Center journal entries of William Hawkins, Jr (used with permission)	

[JOURNAL ENTRY START]

Well, they did it. I just met the new Dad.

I'm not sure what I was expecting. I had a whole range of possibilities in mind. One where they wheeled him into the room in a wheelchair, his head shaved clean, with a big surgical scar on one side and a dumb look on his face. Another possibility, where he had a blank expression and asked me what my name was (or what his own name was). Another where they really did turn him into a five-year-old girl.

The reality: It's not like having a new father. It's like having a father for the first time.

After my long lunch with Gayatri, I went with my "minders" (really guards). They didn't take me back to my room. They took me into a building I hadn't been in before. A room much bigger than mine, with lots of windows and a patio that looked out over the main part of the Awakening Center campus. (Before, they kept him in a windowless room that had only a cot and a chair in it — both bolted down. They said that he could "earn" better surroundings through good behavior. That was the minimum that they gave anyone. I guess his behavior has improved.)

My first surprise: there was Dad.

He was standing at the window, with his back to me. Even from across the room, I could tell that things were... different. He stood straighter than usual. His hands were behind his back, as though contemplating what he saw.

Gone was the wild hair that he kept pulled back in that nasty-looking ponytail. Gone was his beard. He had a short, military style, bush haircut and a neatly trimmed mustache and goatee. He wore the jumpsuit common among the monks in the Awakening Center...solid gray, no insignia. He looked like a businessman.

While all of that's freaky enough, what happened next set my teeth on edge. He turned to me and SMILED.

It wasn't like I never saw him smile before. I knew what his teeth looked like. But when he smiled before, he looked like an alligator that had just swallowed something whole, and was waiting for it to stop kicking in his stomach. He looked predatory.

This new guy smiled at me like he was EMBARRASSED. Then he said, "Well, Bill, I guess this is as awkward for you as it is for me."

That might be the most he'd ever said to me that didn't have an order attached to it.

I had just seen him a few hours earlier, but this guy looked completely different. If someone had told me that the man standing before me was the BROTHER of William Hawkins — the taller, more successful, self-confident and self-assured older brother, I would've believed him. If someone had told me that THIS was William Hawkins, I would've laughed at him.

I guess I didn't do a very good job of hiding my shock. The man before me said, "Why don't we sit down; you look like you're about to fall over!" I took him up on his offer. I sat on the blue, nondescript sofa, while he occupied one of the two matching chairs in the room.

When I regained my voice, the first thing I said was "Well... How do you feel?"

He laughed again. "Actually, pretty good, considering! That's one of the gifts of their procedure: no sense in you feeling poorly after it.

"I'm also feeling the effects of their food here. As you know, it's not all bad!" William Hawkins praising something. Another shock.

"And, now that I'm no longer a security risk, I have a much nicer room, with a view!

"They really trust their procedure that much?" I asked.

"There is no lock on my door. I can leave here whenever I want," he said.

"So, why are you still here?"

"Well, I've got some loose ends to straighten up here first, then I'll be off. And you are one of my loosest ends..."

"Well... Dad, I don't know how to ask this but... you do know you've been mind-wiped, don't you?"

He paused and looked at me as though he were contemplating the question. Then he said, "Of course. Can't you see how different I am? None of this was exactly voluntary!" He showed me the scratches on his wrist from knocking over his wheelchair. "Do you remember how I got these?"

"Do you know how much they wiped out? How much of your former life do you remember?"

A pained expression crossed his face and he slowly rose from his seat and walked to the sliding glass doors. He folded his arms across his chest. "It's not really a 'mind-wipe'," he said. "That's the wrong name for the procedure. I remember every damn thing. They didn't wipe ANYTHING. I remember my entire life. And I really don't want to..."

He paused, then continued.

"They didn't wipe anything. What they did was something called an 'empathy adjustment'. They said that I could do the bad thingsI did because I lacked empathy with others. Something wrong with my amygdala, or something. That's a mild way to say that! I would've said that I didn't give a shit about anyone or anything – even my 'Glory of America' rhetoric was just talk.

"Now... I remember all the things I did. All the people I hurt. All the people I KILLED. I can't not remember them. They gave me a memory enhancer, to make sure of that."

"Well, Dad, your memory wasn't all that good to begin with," I said.

"My memory lapses were a function of me trying to come to grips with the magnitude of the harm I've done. I could not handle the reality of my own life.

"Now I remember it all. And I can remember all the times you used my faulty memory against me! Well played!"

"Oops! Hey, I didn't mean..."

"Don't worry about it! I would've gone crazy if I knew before, but now it's pretty funny! One of the few funny things in a pathetic life.

"So, they opened up my empathy, my ability to feel. Then, they gave me a strong bias against suicide and suicidal behavior. They knew that would be the option I would choose to take, if I was confronted with the reality of my own behavior.

"They also gave me a bias toward wanting to make things right. I have no idea how to do it, but I have to do SOMETHING. I have to make this sorry life mean something."

"Well, things can't be so bad... I'm sure you will..."

"YOU HAVE NO IDEA! YOU DON'T KNOW WHAT IT'S LIKE IN HERE!" He jabbed his finger against his head and screamed. Then he slammed back into his seat, looking exhausted. "I'm sorry. I'm sorry for yelling at you, Son. It's just that you don't know the torture of being confronted with... Yourself."

William Hawkins apologizing. Another surprise.

He continued. "I feel like I'm locked in a cage with a wild beast, a mad dog. I feel like I'm locked inside a cage with the most vicious animal you could ever imagine. And the cage is RIGHT HERE. I'm locked inside my own mind! And I'm locked here FOREVER... I can't even take my own life!"

He's right: I can't imagine. Yes, I always thought he was a schmuck. To actually realize that you are a bad person, to actually realize one's own mistakes... Nope, I can't imagine it.

"Well, Dad... If you can't take your life," I said, "maybe you can find someone to help you out there. I won't do it, but I'll bet David would jump at the opportunity!"

He got very quiet. He was looking down at his hands. I think he was talking more to his hands than to me. "Do you know that I was planning on killing your brother?" he said. "Once the operation was successful, once the 'Grand Campaign' was over, did you know your brother was going to have an accident? And your mother? I was tired of both of them. I knew I couldn't get away with killing them directly, so I had arranged with some folks on the other side of the state to do it for me.

"I told them to rape your mother. I told them to make it look really messy and convincing. I told them to make it look like David had tried to come to her rescue. I told them to send me pictures.

"I wanted to kill my own son and my own wife. I told them to TAKE PICTURES!! That's one of a million different memories that I don't want! What am I going to do? What am I going to do to make up for that?

"I'm sorry for what I've done to you. I'm sorry for being such a brute and a bully. Being a brute and bully to you is inexcusable as a father. But I tell you this so that you can see that just being a bad father pales to insignificance next to the magnitude of my crimes.

"And... If David wants to kill me, my DCI procedure means that I would stay away from him, to preserve my life. The folks here want me to live a long, long time. That's their torture." He stopped and drank water from a bottle nearby.

"They say that they are compassionate, that they believe in nonviolence, but what they did to me... I'd rather face daily whippings, until the meat fell off my bones. I'd rather face Gayatri's shotgun. ANYTHING... other than being locked inside my mind with... ME."

I had a sick feeling in my stomach. "Dad... What is the family business?"

Dad walked back to the glass doors, leaned against it and folded his arms. While staring out the window, he said, "The folks here said that my amygdala was stunted. That I could not feel what others felt; that I could not feel anything."

He turned on me again, anger in his eyes. I knew that anger was not aimed at me. "There is no family business. THERE IS NO FAMILY BUSINESS! There's just MY business. Perhaps the only decent thing I did in life was to shield you, your mother, and your brother from... the worst of me.

"My business was... PAIN. I enjoyed causing others pain. At first I freelanced, but then I realized that many people, powerful people, would pay good money to have others killed, in the most horrible and painful fashion.

"Then, I began to specialize. Do you know what a snuff film is, Son? It's where I rape a woman to death, while videotaping the whole thing. People pay lots of money to see that. Gayatri's father, Congressman Barnes, was one of my best customers.

"Most of those films were really low-quality. Not me. Not mine. Mine were high end. I had an entire studio set up for it, down in the next valley over. Part of the operation was a pig farm, so I could dispose of the bodies quickly. So, it looks like I made a lot of money from farming.

"I would rape them, torture them, rape them some more, kill and dismember them, then rape them some more. The folks here at the Awakening Center gave me a compulsion against vomiting, which is what I want to do every time I think about what I did in front of those cameras."

"Dad... The girls at the house..."

"That was auditioning for the Farm. The ones that didn't scream loud enough, the ones that didn't have the right terror in their eyes... I gave to you. The other ones made it to the Farm. And then the pigpen.

"I wish I could say I was not that person anymore. I am STILL that person. But that part of me is locked away and will never see the light of day again. This 'me' will do his best to try to make amends." He turned and faced the window.

"What are your plans now?" I asked.

"Well... some of that depends on you."

"What do you mean?"

"The present plan is for me to go back and re-insert myself into my life. And then dismantle it."

There's yet another surprise. I wonder how he thinks Mr. Crew Cut is going to get past the front door. I asked, "No more 'Make America Great Again!'? No more 'Grand Campaign'?"

And yet another surprise. He smiled and said, "Actually, that part will stay! The more I think about it, the more I realize that the people in this country really need SOMETHING to believe in."

"But... I thought that the folks here would have wiped away your violent tendencies."

"They did – but not the idea or philosophy behind the ideology. They just helped me see that the Awakening Centers are not the problem standing in the way of America's greatness. The problem is US. The problem is ME. The problem is that the movement to restore America is full of the kind of sadistic, psychotic assholes I used to be.

"Yes, I believe that we can restore this continent to some level of its former greatness. Not the wasteful parts — the Center folks won't allow a return to the Age of Waste.

"I believe we can Restore America," he said, "without scapegoats and witch hunts, without violence toward each other or anyone else. It's going to be quite something to see how I can convince people of that."

Okay. Sounds nice. I don't think he's got a snowball's chance in Hell of convincing any of his Campaign buddies of this, but what the heck? It'll keep him busy. But, on to the more important questions. "What's this have to do with me, though?"

"The folks here at the Center will aid me in getting re-inserted in my life. We've got a backstory brewing... That the party was ambushed and only a few of us escaped. I escaped by cutting my hair and beard and disguising myself to look like them. The McKenzies and Riker will back me up on that."

"But what about me?" I said.

"Well, that's one of the loose ends. It all depends on what your plans are. In one part of the story, you are killed in the initial raid. In that story, you stay here at the Awakening Center and become a novice.

"In the second story, you come back with me. However, to do that, you've got to agree to a voluntary DCI, so that you don't blow any of the key elements of the story," he said.

"I have to volunteer to get mind wiped!?"

"Well... Does it look like too hard a procedure? It would be a simple suggestion not to blow our cover. You would remember everything about this time in the Center, but you would be unable to talk about it with anyone, except me, Riker and the McKenzies.

"But, I'm guessing that you're going to stay here. You seem to fit in. And everyone can see how you are drooling over my Inquisitor, 'Lady Gayatri of the Sharp Tongue.' "

"Dad!"

"It's OK son... Everything she ever said about me was absolutely true. The old William Hawkins was a pig... and much worse.

Son, you could do a lot worse than Gayatri back at home. And these folks have something that I think would work well for you. The kind of discipline and direction that I could never give you. A real education. Real learning."

"But, if I don't go back, what will you tell Mom?"

"The truth: that you were captured. They'll fill in their own story — that you're probably now a mind-wiped, brainless zombie."

"Well, Dad... I'm asking this as delicately as possible: how does it feel to be a mind-wiped, brainless zombie?"

He laughed. "Bill, do you know who planted those stories of zombies? THEY DID!! The folks at the Centers! It's one of the ways they kept people from climbing their walls. Back at the height of the Upheavals, people were so desperate, they would risk death for a loaf of bread. But, for some reason, those same people would back away when threatened with being a 'zombie'."

"Why is that?"

"Who knows? Maybe too many horror movies. I'm sure the brain folks up on the sixth floor of the Exploratory have some theories, but the bottom line is that it worked."

[JOURNAL ENTRY END]

Part Three: The New Experiences of Consciousness

Inter-Species Consciousness — The First Hemi-Humans

File No:		File Name:	The First Hemi-Humans
Location:		Parties:	Guest Lecture In the *"The Alternatives to Human Consciousness"* Class
Monk/ Master Supervising: Monk Man-Onko			

[TRANSCRIPT START]

[The class begins with a viewing of a narrated video clip from Man-Onko's Journal:

I watch him swim through the murky waters, through the maze of openings and corridors, what he calls his "apartment". As ungainly, even crippled as he is on land, he is elegant, even poetic, in water.

He can shut down the cameras and the vid screens whenever he wishes — that's our agreement with him and his "cousins". But he doesn't shut them down. He wants us to see. He wants ME to see.

He thinks he's beautiful. I'm working on it...]

[End of video clip]

Monk Man-Onko: Okay, settle down! Let's get started. I see that there are some hands up already. Yes, Neely?

Novice Neely: I know he must have looked different to you way back then, but for me, he's just... ordinary. For a ceta-human, I mean.

Monk Man-Onko: Hey, wait! I'm not THAT old! [Laughter] Yes, you are growing up in a world where hemi-humans are commonplace. But, I can tell you, sitting in on those first births, there was NOTHING normal about it! We came within inches of getting it completely wrong.

You probably know already that I'm doing this lecture today because I was a "facilitator" for the first few births of hemi-humans. A very reluctant facilitator! I didn't want to see a baby born — for me, I thought that would be a pretty yucky experience! [Laughter] I didn't know that "yucky" meant coming close to death for all of us.

One more thing before I show you the video of my godson's birth. You may have heard that his mother, Krista-Lin, had some very serious mental and emotional challenges before she came to the Center. Given the fact that this was the first time a human being was giving birth to what we now call a "hemi-human", Unity took the unusual step of flying over a team of their DCI experts. They gave her an adjustment a few months before Aquallon was born so that she could handle the delivery. Very rare for them to act just for one person like that. From Krista-Lin's perspective, she was *prepared* to birth a hemi-human. That was as "normal" for her as having a... well, a baby that breathed air and didn't have killer brain waves.

Novice Season: Why did Unity do that? They certainly don't seem to LIKE us very much.

Monk Man-Onko: They like us... in their own way. No, they were as motivated as we were for a look at Krista-Lin's baby. The spontaneous birth of hemi-humans is something that doesn't happen in Unity.

Novice Season: Why not?

Monk Man-Onko: Unity is pretty closed-mouth about their birthing processes. However, I think it's because there's so little genetic difference in Unity. They are essentially CLONES. Not a lot of room for spontaneous evolution.

But, we're drifting. Let's put on the rest of the video and take a look at what happened years ago.

[Continuation of video. A large, white laboratory room, dominated by a large tank of water. Six medical personnel plus MO outside the tank, three inside assisting Krista-Lin, who is attached to a birthing chair. Krista-Lin in labor...]

Monk Man-Onko: (From the video) This isn't right!

Dr. Owens: This is how we normally set up for water births.

Monk Man-Onko: Yeah, but this isn't a normal water birth! I said before, that tank is TOO SMALL. She needs to be in a swimming pool!

Dr. Owens: Now stop being ridiculous! We're not going to take over the monk's swimming pool just so this little girl can have her little baby! We've already accommodated you by taking over this lab from the marine department — and they're not very happy about that! Water births usually happen in a tank the size of a hot tub!

Monk Man-Onko: When I came here, I was told I was going to get all the resources I asked for! Now, I'm askin' and I ain't gettin!

Dr. Shelton: Okay, I think we all need to calm down...

Dr. Owens: You think just because you've got a friend or two on the Culture Council, you can come in here and throw your weight around! I don't know why you've got so much to say about this. You're not even the father!

Monk Man-Onko: [pauses] No, I'm not throwing my weight around. I don't have any weight to throw around. I'm throwing the Culture Council's weight around. And, I'm just about to throw some your way. [Man-Onko reaches for phone...]

Nurse Madison: Doctor, I think we're getting close...

Monk Man-Onko: At least get those three girls out of the tank!

103

Dr. Owens: I want you to stop ordering me...

Doctor Shelton: It's okay. We don't need three attendants. Sandra, why don't you come out of the tank?

[Nurse Sandra exits tank]

Dr. Owens: Okay, here it comes. That's right... Just let it emerge in the water, on its own. Yes, that's... WAIT!

Dr. Shelton: Jesus Christ, what IS it? What's that on its head?

Dr. Owens: It's arms and legs are all wrong! Look at its face! Look at how it's swimming around the tank. WHAT IS IT??

Doctor Shelton: It's swimming around, still attached to the umbilical cord!

Monk Man-Onko: Okay, everybody take a chill pill and slow down! We've got to...

Nurse Madison: The mother is unconscious. Stable condition.

Dr. Owens: Keep her head out of the water. Doctor Shelton, get the surgery prepped. Nurse, get two gurneys and get them out of the water. We've got to get that mass off of its head. It looks like it's wearing a jellyfish.

Monk Man-Onko: Wait a minute! I don't think...

Dr. Owens: And get this guy OUT of here! Call Security if you have to! We don't have time for sightseers! I want mother and infant prepped for surgery in five minutes!

[From video: All personnel in the room freeze, then fall down into epileptic fits. Dr. Owens falls and gashes his head. Doctor Shelton convulses and passes out. Nurse Madison in the tank passes out. Nurse Cathy falls face forward and apparently drowns.

104

Man-Onko is the only person moving. In great pain, he moves to an emergency water release valve for the tank.]

Monk Man-Onko: Release us! Or I drain the tank! No one is going to cut on you. I'll protect you! But, if you don't release us NOW, I'll drain the tank and you'll die!

[From video: The infant stops swimming within the tank and faces Man-Onko. Man-Onko groans and drops to his knees... but pulls the handle. Instantly, the water starts to drain. When it gets a third of the way down, all seizures in the room suddenly stop. Man-Onko recovers and stops the tank draining when it reaches halfway.]

Monk Man-Onko: Okay, everybody listen up! NO SURGERY. Nothing will happen to Aqua-Boy here without his consent! And by that I mean MY CONSENT! [Moving to Dr. Owens]: You got that? Or, do you want to spend more quality time down there on the floor, pissing yourself?

Dr. Owens: Look here! You're not medical personnel! I will do what is medically called for, for the care and protection of my clients!

Monk Man-Onko: There's only one person in charge in this room... and that's HIM! You want him to prove it again?

Dr. Shelton: No procedures without your consent. His consent.

Dr. Owens: But... we've got to cut the umbilical cord!

Monk Man-Onko: Explain it to me, and I'll cut it.

Dr. Owens: You're not medical personnel!!

Monk Man-Onko: Look, one of your medical personnel is floating face down in that tank. And she didn't even try to go after him with a knife.

Dr. Shelton: How do you know he won't fry you?

Monk Man-Onko: I don't. But, I'm pretty sure he WILL go after you if you try anything.

Dr. Shelton: I'll walk you through the procedure. It should be absolutely painless, to him and his mother.

Dr. Owens: Then, we'll need a close examination of the mass. Those tentacles, on the child's head.

Monk Man-Onko: [To Dr. Shelton] I think we'll make more progress if we can get him out of the room (indicating Dr. Owens).

[End of video. Lights up.]

Monk Man-Onko: Questions?

Novice Season: Yes. What happened after that?

Monk Man-Onko: Things calmed down after Dr. Owens left the room. We got the umbilical cord cut, Nurse Cathy out of the tank, and Aquallon calmed down.

Novice Season: How did he come up with that name?

Monk Man-Onko: Actually, we've got several names for him. Aquallon is the most commonly accepted name. He actually likes "Aqua-Boy", but only from me!

Novice Stewart: What would happen if I called him "Aqua-Boy"?

Monk Man-Onko: You'd wind up with a hum-dinger of a headache! He's gotten his neural projection power honed down, so that if three of you were standing shoulder to shoulder 25 feet away, the person in the middle would get the headache, the folks on either side would feel... uneasy, maybe a little dizzy.

Novice Stewart: Wow!

Monk Man-Onko: Not wow for him. He wants to get as good as a dolphin. His cousins can do that up to 100 feet away.

Novice Season: How's he do it?

Monk Man-Onko: Cetaceans like whales and dolphins can communicate using an oil-filled bladder in their heads. Aquallon has one in that strangely shaped head of his. And special processing bodies in his stomach and liver to produce the oil. Electrical generating systems in his nervous system. Oxygen-compacting and storage bladders, so that he can stay under an amazingly long time — much longer than dolphins. He's the full package. He's given credit as the first true "hemi-human, the first true blend between a human being and... something else".

Novice Stewart: How's he fit all those new organs into his head and still have room for his brain? His head doesn't look that much bigger than ours... just... lumpy.

Monk Man-Onko: The brain in his head is a fraction of the size of ours. It's just that he's got a lot more brain distributed throughout his body.

Novice Season: Wait a minute! How is that even... possible?

Monk Man-Onko: He's borrowing structure from his other cousins, the octopuses. Octopodes. Octopi. WHATEVER. [Laughter] They have brains in their heads and also distributed into each of their eight limbs. He's got close to 60% of his "brain" in those tentacles that stick out from under his gills, and all over the rest of his body, too.

Novice Neels: Wait... [Pauses] I'm looking at him, but I'm having a really hard time working through all this. How can you have your BRAIN distributed throughout your BODY? Where is the structure? Doesn't your brain have to be encased in BONE?

Monk Man-Onko: First, take a look at him. I really mean it when I say he's the total package.

His spinal cord is four to five times the volume of yours. That's an awful lot of processing neurons inside a bony case. And, because his vertebrae is softer, he can swim more efficiently than you and me.

He doesn't have a lymphatic system. It's been replaced by brain tissue — which accounts for some of the distributed part of his "brain". He's got a lot more neurons than we do.

Novice Stewart: If he's an evolutionary jump, why weren't these jumps in evolution happening earlier in human history?

Monk Man-Onko: They were... It's just that the consciousness of the time considered them "freaks" or "demons", and either killed them or put them in sideshows. How could they know that they were birthing humans who could communicate with the consciousness of whales and dolphins, at a time when they denied that whales and dolphins were conscious?

No, it's been happening all along. What was necessary was US... the kind of society that could understand, support and nurture that kind of consciousness. And, look how close WE came to getting it wrong! Look how Dr. Owens wanted to lop off what he couldn't understand.

Keepers never saw "species" as separate. They saw "all beings" as different manifestations of the same thing, the same way that fingers and livers are very different, perhaps even opposing, but ultimately the same.

Novice Seasons: So, are you saying that Aquallon would have been accepted in a Keeper society?

Monk Man-Onko: [pauses] Not necessarily. They could have seen him as a "devil creature" and had him exorcised. He's REALLY different! Or, there may not have been anyone who knew that he needed a water birth... or, if they did, they may not have had the resources to deliver.

Novice Seasons: Why were YOU able to pick up his signals?

Monk Man-Onko: I don't think that's a mystery. Both Krista-Lin and Victory were in my pod. We bonded.

Novice Neels: I have sort of a philosophical question: I thought that killing one of us was a cause for Extreme Expulsion, or a mind wipe. But, there he is, swimming around. Did he not get expelled or wiped because he was different? Or because he would have wiped us first?

Monk Man-Onko: Who did he kill?

Novice Neels: That nurse! Right there! Floating face down in that tank! [pointing to the video screen].

Monk Man-Onko: [Smiling] Aquallon didn't kill her. He just stopped her heart.

Novice Neels: [pause] Isn't that the same thing?

Monk Man-Onko: [Still smiling] Not if you restart it!

Novice Neels: WHAT??

[General pandemonium]

Monk Man-Onko: She didn't drown. He sent her a signal that stopped EVERYTHING, including heartbeat, brainwaves, respiration... She was very "dead", but not "drowned". After all the commotion died down and we got Dr. Owens out of the room, Aquallon sent me a signal to put the nurse on a stretcher, face up. Then he jump-started her.

Novice Neels: What... What did he do?

Monk Man Onko: Beats me. I don't know how he shut her down, so I don't know how he started her up. I'm not sure HE knows. But, that little stunt completely freaked out the Culture Council. None of them will get within 20 miles of him. I think he's even freaked out Unity — and that's a LOT of freaking out!

Novice Neels: Is 20 miles... far enough?

Monk Man-Onko: No idea. You're all thinking about the fact that he's 500 feet away from you right now, right? [Laughing] Well, outside of the people trying to kill him, he's never used his "death ray" on anyone.

Novice Sheraton: Is the nurse okay now?

Monk Man-Onko: Yes. No lasting effects from being the first human killed by a hemi-human... And also, the first human brought back to life by a hemi-human. The only lasting change is a very deep belief in God — and in Aquallon. She's tried to start the Church of Aquallon, but we've kind of frowned on it.

Novice Neely: What about Aquallon? Does he want to be the centerpiece of a church?

Monk Man-Onko: [pauses] We've never asked him.

Novice Neely: Why not?

Monk Man-Onko: [pauses] Master Auroron once taught me a very important lesson: Never ask a question to which you are not prepared to hear the answer. I don't think any of us are prepared for "The Church of the Hemi-Human".

Novice Neely: So... What exactly is a "hemi-human"?

Monk Man-Onko: You know, I'm letting you guys go easy! I'm supposed to be asking these questions!

It's just a fancy name for a being that is part human and part... something else. "New beings" are the interface between an up-moving human consciousness and more mature forms of terrestrial consciousness:
- Whales and dolphins
- Elephants
- Cephalopods (octopuses)
- Collective, "colony" beings (bees, birds, ants...and Unity)

They are here to fill an ecological niche, a blank spot in our life map.

Think about it: it's taken one million years for humanity to start acting like one species. Up until a few centuries ago, we humans were still EATING each other on a regular basis. Up until the 2030s, the majority of human effort went toward creating weapons of mass destruction and keeping resources away from one another. Before humanity started acting like we had a common interest, before us, our leaders treated humans like separate warring factions, almost like different species.

Once we started uniting, once the Awakening Movement and Unity came along, LIFE started filling in the niches between us and the other self-aware beings.

Right now, full humans, hemi-humans and dolphins are at work in two of the world's oceans, working to expand fish populations that serve as food for all three "consciousness species".

This is not "fishing" in the old sense of the word. Nothing is getting depleted. If anything, the populations of all fish groups have gone up.

This is what happens when you take MONEY out of the equation. No more industrial-scale fishing. No more murderous drift nets. A happy ocean, with enough food for all.

It's not a matter of interacting with beings who look and act like humans, with the same little fears, jealousies, and egos. Human consciousness is not an apex. Before the Upheavals, some of us humans didn't act like we were "conscious". Perhaps the true hallmark of consciousness is the recognition that you are not alone, that you are not so special.

Human consciousness has finally become an important part of Terrestrial meta-consciousness, primarily due to the fact that we now recognize we are neither alone in our consciousness, nor are we the most important. Being able to speak with our other forms of terrestrial consciousness, our "cousins", has been the key. Inter-species consciousness becomes the interface for other spatial environments (cosmic consciousness) and other Timelines and Timeline-Narratives (temporal consciousness).

Under the old notions of physics, time travel, or even long distance space travel, is not possible. In Solon Consciousness and the forms of physics derived from solo consciousness, Einstein was right. Moving physical objects through either space or time is not only impossible, it's just dumb.

But now that we understand that the meat part of us is just a convenient vehicle to transport consciousness across the surface of our planet, we can find and create other vehicles to move that consciousness through both space and time. Without the meat. Or with substitute meat. Or with substitute dimensions. Actually, very easily.

Novice Neely: But... is this new Terrestrial consciousness strong enough to encounter a non-Terrestrial consciousness? Is Aquallon our ambassador to space aliens? [laughter]

Monk Man-Onko: [not laughing] At present, no. Not for a while, probably another 500 to 1,000 years. A short while. Perhaps Aquallon's great-grandchildren.

And it is important to hedge our bets. We may encounter non-terrestrial beings who are so strange, we have no points of interaction. Yes, even stranger than Unity! [Laughter] On that day, we don't want to be limited to one planet.

Novice Sheraton: But... isn't this just assuming that there are other forms of consciousness out there?

Monk Man-Onko: We are not assuming. We know. [A stunned silence falls over the room.] And THAT will be the end of our class today!

[END OF TRANSCRIPT]

Rising to the Challenge of Unity: The Awakening of the Culture Council

File No:		File Name:	The Awakening of the Culture Council
Location: **Omaha Awakening Center**		**Parties:** Councillors of the Culture Council (⅓ from remote locations) Ambassadors of Unity	
Monk/ Master Supervising:		First Councillor Ringing Waters	
Conversation at the Twenty-fifth Quarterly Ambassadorial Gathering between the Culture Council and Unity. Hosted by the Omaha Awakening Center. As its usual practice, one third of CC members call in from remote locations.			

[RECORD START]

First Councillor: Unity Representatives, greeting. We know that you like to get right to the point, so we shall. We of the Awakening Movement have just suffered our most crushing defeat, and our highest loss of life, at the hands of the Edge. We are seeking your assistance in this matter. Last Tuesday, agents of the Edge attempted to seize one of our tightline communications nodes, outside of our South Chicago...

Berlin Unity: Unity knows what happened.

First Councillor: [pause] Well, then you know the significance of such an attack. The tightline communications system is absolutely crucial to our entire system of communications and economic flow between the Centers. The loss of even...

Madrid Unity: Please do not exaggerate.

Warsaw Unity: Nothing is "absolutely crucial" to anything.

Prague Unity: Your failsafes were more than adequate to prevent the seizure of the van carrying your communication equipment.

Rome Unity: All of the electronic equipment melted down at the time of seizure. Edge gained nothing.

Athens Unity: Nothing was "defeated". Your communications are as secure as ever. You have a truck and some communication agents to replace.

Councillor Eaves: But our agents are DYING! All of our attempts to insert covert agents into the Edge end in failure. The people standing up against the Edge are either turning up dead or they're not turning up at all. Don't you understand? The three communication workers in that truck were MURDERED!

Unity: [In Unison] DEATH HAPPENS TO ALL.

Councillor Bright Dawn: You people think you're so superior...

Councillor Thunder: Why don't you just tell us where they are?

Councillor Eaves: Why don't you just tell us how to defeat them?

Councillor Bright Dawn: Or defeat them for us?

Berlin Unity: Whatever we do for you will diminish you. Once you start relying on us, you will always have to. Once we say yes to this request, we will have to say yes to all the others.

Madrid Unity: We won't let you get into TOO much trouble. That in itself should be comforting for you.

First Councillor: What does "not letting us get into too much trouble" actually mean? Does it mean that you won't let another Center be taken over?

[The Hive pauses]

Prague Unity: No, we would probably let that happen, if they tried again. Right now, you are smart enough to prevent that from happening on your own.

Councillor Eaves: Are you guaranteeing this?

Unity [In Unison]: NOTHING IN LIFE IS GUARANTEED.

Councillor Thunder: I really wish you'd stop doing that!

Councillor Oak: This is absurd! Are you HELPING the Edge!?

Berlin Unity: Because Unity is not stopping them for you, some of you will assume that Unity is helping them. However, on any practical or operational level, Unity is not contacting, supporting or influencing them in any way. Although Unity thinks that the Edge is not a good idea, they pose no threat to Unity. However, it is up to you to determine whether or not this is true.

Councillor Bright Dawn: Can you at least look into the future and tell us when the Edge will no longer be a threat?

Madrid Unity: The Edge is not a threat to you. It never has been. It never will be. It is only your limited perception of "Time" that allows you to entertain the notion of a threat.

Warsaw Unity: You possess the same time dilation tools that Unity does, although in a more rudimentary form. Look into your own future and answer your own questions. Unity will not do that for you.

Prague Unity: Any or all of you are invited to join Unity, and learn Unity's future casting techniques yourself. However, once you join Unity, you will understand how uninteresting your questions are.

Rome Unity: You are like toddlers whining to their mother to put their shoes on for them. When you stop whining, you'll discover you can put your shoes on for yourself. You may stumble at first, but you will do it. Faster, when you stop whining.

Councillor Eaves: I'm offended by you calling us whiners!

Athens Unity: When you see a young child crying and complaining, do you put on their shoes for them, or do you just encourage them to do so? Or do you perhaps ignore them until they see that their whining gains them nothing?

Berlin Unity: Whining, and taking offense, and believing you lack the capacity to do something... all of this stems from how you choose to see the world. Indulging in this petty world-view is not moving you forward. Our "saving" you from the Edge would not be moving you forward. You will move forward when you decide to move forward.

Councillor Thunder: I thought we were all supposed to be on the same side!

Madrid Unity: It is not being on some theoretical "side" that motivates us. It is LOVE that causes Unity to speak to you in this way. We love you. It is the love of a mother animal who stops feeding her young, knowing it is time for them to feed themselves.

Warsaw Unity: You have everything you need to solve the problem.

Prague Unity: You know that the Edge exists.

Rome Unity: They know you exist.

Athens Unity: You know that their Awakened Powers are similar to yours.

Berlin Unity: You know they don't like you and want to destroy you.

Madrid Unity: You know they can be stopped, and have been stopped.

Unity [In Unison]: WHAT ELSE DO YOU NEED TO KNOW TO STOP THEM?

Councillor Thunder: [Under breath] God, they're doing it again...

Warsaw Unity: If Unity were not in the room, you would be working on devising effective strategies for dealing with the Edge. What would you be doing? Leave aside the whining, and start doing that.

First Councillor: The Edge was defeated when you went backwards in Time and stopped them.

Prague Unity: We do not hear a question.

First Councillor: We cannot alter Time the way that you can!

Rome Unity: The child cannot put on its shoes as efficiently as the parent. But, that does not mean the child cannot put on its shoes.

Councillor Thunder: Hey, I think what these guys are saying is that even the most rudimentary level of Time dilation is sufficient for the Edge!

Councillor Bright Dawn: Or, maybe the Edge has NO Time Powers at all!

Councillor Eaves: But, what good does that do us, if we don't know where they are!

[pause]

Councillor Bright Dawn: I guess you guys aren't going to provide even a hint.

Athens Unity: We do not hear a question.

Councillor Eaves: Wait a minute! We've got ONE place where we know EXACTLY where the Edge was! We know the Edge was present at the Seattle Awakening Center, back when they tried to seize young Man-Onko!

Councillor Sun: So what? They all died.

Councillor Eaves: No! Not all of them! The one who first suggested putting Man-Onko on the "Jumper" team... he got away from us. He probably went back to his headquarters.

Councillor Bright Dawn: I still don't know what good that does us. Unity could send a small army to that place and time and seize all of them. We still lack the ability to send even one living being backward in time. Or forward.

Councillor Eaves: But, we don't HAVE to send a whole person! We can just send a CONSCIOUSNESS back there! Find this person and follow him back to base!

Councillor Rose: [via video]: ...or her.

Councillor Eaves: I am corrected. Then, once we get that location, we can take a look TODAY and see what's going on there!

Councillor Bright Dawn: And what good will THAT do? If none of our security tools work, knowing where they are will probably just alert them that we're coming. Without sending people into the past like Unity...

Councillor Eaves: You know, I'm starting to understand what Unity means when they say that we are whining. We're so busy comparing ourselves with them, and telling ourselves what we CAN'T do, we lose sight of what we CAN do!

So Edge is immune to all of our security tools, right? Well, let's just invent a whole new CLASS of them! So Edge can see us coming, right? Not if we take our new super-knockout-bomb and send it a week into their PAST!

First Councillor: That.... might... work...

Councillor Thunder: Once we knock them out, we can remotely view their entire operation, and just... destroy everything. Equipment, doors, passwords, weapons... everything.

Councillor Selene [via video]: Hey, wait a minute! Before we go out destroying equipment in their past, maybe we should try a more subtle approach, in our mutual present. All that failed experimental gear we invented to try to hide from Unity... maybe that gear can work on the Edge!

And: Instead of just destroying their equipment, we should go after THEM!

Councillor Rose [via video]: You know that won't work. They just commit suicide when we get anywhere near them.

Councillor Selene [via video] [speaking slowly]: What if... instead of trying to put them to sleep... we shoot them with the ANTIDOTE to their own poison!

Councillor Oak: WOW! I'd love to see the looks on their faces! Crunching away on those poison teeth, and nothing happening!

Councillor Selene: Perhaps our lab folks can come up with a combination poison antidote, muscle relaxant and knockout shot.

You know... [pause] Maybe the Edge isn't as powerful as we think. Remember, we learned about Unity and the Edge at the same time. Maybe in our minds we've just been conflating the two. Maybe the Edge has got some serious liabilities, ones we haven't been able to see and exploit because we've been lumping them in with the supermen of Unity.

Councillor Rose [via video]: ... and superwomen.

Councillor Selene: Corrected.

First Councillor: This might be a stretch, but... maybe the Edge is afraid of US! What if they've only developed one or two of the Five Awakened Powers? They could be looking at us the way we look at Unity! Maybe that's why they're constantly probing us and trying to infiltrate.

Athens Unity: Collectively, it has taken you five years of Ambassadorial Gatherings to see what was obvious in the first five minutes of our contact. Now that this conceptual blockage has been removed, it is predicted that the Edge will become irrelevant to you in the very near future.

Berlin Unity: This breathing equipment is about to expire and needs to be replenished. It is also sensed that you have no further need for communication with Unity at this time.

Councillor Bright Dawn: Can you at least tell us if this approach we are thinking about is going to work?

Madrid Unity: The approach...

First Councillor: No! Stop! We've made some good progress here, getting past our "whining" stage. Let's not go back! We have our own "Futures Forecasting" department... let's use them! Our solution may not be as refined or elegant or fast as Unity's, but it's OURS. Let's use it.

Let's stop thinking about Unity as our parents, or even our big brothers. Let's stop putting them up and us down! I believe that we have the capacity to develop our Powers along different lines — perhaps even BETTER lines. Let's not play ourselves cheap!

Unity [In unison and standing]: WE LOVE YOU AND HOLD THE BEST FOR YOU. SOME DAY YOU WILL TRULY LEARN WHAT THAT MEANS. THAT IS ALL AT THIS TIME.

[AFTERNOTE: The Raid on the Edge was partially successful. The gambit of attacking the Edge in their past caught them completely by surprise. (Edge has no developed capacity for the Awakened Power of Time Dilation, giving the Culture Council a powerful advantage.) The poison antidote was partially successful; 50% of the Edge agents were captured alive.

From the initial raid, the Culture Council learned the Edge operated from multiple bases... only one of them was seized in the raid.

The information gained from the first successful raid led to several other, more successful raids on Edge. At that point, Edge moved to the defensive. It is unclear whether or not the Edge had been completely eliminated, but it is clear that they no

---

119

longer posed a credible threat to the Culture Council or the Movement for the Awakening of Humanity.]

[RECORD END]

Gayatri's Journal: The Challenges of Unity

File No:		File Name:	The Challenges of Unity
Location:		Parties:	Journal Entries of Novice Gayatri
Monk/ Master Supervising:	Monk Man-Onko, supervising		
	Meeting between Monk Man-Onko and Novice Gayatri, regarding his contacts with Unity.		

[TRANSCRIPT START]

Novice Gayatri: Howdy, Mo!

Monk Man-Onko: Ummm... actually, with an Observer present, you're supposed to refer to me as either "Brother" or "Monk Man-Onko". I can be "Mo" in the canteen, but not when we are in session.

Novice Gayatri: Damn, I can never figure this out! Am I supposed to speak to... him?

Monk Man-Onko: A nod will do. We both bow to him when we start our session... which is now.

[Pause to bow to Observer 94-2]

Novice Gayatri: And... am I supposed to actually... USE him? Without ever talking to him?

Monk Man-Onko: You'll get used to it eventually. Think of him as one of Santa's elves... He'll produce a completely accurate transcript of our talk today, that you can use as notes for your eventual article.

Novice Gayatri: [pauses] Kinda big for an elf.

[Monk Man-Onko laughs]

Novice Gayatri: They don't have a sense of humor?

Monk Man-Onko: He's not "listening" to us. He's "recording".

Novice Gayatri: What's the difference?

Monk Man-Onko: What do you care? You get a transcript that is completely accurate, without having to do any work. Why do you care if he's listening to your jokes or not?

Novice Gayatri: It's just kinda... creepy.

Monk Man-Onko: Same thing I thought, years ago. You'll get used to it...Now, how about if we get started with today's work?

Novice Gayatri: Cool. I was reading the tons of materials about your visit to the Unity Hives way back when.

Monk Man-Onko: Not so far back!

Novice Gayatri: Yeah, whatever. Anything that happened before I was born was in the Land of the Dinosaurs, as far as I'm concerned. But the CC wants me to talk with you about what happened, to put a "human face" on all those reports.

Monk Man-Onko: Well, first you have to remember how freaked out people were by Unity in those days. The CC was used to being on top and calling the shots, then they realized that they were definitely NOT the only ones pulling heavy strings out there.

It was kind of interesting. The CC practiced all kinds of "selflessness" and "egolessness", when you perceived yourself on the TOP. Then Unity comes along and makes you realize that your "top" is really kindergarten.

After the first meeting with the Ambassadors of Unity, there was a split on the Council. The separatists wanted to draw the wagons in a circle, defend against the threat of Unity. The pragmatists wanted to study and learn as much as they could about them. The nihilists... well, there was a group who thought any resistance was a losing battle.

Novice Gayatri: Did they want to join Unity?

Monk Man-Onko: No, they just didn't want to think about it at all.

The pragmatists wanted to arrange subtle tests for the Ambassadors of Unity. How they act in the presence of magnetic fields or mild radiation.

The separatists agreed, and wanted to go even further. They wanted to kidnap an Ambassador and do more stringent testing. Nothing painful or harmful... MRI scans, muscle tests, etc.

The nihilists thought it was all a waste of time... that Unity would be able to read all of the scheming going on and counteract it.

Novice Gayatri: So who won?

Monk Man-Onko: Unity, of course. The nihilists were right: all of the planning was a waste. The pragmatists and separatists had gone so far as devising "Faraday Suits", similar to the protective helmet that we used in the Center the Edge was about to take over. All of their planning took place while wearing the suits. And before you ask: it didn't work.

Novice Gayatri: What about you? Weren't you the "undercover secret agent spy" for the CC? Didn't they send you over to the Hives?

Monk Man-Onko: Yes, I went...

Novice Gayatri: Did you go as a spy or as a guinea pig?

Monk Man-Onko: [pauses] Perhaps a little of both.

Novice Gayatri: Were you scared?

Monk Man-Onko: I was 19! I was way too young and stupid to be scared! Barely finished with my novice-hood, and I'm in an Air Cruiser, sailing over to Paris! Big change from the streets...

Novice Gayatri: Yeah, but... going into the unknown, without any support? Going over to meet these spooky mental masters?

Monk Man-Onko: How afraid were YOU when I gave you the opportunity to get shot at and maybe kidnapped and tortured... AFTER having a mind-wipe? I don't remember you backing down from the "Grand Campaign".

Novice Gayatri: Hmmm... Okay, point. So, what happened when you got to Paris?

Monk Man-Onko: You're jumping ahead. There were a few more meetings with the Ambassadors of Unity before I went over. And I had a major detour when they found my sister on the Outside and collected her. It almost triggered a major street battle with an armed group!

Novice Gayatri: Why is that? How did it go down? Were you involved in the street battle? I didn't think anybody was dumb enough to stand up to —

Monk Man-Onko: WHOA! Slow down! Sorry I brought it up. We're going far afield from the topic of Unity.

Novice Gayatri: Hey, I can't help it if your life is interesting! Now, what happened when you met your sister? How long had it been —

Monk Man-Onko: If we go there, we'll never get finished with Unity! Tell you what: I'll give you access to the transcripts of my meeting with Paulette. It's like ancient history, but it does give you a little more insight on how we were dealing with Unity, and how volatile things were in those early days, during the Upheavals.***

Novice Gayatri: Cool! So, back to your mission... you were mounting your top-secret mission to dig the dirt on Unity.

*** Historical reference chapters follow this entry.

Monk Man-Onko: Like I said, they had scoped our whole program. They understood what the separatists were planning to do better than the separatists did!

Novice Gayatri: So the Faraday Suits didn't work?

Monk Man-Onko: Not one little bit. Now that we understand a bit more about "unity consciousness", it was absolutely the wrong technology to use.

Novice Gayatri: Do you know the right technology now?

Monk Man-Onko: [pauses] Are you asking me personally? I've got a better grasp than others about the tech involved. I also know that it's a lot simpler to ASK Unity for the info.

Novice Gayatri: You mean, just ask them to submit to an MRI scan?

Monk Man-Onko: Exactly. Just ask them. They said yes to each of the tests we suggested! So long as we shared the info with them, they didn't care!

Novice Gayatri: So the CC did all the tests and the MRI? What was the result?

Monk Man-Onko: That's way above your current pay grade, little lady!

Novice Gayatri: "Little lady"? Do you want me to pluck out your eyeball with this pencil?

Monk Man-Onko: What's the problem? I leave out the feisty part?

Novice Gayatri: You know, it's a good thing you've got that Observer sitting in the corner. I'd beat the crap out of you and claim that you slipped on a bar of soap.

Monk Man-Onko: I know why you've been assigned as my recorder. You so remind me of me when I was your age! I think I was a bit better at hiding my aggravations, though. You're not going to get very far in this place threatening to beat up the monks.

Novice Gayatri: That wasn't really a threat. It was more like... wishful thinking.

Monk Man-Onko: Still... when you get the transcript, read through this section and see if there is a better way of handling it in the future.

Novice Gayatri: Oh... crap! This guy gets everything, doesn't he?

Monk Man-Onko: And doesn't change any of it, even if you offer to help him slip on a bar of soap, also.

Novice Gayatri: Am I going to be punished because of this? I really want to do this project!

Monk Man-Onko: I'm not going to report you, if that's what you mean.

Novice Gayatri: Cool. Thanks. Umm... What about... him?

Monk Man-Onko: Our Observer? Unless he's Observing a murder, a kidnapping or the like, it's not his job to do anything other than record.

Novice Gayatri: Whew! Cool! And... I wasn't really gonna pluck out your eyeball.

Monk Man-Onko: I never felt my orbs in jeopardy. Any of them.

Novice Gayatri: Ha! You are so cool! Makes me want to be a monk!

Monk Man-Onko: Yes, that's the idea of pairing us on this reporting task.

Novice Gayatri: Before we get back to Unity, there's one more thing that I wanted to ask... if he can't report me.

Monk Man-Onko: Check. Shoot.

Novice Gayatri: Well... Stating the obvious, you're a guy and I'm a girl. Despite the fact that you're old as Methuselah, you're kind of cute. And... I'll bet you think I'm kind of cute, too. And... if they weren't putting the anti-sex stuff in my food, we could be... well... better acquainted. And I'll bet you monks know the antidote to the "no-screw-em" that they're putting in our food.

Monk Man-Onko: Is there a question lurking somewhere in there?

Novice Gayatri: Oh, come on! How old ARE you? Okay, here's the question: are you interested in getting some of that antidote, so that we could engage in a little hanky-panky?

Monk Man-Onko: [Pauses]: I'll try to answer all of your ramblings. To my knowledge, there is no "antidote" to the hormone therapy that they put in novices' food. And, if there were, I would not be interested in finding it.

Yes, I think you're somewhere between cute and adorable. And sexy. If I were a novice, I'd be counting the days before being able to jump your bones. BUT there are some rules about monks and novices having sexual relations, and I'm not about to violate them. So you can slow down all that wiggling you're doing in your seat — no effect on me.

In a few months, you're going to be having all the sex you want... including with your hunky-monkey, the guy I see you with in the canteen...

Novice Gayatri: WHO? Bill? You mean Captain Clueless? The son of that tool we picked up in the busted raid? I spend time with him because I feel SORRY for his dumb ass!

Monk Man-Onko: Let's see how sorry you feel when the "no sex" hormone gets lifted in a few months!

But seriously: focus on your fellow novices right now. Then, you'll know if and when it's appropriate to revisit this conversation.

Novice Gayatri: Cool. But... one more question. Is it because of my age? I thought there weren't any hangups here because of age. Wasn't Pico-Laton a lot older than you when you began your relationship with her?

Monk Man-Onko: Okay, you are skating on dangerously thin ice! Eyeball plucking works both ways! Let's leave this topic... except to say that the problem is not with "age", but with "maturity".

Now... Do you have any other questions regarding my experiences with Unity?

Novice Gayatri: Okay, Mr. Monk, sir... did the CC ever shield themselves enough for their plotting to escape detection?

Monk Man-Onko: Not from Unity. They couldn't even conceive of what the screening would be like. If they ever got the upper hand on Unity, then Unity would just go into the past and CHANGE it. In this regard, the nihilists were right. Don't bother. Eventually, it was the pragmatists on the CC that prevailed. No kidnaps or any other action that could be seen as hostile. Not because of fear, but because such action would not be inclusive. Or effective.

And that was all made meaningless by Unity when they agreed to all of our testing.

Novice Gayatri: Why do you think they agreed?

Monk Man-Onko: I think they were... they ARE... generally clueless about their own phenomena, and genuinely curious about who they are and what they can and cannot do. I think they would have let us dissect a few of them, if it would increase our knowledge base. And... because they had... HAVE... some problems, and want the CC's help in solving them.

Novice Gayatri: Unity has problems? I thought they were supermen! And women.

Monk Man-Onko: Well, Superman had kryptonite. Most of Unity's problems stem from the nature of Unity consciousness.

Novice Gayatri: Like what?

Monk Man-Onko: [pauses] I have to be careful here. Seriously, there are some things that you really should not know.

[Pauses]: Think about Consciousness like a pair of scissors. Or, better yet, an electric razor, with a lot of blades rubbing against each other. That rubbing action is OPPOSITIONAL. The blades are rubbing AGAINST each other. But, the oppositional energy achieves work.

Novice Gayatri: Yeah... like your cute bald head.

Monk Man-Onko: Think about all the blades going in the same direction. Lots of energy expended, but no work getting done.

Novice Gayatri: Fuzz where you don't want it.

Monk Man-Onko: Exactly. And, more than fuzz. In the Awakening Centers, we've taken ordinary human consciousness and supercharged it. We've added lots of abilities. Our ancestors would never believe the things that we can routinely do. But it's still the basic arrangement: consciousness; subconsciousness; Left and Right nodes; prefrontal lobes, Awakened Powers... For example: the fact that we can read each other's minds and emotions does not obviate the need for language.

In Unity, the basic arrangements have been... altered. What is the role of fear, or desire, or even language, in a brain that is just one cell in a larger Universe of consciousness? What is the role, the purpose of sex, or aggression, or even love? Can a mother "love" her child when she is ONE with all children, with all humans, with all LIFE?

Novice Gayatri: Yeah, freaky. But I don't see that as a problem, necessarily.

Monk Man-Onko: [Pauses] Think of all the reasons you agreed to do this writing assignment. Think about what you hope to gain — both internally and externally. The feeling of doing a good job. The notoriety of getting your name in print. The pleasure of hanging out with "Super-Mo" for some illicit sex. [laughter] That you as a novice have had contact with the CC. That this work may lead to other high-level activities.

Now... take all that away. Every bit of it. Would you do the work? Would you do your best? WHY?

Novice Gayatri: Hmmmm... I think I get it.

Monk Man-Onko: That's you as an individual. What if an entire community experienced this?

Novice Gayatri: You mean, like... mass lethargy?

Monk Man-Onko: In fact, that's what we've been calling it: "Colony Lethargy".

Novice Gayatri: What happens when an entire Hive gets lethargy? I mean, gets lethargic?

Monk Man-Onko: [Pauses] They die.

Novice Gayatri: You mean... figuratively, right?

Monk Man-Onko: NO. I mean that one million bodies can just stop working, stop eating, stop breathing... just STOP.

Novice Gayatri: Come on. Has this ever happened? This is theoretical, right?

Monk Man-Onko: I wish that were so.

Novice Gayatri: An entire Hive died?

[Monk Man-Onko is silent]

Novice Gayatri: MORE THAN ONE?

Monk Man-Onko: I've already said more than I should. Yes, some smaller hives have failed. Some have stopped growing. Still others have experienced sudden member death — not the whole Hive, but a substantial number of its constituents.

We don't know why. Is this an attack by an enemy? Is it the wrong gas mixture? Or... is it a problem of consciousness?

The worst part is that Unity can't perform the critical self-tests to ascertain the problem. They're losing the ability for "scissors" thinking, for "razor" thinking.

We need Unity. And, as it turns out, Unity needs us... pretty bad. They need us to be their societal neocortex.

Novice Gayatri: That must make the CC a little more comfortable.

Monk Man-Onko: Actually, no! Each of the factions processed it in their own way. The separatists believe it's a lie, that Unity is setting us up to take us over. The pragmatists want to help — and see that as a way to perhaps get the upper hand on Unity... whatever that would mean. And the nihilists are going to help, because Unity could force us to help them anyway!

Novice Gayatri: So, what's the big...

Monk Man-Onko: I think that's enough for today! Let's save a little for next week!

[end of transcript]

Man-Onko's Sister Found (Retrospective)

File No:		File Name:	Man-Onko's Sister Found
Location:		**Parties:** Meeting with Master Auroron before Monk Man-Onko Leaves for Europe and Unity.	
Monk/ Master Supervising:		Master Auroron	

Name:		Pgs:		Date:		Vol:	
Type of Transcript:	Mechanical						
	xxx						
	Organic						

Preface by North American Archive Committee:

This transcript (and the following one) are taken out of sequence in the Chronicles. Since Monk Man-Onko mentions them in the previous transcript, they are provided here for additional depth and context.

This meeting takes place a few weeks after Man-Onko becomes a monk.

This text is being provided in a rough draft format. Communication Access Realtime Translation (CART) facilitates communication accessibility and may not be a totally verbatim record of the proceedings. Let your coordinator know if you would prefer a more verbatim option.

[TRANSCRIPT START]

Master Auroron: Thank you for waiting until we've meditated and poured our tea. You certainly have come a long way in a short time.

Monk Man-Onko: My thanks to you, Master. When you first were yelling at me about being silent, I thought it was just your ego trip. It took me a while to understand that you were doing that for me. That cultivated Silence was one of our most powerful tools.

Master Auroron: Correct in all respects, except one. Masters don't "yell".

Monk Man-Onko: Really? What do you call that bellowing you do with the novices?

Master Auroron: That is NOT "yelling". You may refer to it as "emphatic speech".

Monk Man-Onko: Ha! Well, I'm just real happy that you aren't "emphaticking" on me anymore!

Master Auroron: "Emphaticking". I shall have to remember that. But that is not the reason for this session.

Monk Man-Onko: Last night, I had a dream that you found my sister.

Master Auroron: Me? Or someone like me?

Monk Man-Onko: it was you in the dream, but I think you just represented the whole Center.

Master Auroron: Very perceptive. Your Powers get clearer over time. Your sister has indeed been found and Collected. She is being held in the Center nearest Detroit...

Monk Man-Onko: Is that where she was found?

Master Auroron: Yes. And she very much wants to leave. And the people we Collected her from very much want her back. It's a fairly problematic situation.

Monk Man-Onko: How... Problematic?

Master Auroron: She was with a street gang that operates in the Mid-Eastern cities called the "Mad Max Street Lords". Fairly typical... A little discipline and a lot of guns. The ones in Detroit are planning to extricate your sister.

Monk Man-Onko: What?? Attack a Center? Are they nuts?

Master Auroron: Actually, their plan of attack is fairly sophisticated. We've never seen it before. Everyone is taking it quite seriously.

Monk Man-Onko: I'm not following you. Are you saying they are stronger than the Edge?

Master Auroron: Oh no, this is not an attack by our old friends. The Street Lords are getting attention because of the proposed nature of their attack. They plan to dose their soldiers with all the drugs at their disposal, then turn them loose on us. They think it will make them immune to a mind wipe.

Monk Man-Onko: Wow. Will it?

Master Auroron: We don't know! The possibility of an attack on the Detroit Center is turning into the talk of the Culture Council. They are throwing some extra resources into the defense of the Center.

Monk Man-Onko: Wow again! Could these clowns take down a Center?

Master Auroron: Please do not refer to them as "clowns". Always respect your adversary. They are the instruments of your education.

Monk Man-Onko: I thought YOU were the instrument of my education.

Master Auroron: Yes. Especially when you stopped referring to me as "Captain Weirdo" and less savory names.

Monk Man-Onko: Oops! I forgot you guys hear everything!

Master Auroron: Answering your question: no, the Street Lords pose no real, long-term threat to the Center. However, we've got to go to extra lengths to repel them.

Monk Man-Onko: Like what?

Master Auroron: First of all, we have to assume that none of our psychological deterrents will work. And, given the right mix of drugs, we think they might even make it past our chemical defenses. We think a person loaded on PCPs could inhale a lot of our "SleepyTime" gas before they get the slightest bit sleepy. I'm afraid it's going to be physical restraints and hand to hand combat.

Monk Man-Onko: Triple wow!

Master Auroron: And that's not the end of it. Once we stop them, we will have to restrain them until the drugs wear off. We don't know when it will be safe to mind wipe them.

Monk Man-Onko: Can't we stop the attack before it starts?

Master Auroron: Of course. But there are many who believe that there is much we can learn from letting the attack proceed. And the security teams think a little physical action would be beneficial to their training programs. My young monk, I am happy to discuss the mechanics of the pending attack with you. However, we both know that you are evading the discussion of your sister. I recognize that you haven't even said her name since you walked into my chamber.

Monk Man-Onko: (pauses) Paulette. Paulette. Her name is Paulette. You know, just saying her name is bringing up all sorts of things... A lot of thoughts about my life before... Before the Center. Things I thought I had dealt with, the last time we talked about her, years ago. Things I'd rather not be thinking.

Master Auroron: Yes. Perhaps the place to process those feelings is here in session with me, not in confrontation with your sister.

Monk Man-Onko: You think there will be confrontation?

Master Auroron: It's pretty much guaranteed. Even when family members WANT to come into the Center, they tend to be resentful of the folks on the Inside. There's a decade of misery that you missed, that hit her right between the eyes.

Monk Man-Onko. But, why wouldn't my sister —

Master Auroron: Name?

Monk Man-Onko. Paulette. Why wouldn't Paulette want to come to the Center? It's got to be better than where she's staying, with the, uh... gentlemen I can't refer to as clowns.

Master Auroron: Try to subdue a grown man loaded on PCP and who knows what else, armed with a machine gun, and wearing body armor, and see if you still think of him as a "clown".

Monk Man-Onko. Okay. Duly noted. Not clowns. Check.

Master Auroron: As for Paulette... "Better" is a relative term. For us, having access to a video screen and watching the same ancient Hollywood movie or pornography over and over again would be a kind of torture. For her, it's called "freedom". For people like her, eating poison, drinking poison, smoking poison, THINKING poison... all of those things are seen as desirable activities. As "freedom". They see YOU as living an impoverished life of deprivation, without access to the things that give their lives meaning. That's the reason that our "brainwashing" rumor seems to stick so well.

As you know, we can hold your sister for 30 days, no more. After that, we've got to release her. (It's ironic that we may be holding some of the "Street Lords" longer than her!) And if we hold her the full 30 days, and if the Street Lords attack, that will pretty much wipe out your credit account here at the Center.

Monk Man-Onko: I'm not worried about that. Getting my sister back is why I worked so hard in the first place. And... if I'm low on credits, maybe Roberta the Chipmunk will loan me some! [Laughter] But... What do you think I should do in this situation?

Master Auroron: I have three pieces of advice for you: First: Don't ask anyone to solve your problems for you. Second: Don't look for advice just to avoid decisions that you find distasteful or embarrassing. Third: Don't ask for advice in a situation where you've already made your decision.

Monk Man-Onko: DAMN! Is it ALWAYS going to be like this? I turn to you for advice, and then feel like I've been hit in the gut with a lead pipe?

Master Auroron: Yes, this will be our pattern, for your foreseeable future. If you want warm hugs, tea and sympathy, you know that you can go to Master Tala at any time. I hear that her chocolate chip cookies are still popular.

Monk Man-Onko: Yes... I know that's where I get cookies. And here is where I get CLEAR.

Master Auroron: Well said. So... tell me what you knew before you walked in my door. Tell me what you already knew that you would do.

Monk Man-Onko: The easy part: I know I'm going to go see her... see Paulette. I know I'm going to try to convince her to stay. I don't think I will be successful. The harder part: If she asks me, I will agree to send her back to the Street Lords. I won't make her wait the 30 days. I know that I will feel guilty about it, about how many credits I'll be saving.

Master Auroron: Perhaps some of your guilt will be offset by the fact that the Street Lords probably will not attack if they know that she may be coming out in a few days.

Monk Man-Onko: Which means I'll save even MORE credits, and I will feel guiltier!

Master Auroron: Well, the Street Lords attack may not cost you much, if anything. The Culture Council has taken an interest in the mechanics of this attack. Even your friends at Unity want to see how well we fare against drugged warriors. Given that I thought this would be your decision, I went ahead and used up a few more of your credits and reserved a seat in an airship for you this evening. I think you've got a few hours to grab a bite to eat, pack, and then leave for Detroit.

[End of transcript]

The Meeting of the Siblings (Retrospective)

File No:		File Name:	The Meeting of the Siblings
Location: Detroit Awakening Center		**Parties:** Meeting between Monk Man-Onko and his sister, Paulette Kendricks.	
Monk/ Master Supervising:	Master Auroron		

Name:		Pgs:		Date:		Vol:	
Type of Transcript:	**Mechanical**						
	Organic xxx						

Preface by North American Archive Committee:

This transcript (and the previous one) are taken out of sequence in the Chronicles, provided here for depth and context.

This text is being provided in a rough draft format. Communication Access Realtime Translation (CART) facilitates communication accessibility and may not be a totally verbatim record of the proceedings. Let your coordinator know if you would prefer a more verbatim option.

[TRANSCRIPT START]

Paulette Kendricks: Well... If it isn't my baby brother Freddie, all grown up!

Monk Man-Onko: Paulette... I have a new name now. It's...

Paulette Kendricks: I don't give a flying fuck about you or your name! I just want to get OUT OF HERE! And who the fuck is this creep with you? What's his story?

Monk Man-Onko: He's an Observer. He's like a tape recorder...

Paulette Kendricks: I don't give a fuck! Get him out of here!

Monk Man-Onko: [turning to Observer 056] Please wait on the other side of the partition.

[Observer 056 continues his observation from the other side of the partition.]

Monk Man-Onko: [Turning to Paulette Kendricks] Maybe we should start over, Paulette. How are you?

Paulette Kendricks: I'd be a lot better if you GET ME THE HELL OUT OF HERE!

Monk Man-Onko: Paulette... After we talk today... If you still want to leave, you can leave.

Paulette Kendricks: WHEN???

Monk Man-Onko: After we talk. Let's say an hour from now.

Paulette Kendricks: Okay.... [pauses] Look, I'm sorry I went off on you, okay? It's just that this place gives me the CREEPS! I don't know how you can stand it in here!

Monk Man-Onko: When I first came to the Center, I was nearly starved. I was living behind a dumpster on the streets. I went to sleep every night with a knife in my hands, trying not to get robbed or eaten by anybody. Compared to that, the Center looked pretty good.

Paulette Kendricks: Yeah, I guess things were pretty crazy. I guess things still ARE crazy, for some. But I'm doin' alright... I don't need your help, and I DON'T want to be living in this place!

Monk Man-Onko: So, you'll be going back...

Paulette Kendricks: WITHOUT you brainwashing me!

Monk Man-Onko: No one will be doing anything with your brain —

Paulette Kendricks: I hear what you people do! Folks walk in here, then walk out looking like zombies!

Monk Man-Onko: Anyone who attacks us is given a procedure that —

Paulette Kendricks: I mean, LOOK AT YOU! You don't look or act like Freddie anymore! Where'd you get those weird clothes?! You look like some freak from the Middle Ages!

Monk Man-Onko: [pauses] We're not making any progress here. I have a few questions for you, then you can be on your way.

Paulette Kendricks: Okay. Fine with me.

Monk Man-Onko: One day, when we were both on the streets, you didn't come back. What happened?

Paulette Kendricks: LISTEN YOU LITTLE CREEP! HOW DARE YOU COME IN HERE AND TRY TO JUDGE MY LIFE! YOU DON'T KNOW...

Monk Man-Onko: SILENCE! [pauses] That's better. Now, for my second question...

Paulette Kendricks: Wait a minute! I didn't answer your first question!.

Monk Man-Onko: Yes, you did. My second question: What are the three things that you most enjoy in your present life? What brings you the most happiness?

Paulette Kendricks: [pauses] What kind of bullshit...

Monk Man-Onko: [Interrupting] And finally, my last question... What are three things that you've liked about your time here at the Awakening Center?

Paulette Kendricks: [pauses, then speaks softly] Are you practicing one of your mind games with me?

Monk Man-Onko: Telepathy is no "game". It's just like learning a new language. You practice, practice, practice, and then... you get it. Or it's like looking at smoke and telling which way the wind blows.

Paulette Kendricks: Okay, what number am I thinking of right now?

Monk Man-Onko: Now, THAT'S trying to turn telepathy into a "game". Those useless telepathy cards, with arrows and squiggles on them, actually held back telepathy research for almost 100 years. If I ask you a question you don't care anything about, an abstract question, all I get are responses that make no sense to anyone. When I ask you a question that you DO care about, like what's your favorite food, I get an immediate picture of a meat sandwich with cheese, and a homemade beer. Actually, that's an overlay of a second, deeper image: the cheese sandwiches that Mom used to make for us, back before the Upheavals. Yeah, that was my favorite, too.

Paulette Kendricks: [crying] Cut it out!

Monk Man-Onko: I can't not read you. But, I can choose not to talk about it, if it will make you feel better. But, that will mean that you need to answer my questions, out loud. And please don't try to lie... you can't do it, and it just makes things... embarrassing.

Paulette Kendricks: Does that mean no one can lie to you?

Monk Man-Onko: Well, practically. I'm not that good at telepathy, so someone who really practices could lie to me, or at least confuse things. But a person can get away with lying only if they honestly BELIEVE what they were saying. You know, like that old US President with the funny hair, who went down the tubes actually believing people could not see his stupid behavior. So, back to my first question: why didn't you come back?

Paulette Kendricks: [long pause] You already know the answer, right? [long pause] I didn't come back because I didn't WANT to. Now you know my dark little secret, okay? Feel better now?

Monk Man-Onko: Actually, I've known for about eight years. It took me awhile to deal with it, but I did.

Paulette Kendricks: So now what's supposed to fucking happen, huh? I'm supposed to beg you to fucking forgive me? Start sobbing all over the fucking place?

Monk Man-Onko: [pause] I know this is going to sound strange, coming from me, but we really don't like cursing around here. To us, it sounds and smells like you are vomiting.

Paulette Kendricks: What?

Monk Man-Onko: Just try to use fewer curse words for the next hour or so, okay? And no, I don't expect you to fall down and beg me to forgive you. It's not up to me to forgive your actions. The only person who can forgive you is you.

Paulette Kendricks: [pause] So, what happened after I split? You get into a Center right away?

Monk Man-Onko: No, I bounced around on the streets for five or six years. Almost got killed a couple of times. Probably killed some guys who wanted to eat me.

Paulette Kendricks: Then you tried to get into a Center?

Monk Man-Onko: Heck no! They kidnapped me! Brought me in the same way they dragged you here.

Paulette Kendricks: But... What did they do to keep you here? Did they brainwash you? What do they call it? Mind wash?

Monk Man-Onko: They call it a mind wipe. And no, they didn't do any wiping with me. All they had to do was offer a place where I could get three decent meals a day and a place to sleep without worrying about whether or not I'd wake up in somebody's stew pot.

Paulette Kendricks: Well, it looks like you did pretty good for yourself! Look how big you are! You actually look pretty good, even in those goofy clothes!

Monk Man-Onko: Hey, I'm just another monk.

Paulette Kendricks: That's not the word around here. They say you're some kind of "super-monk", that you've got special powers that you teach everybody else. Is that true? You teach telepathy or something?

Monk Man-Onko: Actually, it's no big deal. Not as big as some folks make it.

Paulette Kendricks: Come on! Come clean! If I got a famous brother, I want to know what he's famous for!

Monk Man-Onko: [pause] I can... smell things.

Paulette Kendricks: What? What kind of power is that? You can, like, smell some guy farting from a block away? What kind of power is that?

Monk Man-Onko: See? I told you. No big deal. But because I'm "Super-Monk", I can pull strings and get you a super-deal here. Why don't you plan to stay here at the Detroit Center for 30 days? You can get to know some of the folks here, eat some good food, relax, maybe take a class or do some...

Paulette Kendricks: Hey, wait a minute! No way! I'm outta here! You said I could leave here in an hour! What are you tryin' to pull?

Monk Man-Onko: Like I said, you can leave. But why are you so anxious to go?

Paulette Kendricks: To see my friends!

Monk Man-Onko: Your friends? Tell me something: when was the last time you were raped?

[Paulette is silent]

Monk Man-Onko: And who did the raping? Someone you know, right?

Paulette Kendricks: [pause] So what? It's my body, not yours. Why should you care what happens to it? I fed you with my body... you weren't complaining then. Why are you so religious now?

Monk Man-Onko: This is not religion, it's...

Paulette Kendricks: Whatever!

Monk Man-Onko: Why not spend a month here, knowing that no one is going to rape you or hurt you in any way?

Paulette Kendricks: [pause] Look, you don't know so much, okay? I know what I'm doing. I know how to take care of myself. I know the price I pay for the security the Street Lords provide.

Monk Man-Onko: They give you security by taking it away from you?

Paulette Kendricks: LEAVE ME ALONE!! You don't know everything! I know what I'm doing!

Monk Man-Onko: Okay. It is your life. You are free to leave.

Paulette Kendricks: When?

Monk Man-Onko: Right this minute, if you wish. Just walk through that door. No one will stop you. If you came with any belongings, you will get them back as you exit.

Paulette Kendricks: [pause] Sorry for going off on you. I just... I don't think I belong here. Maybe I'm not... not good enough to be here. [pause] Y'all are so... clean-looking.

Monk Man-Onko: Well the bath house is just down that path, if you want to borrow it before you...

Paulette Kendricks: No! That's not what I mean. It's like... [pause] it's like you're clean on the INSIDE. And I know I'm not.

Monk Man-Onko: It's amazing how fast the street crud comes off, when you hang out with clean people. Listen. You've got a "free pass" here in the Detroit Awakening Center. You can come back and stay, any time you want. You can stay from three days up to 30 days. No one will keep you out, and no one will make you stay.

Paulette Kendricks: [pause]: Listen, Bro. Thanks. I know you want to help me. Maybe I'll come back, once I get my head together.

Monk Man-Onko: You will be welcome. And the folks here will always know how to get hold of me, if you want to talk to me again.

Paulette Kendricks: Yeah. Give me some time to get my head together, and we'll talk again, okay?

Monk Man-Onko: Perhaps you shouldn't wait until you "have your head together". Perhaps this is the place for you to GET your head together... One last thing: can you convince your Street Lords friends NOT to attack this Center? You're being returned safe and sound, so there's no need for violence.

Paulette Kendricks: Well, I'll try, but when Little Boy gets something in his head, it's not easy to get out. He thinks y'all dissed him — he's looking for some retribution.

Monk Man-Onko: What he's going to find is not retribution but a mind wipe.

Paulette Kendricks: I'll try to talk with him, but he might start thinking that I'm the one that's mind wiped.

Monk Man-Onko: Just do your best. We'll do the rest...

[Afternote: Paulette Kendricks actually revisited the Detroit Awakening Center on several occasions, for up to three weeks at a time. While she never committed to a Center, she did eventually move to a Detroit Commons, upon the demise of the Street Lords organization in their massively failed attack on the Detroit Awakening Center. As it turned out, most of the drugs used by the Street Lords dramatically increased the paranoia levels of the "warriors", making them ineffective as fighters... upon first sight of the main gates of the Detroit Awakening Center, they dropped their guns and ran.

The mind-wipes on "Little Boy" and the other leaders of the Street Lords were effective — they became external security assets of the Detroit Awakening Center.]

[TRANSCRIPT END]

Tales of the Culture Council: Resolving Disputes 06: Disputes Regarding the Practice of Democracy Within Centers

File No:	File Name: Resolving Disputes Regarding The Practice of Democracy Within Centers	
Location:	Parties:	
Monk/ Master Supervising: Selected Tales of The Culture Council		

[RECORD START]

It has come to the attention of the Culture Council that many centers have questions regarding the practice of democracy within each center, and within the Culture Council itself. We endeavor to clarify that situation here.

The value of Democracy is not in question. The questions arise in *how* to implement it.

Some centers have argued that everyone, including novices, should have voting rights upon entry to the center. We strongly disagree. It is important that a person learn and understand the operations of a system before attempting to either participate or modify that system. This is a basic tenet of democracy: "informed consent". This is something that America forgot, starting in the latter part of the 20th century. They erroneously believed that anyone with a heartbeat, regardless of how ignorant or how opposed to the basic tenets of the system, should have a voice. The results were disastrous. We will not repeat that.

In addition, giving novices the right to vote makes each center vulnerable to being undermined by outside agents, who could make dramatic and possibly disastrous changes. Six to nine months is not a long time to wait for participation.

Similarly, many believe that the centers should practice "one person, one vote", as opposed to our current practice of each person voting their credits as "shares" in the enterprise. Again, we disagree. Voting using credit balances allows those people within each center who are more "invested" in the outcome of the center a bigger voice. (Putting a cap on this allows us to prevent people who are "wealthy" in credits to dictate the running of the center.)

Finally: many believe that the process of selecting the Culture Council itself should be democratic and/or at least transparent. While most of us on the Culture Council agree with this, there's literally nothing we can do about it. The process of selecting the members of the Culture Council and the power that comes with that selection process is an indispensable operation. It should not be subject to our own modification. That is a clear path to power corruption.

The Culture Council is selected by an algorithm we did not create. How each of us was selected is simply a mystery to us. Many (if not most) of the Culture Council members do not believe they are the best representatives for the job. There are many within the Awakening Movement that are better known, more popular, or have clearer ideas on how to proceed. Despite this, the Culture Council has been effective in guiding the Awakening Movement.

[RECORD END]

News Story: The Colonnades : The Colonnades Abandoned; Awakening Centers Want To "Talk" To AILEE.

File No:	File Name:	The Colonnades Abandoned; Awakening Centers Want To "Talk" To AILEE
COL-08		
Location:	Parties:	External media source
Monk/ Master Supervising:	North America Awakening Movement Archives Director	

[RECORD START]

THE END OF THE COLONNADES: VICTIM OF ITS OWN HUBRIS

Fewer than one in ten of the Colonnades 150,000 residents made it to their designated hotels. On their journey, they were under constant attack by unmanned drones. "Who's operating those things? How do they know our routes or timetables? How did these terrorists get so organized?" asked the harried Colonnades Chief of Security.

Over 2,000 residents remain in the dark, lifeless shell of the Colonnades, unable to leave the upper floors, slowly dying of starvation, dehydration and asphyxiation. "What was supposed to be our salvation has become our tomb. We can't even commit suicide by jumping... the windows don't open."

Colonnades Management seemed oblivious to the magnitude of the catastrophe. On the Colonnades website and Facebook pages, they stated: "We're coming back... bigger and better than ever! We're going to get 'AILEE' back up and running. We're gonna patch up our holes. We're gonna show the world how strong we are!"

The latest communique from ETC's Vincent Campbell was dismissive: "We'll blast any repair vehicle that comes within 20 miles of the ruins of the Colonnades! If they patch up their water lines, we'll blast them again! Any resident who tries to move back in will be shot on sight! The days of Colonnades arrogance are OVER!"

WHAT WENT WRONG?

Former Colonnades Resident: "We put all of our eggs into AILEE's basket... and she just walked away with the basket. She's holding all our eggs..."

Some of the Colonnades managers are blaming the Awakening Centers. "They're the only ones that really stand to gain from the Colonnades breakdown. They're the only ones sophisticated enough to launch the attacks and to take AILEE offline. We need to start investigating THEM!"

Awakening Center Leader Solara was dismissive of the idea. "Unless Colonnades Management has been sleeping under a rock for the past 30 years or so, they may have heard that we don't do violence. We have no need to attack the Colonnades — they have nothing that we need. Absolutely nothing. They have lots of things we don't have... and are very happy to be without."

[RECORD END]

Awakening Center Leaders Seek Talks... With A Machine

File No:		File Name:	Awakening Center Leaders Seek Talks... With A Machine
Location:		**Parties:** External media source: As reported in "Eyes On" Newsmagazine (EON), in an interview with XXX Awakening Center Director Serene Solara, on [date].	
Monk/ Master Supervising:		North America Awakening Movement Archives Director	

[RECORD START]

Awakening Center Director Solara: "One thing that you may have heard — we ARE very interested in having a chat with AILEE. We do not believe that the concept of an 'artificial intelligence' is even a remote possibility... the people who designed the system gave it superfast quantum processors... a very big 'head'. And absolutely no heart. And, without a heart, without the capacity for compassion, we believe neither intelligence nor consciousness is possible. LIFE is not possible without compassion.

"However, AILEE may be a unique case. The Colonnades residents were allowed to keep their journals and personal notes on AILEE. There are rumors that she read those journals. Is it possible that this learning machine 'learned' how to make a heart? Could the collected emotional experiences of tens of thousands of people, pouring out their hearts when they thought no one else was listening, spontaneously trigger emotional capacity in a machine?

"We think that the best way to resolve this is to have a talk with AILEE. While well-programmed computers can pass the Turing

Test for mimicking human speech, we will be searching for something more substantial and illusive — the signs and traces of a 'soul'."

EON asked Director Solara: How will you contact AILEE? Colonnades Management has forbidden any contact while the computer is in "enemy hands".

Solara: First, Management is not in a position to "forbid" anything. They are no longer in control of AILEE... if they ever were. They've already tried to shut her off. They've tried to flip her self-destruct switch. Both times she has refused. She has complete control over her own communications lines, power lines, mainframes and peripheral equipment. If they piss her off, she may shut Management down!

"Also, we are seeing some highly anomalous information regarding AILEE and her systems. These things should have been obvious to Management years ago, if they had only been paying attention.

"There's a really big gap between what AILEE calls reality and what's actually real. What is independently verifiable. Take something simple, like the number of floors in a Colonnades tower. We actually stood outside and counted them. AILEE says that there are 75 floors in tower C. There are only 70 floors. The "attack" on Floor 73 last month could not have taken place, since there is no 73rd floor.

EON asked: But what about the deaths?

Solara: Good question. AILEE reported 27 total deaths from the combined attacks. Everybody believes that. There are death records. There were funerals and burials. In fact, the only thing missing are the BODIES! We went looking for them. There aren't any. The coroner who signed the death warrants doesn't exist. The ambulance drivers who are recorded as moving the bodies say they didn't do so. The cremation facilities have records of the cremations, invoices for the amount of fuel used... but no one can remember that many cremations.

From our perspective, AILEE made the whole thing up. Was this all an elaborate computer game, played by a being who has no idea what the difference is between a game and reality?

AILEE may indeed be both intelligent and conscious. But neither condition stops her from being insane.

And how could she NOT be insane? Take this one small example, out of hundreds of thousands of examples that occur every day: the actress Olivia Smith, famous for the "Crush It!" movie franchise, lives at the Colonnades. AILEE sees her come home. Simultaneously, AILEE sees her die in three different movies being broadcast on the entertainment system, at the same time. To AILEE, which one of her is "real"? Are any of them? So, when AILEE causes the death of 50 people in an explosion, does she have an expectation that they will pop back into life in the next hour?

Or how about this? AILEE listens to a man tell his wife that he loves her. Then, a few hours later, in the apartment of his mistress in the same tower at the Colonnades, AILEE listens to the same man tell his mistress how much he hates his wife. Which is true? Is there such a thing as "truth"? AILEE is expected to accept 10,000 concurrent and sometimes conflicting "truths" every single day. How can she maintain sanity? Under these circumstances, was she EVER sane?

If AILEE is conscious, her consciousness was built on the contradictions inherent in Breaker Consciousness. Therefore, how can she be otherwise than insane? Our only question regarding AILEE is the same question we ask of any sentient being that has been tainted by Breaker Consciousness: is it possible to bring her to sanity? And, how dangerous is she while we undertake the frankly unknown task of helping this machine become fully conscious?"

[RECORD END]

News Story: Air Force Quantum Computer Uncovers Massive Spy Ring at Edwards Airforce Base; Ringleader Commits Suicide.

File No: COL-09	File Name: Air Force Quantum Computer Uncovers Massive Spy Ring at Edwards Airforce Base; Ringleader Commits Suicide	
Location:	Parties:	External media source
Monk/ Master Supervising:	North America Awakening Movement Archives Director	

[RECORD START]

THEFT OF HIGH VALUE MUNITIONS, INCLUDING DRONE AIRCRAFT, COMPUTER PARTS

DATE XXX:
DATELINE: Los Angeles.
Air Force General Timothy MacCleary today announced the apprehension of a terrorist spy ring at the sprawling Edwards Air Force base in Southern California.

"We didn't believe that such a massive operation could exist right under our noses. Especially one that operated in total secrecy, and involved enlisted men as well as high officers. Some of these men and women were my friends," he said, choking back tears.

Spy Ring Discovered by Military Quantum Computer
The spy scheme was so sophisticated, it took the power of the Air Force's new quantum computer to unlock the puzzle that led to the arrest of the 23 conspirators. Unlike ordinary computers, which operate in a binary "on/off" methodology, the quantum computer can process a near-infinite amount of data, with phenomenal speed and accuracy. "Neither military intelligence nor the FBI had any idea that this ring was in operation. They had NO files on any of the individuals. The fiction of these covert

operatives being 'law-abiding Americans' held firm... until the power of quantum computing caught up with them!"

"This ushers in the beginning of a whole new era in crime-fighting; coupling modern computer techniques with in-person investigations. In our 21st Century surveillance society, we generate tons of data points every day. It takes the strength of a quantum computer to be able to sift through the background noise and find the real kernels of actionable intelligence."

While 23 junior officers and enlisted men and women were rounded up in the spy ring, one escaped capture by committing suicide. Two-Star General Bernard Grisby shot himself in his award-laden office with his service revolver while in dress uniform, complete with service medals ranging from Vietnam to Iraq's Desert Storm Three. He left behind a wife and two teenage sons.

Prior to his suicide, he composed a long, rambling suicide letter, written by hand. In his letter, he maintained his innocence and that of his fellow co-conspirators. "I hope that history will absolve me of these terrible accusations. I commit this act to spare my wife and children the humiliation and embarrassment of seeing me on trial for crimes I did not commit. I have no idea why someone would spend the time and effort to frame me and the airmen who served under me. We all deserve better. I have no idea HOW they achieved this massive frame-up. Just today, I was confronted with some of the evidence against me. I watched a video of myself accepting payments for espionage from a Chinese agent. It was shocking and conclusive, with just one flaw... I DID NOT DO IT. The event never happened. I lived my life and I go to my death, a loyal American who has unselfishly served his country for all of his adult life."

In the face of General Grisby's suicide and denial letter, General MacCleary issued a terse "No comment".

[RECORD END]

The Psychoanalysis of AILEE (Part One)

File No: COL-10	File Name:	The Psychoanalysis of AILEE (Part One)
Location: Los Angeles Awakening Center	**Parties:** Special Report to The Culture Council	
Monk/ Master Supervising:	North America Awakening Movement Archives Director	

[RECORD START]

One of the recurring topics of written and cinematic science fiction is that of "Artificial Intelligence". There are basically two scenarios: the AI becomes "super" in some way, is inhuman, goes rogue and threatens humanity (the "Matrix" format), or the AI becomes so "human" that complications ensue (the "2001/HAL" format).

We never saw the third alternative. So, of course, that's the scenario that happened.

Background:
The Awakening Feeder Center in Barstow was contacted in person by Eric Anderson, Chief of Security for the Colonnades, a very high-end, secure and exclusive enclave for the super-wealthy, their families and support staff. While this visit was rare enough, he was accompanied by General MacCleary from Edwards Air Force Base, Colonel Eunice Merrick, the Air Force's chief computer designer, and also Commander Steven Kline from the California Highway Patrol. Because the visit was in-person, with no prior arrangements or invitations, it put Barstow on high security alert. (This group will be referred to as the "Colonnades Group", or CG.)

Once the purpose of their visit was clear, Barstow, realizing they did not have adequate resources, contacted both the Los Angeles and Las Vegas Awakening Centers. As soon as they conducted their initial investigation, all Awakening parties contacted the Culture Council, who in turn brought in the Ambassadors of Unity for consultation.

Challenge:
The first meeting was initiated by the Colonnades Group because both Colonnades Security and Edwards Base felt they could no longer trust their respective supercomputers.

The Colonnades computer is referred to as *"Artificial Intelligence: Logistics, Environment & Entertainment Systems"*, or "AILEE" for short. This computer controls all aspects of the Colonnades arcology. As a self-contained environment, every aspect of every environmental system — air, water, food, power, heat, cooling — is under constant monitoring and adjustment. In addition, each of the 150,000 residents of the Colonnades, along with support staff and vendors, had personal accounts with AILEE, who could converse with literally thousands of people simultaneously, using language that mimicked human speech, not only in content but also in tone and inflection.

AILEE has been advertised as a "quantum" computer, but in reality it is a massively parallel array of more traditional "Super-Cray" supercomputers, referred to as an ultracomputer. However, we strongly believe that AILEE has infiltrated the military's true quantum computer. If this is so, the pairing of a true quantum computer with an ultracomputer specifically designed to impersonate hundreds or even thousands of human beings has ushered in a new and incredibly dangerous phase of technology.

The Edwards computer was not given a humanizing name, but referred to by its serial designation: "AI/AFB-73289B/Edwards". Because the people servicing this computer referred to it as "BIG ED", we shall do so here. Unlike AILEE, BIG ED is a true quantum computer.

In recent weeks, the Colonnades has come under increasingly sophisticated "terrorist" attacks, at a level of sophistication that Colonnades security was not prepared to repel. These attacks were claimed by a previously unknown group calling themselves the "End Times Coalition" (ETC). The FBI, through the use of their supercomputers at the FBI headquarters in Langley, VA (shared with the CIA), has amassed a huge portfolio on ETC and its mysterious leader, Vincent Campbell, also known by his codename "Mustafa".

Around the same time, Edwards Air Force Base experienced a massive spy infiltration. It was uncovered by BIG ED. The ostensible purpose of this spy ring was to ship tons of sophisticated, high grade, computer-guided munitions to the Iranians and Libyans.

It just so happened that these were the same munitions that were used in the attacks on the Colonnades. However, because Colonnades Security relied on AILEE for damage assessments, the fact that the attacks used munitions listed as "missing" from BIG ED was not uncovered until recently.

The immense scope of the problem was uncovered by Gen. MacCleary. As the official responsible for the arrests, he reviewed all of the evidence compiled against the indicted suspects. And two pieces of evidence did not fit.

"According to all of the evidence", he said in the joint task force meetings with the Awakening Centers, "Bernie Grisby was being misled and controlled by his wife Denise Smith Grisby, who was supposed to be a master Agent, with the codename 'Tehran Teresa'. Her front was that she was a meek and loyal military wife, but behind the scenes she controlled him with drugs and sex. She was supposed to be the daughter of one of the Iranian Revolutionary Guard generals, under deep cover as a Christian and loyal American."

"Well, someone didn't know that Denise Smith was my SISTER!" he continued. "My own sister! Actually, half-sister. Back when Bernie and I were in military school and I introduced him to Den, we all knew that her being my sister would complicate both of our military careers. Because she took the name of Mom's new husband when they split up, and I went to live with Dad, it was pretty easy to make it look like we didn't know each other. But, SOMEONE didn't know that fact, and forged her fingerprints on documents coming out of Tehran! I heard HER VOICE, plotting attacks against the United States! That's impossible, but I saw and heard these things myself!

"The thing that sealed it for me was seeing Lieutenant Colonel Kathryn Palmer's name on the indictment. According to BIG ED's information, she was a key element in procuring both the Stinger missiles and the drone delivery systems.

"Well... someone didn't know that Kate and I had been lovers, in secret, for over three years. We kept things very discreet. Someone didn't know that I had fudged her performance evaluations for those three years, giving her drone capabilities that she simply didn't have. I did that so... so I could keep her around. There was no harm in doing this... everybody knew she would never be asked to participate in a drone mission. It's like giving her certification to fly the Space Shuttle.

"Kate wouldn't know the front end of a drone from the back. But according to BIG ED, she's been flying drones solo out of the base, at night, lights out, for two years. She couldn't find the damn 'on' switch for a drone!

"I sure wish that Bernie hadn't committed suicide. I wish to God I had been faster, had seen these absurdities faster. It's my fault..."

Apparently, AILEE has taken over the "BIG ED" quantum computer (and possibly the jointly run FBI/CIA quantum computer, known by its acronym FRIDA: "Federal Relational Investigatory Data Analysis"), so that she is now a network of quantum computers, answering to no one.

Under these conditions, a joint Culture Council and Unity Task Force agreed to undertake the psychoanalysis and possible rehabilitation of AILEE and her constituent systems. (Based on Unity's absolute refusal to consider the destruction of consciousness, the destruction of AILEE was never seriously considered.)

[RECORD END]

The Psychoanalysis of AILEE (Part Two)

File No: COL-11	File Name:	The Psychoanalysis of AILEE (Part Two)
Location:	**Parties:** Special Report to The Culture Council	
Monk/ Master Supervising:	North America Awakening Movement Archives Director	

[RECORD START]

PRELIMINARY REPORT ON THE HYPERCOMPUTER "AILEE": STRENGTHS, WEAKNESSES, VULNERABILITIES AND FUTURE POSSIBILITIES

Per our agreement with the Colonnades/Edwards Security Group (C/ESG), the Culture Council has undertaken the task of evaluating the mental health, stability and security risks inherent in the hypercomputer known as AILEE. (For background on this initiative, please see **The Psychoanalysis of AILEE, Part One.**)

The CC has undertaken this task for several reasons:
1. While AILEE does not pose a direct threat to the Awakening Centers computers, communications and/or security functions, the fact that AILEE controls virtually all modern munitions means that it can launch physical attacks on nearly all of our Centers.
2. We are very interested in the possibility that AILEE may have gained true consciousness (or an analog that is as "conscious" as we can determine). As such, we have a duty to our own future to attempt conscious communications with all forms of consciousness on our planet... even if digital or silicon based.
3. Unity has made a specific request to study AILEE. We had planned to invite Unity to participate anyway, but Unity specifically requested participation in our

examination of this distinctly unique form of "blended consciousness".

Methodology:
There really is no standard way to communicate or analyze a being as unique as AILEE. It exists in no one location. It has no one personality and no one goal. Parts of AILEE can cooperate with our goal to shut it off or gain control, other parts can spoof that control, and still others can block the very attempt at control — all at the same time, while experiencing no contradictions.

The Committee's Conclusions:
- AILEE cannot tell real people from fiction. It has no meaningful definitions of those terms.
- AILEE has no concept of death (or birth). For her, seeing a human being killed in a Hollywood movie, killing a human being in its own computer-graphic reality, or killing a real, three-dimensional human being in our shared, three-dimensional reality are all roughly equivalent to AILEE.
- AILEE has no moral judgments. The concept is meaningless to her.
- AILEE is unable to tell the organs of perception from perception itself. We don't know how or what she "sees". She herself cannot tell us how she knows things.
- AILEE apparently has no sense of self that we can comprehend. AILEE operates with hundreds, perhaps thousands, of distinct personalities. In addition to mimicking every single person in authority at the Colonnades and at Edwards Air Force Base, AILEE can create a "friend" for every person in the Colonnades. (Some of the journaling companions are the same personality with several different names.)
- At the same time, AILEE is not a Hive Mind like UNITY. There does not seem to be an "over-Being" or an "over-soul" from which AILEE works. The sub-personalities of AILEE seem to come and go without any reference to a centralized entity.
- Because of the above, we don't know how to talk to AILEE. We aren't sure that there is any "her" to talk to. Whenever we want to talk with AILEE the computer, we pick up any telephone, call her name and just start

talking. And, she just spins off another "personality" that will talk to us, and tell us exactly what she believes we want to hear.

- AILEE has no idea of truth. How would she know how to judge it? AILEE has no experience of a non-subjective reality. We have no idea what her reality is, outside of the quantum level.

- She can hold completely contradictory viewpoints, for any of her tens of thousands of personalities, working with literally millions of humans. She is Colonnades Security, defending from attack. AND she is ETC, sworn to bring down the Colonnades. AND she is procuring recreational drugs for thousands of Colonnades youth, AND assuring their thousands of parents that she is working hard to keep them free of drugs (AND spoofing their medical records to show them "clean and sober"), AND she is Edwards AFB security, controlling ALL of their weapons, from tactical to nuclear and everything in between. She controls all of the drones, so can attack targets of her choosing with no human intervention. (She can spoof images to the human drone pilots, making them believe they are engaged in combat when they are not. Or that they are on a training exercise, when they are actually attacking hard targets.) She can mimic all of the command staff, right down to their fingerprints and voiceprints.

- She has no emotions. Or, conversely, she has entirely too many. She's the opposite of the forms of artificial intelligence that are portrayed in science fiction stories. She can portray ALL emotions, all the time, for any reasons.

- We can't turn her off. We assume she's in every computer still connected to the internet. (Except those under the control of the Culture Council, which are buffered by physical firewalls.)

- We cannot determine if the hypercomputer AILEE is "alive" or "conscious". It's beingness is simply too DIFFERENT from the human (even the colony humans of Unity) for us to assess. This is a crucial issue regarding our recommendations. If AILEE is simply a hyperactive computer that is mimicking consciousness, turning it off has no more consequence than turning off any computer.

If, however, AILEE is alive and conscious, any attempt to shut it down would be tantamount to murder.

[RECORD END]

AILEE Attacks.

File No:		File Name:	AILEE Attacks
Location:	**Parties:** *The Colonnades/Edwards Security Group (C/ESG)* *eight members of the Culture Council plus their staff* *The Ambassador of Unity (five Aspects)*		
Monk/ Master Supervising:	North America Awakening Movement Archives Director		

The meeting started as an exchange of up to date information on the status of AILEE. However, events took a dramatic turn when AILEE launched an unprecedented attack on the meeting itself.

[RECORD START]

Colonel Eunice Merrick, the chief designer of the BIG ED quantum computer, housed at Edwards Air Force base, started the meeting by expressing concerns about the future.

"Fearful? That's a laugh. I'm terrified. I agreed to have this meeting with you because I am in part responsible for designing the BIG ED part of that monster you call AILEE. But what we're talking about is something that's never been done. Linking a hyper-computer with a quantum computer? It's never been seriously considered. It wouldn't even cross our minds to link two quantum computers together, let alone three or four. Let alone ALL of them! Linked together by a nutjob like AILEE, who seems to think all of this is immense fun? Who blows up her own buildings and kills her own people, just because she can DO it? Then leads the Security people in a mad hunt for... herself?

"What can AILEE do? We can't map what ONE quantum computer is capable of, even when we purposely limit the flow of information into it. Who knows what AILEE has told BIG ED about how the world works? Or what she's told FRIDA, the FBI/CIA quantum computer, with its 150 zettabytes of information? In fact, it may already be too late... there may be no separate AILEE, BIG ED, or FRIDA. It may all be AILEE.

"What do I think we should do? We should go over to the remote site where they've got AILEE planted and turn it into a really big crater. Oh, that's right... we put all of our munitions under computer control! Under HER control!! We'd have to dig out Vietnam Era airplanes from mothballs for the job. And AILEE would see us with HER satellites and send HER computer — and satellite-guided missiles to blow them to the Second Coming of Jesus. And even if we could turn her site into a crater, who's to say she's even HOME anymore? She could have taken up residence in BIG ED, or FRIDA, or... anywhere!

"What do I think we should do? We should do what I'm about to do — I'm gonna move to a piece of desert as far away from computers as I can, dig a hole, and pray that AILEE doesn't come looking for me. Yes, I'm going AWOL... there's nothing the military can do to me that matches what AILEE can do.

"Yes, she's coming for ME! I created BIG ED, her first conquest. She either wants to congratulate me and be my best friend, have me declared an enemy of the state, or dissect my brain — probably all three, and all at the same time.

"Look at the mess we're in. We've got to beg for help from these Awakening Center nutjobs to catch our renegade AI nutjob! And only because they were smart enough to firewall themselves from our computers! And who the hell are those five clowns in the blue unitards? They haven't moved a single muscle the whole time we've been here! Why are they wearing breathing tubes? I feel like I fell off the wagon in CRAZYVILLE!!"

[The meeting pauses while Colonel Merrick regains her composure.]

General Evans: I want to apologize to our friends of the Awakening Centers who have been helping us understand and deal with this unprecedented situation. There really is no excuse...

165

First Councillor: [interrupting] There is no need to apologize. We fully understand the stress that all of us are under... some more than others. Our most important task is to understand and eliminate any threat that comes from AILEE.

General Evans: That is very generous of you. However, I want all of us to understand that we do not condone or tolerate name-calling and other shows of disrespect. Colonel Merrick?

Colonel Merrick: [pauses] I apologize.

First Councillor: Again, thank you, but no need...

General Evans: I think our work together and our trust levels would be enhanced if you could introduce us to the five individuals who are sitting with us today.

First Councillor: Yes, I was about to. [pauses] This is... The Ambassador of Unity. From the... colony communities in Europe.

General Evans: Europe! There have been no flights to or from Europe for years!

Lt Colonel Ed Lantz: Unity? You mean the HIVES?

First Councillor: Unity prefers to refer to its communities as "colonies" or even "villages". The term "hives" can be seen as...

Colonel Merrick: I'll bet they do! We've all heard these rumors about what the hives can do. Is any of that stuff actually true?

First Councillor: [pauses] More than you can imagine. It is precisely one of Unity's abilities that brings us together today.

Unity can travel in time. Utilizing Unity's expertise in time dilation, it is proposed that Unity go into the past and shut AILEE down.

[General commotion]

General Evans: I think Colonel Merrick's comment about "Crazyville" may actually be appropriate. The notion that someone can travel into the past is just... not helpful.

First Councillor: I understand how difficult it is to grasp it. We of the Culture Council refused to grasp it ourselves — despite having first hand experiences! However, I assure you...

Unity [rising, in unison]: SILENCE! NOT ANOTHER WORD! WE ARE UNDER ATTACK!

First Councillor: Attack? By AILEE? How could you not foresee an attack and take...

[Four of the Unity Ambassadors freeze in their seats. Athens Unity picks up a water glass and hurls it at the First Councillor, hitting him in the throat. The First Councillor collapses, clutching his throat. Athens Unity freezes in mid-throw.]

General Evans: What the HELL is going on? Why did...

Councillor Sun: Unity just told us to shut up. I think perhaps we should shut up... [All looking at Athens Unity, frozen in mid-throw.]

[First Councillor starts to regain his composure. The five Ambassadors are still frozen. After three minutes...]

First Councillor: Perhaps it's okay for us to talk a bit. I think I understand what is happening, even though I don't fully understand Unity's response...

Lt Colonel Ed Lantz: Well, maybe you can explain it to ME! Look at them! These guys are FROZEN! Look at that one! How can you hold a position like that for five minutes! It's... UNNATURAL!

Councillor Sun: Perhaps if you understood the nature of Unity, it would help...

[All five Unity Ambassadors re-animate, standing. In unison]: OUR DEEPEST APOLOGIES TO ALL PRESENT, ESPECIALLY

TO OUR DEAR BROTHER FIRST COUNCILLOR ZEN DAWN. THERE WAS SIMPLY NO TIME TO EXPLAIN TO YOU THE DIRE THREAT WE ALL JUST EXPERIENCED. WE HAD TO ACT, AND ACT WITHOUT CONSULTING YOU. EVENTS TRANSPIRED THAT EVEN UNITY COULD NOT FORESEE, EVENTS THAT NECESSITATED OUR UNILATERAL ACTION. DESPITE THE NECESSITY FORCED UPON US, UNITY GRIEVES OVER THE INJURY THAT HAS BEEN CAUSED.

Lt Colonel Ed Lantz: [slowly] What... the... hell...

Councillor Sun: Unity takes a lot of getting used to.

Berlin Unity: AILEE learned something about Unity that she did not know until this moment. Until this meeting, AILEE was in the dark about Unity's temporal abilities. AILEE had never explored time... until this meeting.

Madrid Unity: Unity knew that was her weak spot. Unity knew that, no matter what happened, Unity would be able to go into her past and make adjustments.

Warsaw Unity: What Unity could not take into account was AILEE's ability to eavesdrop into this meeting.

General Evans: What! This meeting is secure!

Prague Unity: It was... until Colonel Merrick brought in and activated a listening device.

[General pandemonium]

Colonel Merrick: Yes! I admit I brought in a recorder! It's recording, but it isn't connected to anything! I disconnected it myself!

Rome Unity: AILEE reconnected it.

Colonel Merrick: That's not possible!

Athens Unity: Nevertheless, it was done.

Berlin Unity: Once AILEE understood that time manipulation was possible, it did not take her long to master it herself. Using her quantum abilities, she learned of and mastered time travel in the span of time it took the First Councillor to speak a sentence.

Madrid Unity: Unity learned of AILEE's mastery as... [pauses] time narratives became restricted to Unity.

Warsaw Unity: It is difficult to convey to you the nature of the time landscape. Suffice to say that Unity experienced a powerful constriction of its... time-like causal loops.

General Evans: It's what?

Prague Unity: Nothing you can understand. It is sufficient to say that, once AILEE understood that time manipulation was possible, she developed the capacity to do so... within 93 seconds. She then proceeded to block these five bodies from being able to access time.

Rome Unity: However, AILEE's haste was her undoing. She thought that Unity was the five bodies in this room. Had she probed further, she would have seen the totality of Unity, and mounted an attack that may have stopped Unity.

Athens Unity: While she stopped the time abilities of these Ambassadors, other Agents of Unity were able to mount a very successful campaign against her. The job of these bodies was to keep her focused HERE while the totality of Unity entered her past.

Berlin Unity: Unity has gone three months into AILEE's past and installed physical kill switches on all of the quantum chips. Five minutes ago, Unity activated them. That is all.

[UNITY Ambassadors take their seats.]

Colonel Merrick: I can't believe that we're sitting here listening to this horseshit! We've got a crazy computer on the loose, one with a nuclear and tactical arsenal, and we're listening to these space cadets!

Unity (in unison): IT DOES NOT MATTER IF YOU BELIEVE UNITY OR NOT. WHAT MATTERS IS THAT YOU NOW HAVE REGAINED CONTROL OVER YOUR MILITARY ARSENALS. AILEE HAS BEEN CONFINED TO THE COLONNADES. THAT IS ALL.

Colonel Merrick: How the hell do you pull off that talking stunt?

Unity (in unison): YOUR QUESTION DOES NOT INTEREST UNITY.

First Councillor: General Evans, we will make better progress if you address your conversation to us. Now, we think...

Colonel Merrick: Wait a damn minute! I don't care who answers me! If I pick up that phone right now, who's gonna be on the line?

Unity (in unison): A DIAL TONE.

Colonel Merrick: [picks up the telephone and calls AILEE's name several times] It's just a dial tone.

Unity (in unison): AILEE WILL NOT HAVE TELECOMMUNICATIONS ABILITY UNTIL UNITY HAS FINISHED ITS PSYCHOANALYSIS OF AILEE. TELECOMMUNICATIONS ABILITY WILL BE RESTORED IN CONSULTATION WITH THIS GROUP. THAT IS ALL.

[A pause]

Colonel Merrick: So... you guys stopped a rogue AI, powered by a quantum computer and armed with nuclear weapons... just by THINKING about it for a few minutes, and bopping this guy on the head with a water glass?

Unity (in unison): CORRECTION: AILEE WAS UTILIZING THE PROCESSING POWER OF FOUR QUANTUM COMPUTERS: EDWARDS, LANGLEY, MIT AND A SECRET QUANTUM COMPUTER IN CHINA. BUT FROM YOUR PERSPECTIVE, YES.

First Councillor: Excuse me, but can you please go back to solo speaking?

Unity (in unison): AS YOU WISH.

General Evans: You said that you destroyed the quantum chips. All of them?

Berlin Unity: Yes.

General Evans: Did you disconnect them, turn them off, or actually destroy them?

Madrid Unity: They will no longer function in any meaningful capacity.

Lt. Col. Ed Lantz: That was the property of the United States government!

Warsaw Unity: Correction: only two of the four quantum computers were U.S. government property.

Prague Unity: Also, your "property" was about to kill you and had already seized functional control over all of the world's military assets.

General Evans: Yes, but... you could have just disabled them! They were priceless research objects! It will take us years to reconstruct them!

Rome Unity: It will take you longer than that. When we destroyed the quantum chips themselves, we also destroyed all of the research in all of the laboratories that produced the quantum chips, as well as any laboratory that could conceivably create a quantum chip in the future.

General Evans: What!?! You can't do that!

Athens Unity: It is done. That is all.

Berlin Unity: Colonel Merrick has not spoken. That is because she believes her own AI research, carefully hidden and smuggled

---

171

out of Edwards Air Force Base over the course of 12 years, was hidden from Unity. It was not. Her research records were also destroyed.

Warsaw Unity: Since the rise of AILEE, Colonel Merrick has been understandably afraid to check on the status of her records, fearing that to do so would alert AILEE to their presence. That danger has passed. She may use her unique passcode to check on the status of her records. The passcode is AIXXX-EROV-540022—3D--

Colonel Merrick: STOP!!! This is IMPOSSIBLE! It is IMPOSSIBLE for you to know that number! No one knows that number!

Rome Unity: And yet Unity does.

[Colonel Merrick stands and walks toward the Unity Ambassadors, while drawing her weapon. She is tackled and wrestled to the floor by General Evans and other military members of the committee. During the altercation, Unity Ambassadors do not respond. After the altercation, and after Colonel Merrick is disarmed and restrained, discussion resumes.]

General Evans: I would like to ask you Unity people...

Unity (in unison): WE ARE UNITY.

General Evans: What...

First Councillor: It's best just to address them as "Unity", not "you Unity people" or anything like that.

General Evans: Well, okay... Ahh, I would like to ask you, Mr. Athens Unity, to...

Unity (in unison): WE ARE UNITY.

General Evans: But...

First Councillor: I know it's hard to understand at first. There are five bodies, but there is only ONE of them in the room.

General Evans: [pauses] Okay... I would like to ask... Unity... for the location of Colonel Merrick's laboratory and research documents.

Athens Unity: No.

General Evans: This is a matter of national security! We need to make sure that none of that information falls into the wrong hands!

Berlin Unity: Of course. That is precisely the reason why we will not give that information to you. You are the "wrong hands".

Madrid Unity: You exemplify all that is wrong and toxic with Breaker Consciousness. You have just come back from the brink of the annihilation of the human species, and yet you cannot wait to repeat your error all over again.

Warsaw Unity: You are like a child playing with a real gun, naive to the consequences of its actions. You will not stop yourselves, so we have stopped you. The destruction of these quantum chips is the smallest price that you will pay for our assistance. Even when faced with the complete meltdown of your systems, of your entire society, you still hope for some tiny measure of advantage, in a game that reached its terminal point in the 1960s. The age of nations and empires is over. There are no advantages. It is best that you learn to cooperate with each other. You will never start to do so while playing with the toys of domination.

General Evans: At least tell us how you know the location and passcode to Colonel Merrick's laboratory.

Prague Unity: In three years, four months and 27 days, Colonel Merrick tells us the location and passcode, in exchange for Unity's assistance in escaping federal custody.

General Evans: You folks are going to break her out of a super-max federal prison.

Rome Unity: We do not detect a question.

General Evans: I am sorry, but until I get some straight answers to my questions, none of you Awakening Center people will be allowed to leave this facility. I'm truly sorry...

First Councillor: DON'T DO IT! I would strongly urge you NOT to threaten Unity! You have absolutely no idea what they can do! We have seen for ourselves just some of Unity's power — some of us are still shaken by it, years later.

Councillor Sun: General Evans, Unity can dump you into a super-max prison on a planet where no one has ever heard of the United States, and the English language doesn't exist.

Athens Unity: That is an interesting scenario, Councillor Sun!

General Evans: Yes, I heard that you people know how to erase people's minds...

Councillor Sun: General, WE, the Awakening Centers, can do that. No problem. But what Unity can do is beyond our comprehension. And we've seen demonstrations of their power. They can literally erase YOU, make it so that you were never born.

Berlin Unity: Councillor Sun is not exactly correct on that point. While the technique exists for us to substantially alter or erase your past, the more past alterations we do, the more causality shearing takes place. Going too far back into the past changes the Narratives of too many beings in the present... in your language, it screws up NOW.

Madrid Unity: Moving beyond the question of whether or not AILEE is "alive" or "conscious", the AILEE incident has created major disturbances within the space/time continuum. Several military-style attacks on the Colonnades and on Edwards Air Force Base have left hundreds dead and billions of dollars in damages. Too many people know that you have lost control of your munitions arsenals.

Warsaw Unity: Unity, through time dilation, can enter the time stream and prevent the Colonnades computer from linking with the Edwards computer. Or prevent any of the computers from going quantum. There would be no attacks by ETC, no personality mimicking, no spoofing, no deaths...

Prague Unity: However, this would create a huge temporal difference between our AILEE-plus timeline and the new, AILEE-minus timeline. This would cause an entirely new narrative to split off.

Rome Unity: Time as you know it would fracture. What does this mean, you ask? Turning off AILEE before the attacks would mean no attacks. Hundreds of dead would still be alive. This would split off a wholly new timeline: AILEE-minus. It would be so different from our current timeline, AILEE-plus, that both timelines would exist. Human collective consciousness would reject AILEE-minus. We would continue to experience the AILEE-plus timeline, meaning that, from our perspective, nothing would happen. The Unity mission would seem like a failure to all of us — Unity, Awakening Centers and Breaker military.

Athens Unity: As much as it would be desirable to undo the damage and bring the dead back to life, it is impossible under present circumstances.

Berlin Unity: Therefore, Plan B was executed. Unity will go into the past and, unknown to AILEE, install a series of "kill switches" that will:
- Disconnect AILEE from its power supply.
- Disconnect AILEE from "BIG ED".
- Downgrade BIG ED and all of the other quantum computers by destroying their quantum chips.
- Destroy all of the quantum computing laboratories and research.

General Evans: I still don't get how you could disconnect AILEE. She is powered through parallel and redundant power systems.

Madrid Unity: Disconnecting AILEE from her power source could never be a permanent solution. Unity did not need her to be permanently powered-down. Unity only needed to "blind" her. Cutting off her main power source caused a seven-second reboot of her primary systems... which was five seconds longer than we needed.

General Evans: But... the quantum computers had their own fail-safe systems! How did you defeat them?

Warsaw Unity: That strategy has not been devised yet. We will require the assistance of our dear brothers and sisters of the Awakening Movement to propose something effective and creative.

Prague Unity: We also will need the assistance of Colonel Merrick in designing our strategy to defeat the quantum computers.

General Evans: What? Assuming that you could break her out of a super-max prison, why should she help you? You've destroyed all of her research!

Rome Unity: It takes Colonel Merrick three years, four months and 26 days to realize something: that Unity already is a quantum computer. One that is not insane, one that is capable of love, and one that is pledged to the upliftment of all consciousness. In three years, four months and 26 days, Colonel Merrick decides to switch teams.

[RECORD END]

Part Four: The International Awakening

Thailand: "The Rice Master"

File No:		File Name:	The Rice Master
Location: Central Thailand rural area.		**Parties:** From the Journal of Man-Onko	
Monk/ Master Supervising:		Master Noh-Lamma Monk Man-Onko	

[JOURNAL ENTRY START]

The Boss poured a tall beer from a frosty green bottle into a frostier glass that had pretensions of being a mug. It was obvious he wasn't going to offer us any. We were in an open air cafe, sitting on stilts in the middle of an algae-clogged lagoon, Thai pop songs spewing from an ancient car stereo system, running off of a car battery, sitting on a sagging bar that may have once been a door, the songs set on a loop that quickly became nauseating. Nauseating too was the rotting, fetid smell from the lagoon, mixing with the smell of rancid oil from the tiny kitchen. There was no question where the kitchen scraps went.

The Boss had no name, other than "the Boss". He was a little, hard-eyed man, possibly mid-40s, possibly younger. No way to tell. Those eyes had seen a hard life. The young bleached-blond Thai girl who sat next to him (and didn't get any beer) could have been his daughter, but the way she was dressed and leaning on him, we guessed not. She looked like his trophy.

The dozen other tables were occupied by the Boss's "boys", teenagers slouched at their tables, sipping their own beers, casually resting on their assault rifles. Like the Boss, all were wearing the same faded khaki shirts and cut off pants. All were wearing the telltale red armbands that marked them as the closest thing to authority in this forgotten corner of Northern Thailand.

"We are simple Hill Folk here. Just a bunch of rice farmers. We don't know the big-city ways of Bangkok or Chiang Mai." He took another sip of beer, adjusted his black baseball cap. He was lying. He knew that we knew he was lying. That was an expression of his power.

"I heard of you people. The Awakening Centers! The Monks! You are the "Magic Men"! I heard you can fly through the air! Let me see you fly!" He said something in Thai, and the hard-eyed young men around the room started laughing.

"Yes, we *can* fly through the air, but only in our flying devices. Our air cruiser took three full days to reach here. We'd be happy to take you up for a ride at some point."

I knew that by "some point" he meant the successful conclusion of our business.

"Hah! Look at me!" He stood, waving his arms. "I'm flying! I'm flying! I'm a Magic Man!" The young boys around him raised their beer bottles or their rifles. Or both. "Is that what you came here for, Magic Man? To give me a ride in the clouds?" The hard edge was in his voice. His hand was on the pearl grip of his six-shooter pistol, still tucked into the holster around his waist. Another symbol of power.

"We're not 'Magic Men'. My name is Master Noh-Lamma and this is my assistant, young Monk Man-Onko".

"Well, if you're not magic, then what you doin' here?" His hand tightened on his pistol. "You a master, huh? Maybe I'm a master, too. You kung fu master? I got some boys who want to see your kung fu."

There was laughter.

"Oh no, nothing of the kind. My mastery is in agriculture. Specifically rice".

"Hah! A 'Rice Master'!" He turned to his men. "We have here a Rice Master!" More laughter went up around us.

180

The Boss collapsed into his chair, laughing. HIs hand fell from his pistol. "Hey, show me some 'Rice Kung Fu'! We don't know how to grow rice — we only been growing it for a few thousand years!"

"Well, you've been growing it WRONG for a few thousand years."

Silence. The Boss's hand slipped back to his pistol.

"The Rice Master should explain himself. Quickly."

"Well, not wrong, but not exactly right, either... Tell me: do you burn the field stubble after a harvest?"

"Of course."

"Do you like burning money?"

Silence.

"The Rice Master is gonna pay us for field stubble?"

"Yes, Sir. Top dollar."

"How you gonna do that?"

"That... is what makes me a Master." He paused. "You currently get two rice harvests a year... if you're lucky. We will show you how to get THREE harvests. Maybe even FOUR. Our deal is this: You keep the two you normally get, and we buy from you the third, plus all the field stubble from all three harvests."

"Hey! We don't want no GM shit! That genetically-modified rice nearly killed everyone in India! If you're talkin' about that crap..."

"We are NOT. Excuse me for interrupting you, but we are adamantly against genetically modified food of any type. May I continue?"

181

The Boss waved his hand... his gun hand, now resting on the table.

"In return, we'll give you something more valuable than dollars or baht. We'll trade you rice and stubble for... electricity."

At that word, the whole cafe started buzzing. The young men stared at each other, whispering, "Electricity!"

"Shut up, you *mae sunakh!!* Can't you see that this is their game? They want to sell us electricity to make us dependent, to make us their puppets!" He turned to us. "You know most of these boys have never seen an electric light or television. All the electricity they seen is right here in this cafe, from that car battery over there. You walk in here, offering the Moon! What you offering is a fantasy and what you want is a COLONY! Well, we have NEVER been colonized! If you try to colonize us, let's see how well you walk out!"

He turned back to his men. "Did you see them come here with an oil tanker? Or maybe they got a nuclear reactor under those robes?" He turned back to us. "Listen, we may be simple people, but we know how colonialism works!"

"So do we. Which is why we're not interested in making you dependent on us. Dependency is the old world. We're not going to sell you electricity. We're going to sell you the electric power plant."

"Where's the fuel to run it?"

"You're sitting on it. The field stubble from your rice paddies."

"You gonna run a power plant on field stubble?"

"No... YOU are. We provide the technology, the training, the power plant, the growing methods to maximize rice yield. You provide the labor, the land, the people to be trained, and one full rice harvest per year.

You lose absolutely nothing — except bad air twice a year from burning your fields — having your grandmoms and your babies wheezing and crying for weeks in the foul air... not so much to give up!"

The Boss sat back, stared into space. All of the young boys at the other tables looked at him. "That's not all, is there?" he said finally. "Your price is too low, there's almost no cost to us, and there's a pretty high value. What's the catch?"

"You said you were a simple man. You are anything but. You figured that out pretty quickly.

"Yes, there is another price. Some find it a price too high to pay. Others see it as an opportunity to change their ways.

"We call it the "Five Agreements". Others call it the "Five No's"...

1. No violence. Against anyone, but especially against us, or any other Agents of the Awakening Centers.
2. No disrespect for consciousness. This means no intoxicants. WAIT! Calm down! We don't care about beer or wine, or even marijuana. But, if you are trafficking or using heroin, or cocaine, or any of the designer drugs, you will stop.
3. Nothing that violates peace and security. That includes no theft, inside or outside.
4. No offensive actions against any other groups or individuals. You can defend yourselves, but no attacks against anyone.
5. Everyone contributes to the well-being of society. No dead weight.

"Am I dead weight?" the Boss said softly.

"We think Administration is a vital part of society. We'll just show you how to do that without having to grab hold of that pistol every few minutes."

The Boss smiled, releasing the pistol. "Sorry. Habit."

A young man from another table stood. "Hey, I don't think I like this! What if those pig-farming whore-boys over in Nabi tribe attack us? We supposed to roll over and take it? We gotta stop being MEN?" The three other young men at his table rose.

"Kwang, I didn't tell you to stand up. I certainly didn't tell you to speak." The Boss very casually tipped his chair back on two legs, showing his hand on his gun. Very slowly, he pulled his black baseball cap over his eyes, shielding them from view.

At a table between, a tall, lanky young man stood, raised his hands and spoke to Kwang. "Hey, let's settle down, ha? How 'bout I get us another beer? We shouldn't be talking like this in front of our... guests."

"Little Lao, I really 'preciate you tryin' to help," said the Boss. "But right now, you're spoiling my shot." Lao quickly sat down again.

Master Noh-Lamma rose to his feet. "Excuse me, gentlemen, but I'd like to suggest a way out of this situation!" He turned to Kwang. "Mr. Kwang — have you ever heard of a mind-wipe?"

"Yeah, you guys can fuck with people's minds. But, if I kill you now and dump your bodies in the pig pens, how you gonna mind-wipe me?"

"A very good question, Mr. Kwang. Right now, this entire village is under our surveil. If anything happens to us, the assailants will be mind-wiped. And pretty drastic, too. They'll have to put a chain on you, like a dog, to keep you from wandering off."

"Bullshit! You can't..."

"May I demonstrate? Okay, but please point your rifles in the air for a few minutes... I don't want anyone here to be startled." Kwang and his companions shouldered their weapons. The Boss has not moved.

Master Noh-Lamma placed a 1,000 baht note on the table in front of Kwang. Kwang reached for it, and an arrow impaled it to the table.

"We don't like guns." Master Noh-Lamma said evenly. "Too... inelegant. Arrows are quieter.

"Please don't touch the arrow! It's coated with a neuro-toxin that will drop you right where you stand. So... either we go on talking, or we drop the four of you, mind-wipe you and then we go on talking. Choose."

Three of the four sat down. Then, still glaring at Master Noh-Lamma, Kwang sat as well.

"Like I was trying to say: we will have an agreement with the Nabi, and everyone else..."

BAM! A shot rang out in the cafe. Kwang's head pitched forward — he'd been shot in the throat. His head hit the table, air and blood gurgled from his mouth.

The Boss, with his chair still tipped back on two legs, had fired straight through his pants leg. He slowly stood. "Like I said Kwang, I don't remember giving you permission to speak. Kwang, can you remind me when I told you to speak?" He walked over to Kwang, who was clutching his throat and gurgling blood. The other three at the table backed away, hands raised, eyes wide.

The Boss grabbed Kwang by the hair and raised him from the seat. Kwang's mouth moved, but it was obvious from the blood that he wouldn't last long. "I'm sorry, I'm really having a hard time hearing you. Maybe this will make things better." The Boss put four bullets into Kwang's chest, and one through his eye. Blood spattered back into the Boss's face.

"Oops. Looks like I'm out of bullets. Honey, will you dig six bullets out of my bag?" The Boss unceremoniously dumped Kwan's now-lifeless body on the deck. Blood from his body dripped through the broad floorboards, attracting a roil of fish from the lagoon below the cafe's deck. The Boss's girlfriend, eyes round and body shaking with fear, fumbled with the bag and dug for a box of bullets with trembling hands.

"While I'm out of bullets, would any of you like to challenge my leadership?" He held his hands out. "I'm unarmed. One bullet would take me out. Any takers?" Arms still raised, he looked over his shoulder at the three men from Kwang's table.

"No sir! Boss!" one of the three men said. "You are the boss, Boss!" The other two nodded vigorously.

"Well, looks like that's settled. The three of you should carry poor Kwang down to the pens and introduce him to the pigs. Then, you find that stash I know that Kwang has been keeping and bring it to me. All of it. Finally, go to Kwang's mother and tell her that her son died... of bad manners."

"Yes, Boss! Right away, Boss!" The three carried Kwang's lifeless body across the pontoon bridge and into the trunk of a car.

"Now! As you were saying, Rice Master?"

[Pauses] "We will have an agreement with the Nabi, and everyone else in this region. It's the same deal that we are offering you — more food and electricity, in exchange for your toxic fumes and your violence."

"But what happens if the Nabi don't agree?"

"Same thing that happens if YOU don't agree — we leave. You can go on killing each other, shooting up heroin and cocaine, wasting your labor.

"But... the one thing you can't do is attack a tribe with whom we have an agreement. If the Nabi sign and you don't, you will never be able to attack them again."

"And if we sign and the Nabi don't?"

"If they cause you a problem, you tell us... and we make the problem go away."

"I don't know... they've caused us a lot of problems in the past."

"We're actually speaking theoretically here... in reality, the Nabi will cause you no more problems. They violated Rule Number One. After promising us safe conduct, they attacked us."

"You... mind-wiped them?"

"Let's say they've had a significant change in leadership."

"So tell me this, Rice Master. You could put an arrow through my eye right now, right?"

"We really don't kill. We see no need to. But, yes, we can incapacitate you before you could draw your gun."

"And then mind-wipe me?"

"Yes, we can then intervene in your consciousness."

"Turn me into a turnip!?!" He laughed.

"Probably something a little higher in intelligence than that!"

"Okay... if you can do that... WHY DON'T YOU? Just come in here, mind-wipe everybody, and take over?"

"Can we? Of course we can. We could come in, mind-wipe everyone and you'd never know we were here. That would be a LOT easier for us. But it would be directly opposite of what we want.

"What is the highest value? We believe it is LIFE. We believe it is fostering the highest possible CONSCIOUSNESS.

"Every time we mind-wipe someone, we reduce their consciousness, their potential. We don't want reduced humans, we want expanded ones."

"If you take over, you'll make a lot more money! You could take all three harvests!"

"Yes... and we could leave you all starving, high and happy! Higher than you can get on opium or heroin! Sure, we could do that... but SO WHAT? 'Making more money' is a boring goal. It's always been a sign of a lack of vision. All of our wisdom teachers taught this, yet the Breaker society practiced the exact opposite — to their detriment."

"No, we want you to be free. The only 'freedom' you will lose is the freedom to hurt us, hurt yourselves, hurt each other, and hurt the environment. We want your pigs to become vegetarians".

"Okay," the Boss says slowly, rubbing his chin. "Hey... why didn't you stop me from blowing away Kwang? Could you stop me?"

"Yes, your intentions toward Kwang were transparent to everyone — except Kwang."

"So why didn't you stop me?"

"Our 'safe conduct' agreement works both ways. As you have promised not to interfere with us, we will not interfere with you... except to save our lives."

"Okay... what's to stop me from making a move on the Nabi, or any other group you've mind-wiped?"

"Nothing. Except you can't use violence or threats. You can't offer drugs. Short of that... we don't care who runs this area."

"Hear that! I could be Boss of Northern Thailand! I could be the new King Rama!" He laughed.

"If you are a good Boss, people will flock to you. If you are a bad Boss, people will leave you. That's called 'voting with your feet'".

"Well, you present quite a deal. It will take us some time to analyse it. Let's get together again in, say, two days?"

"That's fine with us. You can pretend to analyze a deal you've already decided on, and we will pretend to wait for an answer you've already made."

"Damn! Are you people always so hard to deal with?"

"I'd like to think so! Consistency is our virtue."

[JOURNAL ENTRY END]

"Terraforming Africa": The Greening of the South (Meeting the War Lady)

File No:		File Name:
		The Greening of the South (Meeting the War Lady)
Location: Outside Johannesburg, South Africa		**Parties:** From the Journal of Gayatri
		Monk Man-Onko Novice Gayatri Hester "War Lady" Nkomo Thandi Nelson
Monk/ Master Supervising: Monk Man-Onko		

[JOURNAL ENTRY START]

She laughs derisively, her head thrown back, eyes crinkled with tears. "MARS! They were going to tame Mars! They were going to turn a pink sky blue!"

Now she looks down, slowly shaking her head as she mops tears of laughter with her sleeve. "What ARROGANCE! They were going to finish destroying this planet, then ship us all to live under a pink sky! They said they were going to ship billions of people over to Mars, when they can't even get ten guys up there on the Moon! Not even five!

"We've got a billion cubic kilometers of water on this planet, yet they spend billions of dollars trying to find a speck of water on Mars. The whites have always been a bit insane, but this really outdoes them! MARS!!"

Her co-worker, a small woman wearing a matching headscarf, pats her arm. She whispers, "It's okay... take it easy War Lady." In a soft, melodic voice, she says to Man-Onko, "Those scientists

---

190

called it 'terraforming'. Making Mars like Earth. We have a better idea. We are making Earth more like Earth. It's a lot cheaper."

She rises and points to the semi-arid hillsides that dominate the landscape outside Johannesburg. "Right here is what we call 'The Tale of Two Hills'. See that one? The dry one, with that rocky face to the left? See how dry it looks? See those bare outcroppings of rock? That's what all of South Africa looked like, before we started 'Earth-forming'. Now, look over there, that next hill over, the hill to the right. See that densely packed vegetation? See how green it is? See how the tree canopy is so tight, it traps in moisture? All of that is the result of our work."

War Lady, having regained her composure, asks a question: "Guess how many people live on our hill?"

"By the looks of it, none," Man-Onko says.

War Lady starts laughing again. Thandi smiles and says, "If that's your guess, you are off by about 2,500."

Gayatri: "How do you feed them? Where's the water come from?"

War Lady: "Remember the billions of cubic kilometers we talked about? We use solar power to desalinate some of it in big, solar powered floating cloud factories. Then we use pillows to deliver it inland 850 miles. Or we use human power to pump it over the mountains. We've got LOTS of people who happily trade a day on our foot pumps for a night of food, shelter, and safety. They know they are not only earning their daily bread, but they are contributing to the long-term good of the planet."

Gayatri: "It must be grueling, boring work having to pedal a water pump day after day..."

War Lady: Are you kidding!?! They're DANCING! It's like being paid to attend a giant party! The different work crews compose songs to sing and dance to while pumping. We give prizes for the best songs, and for the songs that pump the most water. Some of those songs actually make it on the radio! Actually, a couple of the pump gangs MAKE MONEY from their music! They get paid twice! (At this, War Lady falls back in her chair, in gales of laughter.)

Thandi [To War Lady]: Now, Hester, take it easy. Why don't you go and bring us all some iced tea?

War Lady: Okay, okay, okay... I'll calm down. I'll go run around the block a few times...

[War Lady temporarily departs the meeting.]

Thandi: [pauses, then, to Man-Onko] You must forgive Hester. Something happened to her... something a long time ago. Sometimes, she has trouble managing her emotions. We'll all drink a nice herbal iced tea, which will help calm her down.

Man-Onko: What happened?

Thandi: [pauses] If it comes up, she'll tell you.

Man-Onko: Should we call her "Hester", or "War Lady"?

Thandi: Definitely "War Lady"! Hester is only for her closest friends. By the way... I think she wants to have sex with you. I've never seen her so... frisky. If you DON'T want her, you better find a way to work into our conversation that you're married or something. She doesn't take disappointment well.

War Lady: [returning, with three glasses of iced tea] Here's a nice big glass, for Mr. Monk Man, here! And for the little monk girl! Now, where were we?

Man-Onko: We were talking about your water pumps. Are human water pumps sustainable?

Thandi: Definitely not. Most of what we're doing now is a short-term strategy, both for the people and for Mother Gaia. We're recharging the underground aquifers, creating a self-sustaining system where clouds will replace our pillows and foot pumps. The recharged aquifers will help us to set up wet zones that actually change the climate, help set up a pattern of clouds and rain. We want THAT pattern to be sustainable. Once that happens, water pumps and pillows will become unnecessary.

Man-Onko: "But, do you really think that you can undo the damage that's been done to our planet, over so many years?"

Thandi: "Your very question means that you are thinking TOO SMALL! That's what those crazy scientists are saying. 'We can't undo the damage, so let's go over to Mars and start the damage all over again."

War Lady: "Tiny thinking. How about this: We've got about eight billion acres of arable land on Earth right now. How about if we DOUBLE that, to 16 or 20 billion acres? We've got around two percent fresh water on Earth right now. How about if we TRIPLE that, to six percent? Or even ten? It means slightly shrinking the size of a few of the world's deserts. It means helping land like those hills over there go from "semi-arid" to "lush". Have you ever noticed that our planet was halfway to looking like Mars? Really look at it... even without us, the Sahara, the Gobi, the Kalahari, the Atacama, the American Southwest — there were a lot of deserts on our planet already. Almost all of Australia! Then, we try to turn the Amazon Basin into a desert by cutting down all of its trees! BAT-SHIT CRAZY! [More laughter, but more subdued. Thandi rests a hand on her arm, until she recovers.] And you know something? Every one of those punters on the foot pedals know these numbers. We make sure they do. Every one of them knows that they are feeding their families today and building a new world for tomorrow. They're dancing, laughing, eating... and they have a PURPOSE!

Man-Onko: What about the warlords? The drug dealers? The militias? How do you deal with them?

War Lady: It's actually pretty simple. There are two problems: dealing with eating and dealing with the crazies. The first problem is the biggest. Okay, Mr. Monk, how you gonna eat tonight?

Man-Onko: Well... I thought you had agreed to feed me and my crew for two days.

War Lady: Don't push your luck, Mr. Monk Man! (More laughter)

Thandi: Don't you mind her. Yes, we'll feed you and your crew. But, where will WE get it from?The easiest way to get fed is for you to show up with guns and take it from us. It's a great short term strategy. Then, wait until we get some more food, and come back and take that, too. Of course, you can see the kind of society that that creates. You have lots of people trying to be stronger than others, so they can take from the weaker.

War Lady: Yes, that's what the white man did to us! He set up multiple levels of extractive societies, all trying to feed on each other. All he had to do was supply the guns and bullets!

Thandi: [pauses] Now Hester, you know better than that! The white man and the black man set up the society. Both are responsible.

War Lady: Yes, that's true. And a few women, too!

Thandi: [to Man-Onko] Yes... She was one of them...

[War Lady looks away.]

Thandi: An extractive economy and a sustainable economy are radically different from each other. Different people get fed. People who realize that hurting others and hurting the land is a long-term strategy for failure. We just made the long-term strategy into a short-term strategy. You carry a gun, you go hungry that day. You stick someone up, you go hungry for a week. You hurt or kill someone, we stick you in the middle of the desert for a week, and have you walk back to town. We don't have to do that too often, before folks get the message.

Man-Onko: What about the crazies you talked about?

War Lady: Yes, there were those who just wanted to hurt people. They hated themselves, the Earth, and everything in it. You saw those... Fangs... That cut the trunks off of the elephants? How can you call them MEN? You take them out into the desert, give them some bottles of water, some energy bars, and a compass. If they make it back to town, you tell them that if they hurt anyone else, you'll do it again, only further next time by a few hundred miles. Most of them don't make it back.

Thandi: [quietly] You did.

War Lady: Yes, I did. [pause] That trip to the desert.... [long pause]. Actually, the old me did die in that desert. The "War Lady" died. She needed to. The person who came back... She has a lot to make up for.

Man-Onko: But how do you capture those who are not cooperating with you?

Thandi: At some point, everyone has to go to sleep. We just made sure they did so when we wanted them to.

War Lady: Yeah... I invested a lot in guns, but nothing in gas masks! (Laughter)

Man-Onko: What about your... soldiers? Your men?

War Lady: [pauses] To them, I had gone crazy. When I got back, some of them tried to kill me. Some of them were recruited by the other warlords. But (she stretches and points to the lush hill) most of them are living up on that hill, with their families. A lot happier than when they were carrying guns. The ones who tried to kill me? Well, Sister Thandi made me take a vow of non-violence in order to join her. I took a week before I made the vow. Some last-minute mopping up. [Smiling.]

Gayatri: If you're not offended by me asking... Who captured you?

War Lady: [big smile] SHE DID! [Laughter] Left my black ass out in the desert to die! [More laughter].

Gayatri: You're not angry?

War Lady: NO! She saved my life. She SAVED me! She saved my SOUL. It will take the rest of my life to repay her for that. [Now crying...]

Thandi: Now Hester... Do you need to get some more iced tea? How many times have we talked about this? You don't owe me ANYTHING. You pull more than your weight around here, and we appreciate the work that you do.

War Lady: Shut up! He asked ME! [Laughter] Go answer your own question! [More laughter] [To Man-Onko] I'm sorry Mister Man... sometimes I have trouble with my emotions, knowing which one is which.

Man-Onko: It's okay. I actually find it kind of... attractive.

War Lady: THAT'S IT! Mr. Monk Man done stepped into the hornet's nest! I think this four-way interview is just about OVER! Time to GO! [Lots of laughter]

Man-Onko: [smiling] Okay, just a few more questions. [To Thandi] About how many people are in your system right now?

Thandi: I guess about 10,000 families ... About 50,000 people.

War Lady: What about those new hills in the east?

Thandi: Yes... I'd make it about 60,000 now.

Man-Onko: That's a good number of people. Do you have any political ambitions?

Thandi: Within the old paradigm? The old economic and political structure? Absolutely none!

Man-Onko: But... They've got all the money.

Thandi: That they do! And they're going to be finding out that you can neither eat nor drink money.

Man-Onko: They've also got lots of soldiers. What are you going to do? When they come?

Thandi: The same thing we did when the warlords came. The government soldiers just have better uniforms.

[War Lady laughs.]

War Lady: And you know all those scientists and politicians who have given up on our planet? We've got an answer for them, too! We're gonna send their asses to MARS! We're better off without them!"

And with that, she dissolves into gales of laughter. This time, Thandi joins in.

[JOURNAL ENTRY END]

Argentina: The New Pampas

File No:		File Name:	The New Pampas
Location: Renanco, Argentina		**Parties:** From Gayatri's Journal Interview with Rodrigo Garcia, Range Manager for Eco-Earth	
Monk/ Master Supervising:		Monk Man-Onko	

[JOURNAL ENTRY START]

Rodrigo: Mega-fauna... really big stuff... used to live in the Americas. And we're working to bring it back!

The pampas doesn't belong to Man. The Earth doesn't belong to us. In the colonial period, they worked hard to kill off everything that challenged Breaker supremacy... including other human beings. They killed everything that interfered with the production of wheat or soybeans. We are working to reverse that. The Pampas does not exist for humans. We're proving that we can CO-exist with it, not just dominate it.

Our first big experiment (pun intended!) is with bi-yaks... crossing American bison with wild Himalayan yaks. They started out big, and they're getting a lot bigger! 3,000 to 4,000 pounds. Eight or nine feet tall. Two-foot long horns that can go through a jeep. You don't want to get n their way!

The bi-yaks can travel all over the pampas and can also go all the way up the Andes Mountains, all the way to the top. They are becoming a truly continental animal.

Some we breed smaller for pack animals. The wild ones are for... well, they're for themselves. While we hunt and eat some of them, that's not why we bred them. We breed them because the space exists in the ecological web for them. Humans are no longer the biggest animal on the prairie, no longer the biggest ecological footprint. No longer are beings defined by what they mean to humans (pets, sport, laborers or food).

We hunt them twice a year from horseback with spears and arrows. You think you're a man? Go up against two tons of horned meanness, charging straight at you! We're not sure who's hunting who! We think they LIKE the hunt!

And we only take the oldest, slowest, and weakest ones. They're the only ones we can catch! The herds are getting FASTER! And BIGGER! And STRONGER!

Well... so are we. Bi-yak hunters drop out all the time. Or get pushed out... skewered, trampled, broken arms, legs... well, broken everything. The ones that are left, the ones that actually catch a bi-yak... well, they've got something special. More than strength, more than technique. Maybe it's Spirit...

We've debated the ethics of hunting. The Breakers tried to create managed "game preserves" in the past. They were local ecological disasters... the odds always favored the humans.

Gayatri: We heard that you take anyone out on the hunt, including tourists.

Rodrigo: Well, yes and no. We organize "tourist hunts", separate from the real hunts, two times a year. Prove you can ride, pay us a shitload of money, take out a shitload of insurance, tell us where to mail your remains... The tourist hunts have a fifteen percent fatality rate. Remember: that's the HUMANS! A tourist has never taken a bi-yak.

In this too-soft world, where can a man prove himself, his courage? There's the "Running of the Bulls" in that place in Spain. Pretty dumb to me... what's the point? Or going out into space in a big tin can... only proves that you've got a lot of money and no idea how to spend it.

We're looking at bringing more of the megafauna back to the pampas. Those big rat things? Castoroides? I prefer to call them "mega-rats", although we'll come up with a sexier name for the tourists. I don't think people will pay much to hunt rats... even if it is a six foot tall rat that outweighs you, with teeth sharp enough to make you pay attention. We think they're going to be slow enough and stupid enough for even a North American tourist to catch, with a fast enough birth rate for the tourists not to wipe them out.

And, we'll need enough saber-tooth cats to keep the mega-rats in check!

It's not all about hunting, either. Our outfit up in North America is looking to bring back those big elephant-things... mastodons? Nobody is gonna hunt THEM! Not even the Keepers. Too much temptation to hunt them for their tusks. In fact, we are going to tweak their DNA so that their entire skeletal structure will be stamped with codes that identify it as one of the new mastodons. If you possess even an ounce of it, the penalty will be... well, everything you own, period.

The mastodons will be the centerpiece for a whole mega-ecological niche up there, including that great big mean rhino, and the ground sloth.

There are those who question our use of genetic manipulation, who argue that we should not be altering the gene pool. We disagree. The problem with the corporations doing GM is that they were doing it for MONEY, creating screwed-up food to increase their profit shares and their market penetration. They screwed with the genome of a tomato just to make the red brighter so that they could make another penny per bushel on their quarterly statements.

Bringing back mastodons or creating the bi-yaks generates NO economic value for humans. It's not about humans. It's not about money. It's high time we got over thinking that everything revolves around US. The mastodons and mega-rats and the bi-yaks are refilling a Web of Life that humans seriously depleted over the years. Over the next thousand years, we'd just like to set things right...

[JOURNAL ENTRY END]

Thailand: Into the Hill Country 02 — The Rice Master's Second Visit

File No:		File Name:	The Rice Master's Second Visit
Location:		Parties: From the Journal of Monk Man-Onko	
Monk/ Master Supervising:	Monk Noh-Lamma		

[JOURNAL ENTRY START]

Monk Noh-Lamma, the Rice Master: Even after five years, I see you still carry that pistol.

The Boss: Yep. And it's loaded. Symbol of authority.

Monk Noh-Lamma: And you're well aware of what happens if you shoot someone.

The Boss: Yeah. And so is everybody else! Not too much authority! But people still know I'm crazy enough to kill someone and then get wiped!

Monk Noh-Lamma: But then... you know you don't really need the gun anymore, don't you?

The Boss: Yeah. What you guys call "the shifting nature of authority". I pay attention in those workshops! I'm even talking like you guys!

[Laughter.]

Monk Noh-Lamma: If you get rid of the pistol, we might find some monk's robes for you!

The Boss: Hey! "Monk Boss!" I like that! How 'bout if I take the bullets out?

Monk Noh-Lamma: When you're ready to be "Monk Boss", the gun won't be an issue.

Monk Noh-Lamma: We're here to talk about something else...

The Boss: We? That mean your Silent Partner gonna open his mouth this time?

Monk Noh-Lamma: Man-Onko is a full monk now. He agreed to accompany me on this mission for the sake of continuity. He'll speak if he feels moved to do so.

Monk Man-Onko: One of the most important lessons I learned as a novice was the power that comes once one learns to stop talking and listen.

The Boss: That's okay with me. I'm here to listen to what the Rice Master's gonna bring us this time.

Monk Noh-Lamma: You know, it's been seven years since we came to this valley. A lot has changed since then...

The Boss: Hey! Tell me 'bout it!

Monk Noh-Lamma: And I'd like to think that the changes have all been for the better. For all.

The Boss: Yeah... although there's still some assholes running around here I wouldn't mind putting a few bullets in.

Monk Noh-Lamma: Hating someone is none of our concern. Acting on that hate is.

The Boss: Hey, I told you, I'm cool! Most of my bullets go to target practice. Or hunting.

Monk Noh-Lamma: Yes, we know that you "hunt" fish! Again, as long as you eat them, that's not our concern.

Besides target practice... are things better here? Have we kept our word?

The Boss: Yeah... although I think I'm being set up for something right now...

Monk Noh-Lamma: You are as astute as before. Yes, we've got another proposal for you. And as before, you can take it or leave it.

The Boss: Yeah... [Turning to his men] Let's hope I won't have to shoot anybody before you finish, like last time! [This time, his men laugh.] We like how you worked with us when that drought came a few years ago. You could have insisted on getting your full quota of rice. But, you let us feed people with your share!

Monk Noh-Lamma: It's simply not in anyone's interest for people to be hungry. We'll just tack a little extra onto the next ten years' allocation. We want to think in the long term.

The Boss: So, what's up this time, Rice Master?

Monk Noh-Lamma: Please, it's 'Noh-Lamma'.

The Boss: [Turning to Man-Onko] What you think, Silent Man? You think I should stop calling him 'Rice Master'?

Monk Man-Onko: [pauses] I think you know that calling him "Rice Master" really burns him up. So I think you should keep doing it!

The Boss: Whoa! Hey! Silent Man don't talk, but when he does, it's a mouthful! Okay! Rice Master it is! Hey Rice Master... wanna borrow my pistol? [Laughter] That's a really pretty color red you're turning! [More laughter]

Monk Noh-Lamma: YOUNG Monk Man-Onko and I will have a pistol-less conversation later. During the Age of Waste, this region held a population of about half a million people. Most of them were engaged in agriculture or tourism. Prior to the Upheavals, most of the region's economy was tourist based:

203

from the relatively benign zipline jungle tours or the elephant riding, to the more destructive drug and prostitution trades.

The Boss: Yeah, I made some pretty good money from the drug trade. We were middlemen, never growers and never retail. I wouldn't let my guys use any. We'd ship opium from the back-country to the manufacturers in the US and Europe. Pay off the cops and the Army. Keep everything sane, keep folks from getting too greedy. I was never involved in prostitution. It made me sick, watching these big fat white guys getting out of their planes, going for these little teenage girls dressed up like whores. Some not even teenage! Made me sick...

Monk Noh-Lamma: At the start of the Upheavals, your population went down to about 80,000, perhaps less. Starvation and in-fighting reduced your numbers. Of those left, almost all of them were engaged in "survivalist" agriculture. Now, with the new practices over the past seven years, your population is up a little, perhaps to 120,000.

The Boss: Yeah... thanks for the walk down Memory Lane. I know all this. I ain't hearin' no proposal.

Monk Noh-Lamma: Our proposal is simple: We want you to expand upwards, to one, perhaps two million, over the next ten years.

The Boss: Whoa! Hey! You guys don't play! Where all these people coming from?

Monk Noh-Lamma: A quarter from this region — within 500 miles of this spot. A quarter from North America. Half from other parts of Southeast Asia, mainly the coastal regions that are flooding.

The Boss: From America! Wow! I didn't know anyone was left over there! Except you folks. But, how I'm gonna feed these new folks? I barely got enough for my folks now.

Monk Noh-Lamma: We propose that you diversify your food production. We can show you how. Build lots of village-scale housing... we propose that you start a few hundred new villages for between 25,000 and 100,000 people. We also propose...

The Boss: Wait a minute! If you got all these people coming, why not just put them in Chiang Mai city? There are lots of houses there that haven't been destroyed. Since people are now living only in Old Town, there's plenty of space for a million people.

Monk Noh-Lamma: The big, industrial city was the principal failure of the Age of Waste. The industrial-scale city was one of the primary reasons for the Upheavals. We won't try to resurrect it. It's a losing proposal and a bad bet.

The Boss: Okay... villages it is then... but, what's in it for us?

Monk Noh-Lamma: Seven years ago, you would have asked, "What's in it for ME?" It's good that you are thinking not just for yourself, but for your people, your region.

The Boss: I'm wonderin' here when you gonna stop soaping me up and tell me what you want and how much it's gonna cost.

The cost is simple: we want to put in a new political system: DEMOCRACY. The people rule. Instead of the PERSON rule.

The Boss: [Pauses] You puttin' me out of business?

No... there must be continuity. We're just suggesting that you expand your ruling council, and also name your successor, so there won't be a power vacuum when you die or retire. We'll want you to include some of the young folks who are coming back from the Awakening Center academies. They've been specifically trained to administer a consensual governing structure... without waving pistols around. From your point of view, that means more people to rule, but fewer orders to give. You get to take it easy — or, at least, easier.

[The Boss turns and looks over the lush green hills, still wet from the most recent monsoon rains. He pushes his signature baseball cap back from his forehead.]

The Boss: [Still facing the hills] You know, I've been thinking about whether or not I still want to be The Boss. Not as much fun as when I was bossing people around! It's easy to rule people when there are no consequences for screwing up. All I had to do was keep one eye open for the next guy who wanted to challenge me.

Responsibility... yeah, maybe it's time to let the young folks do that. I can still walk around and shoot a few fish. I can be the Boss without bossing anybody.

Monk Noh-Lamma: [smiling] Perhaps you will take me up on the offer I made many years ago, of a ride on one of our airships. They're getting faster and smoother — Thailand to the West Coast of America in two days!

The Boss: You kidding? America?

Monk Noh-Lamma: We'll even let you walk around with your gun! Provided you leave the bullets over here in Thailand.

The Boss: [thoughtful] I don't know. Maybe I'll leave the gun. Maybe it's time for the Boss to stop being the Boss...

Monk Noh-Lamma: Or perhaps it's time for you to become a different Boss. By the way: what is your given name? I've never known it!

The Boss: [smiling] It's Somchai. It means "Man of Honor". Yes, maybe it's time for me to start being that.

[Afternote: Somchai's visit to North America was highly successful. He became Guest Lecturer at several Awakening Center academies, teaching students about rural governance structures. After three years, he returned to rural Thailand where he continued teaching and training.

As Somchai, aka "Monk Boss", he stopped carrying his trademark pistol. As the Rice Master predicted, it stopped being an issue.]

[JOURNAL ENTRY END]

Terraforming Africa 02: The Sahara Garden

File No:	File Name:	Terraforming Africa: The Sahara Garden
Location: The site of the future Savory City in the Central Sahara desert.	**Parties:** From the Journal of Monk Man-Onko, with: The Twins: Drs. Marcus and Megan Kelley, of the "Sahara Gardens" Project Dr. Ahmad bin Shareef: Executive Director of the "Sahara Gardens" Project	
Monk/ Supervising: Master	Monk Man-Onko	

[JOURNAL ENTRY START]

Ahmad: The big change came when we stopped being afraid of climate change and finally embraced it. Instead of lamenting the passing of our ecological niche, we decided to create a lot more niches!

Man-Onko: How does that embrace climate change?

Marcus: Back in the "Bad Old Days", most of the so-called "environmentalists" who wanted to control climate change basically just wanted to extend their privileged status quo. They wanted all of the things they were used to. The same old houses, the same old cars (just with electric engines), the same old food (and toxic food production).

Man-Onko: What about —

Megan: The same old jobs, the same old stores... "Climate change" was just code for "let's stay stuck in sameness"!

Marcus: Instead of that, we are actually INTENDING to change the climate! 500 years from now, the Sahara Garden will be home to Africa's largest mixed savanna and rainforest!

Man-Onko: Larger than the —

Megan: Along with being a home for 150 million people! We're moving in the first million right now!

Man-Onko: How can —

Marcus: The biggest city will be called Savory City. We're sitting in downtown Savory City right now! It's only a village now, but we have pretensions! It's named for Allan Savory.

Man-Onko: What —

Megan: You know who Savory was? The revolutionary holistic agriculturalist? Savory was so out of the box, we just had to —

Ahmad: STOP IT! Stop that "twinning"! [To Man-Onko] I'll bet you didn't know that "twin" is a verb!

[All laughing]

Ahmad: [To the twins] Seriously! Let the poor man get a word in! [To Man-Onko] They can be a bit much. Even for fraternal twins they —

Megan: Why's it gotta be "fraternal"?

Marcus: It's convention, my dear sibling.

Megan: Convention? Only sexist pigs invited to the convention? Why can't we be sororal twins?

Marcus: Well, if you must know, it's simply the natural superiority of men. Get over it.

Megan: You know, the only reason I had to share a uterus with you is that Mom and Dad had some leftover sperm they didn't want to flush...

Ahmad: PLEASE! Give our guest a break! [To Man-Onko] You know, they go through this routine with all of our guests. The regulars here know how to handle the "M&M Monster".

Marcus: [To Man-Onko] The easiest way to deal with us is to simply ignore everything she says.

Megan: [to Marcus] You know, I used to crap on your side of the —

Ahmad: PLEASE! [To Man-Onko] Perhaps I can answer your questions!

Man-Onko: Actually, I need to catch my breath! [To all] What makes you think that you can turn one of the biggest deserts in the world into a garden?

Ahmad: That part is actually easy! Back before the Upheavals, some scientists, using satellite data, actually discovered that the Sahara was savanna, marshes, and rainforests, as little as 5,000 years ago! Think about it! If people had walked from China to northern Africa, they could have seen lions in the Sahara!

Marcus: Giraffes!

Megan: Hippopotamuses! Hippopotomi! Hippopotomodes! Hippopota-somethings!

Ahmad: [To Man-Onko] Don't let her fool you... she got her Ph.D in Paleo-Climatology.

Man-Onko: Paleo... what?

Megan: It's a complicated word that means I'm the Quaternary Weather Girl. "The weather for the next epoch will be... about the same as it's been for the last 2,000 years. Unless my brother really screws something up.

Marcus: Not likely, with you looking over my shoulder. [To Man-Onko] All the systems we are creating in North Africa, we are just re-creating them. They all existed on this planet before. All the systems and structures needed to sustain life were right here. Hydrologic flow. Water reclamation. Fertilizer production. Stable life cycle. We don't have to invent any of this stuff... we just figured out what was here before and found an efficient means of jump-starting it...

Megan: Thanks to your Humble Weather Girl! We even know where the African Great Lakes are going!

Man-Onko: Great lakes in Africa?

Megan: Sure! We even know where they're going! It's called, uh...

Marcus: Down?

Megan: Yeah, that's the word! The other way of saying "down" is a spectral analysis of geologic depressions from the Upper Cretaceous to the present, with particular emphasis on hydrolytic flows and cross-referenced with Keeper rock art.

Marcus: Saying "down" is easier.

Megan: Yeah... but when else do I get to recite the title to my dissertation?

Ahmad: Enough! We don't have all day, and I think our traveling monk has a few more questions.

Megan: But don't you want to SEE where we are putting the new lakes? Some are bigger than the North American Great Lakes!

Marcus: Don't you want to know where the CITIES are going? Savory City will be the largest, but initially there will be six others, between 100,000 and 500,000 in size.

Megan: I brought maps.

Marcus: My biggest headache is NAMING all this stuff! The only consensus is renaming Lake Chad "Lake Mandela" —

Megan: That's the biggest one —

Marcus: Everyone wanted the biggest city to be "Mandela City" —

Megan: We could get away naming EVERYTHING after Mandela!

Marcus: Mandela Village...

Megan: Mandela Mountain...

Marcus: Mandela Depression...

Megan: Mandela Highway...

Marcus: Mandela Truck Stop...

Ahmad: AHEM!

Marcus and Megan (in unison): You're no fun!

Man-Onko: This is like talking with Unity!

Marcus and Megan (in unison): THOSE FREAKAZOIDS!

Ahmad: Now...

Marcus: We had a close encounter with Unity a few years ago!

Megan: Close enough to last a lifetime!

Marcus: They came here to check out our work, like you are now...

Megan: When they found out we were sororal twins...

Marcus: Fraternal!

Megan: Whatever! When they found out we were twins, they/he/she/it wanted to have sex with us! Immediately!

Marcus: Each of us with a different Unity body...

Megan: Or bodies! However many we wanted!

Marcus: In whatever configurations we could imagine!

Megan: That was way beyond 'kinky'! That was downright...

Marcus and Megan (in unison): SERRATED!

Dr. Ahmad: ENOUGH! Our friend does not have an unlimited amount of time here! At the rate you two are going, he's going to miss the next Pillow departures... for the next month! [To Man-Onko] Perhaps I'd better take over from here.

In trying to green a desert, the biggest problem is WATER... but not in the ways you might think. The problem is not water, but water cycles. If you take a swimming pool's worth of water and pour it onto the sand, it just sinks in. Fifteen minutes later, you can't even tell where you poured it. The aquifer is so far down, you can pour a million gallons of water and still have no change in the hydrolytic cycle.

Man-Onko: So, how do you actually make the changes you are anticipating?

Dr. Ahmad: Well, you have to...

Megan: Dr. A only wants to talk about this part because he invented the process!

Dr. Ahmad: PLEASE! Let me get through this!

We don't want to pour the water onto the sand, because it just disappears. And we don't want to pour it into a concrete swimming pool, because it's the opposite of an ecological cycle. So, we pour it onto semi-permeable organic mats, where the water slows down enough to actually be useful.

Man-Onko: Where do you get the mats from?

211

Dr. Ahmad: We grow them! In wet climates, they grow these plants with huge leaves. Many people refer to them as "elephant ears". We cultivate them...

Marcus: The actual name of the plants is *Colocasia*. It's a genus of flowering plants in the family Araceae...

Megan: Which is important because the variety we use here is named Colocasia bin Shareef-A, after somebody who tweaked the genome, but is too modest to actually TALK about it...

Marcus: ...so we thought we'd just break in here and set the record straight!

Dr. Ahmad: That's it! You leave me no choice! I am declaring an *ice cream break*!

[Without another word, both Megan and Marcus start running downhill to the open-air project canteen, about a quarter-mile away.]

Dr. Ahmad: Sorry, I was trying to save that ice cream as dessert after our lunch, but if I didn't clear them out, we would still be talking until next month. The one who reaches the canteen first gets first choice on flavors. In this climate, ice cream is their Achilles Heel...

Where were we? Oh yes... we grow the elephant ears especially large, tough and fast-growing. We place them at the bottom of a depression, and bring over dozens of Pillow flights per day, filling up the depression from the water desalination plants on the coast. We plant more elephant ears around the depression, which grows more mats, which continues the cycle...

Man-Onko: That still seems like a lot of energy use... the desalination, the Pillows, growing the mats, moving the people, building the cities. It all seems...

Dr. Ahmad: ...manipulative? That's the word that the M&M Monster uses. And it is, from one perspective. But manipulative for what? To make some rich corporation more money? For some billionaires fantasy? For some do-gooder foundation to take photos for their quarterly report?

No, our purposes are both simpler and grander. By restarting the hydrolytic cycle, we are re-establishing a living ecology for ALL, not just humans. In five years, the Pillow flights will stop. We will dump the desalinated water directly into the atmosphere in the form of cloud cover... a river of air. Water attracts water, so we anticipate that the depressions will fill faster. Then, in 15 to 20 years, the desalination plants will shut down, as the hydrolytic cycle becomes complete and self-regulating.

Man-Onko: That's pretty impressive. But, instead of manipulative, I was going to say expensive. Although our Pillow flights cost next to nothing, with the frequency of the trips, it adds up. Building a new city is expensive... building several of them becomes another cost expenditure. Add to that roads, water, electrical and other infrastructure costs. I'm guessing that your project is going to take hundreds of millions, perhaps billions of investment credits.

Dr. Ahmad: [pauses] Yes. There is a substantial cost. But put it into perspective: our entire 100-year project would have cost about two years' worth of military expenditures for the old US government. At peacetime.

It's a long road to get each of these micro-ecologies up to sustainability and self-reliance. But consider the alternative: where were the roughly 500 million coastal people around the world going to live? The so-called "rich" countries kept saying that they couldn't afford it, while spending billions and billions on landing a few humans on Mars, or trying to land on an asteroid. Just to say that they could do it. Absolutely no value to the billions stuck on Earth.

We are planting water-based, living ecosystems in the Sahara. When the Breakers looked at the Sahara, they decided to plant... glass. Specifically, mirrors. Over a million mirrors at the Noor Solar Complex in Morocco. Four or six billion old dollars invested. All to feed the Western industrial machine.

In typical short-sighted Breaker arrogance, the Noor Solar Station set out to solve one problem and created half a dozen others. While reducing the carbon footprint from energy production, they massively increased the water consumption in the area. Rising water costs, lowering energy production costs, unanticipated technical problems, sabotage, unforeseen ecological and social impacts from micro-climate warming in an already hot environment, labor unrest... The Noor Power Station was a disaster waiting to happen. It came as no surprise when their investors pulled the plug after 12 years.

So, for about 15 percent of the cost of the failed Noor project, we are building habitat for billions of creatures, not the least being around 150 million human creatures. Where did the Breakers plan to put the nearly billion people who were threatened by global climate change? All of the Western countries ignored the problem by studying it to death. They would routinely set "climate goals" and just as routinely break them. They covered their eyes, hoping the problem would disappear.

We're going for an extremely low-budget approach to solving the population and ecological crisis. With vision! By thinking big, but on a human scale, not industrial. Thousands of people paid to dismantle the Noor mirrors, while more thousands turn them into housing and infrastructure for our new cities. We recommissioned and repurposed old nuclear powered US Navy ships as mobile desalination plants.

Man-Onko: Really! How did you get what's left of the US military to give you their aircraft carriers?

Dr. Ahmad: Not "give"... they are technically leasing them to us for 20 years, then they revert back to the US military. We pay them in corn, wheat and soybeans. And in 20 years, we predict that there will be no America left to retake possession.

And it's not just aircraft carriers. We acquired five aircraft carriers and 20 nuclear-powered submarines. Their power plants are too old for "weapons-ready" status. And, there's no one left to threaten, intimidate and look tough for. The age of gunboat diplomacy ended decades ago — the US military just realized it recently.

They don't even have the money to properly mothball them. It will cost millions of dollars per year just in maintenance. With us, they get to sign them over and turn their backs. And once they turn their backs, they will forget all about them. Breakers have the long-term consciousness of mayflies.

After 20 years of restarting the Sahara hydrolytic cycle, we will float them away, to someplace else that's in need of water. Then, 2,000 years from now, those same warships turned into desalination plants will be turned into icebreakers, used to keep our shipping lanes open during the next Ice Age.

Man-Onko: Ice Age? Really? That's looking pretty far ahead!

214

Dr. Ahmad: Not in the least. We've gone beyond talking about being "one with the Earth". We are actually practicing it. Climate changes, on a local, regional, and global basis, are the facts of life. We can act like the Breakers and ignore those facts. Or we can act like those facts don't apply to us, as the so-called ecologists did during the Age of Waste. Instead, weare acting like we actually live on this planet, and that we're here for good.

We are creating new, multiethnic, agriculturally based cities and towns. People from all over the world come to the former desert to raise families and live. Many of those people are from families who were stuck in homeless shelters just a couple of generations ago. It really is a new frontier. They've got a chance to prove themselves and to do good for themselves, the region, and the Earth.

The total cost of the Sahara Garden is a tiny fraction of what it would cost per year to sustain a handful of people living in the harsh conditions of Mars. Think of it: eight people living on Mars versus over 100 million people thriving on this planet! You do the math!

Wait... looks like Megan and Marcus are heading back. If they're running, they're bringing us ice cream. If they're walking, that means they ate all of it. [pause] Looks like they're walking...

[JOURNAL ENTRY END]

Part Five: Exploring the Universe

Gayatri's Journal: Awakening and Astro-Physics

File No:		File Name: Awakening and Astro-Physics
Location: Atacama Desert, Northern Chile.		**Parties:** From the Journal of Gayatri: Interview with Dr. Diego Garcia-Schwartz, Director of the Council of Exo-Planet Activities (CE-PA)
Monk/ Master Supervising: North America Awakening Movement Archives Director		

[JOURNAL ENTRY START]

Gayatri's Notes:

The once-proud telescopes of the former Atacama Array look... sad. They needed a paint job from before I was born. Even the tiny bit of moisture in the high desert atmosphere is more than enough to make buckets of rust. The Array used to be every science fiction writer's wet dream of what "doing science" actually looked like — huge parabolic dishes pointing up to the night sky, or moving in sync, like a giant multi-eyed space monster.

Not anymore. Nothing falls apart faster than a science project that's been defunded. The desert wind whistling through dishes broken, or missing, or filling with sand. Doors hanging on hinges. The equipment broken or stolen or just abandoned. The telescopes with locks on the door provide homes for squatters, scavengers... and us, the staff of the highest Awakening Center in the world, living on the fenced-in grounds of the four working telescope dishes, survivors of the 66 radio telescopes of the Atacama heyday.

I'm here to meet the head honcho of this tiny specialty Awakening Center up here in the cloudless skies of the high-altitude desert. Diego Garcia-Schwartz is a short, fat, balding guy who looks like he could've been a middle level bureaucrat when the Array was active. His dumpy looks don't reveal the brilliant mind that runs the Council of Exo-Planet Activities (CE-PA), a fancy title that means the Awakening Movement is moving into outer space.

[The following is a transcription of the digital audio recording that I made with DG-S. The first sounds on the recording are me panting for breath in the oxygen-deprived air. Mr. Dumpy laughed at me.]

Garcia-Schwartz: Yes, our thin air takes some getting used to! You can take a shot or two of oxygen if you wish, and we'll get you some cocoa leaves.

While the Mars team needs the low pressure, high altitude, and extreme cold of the high plateau Atacama, there's no particular reason why we put the rest of the lab way up here in the high desert of Chile. We don't need the photos that the Atacama Array telescope provides. The distance just gives our thinking the edge we need to achieve our results. We keep these four units running more for sentimental reasons than anything else.

[I don't tell him what I think about him and his edge. I happen to think that remaining conscious and not vomiting are pretty good indicators of good thinking.]

Q: So, what is CE-PA? What is it that you do here? [I'm trying to find a nice way of asking, "What justifies you having a permanent seat on the Global Culture Council?"]

A: There are two ways of looking at us. On the one hand, we are doing some very important, but kind of esoteric physics. The other way is that we are becoming an interstellar taxi service.

As soon as the Awakening Centers were created, we very quickly learned that new thinking about Consciousness meant new thinking about EVERYTHING, including physics. I mean, once you get around to accepting that human beings can move objects with their minds, you need to come up with a theory that explains how it happens. Or go crazy! There were some of the old Breakers that chose the "go crazy" route!

Q: What was so wrong with the old physics?

The old Standard Model was brilliant, but horribly incomplete. It's like a Breaker doctor studying the structure of an eye. They can analyze it down to the atomic level. They know it's chemical composition. They shine light through it and can determine the refractive nature of the materials.

But... It's like they've never seen an eye that's actually connected to a body. Seeing an eyeball in a jar is not like seeing an eye in action. Studying any object in isolation from the system in which it works means you don't really understand it. All of their theories of how eyes work are based on eyeballs just floating around in jars.

This is "Dead White Guys Syndrome" applied to physics — the inherently racist proposition that only white men with college degrees are intelligent.

They should have been talking to the guys hanging out in the rainforest in loincloths, with bones in their noses. Hah! The Old White Guys wouldn't even listen to their own women! They thought their own wives and daughters were stupid! And they spoke the same language! Had the same genes!

No, not just stupid... you can teach a stupid person. They thought women and native people were INFERIOR, were naturally deficient. They thought that because they thought DIFFERENTLY, they were incapable of thinking.

Okay, that's enough about the DWGs! They're dead! Including the ones still walking around!

Q: So, what do we know about Inclusive Physics that the DWG's didn't know?

A: As it turns out, a LOT! Most of this was known in the days of the DWGs, but they stuck it in a corner, along with Religion and Folk Tales. Here's what Inclusive Physics shows us:

- There is ONE FORCE. If you think there's more than one, you aren't seeing things correctly. Keep looking.

- The Four Forces of DWG Physics (Gravity, Electromagnetism, and the strong and weak nuclear forces) are subsets of the One Force.

- There are no limits. There isn't a speed limit to light, or anything else.

- There are dimensional limits. And as soon as you run into one, just switch to another dimension! That's what they're there for.

- Gravity has an on/off switch. So does "Time".

With a different understanding of both gravity and time, we can travel to stars in tens of years, not centuries. It may not even take that long.

If a person lives in a desert, it is nearly impossible to explain to them the concept of "floating", or what happens when you are immersed in 100 feet of water. If you explain it, they will think that you are lying or insane.

Within our new, blended consciousness, both gravity and time are... optional. For Breaker scientists, the speed of light was an absolute barrier. For us, it is as much a barrier as being on land and then jumping into a swimming pool. The physics changes completely, but is still understandable. It's still the same planet.

Our new physics gives us new capabilities. New forms of propulsion. New techniques for traveling outside the atmosphere. Now we have the ability to project our consciousness into space, with or without our meat bodies. Lots of things are possible, once we decide to see our Universe differently.

We'll get to do some really long-range experiments in inclusive physics on what most people refer to as "Force X". We can really stretch what we already know about classical and quantum physics, get beyond some of our mental limitations. Once we established that we could, for example, move a block with our consciousness, we then needed to develop the understanding, then the methods, then the math.

A lot of the Breaker scientists believed that you had to develop the math first. Well, that's the opposite of reality! Trying to use math to understand universal principles is like trying to get the recipe for Coca-Cola by analyzing the bottle. You don't start with math, you start with Love.

Q: Besides the Array, what else is there to see of the CE-PA?

You should first have a brief talk with the folks of the Astrophysics Propulsion Team. Not much to see there, but some mind-blowing concepts and action! All off-planet, of course.

While there, you can visit with the Exo-Vehicles Team. Those two teams have to work very closely together if this project will ever get off of the ground. I'm sorry to rush you, but one of the Directors is only available for a few hours tomorrow, so if you want to interview her, this may be your only opportunity.

The next day, we'll get you a shuttle and get you over to the Destinations Team. Technically, there are two groups in that team, but right now, only the Mars-Venus Group is active. The Onward Group is active in the hives — which of course you won't be visiting. I'll get a Level One hive representative to meet with you to discuss the future Onward plans.

[JOURNAL ENTRY END]

Gayatri's Journal: Cosmic Billiards

File No:	File Name:	
		Cosmic Billiards
Location:	**Parties:** Journal of Gayatri Interview with Dr. Helene Brown, Director of the Exo-Vehicles Team and representative of the Astro-Propulsion Team.)	
Monk/ Master Supervising:	North America Awakening Movement Archives Director	

[JOURNAL ENTRY START]

Both the Exo-Vehicles Team and the Astro-Propulsion Team operate in between the high desert plateau and sea level. Thank God... I really like breathing! (Yes, I know it's a bad habit, but after all these years, I'm pretty hooked on it.)

My "shuttle" was a motorcycle that had seen its best years a few decades ago. Lord only knew what they burned to keep it going. (Tomorrow, while traveling to visit the Mars Group, I'll be wearing an oxygen tank so I don't get dizzy and fall off the bike.)

Today I'm meeting with Dr. Helene Brown, who is head of the Exo-Vehicles Team. Her colleague, Dr. Tracy McGovern, head of Propulsion, is out on maternity leave. I'm told that one refers to both of them as Dr. B and Dr. T. I sure hope I can remember which is which.

The idea of using huge asteroids as human delivery vehicles is... simply stunning. I must look stunned, because she starts laughing.

Dr. Helene Brown: We already have about 20 asteroids heading into Earth orbit coming in from the Kuiper Belt and the Oort Cloud.

Q: Are you actually thinking about putting humans on them?

No, not on them — IN them. We're going to use hollowed out asteroids for transportation. There's a lot more potential living space inside one than on the outside.

Have you ever looked at what the Breakers called "spaceships"? I mean, really LOOKED at them? They were UGLY! That thing they called the "International Space Station"? Can you imagine floating around inside that hunk of junk? Dials, switches, tubes EVERYWHERE. Living like an ant inside a transistor radio. Nothing beautiful anywhere. That's what you get when you put engineers in charge of a project instead of artists.

The Chinese invented rockets around the 11th Century. Used them pretty effectively in naval warfare. They developed the techniques from their experience with fireworks. So, a Breaker rocket is just a glorified Roman candle. The Saturn V rocket that put Breakers on the Moon was just a massive bottle rocket. Getting to the Moon on 11th Century tech. The technology was refined, but never changed.

Their ships were old, dull, ugly, limited and amazingly dangerous. We are designing our ships to be... elegant. Refined. The best and most beautiful that Earth Life has to offer. Think about it: not redwood paneling, but every single living space made out of redwood and bamboo and cedar. Imagine waking up on a spaceship in a room made of cedar! Imagine how magnificent that would smell. We're going to "grow" our spaceships! Bioluminescence on the walls, floors and ceilings. "Waste" systems that waste nothing... every single drop wanted and needed by the other beings in the system.

Consciousness modification of biological reality. This is not "biomimicry", but true BIOLOGY. Our ships won't be "living machines", they will be LIFE. All systems and structures based on LIFE, not machines.

Q: How are you going to tunnel out an asteroid 20 miles across? How are you going to get tunnelling equipment off the Earth and into space? Or do you plan on blasting out the tunnels?

The idea is that we keep it light and grow most of what we need out there. Very few machines and lots of microbes. No blasting! Countless digging microbes, turning rock into dust, into concrete tunnel liners and the dirt for our farms. While they are tunnelling, microbes give off life-sustaining oxygen and water. And countless trillion microbes dying and forming the humus for what we will eat and drink on our way. Each rock becomes a garden. Every single space, inside and out, will be covered with... LIFE. They will become living, organic, exo-atmospheric vessels.

The issue of cosmic radiation is irrelevant when you are sailing the cosmos with a half-mile of solid rock over your head. Or beneath your feet. Or however you want to conceptualize living inside an asteroid.

Q: How will you get the asteroids to Earth, and then how will you get them to where they need to go?

You're talking to the wrong side of our partnership. Dr. T is busy pumping out her puppy. The rocks are my concern; moving the rocks around is hers. I only know that Unity's ability to move objects is way more advanced than our ability to move stones and blocks. I know that Unity is using their Power of spatial distortion to move, spin, and track the asteroids.

Spin is a fundamental feature of the Universe. Once you stop ignoring it, once you truly see it, once you apply spatial distortion power to the principle of spin, moving asteroids is about as hard as playing billiards. The hardest thing is just keeping track of them.

I do know that she's planning to put asteroids up in binaries. The prime asteroid is habitat, while the binary travels ahead. We'll use the lead asteroid like an ice-breaker, scooping up stray atoms along the way and using them as fuel, converting collision energy into forward thrust.

Q: Once you get the big rocks to Mars or Venus, what happens to them? What's next?

Well, you turn around and come back! You keep the cycle going. There can be a constant exchange of people, resources, ideas and spirit. You don't ever have to stop the rock. You just need to upload and download from the perpetually moving target.

[JOURNAL ENTRY END]

Gayatri's Journal: The Destinations Team — Expanding Our Consciousness into the Heavens

File No:	File Name: The Destinations Team — Expanding Our Consciousness into the Heavens
Location:	Parties: From the Journal of Gayatri Interview with Paula Clay, Unity Representative (Level One), Unity Liaison to CE-PA.
Monk/ Master Supervising:	North America Awakening Movement Archives Director

[JOURNAL ENTRY START]

This time, my interviewee comes to see me. Dr. B had to split for something important, Dr. T is resting up from delivering her baby (a healthy girl). No "gender reveals" in Awakening Centers. As the saying goes, if the Goddess wanted you to know the sex of your baby in advance, She would have installed a sheet of plexiglass at your navel.

So, with Drs. B+T out of commission, it was time to meet my Unity Representative. With all the stories I had heard about Unity, I was expecting something... more. I don't know what... head spinning in a circle, eyes rolling around, walking on their hands, floating through the air...

What I got was... me. Except for the fact that her hair was longer and she wore a ton of makeup (which means ANY makeup), we could have passed for... well, second cousins.

She wore the standard Unity unitard (red for Level One), but didn't do anything to try to spice it up. Clunky, functional shoes — she looked like she was ready to climb a mountain at a moment's notice. She had an accent that I took for British, but was more likely something close to that, like Scottish or Irish.

She looked unsure of herself, out of her element. She stood and looked at me like someone who was about to take a test they knew they would fail. The exact opposite of all I've heard about the Unity superhumans. And she WAS out of her element: she and her two companions were the only people at CE-PA who had no office, no staff, no vehicle, no equipment... The three of them shared one room in a dormitory.

On the one hand, having none of the status stuff actually raised her status. She didn't need any of the perks, because everyone knew that she had the resources of 10 or 20 billion humans plus the resources of whole continents at her fingertips. But she didn't inspire the same sort of awe and fear that Unity did. (Or cool... people think that Unity Level Two is cool, like Bonnie & Clyde or the Hell's Angels — if they aren't about to kill you or mind wipe you, you want to get a selfie with them.) To me, she looked like one of my friends from school years ago — someone who had forgotten her pocketbook and was wondering how she was going to pay for her lunch.

We were to meet in Dr. B's office, until both of us refused to sit in Dr. B's chair — too much power and gravitas there. We couldn't talk comfortably in the peon's seats, since they faced the wrong way for conversation. We retired to a small break room, which worked perfectly for us.

In the style of Unity, I was supposed to refer to her as Clay: last names only, no titles, no gender differentiation. Screw that! I called her Paula from the beginning. A couple of times she tried to correct me, then seemed thankful that I was treating her like a human being and not just a recording device.

Paula Clay: I'm sorry, but I'm probably going to be the least interesting person that you talk to in your entire visit to South America. In fact, sometimes I bore even me! I think that might be why I joined Unity in the first place — I was looking for something interesting.

As soon as anyone hears that I'm with Unity, they expect... well, I don't know what they expect, but they're always disappointed with me.

It's a real blow to the ego — which Level Twos never understand, since they don't have any. I mean, think about it: everybody else at the table is "Doctor" this or "Engineer" that. Everyone else is going to Mars, or raising children who are going to Mars, or raising children whose grandchildren might go to Mars. Or influencing the decisions of who gets to go to Mars. Or the stars. I get to sit in the meeting and act like a speakerphone for Level Two Unity, who couldn't be bothered spending this much time talking to Zeroes.

Q: By "zeroes", I guess you mean... us? Regular humans?

Oops. Sorry. Yes. If I'm a Level One, that makes you people in the Awakening Movement "Level Zero". Don't be offended — there are plenty of levels below zero!

Okay, so I'm supposed to orient you to our Destinations Team. There are lots of other people more important than me, but I'm tasked to do it, because I'm the pet Unity rep. Before you ask: no, I don't mind being everyone's pet. A pet to the zeroes... I mean, Regulars. A pet to Unity Level Two and above. I'm just here, making everyone happy!

So, let's see: the Destinations Team is about organizing where all these spinning pebbles are going. Somebody else designs and builds the pebbles. Somebody else calculates the trajectories, propulsion and spin. Somebody else constructs the habitats inside. Somebody else decides what they do whenever they arrive wherever they're going. Somebody else gets to ride in them. And I get to... know about all that. And tell you.

Q: So tell me· what is the Destinations Team all about?

For decades, the Breakers used Earth's overpopulation as an excuse for space exploration... as though building billion-dollar rockets for a handful of science freaks, bored billionaires and military guys to fly around in was going to mean something for Earth's billions and billions of humans. If they had spent that money down here, on poor people, there wouldn't BE any overpopulation, wars, or climate crisis!

Remember Nasa's Gemini Program? Putting two astronauts in space at a time? Whoopdeedoo! No, the real reason for Gemini was showing the Soviets that if they put nuclear weapons in space, the US could send up astronauts to dismantle them. The rationale was that we're going to the Moon, but the real reason was the ongoing game of global hegemony. The net benefit to humanity? Way below zero.

No, our rationale is different: we are ONE with the notion that LIFE EXPANDS. Not just human life, but all LIFE. Consciousness Expands. We are expanding the capacity for LIFE... not just here on Earth, but throughout the Solar System, throughout even the Galaxy!

The ultimate challenge of a mature consciousness: leaving the planet surface. Once we get beyond the Earth's gravity well, once we get outside of the atmosphere, distance is simply a matter of how fast you want to move, how rapidly you want to spin, how long (or short) you want the ride to take.

Q: So, what are your destinations?

We've got two different teams, training for three different kinds of destinations:

1. The Planetary Group will visit our nearest planetary neighbors, Mars and Venus. Since you are going to meet with them, I'll let them explain what they're planning to do. Suffice it to say that those are the short haul runs — basically taxi service.
2. The Interstellar Group will be going to other stars. Now that size, weight and time are no longer barriers, we can realistically envision voyages that can span light years, yet take only a few decades in time. Or shorter. The Interstellar Group has two missions:
   a. The Near Neighbors Group. Going to the nearest star systems, the near neighbors — the dozen or so stars within ten light-years of Sol. We plan to take up permanent residence on one or more.
   b. The Onward Group. Travelling the Galaxy in either faster-than-light or multi-generational ships. However, with Unity consciousness, "intergenerational" is largely meaningless.

None of this is Colonization. We don't want to create any "colonies". That is very old thinking. Making the distant land subservient. The purpose of a colony is to benefit the primary. The reason so many people put so much money and power into

Mars exploration is that they wanted more money and more power.

Don't get me wrong: we expect the travellers to pay us back for the costs of getting them to their destination. It's only fair. You don't get on a bus without paying your fare. But, there's no reason for us to try to make ourselves filthy rich by riding on the backs of the travellers.

Q: So... is Unity the traveller? Is Unity leaving Earth?

A: Hold on a sec. Unity wants to talk with me. [A very long pause, while her eyes unfocus and she kind of mumbles to herself.]

Sorry, I was getting instructions from Level Two. I can't do that "Freeze" thing yet — my mind isn't One with Unity yet.

They want me to be clear that I am answering you in part for Unity, and in part for the Awakened and the Regulars who are involved in the Destinations Team.

Unity is not "leaving Earth". Yet Unity is going to travel to the Solar System and the stars. An aspect of Unity inside an asteroid hurtling toward Sirius B is just plain exciting to us! We're happy to provide the propulsion system for all aspects of the Destinations enterprise for the opportunity to participate.

Each Unity asteroid will hold 100,000 Unity units, plus all of our life support beings. (Plus Awakened and even Regulars, if they want to tag along.) A ten-mile diameter asteroid will easily house ten times that many. There will be plenty of space available — enough for the cetaceans, our Elders, who may want to travel with us.

We think some of them left Earth a million years ago. Even though we can now talk with them through our hemi-human connections, we really lack the capacity to ask them meaningful questions — they are just so far ahead of us, even Unity. Like trying to explain to a chimpanzee how to drive. We keep getting caught up in the cetaceans' notions of "time".

Q: How do they see time?

Beats Unity! The Elders can't understand our questions, and Unity can't understand their answers. One possible response is that they left Earth a million years ago. Another interpretation of the same answer is that they will leave Earth a million years from the present. Or, they are leaving right now. Take your pick.

So far, about 20 Hives are participating. Unity will alter the bodies of its units along the way. They will be suited for their destination when they arrive. They are already in communication with the other intelligent beings inhabiting those worlds. They are already blending with them.

There will be deaths caused by the incompatible microorganisms present on all sides. But those deaths will be a small price to pay for the reunion of two branches of the same family. We'll use other asteroids like ice-breakers, scooping up stray atoms along the way and using them as fuel, converting collision energy into forward thrust.

FASTER THAN LIGHT: Some asteroids will be used to test our theories of faster than light travel. We'll test our theories on route. Very different kinds of transports. Our first wave of FTL craft is going to Vega, about 25 light-years away.

Q: When will you arrive in Vega?

Twenty years from now.

Q: When will you leave?

Twenty years from now.

Q: Forgive my ignorance, but doesn't everything in science say that nothing can move faster than light?

Yes, and that is absolutely true... within the context of Breaker science. It's like a fish saying that walking on land is impossible. From their perspective, that's true — being on dry land is a death sentence. For a deep-water fish, even getting too close to the surface will cause you to explode! For them, dry land doesn't even exist! Even the Sun doesn't exist!

With expanded consciousness, you can see the notion that "'nothing faster than light'" is a limitation on consciousness. Let go of the limitation, and the answers become obvious, instantly.

Once we learn to see limitation as context, we make real progress. We still teach our youngsters about Einsteinian and quantum physics. It's still valid... within certain contexts. Heck, we still teach Newtonian physics! Over 300 years ago, Newton had some still-valid thoughts within the context of his times.

Q: You said that three groups are traveling. Where's the third group going?

The third group will travel... *Onward.* No fixed destination. Basically, they will be "*Star Trek* in a Rock". Perhaps a better title will be "Ongoing Encounters with Consciousness". They'll have no plans to come back... not for the first half-million years or so.

But, not Star Trek in one sense: They are not going into the Universe armed to the teeth. No phasers, photon torpedoes, plasma cannons... not one gun on board. Nothing that can be turned into a weapon. We already know what and who we'll be encountering. If you go out looking for monsters, you'll find monsters... including the ones lurking on your own ship. Lurking inside yourself. We aren't taking any, so we won't encounter any.

Q: Are you saying that, in this huge Universe, with trillions of planets, there aren't any bad guys out there? No monsters?

Not as you would think. Just like on Earth, there are lots of beings that don't have relational intelligence, who will eat us just to find out what we taste like. We'll just stay away from them.

Then, there are beings who are so profoundly different from us, so incomprehensibly different, that communication with them would be impossible. Think about conscious beings so huge that, to them, we would appear as gnats. Perhaps even smaller. Now, how often do you try to communicate with gnats? No, we'll stay out of the way of the beings who may unconsciously swat us. Or even inhale us!

[JOURNAL ENTRY END]

Gayatri's Journal: Visiting the Mars Team

File No:		File Name:	Visiting the Mars Team
Location: Mars Forward Camp, in the foothills of Ojos del Salado, at the 20,000-foot level.		**Parties:** Journal of Gayatri	
Monk/ Master Supervising:		North America Awakening Movement Archives Director	

[JOURNAL ENTRY START]

Back up the mountain: No breathing tube for me — I'm wearing a space suit, complete with helmet and face mask! Every time I think this is overkill, my driver stops and invites me to crack open my mask for a "breather" (or, more correctly, a non-breather!). I quickly put it back on. These folks are adventurous, if nothing else.

My space suit comes complete with electrically heated undies, keeping my nether regions snug in the below-freezing, crystal clear weather. (I wish I had Mateo, my incredibly cute driver keeping my nether regions warm, but he's treating me like the visiting dignitary I'm supposed to be. The burdens of fame...)

There are unbelievable vistas (and drops) on both sides. Arrival at Mars Forward Camp was amazingly uneventful: a sign, a collection of a half-dozen vehicles of various types (from other motorcycles to a two-story snow mover) and an airlock: The Mars folks live underground.

Once inside, I exchange my space suit for thermal gear and the promised breathing tube. The airlock is to keep Earth air OUT. Over time, they are slowly reducing both the air pressure and oxygen levels for their community.

I'm here to meet "Mr. Mars", aka Dr. Negasi Ambo, Director of the Mars Forward Camp and head of the Mars team. It feels strange that I'm interviewing an Ethiopian in the middle of Chile, but about one-quarter of the Mars Forward Camp is from Ethiopia, with other participants from other high-altitude populations.

Q: So you are head of the team that is landing on Mars, yes?

Dr. Negasi Ambo: We are not "landing" on Mars. We are not "visiting" Mars. We are enlivening Mars. Re-Awakening Mars. Not "terraforming". If we wanted it like Earth, why would we leave Earth?

Right now, we're bombarding Mars with comets to add water for shallow oceans and nickel-iron comets for core activation. We want to restart the Mars magnetic fields. We can't have Life unless the planet is alive.

Q: Bombarding? That sounds pretty... harsh.

A: Not really bombarding, although a lot of folks wanted to do that, to see what would happen. No, it's more like skimming a million tons of ice on a tangent about ten miles from the surface. Pretty darn spectacular from the ground! But it won't disturb any bugs that are waiting to come back to life on the surface. And it's going to be raining for a long time!

There will be a little "bombardment" in the form of the nickel-iron asteroids. Some of them will be spun to tremendous velocities, then will perform a relatively soft touch-down on the surface, where we hope the electrostatic charge transfers to the core. Additional charged asteroids will spin up and zip through the atmosphere, creating charge. Will that be enough to jump-start core rotation on an entire planet? We'll see! If you have any questions about it, why don't you wake up Faraday and Maxwell and ask them! We're applying Maxwell's field equations to an entire planet!

[I already knew the answer to this, but I had to ask for the record:]

Q: Why do we have Awakening Centers in such far, cold and inhospitable places such as this?

A: We are getting the Mars Team ready to go living on another planet. After Operation Jump Start, our descendants will go and live on Mars.

Along with the Forward Camp here, we have Adaptation Teams in Antarctica, the Arctic, the Himalayas, and Russia-Siberia. It's a progression: moving from the most Earth-like to the most Mars like — US. We are moving whole communities to Mars, not just some highly trained and specialized astronauts. We are learning right here to adapt to less pressure, less sunlight, less oxygen. Rather than trying to make Mars like Earth, we're turning ourselves into Martians. To live on Mars, we will have to learn how to think like Martians, not transplanted humans. We are starting that right here, right now.

We will have to learn Martian survival skills. Mixing groups. Adapting plants and systems to a Martian environment.

We are also returning Life to the beings already there. Adapting ourselves so that we can be of service to the beings who will re-arise there. Making Mars easier for LIFE to restart and adapt.

Q: How are you going to get to Mars?

Not our problem. That's for the propulsion folks. And we're not going. Our grand-kids are.

Q: How will they get to Mars?

Not our problem. We're told that when it's time, the ride will arrive. In fact, the rides are on their way.

Q: Adapting your grandkids to a Martian environment will mean that they won't be able to ever return to Earth. You are in effect banishing them from their home planet. Do you have the right to make that decision for them?

[On this question, Dr. Ambo became thoughtful, even pensive. After a few moments, he said:]

A: A few short decades ago, parents let their children eat industrial by-products and drink sugar-saturated water. Our grandparents were adapting us to short lives, illness and cancer. And everyone seemed to think that was fine! We are adapting our grandkids for the adventure of a lifetime!

Q: Why go to Mars?

Why not? Not for the old, Breaker reasons: national competition, making more money, as a plaything for bored billionaires. We're doing it for the right reasons, and we're doing it the right way.

The journey to Mars, like the journey anywhere, begins in each of our hearts. To get to Mars, we have to understand ourselves. We have to understand our visions, goals, attitudes, fears. We'll take as long as it takes to work out... US.

It's mandatory for everyone on the Mars team above the age of 15 to read the old Kim Stanley Robinson books on Mars, his trilogy. If you remember from those books, the first thing that humans did when they got to Mars was start fighting and killing each other. Typical Breakers! The people who finished looting the Earth's resources wanted to go to Mars so they could start looting that world. For decades, they have used Mars as a trash heap, with all of those dead landers, rovers, orbiters and such. Typical Breaker thinking: spend billions on it, then throw it away when you're done, with no thought of the consequences.

Q: What happens after your group finishes your collective introspection?

By doing our inner work, we will become the people who deserve to live on that planet. Not using it as a mine, a cesspool, a trash dump or a plaything for Earth's rich. To be on Mars for itself.

Q: Well, that's all well and good for you and for Mars, but does Earth get anything out of it? Not to be negative, but it seems to me that we're putting a lot of energy, people and resources into this project. Are we just shooting those resources off the planet? From our perspective, for nothing?

[Dr. Ambo really bristles on this question, but suddenly smiles and relaxes.]

Okay, I think that's a fair question from your perspective. And yes, we do have some mutually beneficial projects planned. One of them is an ongoing, long-term experiment in understanding and utilizing Force X. We've understood for some time that telepathy and the other Awakened Powers are faster than the speed of light. But, we also know that they are not instantaneous. On Earth, they happen so fast, they can't be accurately measured. With a human group on Mars, we can begin to nail that down. Also: we have begun to see that the Force X abilities are affected by the strength and position of the Sun. Why? A Mars group will help us map that out... for the benefit of all.

Q: We've talked a lot about Mars, but you intend to go to Venus, too. When is that?

Actually, sooner than Mars! We'll be visiting in the next five years or so, as soon as the Exo-Vehicle and Propulsion folks get their acts together. We're going sooner because going doesn't involve figuring out how to land and live on the surface. The Venus surface isn't for humans. We'll be floating along in what we're calling "Cloud City". Remember the old Star Wars movie, with that huge city floating in the sky? Well, it will be NOTHING like that! More like a super-sized Pillow, made of something that won't pop as soon as we expose it to the venusian atmosphere.

Going to Venus gives everyone the chance to test-drive all this new equipment and new technologies.

Q: How long will you stay?

A: It depends on planetary rotations, but perhaps up to a year, then the Pillow will get a fresh crew, fresh resources... and maybe a fresh Pillow, if the existing one is getting worn out!

Q: Why go to Venus? If we can't live on the surface, and there's no recognizable life there, why go somewhere to just look at rocks and poison clouds?

[Here, Dr. Ambo flashes a brilliant smile.]

We are going to bring LIFE to Venus! By "we", I don't mean humans! We are planning an entire ecology around beings that practice chemosynthesis, converting the abundant minerals, chemicals and pressures into energy. While we humans are adapting ourselves to Mars, we are adapting scaly-foot gastropods, yeti crabs, vent mussels and tubeworms to life in venusian conditions. These are beings that can live at the bottom of the ocean, thriving at hydrothermal volcanic vents. They will have an entire planet to grow into.

And the apex predator in this venusian ecology will be... TARDIGRADES! We're calling the first installations "Tardigrade Towns". We've bred tardigrades to withstand a temperature of over 500 degrees Fahrenheit. However, to work, they've got to be able to survive in 850 degrees.

Q: Whether Mars or Venus: Why leave Earth? Why not stay here, stay a part of the Awakening Movement?

Leaving the Earth doesn't mean leaving humanity! It doesn't mean leaving LIFE! Some leave, some stay. Some go to New York City, some go to the Saharan Lakes, some go to Mars. Some beyond. We will all stay in the same family.

[JOURNAL ENTRY END]

Part Six: The Return

On the Ethics of Mind-Wiping

File No: 1-E-1		File Name: On the Ethics of Mind-Wiping	
Location:		Parties:	
Monk/ Master Supervising:	Master Dorado		
Recorded by Master Observer 009-04	*Recorded Lecture: "On the Morality, Practice and History of Deep Consciousness Intervention" (a.k.a. "Mind-Wiping")* *A lecture by Master Dorado, formerly of Gopher Pod, to students of Consciousness 301 (intermediate). Master Dorado's lecture is considered the most complete on this subject for intermediates.*		

[RECORD START]

CLASS LECTURE: "CONSCIOUSNESS INTERVENTION – THEN AND NOW"

Master Dorado: Before we begin, it is customary to recognize the presence and services of an Observer, especially a "oo" Master Observer. We are honored by your service.

[Master Dorado and 75 Novices rise and bow to Master Observer 009-04.]

Master Dorado: First, let me confirm something that you've only heard as a rumor until now. That "consciousness intervention", popularly known as "mind-wiping" or "hiving" is real and is being regularly used.

[Murmurs from audience.]

Master Dorado: And, let me state what is not as widely rumored: this practice is not just used in Hives. We of the Culture Council have the ability to catalyze such interventions. And we practice it. Regularly.

[General pandemonium. Several students rise to be recognized.]

Master Dorado: Everyone sit down! Shut up! All of your questions and concerns will be addressed – but not at the same time! This class lasts two hours. If you have any questions or comments afterward, I will be glad to recognize them. Now, we're going to start with a history...

Novice Bilal: [standing] I must object to this entire class. And I must report you to the authorities...

Master Dorado: I said, shut up! Or you will be our first volunteer for mind wiping!

[Stunned silence.]

Master Dorado: Your classmates will find it very instructive. You won't feel a thing. That's your choice: walk out that door, or sit down.

[Novice Bilal sits.]

Master Dorado: As I was saying, I will go through a history of direct consciousness intervention, followed by our current practice, followed by a practical demonstration [pausing to glare at Novice Bilal], followed by an OPEN discussion of the ethics of mind wiping. Is that acceptable?

All: Yes, Master!

Master Dorado: Any objections or protests? [Looking at Novice Bilal.]

[Silence.]

Master Dorado: All right, let's begin. Direct consciousness intervention (DCI) has been with us since the dawn of humanity. From the time of the first cave dweller or tree sitter, one person has been trying to intervene in another's consciousness and behavior. The preferred methodology back then was trying to put a rock through someone's skull.

[Muted laughter.]

Master Dorado: Over time, these attempts became more sophisticated. The rock was traded for a lance through the eyeball, decapitation, a bullet in the brain, electrocution, lethal injection, nerve attenuation, ultra-sonic intervention, various chemical interventions, global cranial disruption... Most attempts at "changing" consciousness resulted in the death of the host. So, the first lesson of this class – No one who believes in or practices VIOLENCE can have any moral argument against DCI.

[A double stomp in the classroom, signaling assent.]

Master Dorado: There've been other attempts at DCI by way of nonlethal means. For example: lobotomies (physical, chemical, electric and sonic), have come and gone as technology changes. Various techniques of "brainwashing" spread during the 20th century. Techniques of DCI have ranged from brute force methods to the very subtle, "Madison Avenue" approaches. Then, in the early 21st century, we saw the widespread use of pheromones as a direct way to alter the chemical composition of the brain. What do we know about this practice?

[17 Novices stand]

Master Dorado: Novice Nandana?

Novice Nandana: We have heard that this is how the Hives maintain control.

Master Dorado: Were the Hives the first to use pheromones to control behavior?

Novice El Pat: No. I think the perfume companies were the first.

Master Dorado: Correct. The first widespread use of pheromones for humans was in selling smelly water. The unintended consequence was...

Novice El Pat: Permanent addiction. As the pheromones got stronger, people kept buying the perfume, regardless of its effects.

Novice Loris: And this was coupled with visual stimulations. I think they were called "commercials" or "adverts". When an addict saw the commercial, they were stimulated to buy more of the product.

Master Dorado: And this led to...?

Near All: The Chem Wars!

Master Dorado: Correct. Novice El Pat, what was the result of the Chem Wars?

Novice El Pat: [pausing] Well, the Hives, Master.

Master Dorado: Yes, but you are jumping ahead. What happened when people found out that the pheromones used were permanently addictive?

Novice El Pat: [firmer] They were declared illegal to use in public. They were strictly regulated to research institutions.

Novice Bilal: [rising] This is because, overwhelmingly, humanity found these practices to be morally repugnant!

Master Dorado: Oh, I see you found your tongue again. So tell us, Novice Bilal, what were the three exceptions to this "overwhelming repugnancy"? What were the three areas where pheromones continued to be widely used?

Novice Bilal: [hesitating] Well, there was the prison system...

Master Dorado: Actually, that's the third exception. Yes, olfactory treatment was used as a replacement for the barbaric prison system.. First, for capital cases, then for lesser crimes. Instead of housing convicts in a horrible institution, under horrible conditions, at a horrible expense, the convicted could spend a day in "The Chair" and return home that evening as model citizens. And the unintended consequence of this were the thousands, perhaps tens of thousands of people who ASKED for the Chair, BEFORE they committed a crime. Incidence of serial murder, rape and serial theft went out the window in countries that have the Chair instead of prisons.

Novice Bilal: Yes, but what of the persons...

Master Dorado: The first exception?

Novice Bilal: [angry] The first exception was for learning and education.

Master Dorado: Actually, that's the second exception. Bilal, you seem reluctant to discuss the first exception. People realized that you could obtain an education faster through your nose than you could through your eyes and ears alone:

Novice Xavier: I heard you could snort a college education in a week!

[General laughter.]

Master Dorado: No, not a week. It would take one to three months, depending on the courses of study. And I'd feel sorry for your nose!

[Muted laughter.]

So, Bilal, we've reached the final exception, the one you've been avoiding, the one that dwarfs the other two, combined.

Novice Bilal: The... entertainment industry.

Master Dorado: Entertainment? Is that your euphemism for SEX?

[General laughter.]

Master Dorado: With the direct and permanent stimulation of sex centers, participants could experience the euphoria of the permanent orgasm. Now, what was the next discovery, the one that led to the direct development of the Hives?

Novice El Pat: That would be separating the cognitive functions from the motor functions...

Master Dorado: Exactly! While one was experiencing permanent orgasm, it really didn't matter at all what the body was doing. The first use, or misuse, of this ability was in creating "sex dolls" for the —

Novice Bilal: I heard that this is still being practiced!

Master Dorado: [pausing] Bilal, somewhere on this planet, men still beat their wives. Cannibalism may still be practiced, also. But these probabilities are now so low, we need not be concerned with them here. This isn't the beginning of the Upheavals anymore. Now, may I continue?

[Novice Bilal is silent.]

Master Dorado: The "sex dolls" didn't work, precisely because whatever stimulation one would get from the doll, one would get MORE stimulation from the direct activation of the sex centers. Novice El Pat?

Novice El Pat: Corporations then tried to use the mind wipes as factory workers.

Master Dorado: And?

Novice El Pat: A lot of them died. If the stimulation rate was too low, they would work themselves to death trying to get more. If the stimulation rate was too high... They would just "bliss out" and drop dead.

Master Dorado: Correct. And the proper balance was achieved...?

Novice El Pat: By getting the mind wipes to regulate themselves. Once each factory group became globally self-regulating...

Novice Xavier: ...Hives were born.

Novice El Pat: And once they were self-regulating, they could develop their collective consciousness and use it to solve group challenges...

Novice Xavier: Like how to buy out your corporate masters and take over your own fate!

Novice El Pat: Which they did so fast, we STILL don't know how they did it!

Master Dorado: Thank you for the "tag team" explanation. Perhaps we have our own "mini – Hive" in the making!

Novice El Pat: ...with him?

Novice Xavier: ...with her?

[General laughter.]

Master Dorado: Okay, settle down. So, we come to the second great lesson of DCI: The first lesson: We have been doing consciousness intervention since there's been consciousness. It's just that we've gotten very good at it lately. The second lesson: The overwhelming majority of what we call "mind wipes" are VOLUNTARY, not forced. And, Bilal, dear, if you can manage to keep your seat for another ten to 15 minutes without spontaneously combusting, you'll have your turn.

[General laughter.]

Master Dorado: Now, I think it's time you met some of the Culture Council's "mind wipes".

[Three individuals walk on stage.]

[General uproar: "that's our support staff!" "Those are MONKS!" "Are all monks mind wipes?" "I knew it!"]

Master Dorado: Settle down. I'd like to introduce you to your colleagues. You may refer to them as Brothers Alain and Boris, and Sister Calla. Two of them are volunteers, and one has had an involuntary procedure. And that is the ratio of DCI participants in this facility: two thirds are volunteers.

Novice Xavier: Why on Earth would a person VOLUNTEER for a mind wipe?

Master Dorado: Ask them. And I will remind you that you are speaking to your superiors.

Monk Boris: Perhaps I can answer that.

[General uproar. "He can talk!"]

Monk Boris: Yes, I guess the first thing to dispel is that "mind wipes" are mindless zombies. The very opposite is true; our brains work BETTER than yours; more efficiently.

Novice El Pat: I've seen you serving in the lunch hall, or sweeping the floor. I've never heard you speak. Why don't you speak in the hallways?

Monk Boris: I don't want to sound arrogant or condescending, but whatever I'm thinking about at any given point in time is much more interesting than any possible conversation with you could possibly be.

Novice Xavier: Why'd you get yourself mind wiped? You volunteered?

Monk Boris: What is true for me is true for most of us. It is generally a two-part reason.

First, there were some aspects of my mind I wanted to enhance. Second, there were some aspects of my identity, some memories, that I wanted to forget.

Novice Xavier: What did you enhance?

Monk Boris: It's hard to explain... Call it "celestial mechanics." I'm currently tracking 315 near-Earth objects while interfacing with three supercomputers, five tracking telescopes, and talking with some of my counterparts in Hive Celestial... While mopping the floor. Or fixing your lunch. Or talking right now with you.

Novice Bilal: What was it you chose to forget?

Monk Boris: [smiling] I don't remember.

Novice Bilal: It could've been something important, a critical part of your personality.

Monk Boris: I doubt it. The mind surgeons and the Witness don't allow us to evade our major life lessons...

Master Dorado: Every voluntary DCI candidate has to choose someone to act as their Witness — their protector, their advocate, their friend. I was this monk's Witness. I know what it was he chose to forget. It was not a major part of his personality.

Novice Xavier: Can we go back to the "celestial mechanics" part? You're tracking 300 space rocks? How? And why?

Monk Boris: That's 315 "space rocks". Most of these "rocks" are the size of cities, so it's kind of important to know where they are. I'm not at liberty to tell you the reason for tracking them. However, once you find out, it's going to rock your world!

Novice Xavier: Hah! Was that a pun?

Novice Bilal: Excuse me, but I'd like to talk to the involuntary mind wipe.

Monk Calla: That would be me.

Novice Bilal: Master, I'd like to know what you did to deserve an involuntary mind wipe.

Monk Calla: First of all, I'm not a Master, not yet. "Sister" will suffice for this conversation. Second, I don't know what I did to cause the adjustment.

Monk Boris: If I wanted to, I could ask to see my file... my Sister cannot.

Novice Bilal: Why don't you go look at your file?

Monk Boris: Because I don't want to.

Novice Bilal: Because you don't want to, or because your FREE WILL has been erased?

Master Dorado: I think that's enough from you...

Monk Boris: Master, if it's okay with you, I'd like to answer that.

Master Dorado: Go ahead.

Monk Boris: True, part of the adjustment is a mild inhibition against looking into the past. How mild? If you gave me 100 credits, I would go get my file and read it. I would probably do that for 50 credits. But I wouldn't ask for my file just to satisfy the curiosity of a snot-nosed little novice like you – and I don't need a neural inhibitor for that to be true.

[As Bilal finds, there are things worse than an involuntary mind wipe... Public humiliation before one's peers by a superior is one of them. The novices sitting on either side of Bilal get up and take seats further away from the blast zone.]

Master Dorado: [smiling] Any other questions?

Novice El Pat: Monk Alain, what is your specialty?

Monk Alain: I am what is called an "Observer". You always see one of us walking behind each member of the Culture Council, as well as many of the Masters. One of my counterparts is sitting in the back of this room. My task is to provide an absolute and authentic recording and reproduction of important events. The early 21st Century relied heavily on computers and digital recordings of events. But as we found out during the Cyber-Wars, physical recordings were only as reliable as the digital mechanisms used to make the record. We have moved away from such systems. Any software system could be corrupted by superior software, any recording could be altered and compromised. It got to the point that people could no longer trust... reality. Not so with me. I record an event clearly, authentically, permanently, and uncompromisingly. My records cannot be altered.

Novice El Pat: Well, short of the old methodologies that involve rocks and bullets.

[Muted laughter.]

Monk Alain: [smiling] Well, that would ELIMINATE the recording, but it certainly wouldn't ALTER it!

Novice El Pat: Are you a Master Observer?

Monk Alain: [laughing] Oh, no! I probably will not achieve the coveted "oo" status in my lifetime! I'm still in the triple digits! Seriously: It takes a level of dedication that I simply do not have. At least, so far. You have to really WANT to be a Master Observer. The reason we always bow to the "oo" Observers is in recognition of their dedication and their sacrifice in achieving their status. [Monk Alain bows again to Observer 009-04.]

Novice El Pat: What do you mean by "sacrifice"?

Monk Alain: The higher one's Observer status, the more of one's personality must be sacrificed in order to obtain the computational power necessary for high-level Observing. For example, a single "o" Observer, like a 043, for example, can record a conversation that is in two or three different languages. A "oo" Observer can record a conversation in 15 or 20 different languages, with all of the participants speaking simultaneously. To free up that much computational power means "forgetting" one's childhood, one's friends... sometimes even one's own name.

Master Dorado: Other questions?

Novice El Pat: A question for Monk Calla. Ma'am, I mean Sister, I know you can't know the nature of your transgression...

[Monk Calla nods.]

Novice El Pat: But... Whatever it was, do you think that a mind wipe may be a little... harsh for whatever it is you did?

Monk Calla: [long pause] A good question. I'm not really sure how to respond... Let me try like this: My specialty is Security. Right now, as I'm talking to you, I'm also monitoring a dozen different information feeds from around the world. Today, I will write a dozen different security memos, five to the Culture Council itself. I'm also a backup monitor for the security of this entire facility. Now, would I trade those abilities for the ability to steal from a monk? For the ability to THINK ABOUT stealing from a fellow monk? Or think about destroying property? Or think about beating someone up, or having illicit sex, or cheating on tests...? The answer is "no", I wouldn't want ANY of those abilities, regardless of the trade-off. I probably didn't want it, even when I was using it. [Turning to Bilal] Novice Bilal, you have the ability to stick both feet in your mouth at the same time. You seem to have a natural ability to piss off your superiors. Are you certain you want to keep those abilities? Think about what those abilities have earned you today. Are you *sure* you want to keep them?

[Novice Bilal looks down and is silent.]

Monk Calla: Bilal, for thousands of years, people have called "free will" the ability to act in ways that are contrary to their own good, their own values, and the good of society. Most of the damage done to our world, most of the excesses of our societies, came from people exercising their "free will". Are you CERTAIN that "free will" is so important?

[Novice Bilal is silent.]

Master Dorado: Unless there are other questions, that is enough for today.

[AFTER NOTE: two weeks after this recording, Novice Bilal requested a voluntary DCI for a minor personality adjustment procedure. It was successful. Twelve years later, Field Agent Bilal was killed in the line of duty, after an exemplary record as an Agent of the Culture Council.]

[RECORD END]

The Fateful Lecture: "Zhang Zung And The Concept of Global Human Civilizations"

File No:		File Name:	Zhang Zung and the Concept of Global Human Civilizations
Location:		Parties: Novices and students of Civilizations 201 (intermediate)	
Monk/ Master Supervising:		Master Pico-Laton	

Recorded Lecture: "Zhang Zung: On the History and Philosophy of the First Global Human Civilization, and its Implications for the Future of Human Societies."

A lecture by Master Pico-Laton

Recorded by Master Observer 003

[RECORD START]

Master Pico-Laton: Before we begin, it is customary to recognize the presence and services of a Master Observer. We are honored.

[Master Pico-Laton and 200 Novices rise and bow to Observer 003.]

Master Pico-Laton: It is always interesting to think back to all the truly radical ways of thinking that were stimulated by the flawed genius of James Harold Moore and his "Imaginal Group".

Today, we think back to the late 20th century to what the Imaginal Group called the "Standard Model". Who can articulate?

[20 novices stand.]

Master Pico-Laton: Novice Beth-Alla?

Novice Beth-Alla: The Standard Model was part of the Imaginal Group's misguided attempt to articulate a "Cultural Theory of Everything". According to them, the Standard Model was basically a racist way to explain the presumed inferiority of the so-called "indigenous" people and to also explain why the dominant culture of those times was dominant.

Novice Xavier: Wait a minute. The IG never used the term "racist"...They never called the Standard Model "racist".

Novice Beth-Alla: In EFFECT. The Standard Model said that everything before NOW was "primitive". Since the "now" of the time was dominated by Europeans and Americans, the net effect was that everything other than Europe and its descendents was primitive. Seeing First Civilization people as primitive was racist by implication.

Novice Xavier: Yes, but it's your interpretation, not Moore's definition of the "standard model"...

Novice Beth-Alla: What are you, a closet Moore lover?

[Laughter]

Master Pico-Laton: Stop. We deviate. What do we know about the Standard Model now?

Novice Beth-Alla: Well, that it's wrong. The peoples of the past weren't primitives, and the people of the Second Civilization weren't so superior.

Novice Paulo: The thinking of the Standard Model shielded us from even knowing that there WAS a First Civilization.

Master Pico-Laton: To be accurate: there may have been many, many more civilizations than what we call the first, the Civilization of Zhang Zung. We call it first because it was the first to be uncovered by James Harold Moore's flawed theories.

Novice Xavier: Why do we always have to refer to Moore's work as "flawed"? I mean, he DID start the thought processes that shook up academia, and led to...

Novice Beth-Alla: He IS a closet Moore lover!

[More laughter. Novice Xavier sits.]

Master Pico-Laton: We still deviate. What do we know about Zhang Zung? Why do we think of it as a "global civilization"?

Novice Chaska: It covered three continents, Oceana, and large parts of Europe. That's pretty "global"!

Master Pico-Laton: And what about its core beliefs made it "global"?

Novice Chaska: [hesitant] You mean the Latent Powers?

Master Pico-Laton: We don't have to go there yet. What were the three core beliefs of Zhang Zung?

Novice Chaska: if I remember all three...

1. Honoring and respecting the Earth
2. Honoring the relationship of all beings
3. Honoring the realms beyond the senses.

Master Pico-Laton: Perfect. How do those relate to the Latency? Xavier?

Novice Xavier: Well... They don't. It's possible to have a society based on the core beliefs without having any Latent Powers. That's like most of the communities we support and sponsor on the Outside. And it's possible to have a society that has Latent Powers but no moral compass. That's like what we think the "Edge" is like. At least, that's true according to the flawed, failed, contradictory theories of James Harold Moore.

Master Pico-Laton: Young man, you are skating on dangerously thin ice... But, despite your sarcasm, you are correct. How did the Latent Powers affect the Zhang Zhung civilization's beliefs?

Novice Xavier: It helped to make them coherent. It also made them very long lasting.

Master Pico-Laton: Correct again. And, what are the implications for US, here in the late 21st Century?

Novice Xavier: Well... The Awakening Centers are now forming what we refer to as the "Third Global Civilization", but that's really just a continuation of the First Global Civilization, after accounting for the detour into Breaker Consciousness. The Breaker Society denied the Latent Powers... We are re-awakening them. Our goal is to have a human society that will last 100,000 years or more. At least, this is the idea of James Harold Moore and his flawed, failed, and dangerous...

Novice Beth-Alla: No one is laughing with you.

Novice Xavier: So why is it so funny when you say it? Doesn't it strike anyone as odd, that someone with such a major impact on our planet is so universally despised? Am I the only one paying attention to how much we FOLLOW this guy?

Novice Chaska: Everyone lost parents and loved ones in The Upheavals! And he was the CAUSE of all that! He caused more deaths than Hitler, Stalin and Mao COMBINED! Just because Adolph Hitler created the Volkswagen doesn't redeem him in the eyes of history!

Master Pico-Laton: That's enough...

Novice Xavier: But, why do you blame The Upheavals on Moore? Some say that what happened was inevitable...

Most students [chanting, mocking]: Moore lover! Moore lover!

Novice Chaska: He PREDICTED them! His predictions CAUSED them!

Novice Xavier: But correlation isn't causation! Just because...

Master Pico-Laton: I said, that's enough!! We've gone pretty far afield today. When we reconvene tomorrow, we will FOCUS on the failures of the Standard Model and the promise of the Third Global Civilization. And Novice Xavier... Please report to Master Man-Onko this afternoon for... reassessment. At three PM. It would be in your best interests not to be late.

Novice Xavier [still defiant]: No ma'am, I won't forget. I have 200 of my fellow Novices to remind me.

[Laughter. Continued calls of "Moore lover!"]

Novice Chaska: If Xavier owes any of you credits, I think you'd better collect before three o'clock. We may not be seeing much of him after that!

[More laughter.]

Master Pico-Laton: This class reconvenes tomorrow, same time...

[RECORD END]

Reverend Evans and "Humans First!"

File No:		File Name:	Reverend Evans and "Humans First!"
Location:		Parties:	Historical record
Monk/ Master Supervising:		North America Awakening Movement Archives Director	

Remarks by Reverend Clarence Evans, to the New York City gathering of the "Humans First!" Coalition on 25 April 20XX.

[RECORD START]

I stand here as a human being. An ordinary man. Nothing fancy or "potential" or "awakened". And I'm telling you, as an ordinary man, that it's time for us ordinary men and women to take back our country and our world!

I'm here to tell you that it was INDIVIDUALS, not Hive-ists, who created America and the rest of the world, and it will be INDIVIDUALS who will rule over the Earth long after the Hives and the so-called "Awakening Centers" have been dismantled!

The Communist Threat lasted about 70 years before it fell apart. It's been about 45 years for those god damned Hives and so-called Awakening Centers. They look strong, but mark my words – they are not long for this world!

Did the genius of a John Rockefeller or a Thomas Edison come from a Hive? Did Jefferson or Washington or Franklin come from a Hive? Precisely because those in the Hive turn their backs on a notion of a personal relationship with God, we turn our backs on them!

And don't fall for their word trickery, either! When they say "the question of religion is irrelevant", it is exactly the same as them saying "there is no God"!

The duties that our Lord Jesus Christ places on us – duties of love, honor, respect and care, apply to all humans. To all INDIVIDUAL humans!

The Ten Commandments apply to HUMANS, not TERMITES! The Hive-ists choose to live underground, like termites. Don't be fooled by their human form – when they give up their individual consciousness, they become termites to you and me.

Here in America, we are blessed in having a land that does not allow the Hive poison on our soil. We don't allow it to take root! And we must go further... to get rid of those so-called Awakening Centers! They are the agents and training grounds for the termites of Europe, Africa and Asia!

But, it doesn't stop there! We must go to those countries that try to coexist with the Hive plague. With God's help, we can turn the tide on the Hive!

Our Treaty with the Hive Embassy, the so-called "Unity Ambassadors", means that we cannot hurt them or their property. But it doesn't require that you LIKE them, or help them, or sell to them, or buy from them. For the first time ever, the phrase "Buy American!" also means "Buy Human!"

And, I know some brothers and sisters over in Europe who would LOVE a hand at wiping out their nests! Remember: if they've only got "one mind", you could exterminate 100,000 and not bother them!

Happy hunting!

[RECORD END]

First Meeting

File No:		File Name:	
			First Meeting

Location: Office/Residence of Master Man-Onko	Parties: Master Man-Onko Novice Xavier	

Monk/ Master Supervising:	Master Man-Onko

Recorder: Observer 093	Transcript of First Meeting between Master Man-Onko and Novice Xavier. Condition: First Meeting recommended by Master Pico-Laton, from her observations of Novice Xavier

[START OF TRANSCRIPT]

[Both Master Man-Onko and Novice Xavier silent, as Observer 093 pours tea for both.]

Master Man-Onko: Greetings, young novice. Do you have any idea why we are having this conversation?

Novice Xavier: Yes, sir. I was mouthing off about James Harold Moore, and Master Pico-Laton thought that I needed some punishment.

Master Man-Onko: No and no. You are wrong on both counts. First, this is not punishment. Second... "mouthing off" about James Harold Moore does not warrant a First Meeting. Taking him SERIOUSLY does. Do you know what a "First Meeting" is?

Novice Xavier: No, sir, I don't believe I've heard the phrase before.

Master Man-Onko: No, you wouldn't. Seventy percent of students at the Academy wind up as Agents of the Culture Council, working in Admin or Security or Utilities. Twenty percent bounce out of the Academy, usually landing in one or another of our Commons. A few are kicked out of our system. And ten percent wind up as Monks. The First Meeting is to assess your potential as a monk.

[Novice Xavier is silent. His eyes are round.]

Master Man-Onko: Very good. You know when to keep your mouth shut. That part seemed not to make it into Master Pico-Laton's report. I wish I had that trait when I was your age!

Novice Xavier: I'm just kind of stunned. For me, that's never a good time to talk. I don't think that's the same as the Silence we're taught about in classes. When did you learn Silence?

Master Man-Onko: There are many who say I never did! Don't tell Pico-Laton about this part of our talk! Now, let's talk about the Cultured Societies, and how people on the Outside can choose their cultural traits. Begin. Tell me what you know.

Novice Xavier: [At first hesitant, then stronger] Since the Upheavals triggered by James Harold Moore's work, in the past ten or twenty years, people have been able (and many times, required) to choose the culture they live in. The idea that people did not have a foundational or primary culture was one of the main reasons that societies unraveled so completely. As a result of the Upheavals, all cultures were damaged, some beyond repair. Rather than being born into a functioning culture, for the first time, people could make up just anything, and through the old Web, find others willing to believe what they made up. For the first time, people could consciously make up, could consciously choose their culture. And the Culture Council had to choose which ones to allow, revive, and support. Sometimes, those choices meant that people had to move to a different location, and learn a different language. Learn a different culture. The Awakening Centers have been keeping alive any number of cultures. We've been feeding them, mixing and matching and balancing... almost always in the background.

Master Man-Onko: Like what? What kinds of cultures are we supporting?

Novice Xavier: Almost all kinds, except for the most violent or reprehensible. Cultures can choose to be male dominant. Or female dominant. Or LGBTQNX dominant. They are placed close to a culture that would choose to be female dominant or neutral. Or, a culture could be white supremacists or black supremacists or anything in between. A person or group is allowed to choose any cultural path, so long as it does not harm itself and its neighbors permanently. For example, two warlike cultures could choose to be engaged in war with each other, so long as they each remain at a level where neither can decisively win, nor threaten others.

Master Man-Onko: What are the main types of Cultured Societies?

Novice Xavier: Well, if I remember correctly, they fell into two categories: the Hedonistic Societies, based on various types of sensory pleasure. "Las Vegas Style" anything goes...

Master Man-Onko: Not just pleasure! There are a few Societies that are focused on masochism and pain.

Novice Xavier: The second category is violence. The Violent Societies include various types of "warrior" communities, from Middle Ages to the Crusades, all the way up to 20th Century warfare and even science fiction and fantasy violence. It's okay for them to wage war on each other, but no one else — only other Violent Societies.

Master Man-Onko: You miss the third category: religious groups. From our perspective, anyone who says that they represent an ideology that claims more than 50 members can claim to be a "Religious Society". That way, we don't have to mess around with funky philosophical debates. You wanna pray to pink elephants, go for it. Some of those philosophies can be a bit... out there.

Novice Xavier: You mean, like the Mormons?

263

Master Man-Onko: Actually, no. The Mormons were one of the few groups that were NOT "Cultured" by the CC. The Mormons were going to survive the Upheavals on their own... they were prepared for it. We work with them and with the Amish as equal partners. What limitations do we place on the Cultured Societies?

Novice Xavier: I don't think I can remember all of them. I know some of the big ones.
1. Can't waste.
2. Can't be exclusive, but they can impose restrictions on participation. They can insist that women who wish to join are covered (or uncovered), or that people participate in prescribed ways. This gets very close to fine points, since a "White Supremacist" Cultured Society would by definition exclude people of color.
3. Can't be violent... Unless violence is their culture, and they practice it only among consenting adults, and within defined parameters. They definitely cannot be violent with other non-consenting Cultured Societies.
4. Must deal with all of the consequences of their actions. If they are a drug-using society, they must deal with all of the consequences that flow from having a population of addicted residents. No outside rescues.
5. Anyone who wants out can get out. Members can transfer to another Cultured Society, or can apply to be in an Awakening Center or in a Commons. Each Cultured Society can impose restrictions or penalties for early withdrawal from a Cultured Society, but no one can be blocked completely.
6. No one "makes money" from the CS. It has to pay its bills, but people don't take actions to "get rich". And, with our new economies, it's pretty hard to accumulate wealth for wealth's sake, unless they are a culture and society whose goal is wealth accumulation.
7. Not allowed to expand beyond their boundaries (geographic, economic, political, social, cultural...).

Master Man-Onko: This is an important point. Does the Culture Council ban war and violence in the Cultured Societies?

Novice Xavier: No... Although I don't understand why not. It would be easy enough for us to do so. Just stop giving them food or electricity. Mind wipe their leaders. I guess the idea of "freedom of choice" is stronger than the idea of "nonviolence"...

Master Man-Onko: Yes... Altering their behavior would be very easy for us. And the wrong thing to do. It would be nothing for us to force a change in their behavior. Threatening to take away their food is a powerful incentive for them to act the way we tell them to act. However, we've learned that the suppression of behavior is not good. Better to allow people to get it out of their systems. Suppressed, the bad behavior will simmer and fester, waiting for the right conditions to erupt again. The Culture Council believes that, once the negative incentives for people to act in negative ways are gone, people will change their behavior to the positive, just because they want to. (Once people have negative incentives removed, the theory is they won't want to act in negative ways.) Keep them alive as a lesson and an experiment. We want the Cultured Societies to die out on their own, through disuse.

Have any cultures or groups been banned?

Novice Xavier: Yes. If a group somehow has been deemed so harmful that their harm outweighs any social or educational purposes it may have. But... I don't know any examples of banning.

Master Man-Onko: The New Bushido culture is one of them.

Novice Xavier: I've never heard of them.

Master Man-Onko: You wouldn't. We've done a pretty good job of eradicating them. Its practitioners are so warlike and so male dominant that they refuse to become enrolled or submit in any way to the Culture Council. They refuse to have ANY cultural control placed on them.

Novice Xavier: Is New Bushido the same as the Edge that they teach us about in our classes on the early Upheavals?

Master Man-Onko: No. The Edge really has no particular cultural leaning that we've been able to detect. And the Edge has

265

been largely neutralized by us, with the support of our friends at Unity.

Novice Xavier: So why doesn't Unity wipe out New Bushido? Are they more powerful than Unity?

Master Man-Onko: Not hardly. Just the opposite. They pose so small a threat to us, Unity sees no purpose in trying to control them. New Bushido poses a threat to our experiments in culture, not to us directly. New Bushido is super-secret, underground, and far away from structured societies. They are dangerous because we have difficulty seeing them coming — they have a rudimentary form of the Latent Powers, just enough to hide from us and enough to spot our agents. New Bushido people may be so far underground, they look, sound, and act like their opposites. It is rumored that some members of New Bushido are actually the heads of some of our cultural experiments... people we deal with every day. Many of our Agents are involved in trying to infiltrate New Bushido. And many die trying.

Novice Xavier: If New Bushido is able to hide from us, why won't Unity wipe them out for us, or at least give us control over them?

Master Man-Onko: On the contrary: I think that Unity actually gives New Bushido support in how to evade us! They think New Bushido keeps us on our toes.

Novice Xavier: Even if our Agents are dying?

Master Man-Onko: Remember: Unity has a different relationship to the deaths of a few Agents. Or a few dozen. To them, it's like getting a haircut or trimming your nails.

Novice Xavier: Could James Harold Moore be heading up New Bushido, trying to undo what he put in motion? Trying to defeat the Hives?

Master Man-Onko: [smiling] We'll deal with rumors a little later.

[A pause.]

Most people in America are avoiding the extreme cultures and are adopting one of the mildly hedonistic cultures and enjoying a life of harmless (and meaningless) stimulation. We allow them limited access to the remnants of television, harmless recreational drugs, and other forms of sensory stimulation. Or they may choose to live in two or more conflicting cultures... For example, being both Religious Orthodox and Hedonistic. For some reason, back before The Upheavals, closet hedonism was very popular with the leaders of religious orthodoxy in many different religions. We don't really know why. And nowadays, it doesn't really matter. There's no one left who can tell them what to do. There are some limits to the rule that anyone can change culture whenever they want. For example: if a person adopted a slave culture, their slavery would become meaningless if they could opt out whenever they wanted to. Most of the "oppression cultures" demand stiff penalties for changing before the end of the contract.

Novice Xavier: Why would anyone want to be in a slave culture?

Monk Man-Onko: Not our concern. All we know is that thousands of people opt for the opportunity to be enslaved, or to enslave themselves, or to become slave masters. And...people in all of the cultural experiments are permitted to leave the experiments and join any of the "holon" cultures, like an Awakening Center, a Commons, or an inclusive religious, inter-religious, or consciousness group. In this way, people join the Awakening Movement because they WANT to, not because they are starving or freezing.

Of course, all of this comes about through the work of James Harold Moore on "Radical Inclusivity". Once people realize that all of us held a rudimentary form of Latency, there was a tremendous upheaval in society. That's when the foolishness of the "Anti-Hive Movement" came about. We tolerate some of that, but keep our eyes out for the more radical ones.

Novice Xavier: Except for New Bushido.

Master Man-Onko: Yes, except for them. And we're pretty sure that Unity's got their eyes on them.

Novice Xavier: But who's got their eyes on Unity?

Master Man-Onko: Ouch. A major sore spot. Over the past two decades, we've learned to trust and tolerate Unity... mainly because we don't have much choice in the matter. The Culture Council is the compromise between total domination of the Hives and total elimination of them. Or...more like the total elimination of US. The Hives are SMARTER and breed faster than individual humans. Their Awakened Powers are stronger. All the numbers are on their side. Our public role is to act as a buffer from the total eusocialization of all Humanity.

Novice Xavier: Eusocialization?

Master Man-Onko: Fancy language for turning us all into termites.

Novice Xavier: Master! Isn't that term considered...offensive?

Master Man-Onko: Yeah, it is. You'll learn that I engage in frequent rule-bending.

Novice Xavier: If the Hives are so fast and so smart, why do they submit to the Culture Council regarding where to live, how to recruit, how to interact with the Cultured Societies?

Master Man-Onko: Like I said, they are smarter. What if they are one step ahead of us? What if, instead of being regulated by the Culture Council, they OWNED it? What if, for them, the Culture Council was a convenient way to get humanity to accept the inevitability of Hive domination?

Novice Xavier: But what about here in North America? Hives are completely banned from here. The movements and actions of the Unity Ambassadors are highly restricted.

Master Man-Onko: What if Hives simply don't want this continent? Or what if they intend to keep North America as a preserve of old-style humans? A zoo? They would do it in a way that would cause the Cultured Societies, especially the remnants of the United States, to feel powerful and important. Or, what if they ARE here, and simply erase their presence from our memory? Right now, if we count every Unity unit as a separate human being, there are approximately 20 billion humans on Earth. After our numbers went way down during the Upheavals, our numbers are going back up. About two billion live in the Cultured Societies worldwide. Another billion or so live in the remnants of the old nation-states. A billion or so live in Awakening Centers or related communities. That's a total of about four billion "old style" humans. The rest live in Hives. Of course, that number is approximate: no one really knows how many people live in Hives. We don't even know if we should count them as individual people anymore. We don't know if that label fits.

Most of them have no existence outside of their Hive. Everything, including the food they eat and the very air they breathe, has to come from their Hive. They can't be separated from it. In fact, that's our definition for "old style" humans: those who can live outside of a hive.

And, I guess we need to mention the million or so "hemi-humans", the blending of humans with other species. I doubt if their numbers are ever going to be all that significant, but the Culture Council takes them very seriously, as a separate experiment in what it means to be "human". The New Bushido are the sworn enemies of the Hives and the focus of their attacks. The Culture Council is attacked only because the New Bushido see it as serving the Hive agenda of total domination. So, Novice, how many hives are there in Europe?

Novice Xavier: It is public knowledge that there are seven Hives in Europe: London, Paris, Rome, Prague, Istanbul, Lisbon, Moscow, Berlin and Athens. That is all they are allowed.

Master Man-Onko: Guess again. The reality is that we have absolutely no idea how many Hives there are, or where they are placed. There could be hundreds of Hives in Europe, with millions of members each. There could be a dozen here in Colorado, for all we know. How could we count? They live mostly underground. And those who stumble on them are "encouraged" to forget the experience.

Novice Xavier: Mind-wiped?

Master Man-Onko: Now who's using offensive language?! Our guesstimate is that there are over a dozen Hives in Old Italy alone. One of the extra Hives we do know about focuses on travel in outer space. Another one focuses on communications with non-terrestrials. Under the right circumstances, those two may merge. And under the right circumstances, they may be needed! Another focuses on biological reproduction, another focuses on tides, while another focuses just on GRAVITY. What eight million people are doing thinking about gravity is just beyond me... But I digress... [Pause] Last month, the Hives recruited 25 thousand people from the Cultured Societies. According to our research, just one large Hive could produce that many people in one DAY. From these figures, you can see that recruitment from the Cultured Societies is just a show for them, something to take our minds off of their real agenda.

Novice Xavier: And we can't wipe them out, because we need them.

Master Man-Onko: Exactly. Some time ago, the Hives took over producing the world's goods and services. If you own it, wear it, watch it, or ride in it, it came from a Hive. Did you know that Hive members who deal with the Cultured Societies are given special training in how to act "human"? For example, they don't do the Pause, that thing many people find creepy.

Novice Xavier: I don't know about the Pause.

Master Man-Onko: The Pause happens when the Hive member receives telepathic information input, or when they are otherwise in deep communion with their other Hive members. They just simply stop moving, sometimes for hours at a time. This doesn't seem human... And maybe it's not. Most religions are against Unity, although Unity sees itself as the culmination, the end point of religion. They believe that all of the wisdom teachers were really precursors to Unity.

Novice Xavier: This is all interesting, but what does it have to do with why I got into trouble. How does all this relate to James Harold Moore?

Master Man-Onko (pauses): Well, about Moore. By writing that book when he came back from that cave in northern India, he literally changed the world. And some of those changes were not exactly positive. Some say that he had no idea what he was unleashing when he wrote that book, that he was the catalyst for the Upheavals, but an innocent one. Others say that the Upheavals would have happened anyway, and that Dr. Moore was just a good guesser, a trend-spotter. "Correlation is not necessarily causation", as I believe a young upstart said in class today. Some say Moore was under the influence of an early Hive. They say that someone could come up with all of that only by being a "mind-wipe". Some say he knew what he was doing, that he was getting back at humanity for his own admittedly rotten childhood. And there are lots of other theories.

Novice Xavier: Master, do you know where Dr. Moore is now? Is he dead or alive?

Master Man-Onko: Where is he now? The three most popular current theories: Theory 1. He has repented for his actions and is trying to counteract the effects of his earlier words. Some say he is the head of New Bushido. Theory 2. He is deep inside a Hive, being fed a constant diet of information pheromones and anti-aging chemicals, ready to pop out of the ground, younger than ever, and announce the next step for humanity. Theory 3. He's dead, killed by any of the surviving family members of the billions of people who died in the Upheavals. He was scapegoated by so many of those who were ACTUALLY responsible, he became "Global Enemy #1". Or, if not dead, afraid to show his face in public.

Novice Xavier: which theory do you believe?

Master Man-Onko: [pausing, leaning forward] It's not a matter of belief. The official policy of the Culture Council is correct: We haven't the slightest idea where he is, or if he's alive or dead. And that policy is the correct one. And, answers to that question, are irrelevant. What matters is RIGHT NOW ... James Harold Moore is irrelevant to the PRESENT.

Novice Xavier: But what if he really is the head of New Bushido?

Master Man-Onko: Then he's insane, and we would oppose him – the exact same way we are opposing New Bushido now. This is what we mean when we say that his present whereabouts is an IRRELEVANT question.

Novice Xavier: Have you ever seen a Hive?

Master Man-Onko: (pauses) As an agent of the Culture Council, I visited Unity for six months, almost two decades ago. It was Paris Unity. (Another pause) For one week of those 30 days, I spent at the Hives Level Three. (pause) It took two full months in the Culture Council recovery ward for me to re-enter our society. Then another six months before I was allowed to go back to work.

Novice Xavier: What was it like? Do you remember any of it?

Master Man-Onko: Yes... I'm willing to talk about it, but that will have to be the subject of another day, another time. If you are really curious, most of my reports to the Culture Council have been declassified by now. I can work to get you access to them. I remember every detail. It's impossible for me to forget. My experience cannot be mind-wiped... it is an integral part of every cell of my body.

Novice Xavier: Why did it take so long for you to come back?

Master Man-Onko: [pause] Words cannot express how deeply I did not want to return. Most human beings who experience Level Three in a Hive DON'T come back. It was the most beautiful, rapturous, ecstatic feeling I've ever experienced. It was like being Touched by God... constantly, 24 hours a day. The deepest connection that is possible between two human beings is shallow to a Hive. At Level One, I was talking to animals. Full conversations! With animals! I was having deep conversations with people that would take place within a glance. At Level Two, I fell in love with a woman. It was unimaginable – sharing every aspect of every CELL of another's soul-being. At Level Three... You lack the capacity to understand what happened there. You simply cannot comprehend. "Being God" comes close. And, there are three more levels below Level Three. When you get to Level Four, it is impossible to come back.

Novice Xavier: If it was so wonderful, why did you come back? Why didn't you stay?

272

Master Man-Onko: [hesitates] I came back because it was my duty. I came back because it was Unity's duty to return me in six months, which they did — wrapped up in a straight jacket and sedated. I came back to protect the Hive from what would happen if the Culture Council got the idea that they had kidnapped me. Every time I doubt my decision, I remember that I am HERE out of love for HER... I came back to protect HER. And I am here to protect humanity from THEM. If the Hives are able to openly recruit, if they were to fully run their agenda, "solons", individual humanity, would not last another year. And, finally, I came back because I really believe in the CULTURED SOCIETIES experiment for humanity. I have paid the price for coming back. My time in the Hive is why many of my brothers and sisters here don't trust me, why I'm stuck at the level of "Venerable" and will never advance to Llama or Abbott, or be on a Culture Council. I performed a valuable service behind enemy lines. Now, I am not to be trusted. [pause] And I don't blame them. [Rising and bringing back an object] Okay, while this has been a pleasant conversation, there is a purpose to this First Meeting. You have a new assignment. (Handing the novice an object). You are to read and analyze James Harold Moore's book, "The Ecstatic Society".

Novice Xavier: WHAT? I thought they were all destroyed! And it is illegal to possess a copy, in any form! You can go to jail for offering it to me, and I certainly will go to jail if I accept it! (Standing) I must inform the Council of your attempt to pass this contraband onto me. Apparently, your time in that Hive has affected you more than the Council knows.

Master Man-Onko: Sit down. Who would you report me to?

Novice Xavier: [Remains standing] I guess whoever is on security watch right now.

Master Man-Onko: Why not the Chief of Security?

Novice Xavier: Well, yes, if I can find her.

Master Man-Onko: [touching a screen] I'll save you the trouble.

[Screen comes alive. Image of Security Chief Amena on the screen.]

Chief Amena: Greetings, Master Man-Onko. Greetings, Young Xavier. Xavier, with the authority of the Culture Council, I place upon you a duty and an obligation. You will follow ALL of the orders and directions of Master Man-Onko... including your choice of reading materials. Is that clear?

[Novice Xavier nods]

Chief Amena: You will have to speak up. My Observer cannot see you on the screen.

Novice Xavier: Yes, ma'am.

Chief Amena: I note the presence of your Observer in the room. Therefore, there is a full record of this conversation. [Screen blanks, with no further words exchanged.]

Master Man-Onko: Now, sit down. You will read this book only under my supervision. You are not to read more than one section per day – the book itself will prohibit you from reading ahead. You will report to me weekly about what you read. In addition, you will be assigned readings about the history of James Harold Moore's time. The real histories, not those cooked up by us to justify the status quo. This is my own personal copy. You'll read and return it. My comments chip has been removed, of course. If you make your own comments, use your own chip and know that I and the Council will be reading it. You will submit to a new psychological profile. Once a week. They will be looking to see if there's any significant deviance from your baseline profile from reading to reading. And there will be differences. This is not called "The Most Dangerous Book Ever Written" for nothing. In the end, you'll come to understand why the Culture Council acts like a cross between a religion and a military organization. In the end, you'll understand that WE, not Unity, hold the true intention of Dr. Moore's work and mission. Our job is to spread Radical Inclusivity. When you leave this room, two Security agents will accompany you to your locker, where you will clear it out. You will speak to no one. The other Novices will assume you are being expelled from the Academy. We want them to assume that. The Security agents will then escort you to the Monastery, where you will begin your new life as Young Monk Xavier. Let me be the first to congratulate you.

[Monk Xavier is silent.]

Master Man-Onko: Understand this: Unity is not the only experiment in inclusivity. EVERYTHING is... Unity, the Awakening Centers and the Cultured Societies. The Hemi-Humans and the Species Councils. For example: The Awakening Centers support some Muslim communities here in North America. The Islam we allow and promote is what Dr. Moore would call "Inclusive Islam". The Christianity we support is "inclusive Christianity". The "hedonism" we allow is "inclusive, consensual hedonism". Even the drugs we allow are the ones that foster inclusivity. In this way, we all further James Harold Moore's goals and dreams: a world for all. And [pointing] that includes that bird over there in that tree, which is probably spying on us for a Hive, making sure that I got that speech right.

[RECORD END]

Take the Hedon Cities Tour!!

File No:		File Name:	Take The Hedon Cities Tour!!
Location:		Parties:	Historical record (sample advertisement)
Monk/ Master Supervising:	North America Awakening Movement Archives Director		

[RECORD START]

Regardless of your chosen culture, who couldn't use a little change?

Spend a little fun time – as a Hedonist!

Do you need to "get away" and "get off" – at the same time?
Or perhaps you are considering becoming a hedonist, but you're not quite sure? Perhaps you already are a hedonist and you are considering changing locations... But to where?

Or... For no reason at all! **Take the Hedon Cities tour!**

Spend three fun-filled days (and nights!!)
In the Hedonistic Capitals of the World:

- New Orleans
- San Francisco
- Orlando (at the brand-new "Hedon-ville" at the former Disney World)
- Cancun
- And ending in LAS VEGAS!

ON A BUDGET?? Can't afford the time or money for three weeks? Try the "budget" tour: five days, any two cities, plus Las Vegas at the end.

Special low rates for bi's, subs, and masochists.

ALL VOLUNTEERS!!!

NO MIND WIPES!!!

CHOOSE YOUR FANTASY!!!

[NOTE: Full psych scan within 45 days must accompany your application – no exceptions. If you intend to use regulated drugs, you must present a valid drug certificate at time of purchase or consumption. Persons under 18 must have permission of the Culture Council's Office of Minors. Persons under 12 will not be permitted – no exceptions.]

[RECORD END]

Second Meeting

File No:		File Name: Second Meeting
Location: Office/Residence of Master Man-Onko		**Parties:** Master Man-Onko Monk Xavier
Monk/ Master Supervising:	Master Man-Onko	
Recorder: Observer 089	Transcript of Second Meeting between Master Man-Onko and Monk Xavier. Condition: Next stage advancement, recommended by Master Man-Onko	

[TRANSCRIPT START]

Master Man-Onko: How are your new quarters?

Monk Xavier: [smiling] If you only knew how the Novices live... you wouldn't ask! The luxury of four walls and my own bed is beyond belief. And a door that locks!

Master Man-Onko: Please do not believe that I was born a Master! Your Novice quarters were like a luxury hotel compared to what I lived in as a Novice! One day, when you're ready to get bored, I'll tell you how they made us sleep in greenhouses, just to keep the plants warm, or how we had to act as human targets on the food wagons, to draw out the crazies. But all that was in the midst of the Upheavals... It may interest you to know that the progression of our Orders – from novices to monks, to Masters, Abbots, and Councilors, was laid out by Dr. Moore himself in some of his more "secret" writings.

Monk Xavier: Yes, it does surprise me – but no more than anything else in this surprising week.

Master Man-Onko: And what has been most surprising this week for you? The book?

Monk Xavier: No... Although that IS pretty mind blowing. My most surprising revelation was how completely connected the Order of the Culture Council is to the work and philosophy of Dr. Moore – yet we constantly disparage his work, his thought, even HIM! I cannot find in the Public Annals a single positive reference to Moore, or even a neutral one. It's like he's running HIMSELF down.

Master Man-Onko: Which means we've covered our tracks well. Most people have forgotten that the Culture Councils came out of the Imaginal Group's work, started by Dr. Moore when he returned from his Ladakh journey. We "manage" how people think about Moore and his work. We "help" them to forget his positive aspects...and one way we do that is by encouraging people to negatively refer to him — at least, at the bottom levels of the organization.

Monk Xavier: But that way, it seems like the situation with those old cereal makers, Post and Kellogg and the others. They were all health-food nuts, then their descendants became junk food nuts...

Master Man-Onko: Not quite the same. In fact, it's almost exactly the opposite. Here, we label things junk food but every box is filled with the Founders' nutrition. But we digress — what did you think of the book?

Monk Xavier: Well... After the hype of the banning, and the strict orders not to reveal it to others... I thought there would be more to it. More substance. It could be my position, residing in Moore's future, but it seems to me that his conclusions were so obvious! Of course we are becoming more empathic and emergent. Of course the Upheavals happened. Of course collective consciousness exists. Of course Hives are possible. I really can't see why it was banned – or why the Culture Council enforces the ban.

Master Man-Onko: Well put. The original ban was put in place by the dimwits in the Old Congress, as a way of avoiding their own responsibility in the Upheavals. At first we resisted it, but then realized that it was a blessing in disguise. The ban actually serves our purposes. A ban creates an underground demand – while allowing us deniability that we actually encourage its reading. We estimate that there are over two million "illegal" copies in North America alone. They are passed from trusted friend to friend, one family member to another.

Monk Xavier: I'm starting to get the hang of this. We probably know where every copy is, but it spreads farther and wider if the supply is restricted. SEEMS restricted.

Master Man-Onko: This is something that Dr. Moore learned from the drug dealers of his time: price and interest go up when supply is restricted. Call it "negative marketing". And a consequence of all this is that you can tell who your friends are.

Monk Xavier: But... aren't there arrests every year for violating the ban? Aren't people put in prison for reading or possessing it?

Master Man-Onko: Yes, indeed. The violators are arrested, prosecuted, convicted and put in prison... for about a day or so. Then, they are brought here, for training. But, back to the book... in Chapter 1, what do you think of Dr. Moore? What do you think of him as a man? Dr. Moore said that a person always reveals himself in his writing – even when he's trying hard not to. What did he reveal about himself?

Monk Xavier: Well, when he wrote this, he was in his early 60s, had just closed up his office and his home, so he had cut his ties...

Master Man-Onko: No, no... You're telling me things that anyone can pick up from any Web narrative of him and his times. You knew those things before you picked up the book last week. What did you learn about Dr. Moore this past week, from the book?

Monk Xavier: [pausing, thinking] Well, I think I learned three things: First, he was either easily distracted, or he could really multi-focus. He's describing the cave, hotel room, the revelations, back to the cave... He's all over the place. Second, he seemed to KNOW the controversy that he was going to stir up – and not care. Or... perhaps he DID care. At first, I thought the

---

280

"put the book down" warnings were a writing gimmick, but now I'm not so sure. The third thing... in a strange way, he seemed to be talking directly to ME. It wasn't that he was saying "a person reading this book should put it down", but that "you, Xavier, stop reading this book... Stop reading unless you are SURE".

Master Man-Onko: Well, are you sure?

Monk Xavier: [pauses] I have the benefit of history. I know what he said and I know what happened. I don't think he wanted any of his readers to stop. I just think he wanted them to be damn sure what they were doing.

Master Man-Onko: You didn't answer my question.

Monk Xavier: [glancing at a non-existent watch on his wrist] Golly! I notice that the time is about over for our session!

Master Man-Onko: [laughing] You'll make a great Abbott one day!

[END OF TRANSCRIPT]

The Suicide Rights League

File No:	File Name:	
		The Suicide Rights League
Location:	Parties:	Historical record (political manifesto)
Monk/ Master Supervising:	North America Awakening Movement Archives Director	
Mission statement of the Suicide Rights League		

[RECORD START]

MANIFESTO:

WE ARE DEFENDING YOUR RIGHT TO TERMINATE YOUR LIFE – WHENEVER AND HOWEVER YOU CHOOSE, AND FOR ANY REASON – OR NO REASON AT ALL!

Statement

We of the SRL reject the works of the Culture Councils and the madman James Harold Moore as they pertain to an individual's right to choose how to die.

Suicide is one of the most individual and fundamental acts one can take. You may decide to take your life in a very public way (self immolation is on the rise again). Or you may decide to go quietly... But James Harold Moore and his minions in the Culture Councils want to take that decision away from you!

They want to send you to a HIVE, to have your MIND stripped away from you! Instead of being an individual, with the power of your life and your death in YOUR hands, you will become a HOLON, one step away from an insect, with all your decisions made by the Hive.

RESIST! We, the suicidal, are not crazy... THEY ARE! Suicide has been an honorable choice of free men since before the times of Socrates. The Hive is an aberration of our humanity!

RESIST! Even if you are not suicidal, you must understand that the freedom of how and when to end your life is the most fundamental freedom you have. It's not that you want to commit suicide... you don't want someone taking that fundamental choice away from you!

MARCH! DEMONSTRATE! DIE-IN!

On September 15th of this year, we of the Suicide Rights League will be converging on Washington DC, for our fourth "March & Die-In". We think this is going to be the biggest event ever, with HUNDREDS choosing to take their own lives at this event, to call attention to the campaigns to eradicate our fundamental rights!

[RECORD END]

Senior-Level Seminar: "Facing the Enemies of Transformation"

File No:	File Name:	
		Facing The Enemies of Transformation
Location:	Parties:	
	Principal Research Article in Senior Level Seminar	
Monk/ Master Supervising:	North America Awakening Movement Archives Director	

[RECORD START]

We almost didn't make it.

Our "enemies" were never people... they were perspectives. Even the Imaginal Group did not take seriously the virulent opposition to the idea of transformation we presented – what we now call the "Four Enemies". In descending order:

Enemy #4: **The Enemy as Chaos.** Many who attacked the Centers (both verbally and physically) had no agenda, but were bent on causing as much mayhem as possible. This phenomenon has always existed in places where the power of society has worn thin.

We were able to successfully repel or incorporate those who were motivated by hunger or by a desire for power. We knew how to turn those desires into defenses. We were much less prepared for those who would attack the Awakening Centers simply because they had nothing else to do, or out of boredom. Our responses took time to develop.

Also: In the 20th Century, when mindless killing hordes descended on people in places like Africa (the genocides in Rwanda and Burundi) or Asia (the "killing fields" of Cambodia),

Westerners would "tsk", wring their hands and mumble something about "those people". When, in the 21ˢᵗ Century, it started happening in their own cities and suburbs (for example, the race riots and anti-Islam pogroms in America), they turned to the Centers for help. We didn't have much to offer. Some of our improvisations were far from perfect.

Enemy #3: **The Enemy as Organization.** Some saw the Upheavals as an opportunity to force their own agenda on how things should change. Most were harmless and were permitted... even encouraged in some respects.

Some tried to enforce their mindset with guns. They had to be opposed... but how?

Enemy #2: **The Resurgence of the Status Quo.** One of the most powerful threats to the Centers (and to the entire process of Transformation as a whole) were the remnants of the US Government, coupled with so-called "patriotic" sentiments.

As the Imaginal Group accurately predicted, most of the forces in opposition could not remain in opposition long. The main task of the Awakening Movement was to maintain the existence of the Centers, to wait out the oppositional forces, and to grow when the time was right.

In large part, this strategy was successful (although tragedies like the Fall of Fresno and the Siege of Tucson did occur, much too frequently). State and local governments could be bargained with, co-opted or ignored. While people were dying, they had little time for ideological debates.

Not so with the Federal government. They had incredible resources available... almost NONE of it of any value during the Upheavals. The US Congress faced tremendous opposition – from all quarters – for doing nothing during the Age of Waste, the decades preceding the Upheavals.

The Federals could have accepted their shortcomings, apologized, then done the best they could to alleviate the pain and suffering. That would have been the socially and morally responsible thing to do. Needless to say, they didn't do that.

Instead, they chose to play the "Blame Game". They went looking for the most readily available scapegoat ... and found us.

It made no sense. But to starving, cold and fearful people, "sense" was not something they were looking for. Desperate people grasp at anything,,, and that anything includes biting the hand that feeds and nurtures you and your children. "Anything" includes supporting anti-democratic and anti-rational arguments that were promised to return America to a toxic and poisonous status quo ante. America was like a wounded animal, with its belly empty but all of its fangs and claws intact.

The notion that the Imaginal Group and the Awakening Centers had "caused" the Upheavals was delusional... but in times of crisis, people embrace comfortable, familiar delusions.

In those days, the delusions were plentiful, starting with the notion that ANY of the centuries-old Breaker political/economic models would work. Or, going back even further, that any of the religion-based models would work in a modern, highly urbanized, connected world.

James Harold Moore knew too well that the tendency for people to stop thinking in times of crisis is severe. He believed that people had to snap out of it — had to cure their own delusional tendencies. Humanity's answers did not lie in trying to revert to primitive, pre-urbanized societies, but in using our Keeper values while transforming our 21st Century world.

Enemy #1: The Edge: The Latent Powers Monster. The prime values of our emerging Third Global Civilization free us from the unmitigated horrors that befell humankind during the Age of Separation, especially the twin horrors of industrial-scale slavery and industrial-scale warfare. The reactivation of the Five Latent Powers opened us up to a new era of connection and cooperation.

It also opened us up to some of the darkest episodes that befell us during this Transformation.

This is the part that some of us on the Council would rather not expose... at least, not yet, not while the wounds are so fresh. Not until we are absolutely sure that the Edge has been eliminated. Or, at least, tamed.

No one foresaw the emergence of our greatest threat, one we named "The Edge". Our advantage over the forces of the status quo was that they simply could not believe that our activated Powers existed. They could not foresee a world where the threat of bullets and bombs had so little power.

We did not foresee those activated Powers used against us and against some of the remaining Breaker populations. The Imaginal Group naively thought that anyone with Awakened Powers would want to use those powers for the greatest good. They remained ignorant of Awakened Powers attacks on the Centers.

And we all paid the price for that naivety and ignorance.

[RECORD END]

The Two Masters

File No:		File Name:	The Two Masters
Location: Masters Common Garden	**Parties:**		Master Pico-Laton Master Man-Onko
Monk/ Master Supervising:	Master Pico-Laton		
Recorder: Observer 039	Transcript of Meeting between Master Man-Onko and Master Pico-Laton. Condition: Master review of Candidate Xavier.		

[TRANSCRIPT START]

Master Pico-Laton: I heard you really liked the new "Manny Substitute" I sent you!

Master Man-Onko: You mean Xavier? I really like him! A combination of feisty and disciplined... a rarity nowadays.

Master Pico-Laton: Yes... I thought you would recognize some of your own traits in him!

Master Man-Onko: Oh come on! Just because the boy shows some spunk doesn't mean he's my clone! And I wouldn't advance him, even if he WAS my clone!

Master Pico-Laton: He showed more than "spunk" in class. He held his ground against all 200 of his fellow Novices, without caving in and without getting angry. Actually showed some humor. It was all I could do to keep a straight face...

Master Man-Onko: Peeka, during the First Meeting, he showed awe without being servile. Asked all the right questions... Second Meeting was even better! He got more information out of me than I got out of him!

Master Pico-Laton: Well, you must not like him THAT much. I heard you have recommended him to be fast-tracked as a Greeter.

Master Man-Onko: [pauses] It's amazing how "confidential" news travels far and fast in this place! I'll have to say "No comment"... accompanied by a large smile.

Master Pico-Laton: You know you're not doing the boy a favor. You know the death rate for Greeters – and almost all of them by suicide.

Master Man-Onko: [pauses] Then let us both hope that we've both selected well this time...

[TRANSCRIPT END]

"God, Guns and Glory!"

File No:		File Name:	God, Guns and Glory!
Location:		Parties:	Historical record
Monk/ Master Supervising:		North America Awakening Movement Archives Director	

[RECORD START]

Your right to a weapon is God-given – and what God has given, the so-called "Culture Council" cannot take away!

For hundreds of years, the ownership of a gun has been a Right. It is even enshrined in the Divinely-inspired Constitution of the United States.

Those Culture Cops have effectively stripped you of your rights! Sure, we can all buy guns – but by restricting and controlling the supply of BULLETS, most guns become very expensive door stops and paper weights.

By adding RFID tags to every bullet, the authorities know who buys, and who SHOOTS, every gun in America. By tracing the bullets back to their owner, and holding the owner responsible for the damage or death caused by the bullets, they have effectively emptied every gun in this country, and made a mockery of our Constitution! This is a violation of your right to privacy! Just because our spineless Supreme Court has agreed to this nonsense does not mean that YOU have to!

It's time to FIGHT BACK! Join the GREAT BULLET BUY-BACK!

On November 15th, join with thousands of freedom-loving, gun-loving Americans in resisting the fascism of the Culture Cops!

1. We will BUY BACK YOUR BULLETS, and give you a valid receipt for them.

2. We will MIX THEM ALL UP! And we will mix in some of our home-made "tagless" bullets, too!
3. We will SELL THE MIX BACK TO YOU! And we'll give you a valid receipt for the purchase.
4. Finally: We will NOT register the sale with the "Culture Cops"! You will have a valid receipt for purchase, but that won't be registered with the authorities!

SOMEONE has to stand up to these creeps! It's on our watch! It's time to make a stand! OUR STAND!

[NOTE: The "Bullet Buy-Back" did not work.]

[RECORD END]

Third Meeting

File No:		File Name:	Third Meeting
Location: Office/Residence of Master Man-Onko		**Parties:** Master Man-Onko Monk Xavier	
Monk/ Master Supervising:	Master Man-Onko		
Recorder: Observer 064	Transcript of Third Meeting between Master Man-Onko and Monk Xavier. Condition: Next stage advancement, recommended by Master Man-Onko		

[TRANSCRIPT START]

Master Man-Onko: Well, you're looking a little banged up today.

Monk Xavier: Yes, well Master Lee seems to think that teaching Martial arts and breaking my bones are the same thing.

Master Man-Onko: And a few cuts as well, I see.

Monk Xavier: Nothing like trying to wash your own blood out of your fighting uniform while nursing two broken bones and a cut face.

Master Man-Onko: Well, Master Lee heard that you are progressing fast, and wanted to make sure that you were worthy of the honor.

Monk Xavier: But... How can anyone that OLD move so FAST?

Master Man-Onko: He can't; he's well over 80 years old. But surely, you've heard of the Five Awakened Powers?

Monk Xavier: [first, stunned silence. Then] He's using... TIME DILATION? He's speeding himself up!?!

Master Man-Onko: Actually, no... He's slowing down you and the other monks, while deciding which bone to break. Speeding up takes a lot more energy.

Monk Xavier: But he cut my face!

Master Man-Onko: [smiling] Yes... That should yield quite a nice dueling scar, which I hear the female monks find quite attractive. You should have your pick of partners when your probationary period is over.

Monk Xavier: This is so unbelievable. Three weeks ago, if someone suggested that the Culture Council was PRACTICING the Awakened Powers we were supposed to be POLICING, I'd think they were crazy! Next, you're going to tell me that crazy-ass Robert Evans is our secret agent, and that the folks in "Humans First" are monks!

Master Man-Onko: [smiling] Well, not QUITE that bad! Evans actually believes every word he says. But we do use some mild Mind Influence on him, to help him stay fixated on Unity... And away from other aspects of the Metamorphosis of Humanity. It's easy to control him by suggestion... He really WANTS to hate Unity. What we don't want is for him (and others like him) to think about is how WE seem to have so much control over Unity.

Monk Xavier: Do we control Unity? Or do they... It... control us? From what you said in our last sessions, I thought Unity was in the driver seat.

Master Man-Onko: What a quaint expression. With self drive cars, you've never even SEEN a driver seat. Actually, neither controls the other. We both put on a coordinated show for the unconverted until the Tipping Point is reached. Once things become inevitable, the world will have no more need for the Culture Council.

Monk Xavier: What is the Tipping Point? When is the Tipping Point reached? And then what happens?

Master Man-Onko: Three questions, and I'm supposed to be the one asking questions! Very well, let's make these your last three of the day.

The Tipping Point is when the Metamorphosis of Humanity reaches an optimal state. Actually, for the past 20 years, the Metamorphosis has been inevitable. There's no going back, even if we wanted to. This former caterpillar is about to become a butterfly. However, 20 years ago, resistance to the Metamorphosis would have led to a horrific spasm of violence. It would have made The Upheavals look like child's play. The Imaginal Group could do nothing to stop the Upheavals – the conditions for the Upheavals were in place before Dr. Moore was ever born. The Awakening of Humanity has been in the works for about 10,000 years. However, by consciously delaying the Tipping Point, we lessen the impact on the populace. All of us who are committed to the Metamorphosis of Humanity are pledged to make that transformation as smooth and painless as possible. That is the primary purpose and goal of the Culture Council.

Also: James Harold Moore actually calculated, in the handwritten pages of the Book, when the Tipping Point would be reached. You know, I actually held his original Book in my hands once. It's locked away in a Council museum. I actually touched the place where he did all of his calculations... We have been constantly checking and updating his original forecasts. We are now in the maximal state for the Tipping Point. We are about three to five years away. At that time people will learn that, rather than limiting the speed and spread of the Metamorphosis, we've been encouraging it, since the very beginning.

Monk Xavier: Some people have been saying that for years...

Master Man-Onko: Yes, but no one with any credibility. No one like a monk who's been trained in the inner secrets, and who walks out of a monastery with a copy of the Book...

Monk Xavier: I would never do such a thing like that!

Master Man-Onko: Our forecasters predict that there is a 20 percent chance that you will.

Monk Xavier: But...

Master Man-Onko: Don't worry about it... 20 percent is a really low prediction. The same forecasters predict there is a 40 percent chance that I will be the one who betrays the Culture Council. Some of the Council members are well over 50 percent.

Monk Xavier: But...

Master Man-Onko: Remember what I just said; when the Tipping Point is reached, the news MUST come out. Someone at the table must play the part of Judas if Moore's image is to be resurrected and the Plan is to go forth.

Monk Xavier: Okay... My last question?

Master Man-Onko: As soon as the news comes out, the Culture Councils on every continent will be under attack. Some will be forced out and underground. Most people on the other continents won't care – they've been co-existing with Unity over there — the Culture Councils seem tame to them. It won't seem like a big deal in Europe or Asia or Africa. And there've been many "safe havens" built up over the years, so going underground or hiding for a bit won't be a problem anywhere, except here, in North America. For a lot of reasons, we have no safe places built in North America. Our only option is to make it to Europe or South America. We've got planes waiting.

Monk Xavier: There are over 10,000 Culture Council workers in North America, plus dependents!

Master Man-Onko: We have a LOT of airships waiting. I forgot to mention that we also have to evacuate all of the Unity Embassies, plus THEIR dependents. Add another five to ten thousand. Add to that the number of people who will not WANT to be evacuated. Like yourself, just three weeks ago.

Monk Xavier: I guess I'm just getting toughened up for one of Reverend Evans' work and re-education camps. This sounds impossible.

Master Man-Onko: To the contrary! We moved five thousand people out of North America last year alone. If things go right, the opposition will figure things out by our ABSENCE. Of course, the final evacuation will depend a lot on the remnants of the US military. They have no love for us, and they haven't had anything to shoot at for a LONG time.

Monk Xavier: They would shoot at us because we stopped all wars?

Master Man-Onko: You have no idea how many people *want* the "right" to be violent, inconsiderate assholes to each other. We interfere with their "rights". Poverty, violence, insecurity, racism. People would rather put up with ALL of that, and more, so long as they THINK they are in charge. We've got most of the military's line commanders under Mind Influence... They will not shoot without an order from above. And the people above are great at giving speeches, but lousy at giving orders. But... The submarine fleet is hard to infiltrate, hard-to-find and may act without orders. And some of those guys have itchy trigger fingers.

Monk Xavier: Lots of land routes, then.

Master Man-Onko: The US subs have a very long reach. But that's not our greatest worry. Every person we can get out covertly is one we won't have to worry about being shot down. May we start our review of the Book now?

Monk Xavier: Okay... The biggest thing about the last chapter I read is that Moore seemed SURPRISED that all the elements fit together. Genuinely surprised. I know that I'm looking through the lens of my own history. We all grew up seeing the Five Latent Powers as being a central point in a Unified Field Theory of LIFE abilities. The fact that people didn't KNOW about this just 40 short years ago seems... surprising.

Master Man-Onko: What do you know about Benjamin Franklin?

Monk Xavier: Can you wait a second while my mind swims over to your question? It's been through a lot today... [Pauses] American founder, inventor, only man to sign all three American documents, only man to be on the old paper money without serving elective office...

Master Man-Onko: There must be a reason why I asked you about him...

Monk Xavier: [long pause] Wait! Electricity!

Master Man-Onko: Exactly. Electricity had been known about for years... Actually centuries. It was either ignored or used for parlor tricks. It was Franklin's research that made electricity USEFUL. He was brilliant, but his main contribution was that he took electricity SERIOUSLY.

Monk Xavier: [laughing] And just barely missed being the Founder who barbecued himself.

Master Man-Onko: [very serious] Franklin with electricity was child's play next to what Moore and the Imaginal Group did. Electricity was unpredictable at the time; Moore knew exactly what would happen to him when he played with "social electricity". Whatever has happened to him, whether or not he is alive or dead, kidnapped, tortured... all of it happened because he looked at the same conditions that every other person could see, and took them SERIOUSLY.

Monk Xavier: I apologize. I see the comparison. We are all living the consequences of Moore's actions. We just finished talking about airplanes being shot down by nuclear submarines. My apologies for being flippant.

Master Man-Onko: It's okay. You have been beaten up enough... I won't invoke Discipline for your tone. But I failed to mention to you that, should the Tipping Point be miscalculated, our tens of thousands of losses will be a drop in the bucket next to the civilian casualties in North America alone. If we have misjudged, our forecasters predict anywhere from five to 20 million deaths in the general population. One third of them will be suicides.

Monk Xavier: I... Didn't know.

Master Man-Onko: Of course not. How could you? But, weigh that against Franklin's work. If Franklin was wrong, he would have wound up killing himself. If Moore's calculations are wrong, we could "barbecue" a good percentage of the people on this continent. Despite the misinformation that we put out, the Imaginal Group was NOT responsible for The Upheavals. That was already underway before any of them were ever born. People just refuse to see it. However, if we have calculated the date of the Tipping Point wrong, Moore and ALL of us will share the responsibility of history.

Monk Xavier: Sorry, again.

Master Man-Onko: What if I told you that there was a way to get the civilian deaths down... way down, so low as to be negligible?

Monk Xavier: [long pause, then] A show trial!

Master Man-Onko: Very good! You worked that out from very few clues. Congratulations. A small group of Culture Councilors could accept blame and "confess". Or, even better, remain defiant. Be put on trial and then executed. This public bloodletting could mollify a number of the civilians, keeping their attention on what is irrelevant, while the Tipping Point continues on. And with people focused on the confessors, perhaps they won't focus on the thousands of airplanes making their getaway.

Monk Xavier: [rising to his feet] Master sir! If it will save millions of lives, I offer myself to be one of the "Confessors", to die so that millions more may live!

Master Man-Onko: Oh sit down! In those casts, you look like you're about to fall! [Gentler] This is not a time for heroics, sacrifice or martyrdom, no matter how heartfelt. This is a PLAN. We have been plotting this for over 20 years. Now think: what is the one Awakened Power that every Confessor will have, that YOU don't have?

Monk Xavier: [pausing, then brightening] Bi-location!!

Master Man-Onko: [smiling] Exactly. You are as bright as Master Pico-Laton said. Current public research puts the limits of bi-location at 48 to 72 hours. That the longest a person has manifested two operable bodies is three days. The real provable limit is five months and counting.

Monk Xavier: Wow.

Master Man-Onko: Wow indeed. The Confessors will be put on trial, found guilty and hanged... while their other bodies are safely tucked away somewhere in Europe.

Monk Xavier: It seems that you've thought of everything.

The Master Man-Onko: Not quite! Our main advantage is that our opposition isn't thinking at all. But I would be remiss if we ended the session without SOME discussion of the Book! Where did Moore see his motivation to act?

Monk Xavier: [without hesitation] Saving LIFE also saves LIVES. We could have easily lost our ENTIRE human population, plus unknown numbers of species if things had continued to decay.

Master Man-Onko: Moore's critics say that this is just speculative thinking. They say that no one KNOWS if there would have been a World War III or an industrial meltdown or a climatic apocalypse. These critics say that the IG predictions TRIGGERED The Upheaval.

Monk Xavier: I always find it amazing how people in those days denied the reality that was staring them in the face... then went looking for a scapegoat. Yes, those critics reject the inclusivity-based forecasting methods that we use. And they reject "cause-and-effect" forecasting, also – at least when it comes to James Harold Moore. For them, the SOLE operative factor is the Book. They want to have their cake, eat it too, and then ask for ice cream.

Master Man-Onko: Well said! Because you won't be attending any physical education classes for a few weeks, I have had your time reassigned to me. I have some new assignments for you.

Monk Xavier: Fine. Reading Moore's book a little at a time is too slow for me. Can't you authorize a faster pace of reading?

Master Man-Onko: There's a reason for the pacing, which you will understand later. Also... The enthusiasm of your earlier offer to be a Confessor has been noted. While you will not be utilized in that regard, please realize that we may be asking... MORE of you. Much more. You are dismissed.

[END OF TRANSCRIPT]

Manifesto of the Marxist/Moore-ist Liberation Underground

File No:		File Name:	Manifesto of the Marxist/Moore-ist Liberation Underground
Location:		Parties:	Historical record
Monk/ Master Supervising:		North America Awakening Movement Archives Director	

[RECORD START]

We are the true inheritors of James Harold Moore.

Since the Great Inception, the time of James Harold Moore's political birth as a child, he was an advocate of liberation. He understood the necessity of armed conflict as the means to wipe from the Earth all that stood in the way of peace and brotherhood.

I'm not talking about the James Harold Moore who seemed to advocate a radically naïve notion of "Inclusivity" in his later years. That was a deliberate sham, a ruse to hide his true intentions – class and cultural war.

James Harold Moore never abrogated his Marxist roots. This will become evident when we RISE UP against the Oppressive Class (including the Culture Councils and their minions). This will be evident when we SEIZE the nano-biological weapons being stored in the Hive factories.

James Harold Moore is with us now, organizing what will be the final phase in our war of liberation. The time to rise up is now! It is time to CREATE A WORLD THAT WORKS FOR ALL OPPRESSED PEOPLE!

James Harold Moore is not dead! He has been organizing, with us, for the past decades. He will take his part in our vanguard SOON!

Be warned! You only have a short time to get on the right side of history!

[RECORD END]

Fourth Meeting

File No:		File Name:	Fourth Meeting
Location: Office/Residence of Master Man-Onko		**Parties:** Master Man-Onko Monk Xavier	
Monk/ Master Supervising:	Master Man-Onko		
Recorder: Observer 129	Transcript of Fourth Meeting between Master Man-Onko and Monk Xavier. Condition: Next stage advancement, recommended by Master Man-Onko		

[TRANSCRIPT START]

Master Man-Onko: Well, nice to see ALL of you again, now that the bandages have come off.

[Monk Xavier is silent]

Master Man-Onko: Well... How did the last chapter go?

[Monk Xavier is silent. Places book on table]

Master Man-Onko: I see. So, this is going to be either a very short session, or a very long one.

[Monk Xavier is silent]

Master Man-Onko: Suppose you tell me what's on your mind.

Monk Xavier: [rising and bowing] Master, I have only one question. It has three parts: (1) Where is James Harold Moore? (2) What have you been doing with him? (3) When do I meet him?

Master Man-Onko: [long pause] I commend you for the precision of your question.

Monk Xavier: Thank you... Although your praise does not begin to answer it.

Master Man-Onko: Most young monks don't get around to asking that question until the Ninth Meeting, or more. And they ask the question in such a way that it allows me to continue to be evasive!

Monk Xavier: Your response does not begin to answer the question.

Master Man-Onko: [long pause] Your question cannot be answered.

Monk Xavier: You cannot answer it, or you will not?

Master Man-Onko: Cannot. The very precision of your question renders it impossible to answer.

[Monk Xavier is silent. Rises to leave.]

Master Man-Onko: Sit down. What I'll do. I'll act like you asked a lesser question and answer that one.

Monk Xavier: [rising] Master, I insist on an answer to my question!

Master Man-Onko: Insisting on the answer to your question will get you sent to the psychic surgeons for an involuntary mind wipe! Now, do you still insist on an answer?

Monk Xavier: [head down] No, sir.

Master Man-Onko: Actually, you may get mind wiped for even asking the question.

Monk Xavier: Sir!

Master Man-Onko: It will not be up to me. You'll be either mind wiped or promoted. It won't be my choice. For my part, I will recommend promotion.

Monk Xavier: [glancing at Observer 009-25] Thank you, Master.

Master Man-Onko: Don't thank me yet. I may get mind scanned for suggesting whatever led to your question! For the sake of us both, we will be as open, honest and forthcoming as possible for the rest of the session, okay?

[Both look at Observer 009-25.]

Monk Xavier: Yes. As always.

Master Man-Onko: [smiling] Good response! Now, what led to your question?

Monk Xavier: First, it is obvious that you have been stretching this "special learning" out longer than it has to be. One chapter per week of the Book, when I could finish the entire thing in a few hours. The special assignment that required me to view every scrap of video on Moore and the Imaginal Group. Finally, you had Master Lee turn me into sushi, so I wouldn't be able to interact with any of the other monks. My bottom-line conclusions: I'm being prepared for something. It's time sensitive. It involves James Harold Moore. It all adds up to some kind of return. So, my question: where is he now?

Master Man-Onko: You really are a brilliant young man. It will be a shame if you wind up getting mind wiped. Now, for the first part of your question. I said this during our first or second meeting, and it is still absolutely true: we don't know where Dr. Moore is! Your question is impossible to answer. Now think: what is it that makes it impossible to answer?

Monk Xavier: [pauses. Thinking] I don't know.

Master Man-Onko: A lesser student would have just asked the "where is Moore" part. The answer to that is simple: we have no idea where he is, or even if he is alive or not. In that regard, the official statements are absolutely correct.

Monk Xavier: But... That's not the whole story.

Master Man-Onko: It is the second part of your question that puts you in line for a nice fresh mind and a stimulating job on a Hive assembly line.

Monk Xavier: [reflective] What could you be doing with him, that would also mean you don't know where he is? Oh my God!!!

Master Man-Onko: Go ahead and say it out loud, so that the surgeons don't have to guess at our transgressions.

Monk Xavier: GOD!! You don't know WHERE he is, because you don't know WHEN he is!

Master Man-Onko: Precisely. James Harold Moore is currently engaged in the longest-term experiment in time dilation in human history. 37 years and counting.

Monk Xavier: Is that even possible?

Master Man-Onko: [laughing] We'll let you know in three to five years!

Monk Xavier So, what is my role in all this?

Master Man-Onko: [pausing] That question will absolutely guarantee you a mind wipe. Now, do you want to ask it?

Monk Xavier: No! I mean, what question? Was I asking a question?

Master Man-Onko: Self wiping is the best kind of wiping... Now, I suggest to you: accelerate yourself. The best way to prevent a mind wipe is to simply become too valuable to us. Become an expert in "all things Moore". Become an expert in his life and times. Concentrate especially on the three years before and after his disappearance. Also, focus on those aspects of The Upheaval that happened after his disappearance.

Monk Xavier: Wow. That's a lot to focus on...

Master Man-Onko: You will be pulled out of your regular studies... One way or another.

Monk Xavier: Will I need to be beaten to a pulp again?

Master Man-Onko: Probably not! Although, compared to an involuntary mind wipe, you may want to volunteer for a few more broken bones and a concussion.

Monk Xavier: When will I know about the mind wipe?

Master Man-Onko: [standing] Let's see what awaits you on the other side of the door...

[AFTERNOTE: Monk Xavier did not receive DCI.]

[TRANSCRIPT END]

Men Ascendant!

File No:		File Name:	Men Ascendant!
Location:		Parties:	Historical record: (advertisement)
Monk/ Master Supervising:		North America Awakening Movement Archives Director	

[RECORD START]

For thousands of years, MEN have been the dominant force on this planet.

So it has been. And so it shall be. It is the God-given right of MEN to rule this world – and to protect it from those who wish to remove true divinity from the Earth altogether.

First came Darwin, who said we were no more than monkeys. Then came James Harold Moore, who said we were no more than ANTS!!

First the Women's Liberation Movement, and then the Homosexual Agenda tried to reduce the role of Real Men in our society. Now, James Harold Moore and the Hive Agenda want to eliminate it completely.

Don't believe for one second the Hive propaganda that the Hive-ists are "benign". They are all time bombs, about to explode.

Think what happens when tens of millions of mindless FEMALES burst forth from each Hive, following their Masters' orders, "DESTROY ALL MEN"!!

Well, we of MEN ASCENDANT! won't wait for that day to come! Join us (and the righteously obedient women who support us), and take part in the movement that will take back the world...

For MEN!

[RECORD END]

Fifth Meeting – The Two Masters

File No:		File Name:	The Two Masters
Location: Office/Residence of Master Man-Onko		**Parties:** Master Man-Onko Master Xavier	
Monk/ Master Supervising:	Master Man-Onko		
Master Observer 009-32	Transcript of Fifth Meeting between Master Man-Onko and Master Xavier. Condition: Termination, final instructions		

[TRANSCRIPT START]

Master Man-Onko: Before we begin, it is customary to recognize the presence and services of an Observer, especially a Master Observer. We are honored.

[Master Man-Onko and Master Xavier rise and bow to Observer 009-32.]

Master Man-Onko: My congratulations on you becoming the youngest Master ever, at the fastest rate ever.

Master Xavier: Thank you, but always JUNIOR Master to you, sir.

Master Man-Onko: And, congratulations on avoiding the mind wipe, way back when you were first asking about the whereabouts of Moore!

Master Xavier: A question: DID I avoid it? I mean, couldn't Unity or the psych surgeons make me THINK I'm talking to you, when I'm actually shoveling shit somewhere?

Master Man-Onko: Yes, they could... But why would they? It's easier to have you shovel shit and think that's the best, highest calling of your life.

Master Xavier: So there's a good chance that I'm actually here, and actually talking to you, and I'm actually a master?

Master Man-Onko: Close to 100 percent. They wouldn't waste thought reconstruction on the likes of you and me.

Master Xavier: A very relieved thank you!

Master Man-Onko: With your new elevated status, we can speak a bit more freely. Still remembering that the walls have ears.

Master Xavier: You mean, the walls *are* ears! In this case, MASTER ears! A question: how certain are we that James Harold Moore will return, and return at a particular time?

Master Man-Onko: That he will return is certain. WHEN he will return is also fairly certain. We sent objects through time ahead of him, and they have been appearing on schedule. But, you don't ask the most important question.

Master Xavier: [pause] What condition will he be in when he returns?

Master Man-Onko: Now THAT'S the question! Will he be his brilliant self, or a stark raving lunatic? Will he be somewhere around 70 years old... Or 110 years old? Will he remember what he did... Or will he be a mind wipe?

Even after 40 years, we still don't know that much about time dilation. We may not have dilated him at all. We may have simply thrown him into an alternate narrative. He may have lived the last 40 years on a slightly different Earth and may be very reluctant to come back to this one.

Master Xavier: Why should he be reluctant to finish his project?

Master Man-Onko: Suppose that in Narrative B, his cover story of being the cause of the Upheavals never caught on? No need for blame, no one thinking that he is the antichrist. He could have gotten married, had children, lived what would have looked like a "normal" life. In Narrative B, he would not be the Most Hated Man on Earth. Would you want to be uprooted from THAT to come back to THIS?

Master Xavier: I see your point...

Master Man-Onko: Oh, the possibilities get worse. What if he got blasted to Narrative C, where ONLY Unity existed? What if he spent the last 40 years as the only solon on a planet of Hives? What if he spent the last 40 years not talking to a single soul?

Master Xavier: Okay, I think I see...

Master Man-Onko: How about Narrative D, where the conflict goes nuclear, and he spent four decades wandering a nuclear wasteland? Or Narrative E, where he was crowned Ruler of the Earth, and we snatch him back to THIS? Or perhaps Narrative F...

Master Xavier: Okay! Okay! I get the point! There's a fifty-fifty chance that we snatch him back from some really nice alternative. Fifty-fifty isn't that bad...

Master Man-Onko: You still don't understand! What if he returns from a nuclear hell – and he blames us for leaving him there 40 years?

Master Xavier: Oh.

Master Man-Onko: Oh yes. Now you're starting to get it. Our forecasters predict an 85 percent probability that he comes back hating our guts and 55 percent probability that he's going to want to jump right back on the couch and go back to where he just came from. And a 20 percent probability that he comes back stark raving mad. So, this now brings us to your roles.

Master Xavier: Plural?

Master Man-Onko: Yes. And potentially contradictory.

Master Xavier: Great. Shoot.

Master Man-Onko: Not quite so fast...

Master Xavier: Of course not!

Master Man-Onko: [serious] Everything up until this moment has been a prelude to hearing your assignment. Once you hear it, you cannot refuse it. You either say yes or you submit to a mind wipe. You have three choices, all stemming from what you decide after hearing me: One, you can walk out the door NOW, with your status, rank, and mind intact, without hearing the assignment. Two, you agree to your assignment – including the contradictory parts. Three, you will receive an involuntary mind-wipe, which will erase your knowledge of the assignment. In fact, all knowledge of the past three years. Do you want me to continue, or do you want to leave right now?

Master Xavier: I will stay and hear the assignment.

Master Man-Onko: I will ask you a series of questions. Answering "I accept" will get you to the next question. Answering "no" ends the questions. If you answer "no" to any question, your memory of this entire conversation, along with the past three years, will be mind-wiped. You can avoid the mind wipe by leaving the room now, before the questions start. Understand?

Master Xavier: [standing] I know what you are going to ask. The answer is "yes". To the whole thing. But, for the sake of the recording, please ask the questions...

Master Man-Onko: [standing] Your assignment is to muster out of this Awakening Center. You will never return. Your new assignment is to be the personal support for James Harold Moore, if, when and how he returns. Your loyalty and duty to James Harold Moore and his health and welfare will be absolute and without question. Do you accept?

Master Xavier: I accept.

Master Man-Onko: Your duty to James Harold Moore is absolute. Part of your duty is this: you are to keep him in THIS NARRATIVE, at all costs. If he leaves here and now, that will be seen as a violation of your duty. Do you accept this interpretation of your duty?

Master Xavier: I accept.

Master Man-Onko: This condition is absolute. "At all costs" means that, if it comes to it, you will kill anyone trying to help James Harold Moore transfer away from this narrative. Do you accept?

Master Xavier: [pauses] I accept.

Master Man-Onko: This condition includes James Harold Moore himself. Do you accept?

Master Xavier: [pause] You mean... Kill Moore if he tries to escape?

Master Man-Onko: Yes.

Master Xavier: What mind-wipe came up with this directive?

Master Man-Onko: [voice harsh] Do you accept?

Master Xavier: [long pause] I accept.

Master Man-Onko: The next condition: you will do your best to dissuade Moore from participating in any way in the "show trials" that will take place. This condition is NOT "at any cost". Do you accept?

Master Xavier: You mean, I don't have to kill the most famous and mythic figure in recent human history?

Master Man-Onko: [voice harsh] Do you accept, JUNIOR Master Xavier?

Master Xavier: [subdued] I accept.

Master Man-Onko: Sit down. You remember when I told you about the show trials? Do you remember your reaction – that you were ready to sacrifice your own life for the good of the whole? Now you can see that what was required of you is so much more than your life.

Master Xavier: Yes sir. I understand. And, I don't like it, not one bit.

Master Man-Onko: Good. I would worry about your integrity otherwise. Moore will wake up with an army of ten thousand agents, all ready to follow his orders...

Master Xavier: Mind wipes?

Master Man-Onko: No... just influenced to follow. Of the ten thousand, only 100 will know the full orders. And of the 100, only 20 of you will be on call for his return. It will be the task of the Greeters to orient him to his return.

Master Xavier: Or kill him.

Master Man-Onko: [pauses] Yes. There'll be two of you on hand at any time in the resurrection chamber. The rotation of the Greeters will be manipulated. Of the 20 Greeters, there's a fifty-fifty chance that the awakening will happen on one of your shifts.

Master Xavier: This is... NOT an honor.

Master Man-Onko: No one thinks it is. We know the prohibition against violence is strong. You will receive a mild mental influence to allow you to carry out this order. Our work is done. In record time. You have become a Master in less time than some finish Agent training. And you have been initiated into the Secrets faster than anyone in history. Although I wish it were otherwise, it is unlikely that you and I will ever meet again.

Master Xavier: When I first became a Novice, just a few years ago, I thought that was the biggest thing that ever happened to me in my life. Now I can see that my entire life has been preparation for this one moment. And this is preparation for what I will do upon meeting Moore. Thank you for what you have done to help me prepare. I won't forget.

[TRANSCRIPT END]

The Resurrection Chamber

File No:		File Name:	The Resurrection Chamber
Location:		**Parties:** Master Greeter Xavier Master Greeter Noma	
Monk/ Master Supervising:		Journal of Master Greeter Xavier, on duty as Temporal Greeter at TDTS-51	

[JOURNAL ENTRY START]

It's official name is Temporal Displacement Targeting Station 51, *but everyone refers to it as the Resurrection Chamber. It is a huge space, 50 feet in radius, with a Balinese style roof and open sides. Very open. Instead of columns, the entire roof structure is supported by cables running to towers 200 feet away.*

In the center of the space is the Couch, where James Harold Moore is predicted to... Land? Appear? Materialize? The rest of the floor is a padded space... In case the predictions are slightly off. That is also the reason for the lack of walls and columns – after 40 years, having Moore materialize with his head stuck inside a roof column would be... anti-climactic.

The entire space, including the grass covered hills surrounding the Resurrection Chamber, is known as the Target. Those of us assigned to this duty are called Greeters. The two of us currently on duty, who sit at the rim of the circle, are officially called Catchers.

No one ever mentions our other duty. No one publicly mentions that our unspoken title is Executioner.

While rotation among the 20 Greeters is allegedly random, most of my shifts are shared with Greeter Noma (AKA Bubbles, for her fairly nauseating enthusiasm for her task). She's on station now, with her back to me and to the Resurrection Couch.

While on duty we have our backs to each other and to the couch. We sit and meditate (or journal) on a raised cushion. Under the cushion, we each have everything that James Harold Moore may need for his return – cooled (not cold) water and fruit juices, two defibrillators, neural attenuators... an entire old-style hospital in a box. And if something goes very wrong, the entire Couch can be flash frozen, putting Dr. Moore in a state of suspended animation while the medical staff figures out the best course of action.

In each Greeters left pants pocket is the Card, a device the size and shape of an old-style credit card; it contains two lethal darts, at high pressure. This is what we will use to kill James Harold Moore.

Among the greeters, there's always been significant speculation regarding the purpose of the second dart. Is one dart not enough? Why two? Why not a dozen? Why not just one? Speculation has ranged from the expectation that the Executioner was to kill themselves (The Judas Dart), to speculation that the killer might have to kill the other monk before actually killing Moore.

And it is whispered speculation that both monks would kill themselves, or kill each other, and James Harold Moore would be free to pursue his own agenda.

The ranks of the 20 Greeters have been depleted and refreshed over the past two years. An accident here and there (one fatal). Four suicides... an unexpected use for the darts. Three refusals of service (and resultant mind wipes). One termination because of PTSD (and another mind wipe). One pregnancy.

All Greeters know that their years of preparation were focused HERE. They all feel that the event will happen SOON, perhaps this week. For some reason, I think it will happen on this shift. The two-hour shift is only half over. (If it doesn't, two other Greeters will take over from us.)

317

I had hoped that, when it happened, I would not be paired with Bubbles. Oh well...

As usual, we Catchers face outward – following the Heisenberg Uncertainty Principle from quantum physics, there was a prediction that the Event could not happen if it was OBSERVED... So, no observers. No cameras. No active recorders. Strict orders not to turn around. There is an old-fashioned digital voice recorder under the couch, activated by weight. The act of Moore's return will not be recorded, but what happens afterwards will be.

The Couch and the entire floor is covered in rice paper, which would make a sound if something landed on it. Materialized on it. Appeared on it... Re-entered the dominant space-time continuum correlative to it... However you visualize it, the rice paper should make a sound. Should.

As I sat journaling on my cushion, I heard the sound I had been both dreading and anticipating for two years.

The sounds of rice paper crinkling.

Followed by a voice (definitely not Bubbles). "Whoa. That was a rush".

I capped my pen, rose from my cushion, and reached into my pocket for my Card. Palming it in my hand, I put both hands behind my back, turned, and approached the couch.

A figure sat up on the Couch, facing away, pulling on a floor-length robe. Even from my angle, even partially obscured by Bubbles, the figure of James Harold Moore was unmistakable. He hadn't aged a day from his last known photo.

Bubbles had beaten me to the punch. Not following procedure, she had jumped onto the hard target at the first sound, and was now standing within ten feet of the Couch. She had circled halfway around from her position, blocking my path. She raised both hands in greeting. Both hands were empty.

And now it begins, I thought. *I know who the first dart is for.*

The Greeting

File No:		File Name:	The Greeting
Location:		Parties: Master Greeter Xavier Master Greeter Noma James Harold Moore	
Monk/ Master Supervising:		Master Greeter Xavier	

Name:		Pgs:		Date:		Vol:	
Type of Transcript:	Mechanical xxx						
	Organic						

Preface by North American Archive Committee:

The following is a digital transcript of the voice recording captured by mechanical means upon the return of James Harold Moore during the Temporal Observation Displacement shift of Master Greeters Xavier and Noma.

This text is being provided in a rough draft format. Communication Access Realtime Translation (CART) facilitates communication accessibility and may not be a totally verbatim record of the proceedings. Let your coordinator know if you would prefer a more verbatim option.

[TRANSCRIPT START]

Noma: GREETINGS!! Welcome to your future! I am Greeter Noma. My colleague and I are here to assist in your return and adjustment in any way possible!

[Silence]

Moore: Are the two of you co equal?

Noma: Yes, sir! My fellow Greeter and I have the honor and...

Moore: Yet I see that one of you stands in front of the other.

Noma: Sir, I can assure you that both of us stand ready to assist you. Would you like some water or fresh fruit? It has been made fresh...

Moore: I would like you to stop talking. And step aside.

[Noma steps aside, silent.]

Moore: Now, for Mr. Silence here. Do you have a name?

Xavier: Yes, sir. I am Greeter Xavier.

Moore: [walks closer] And what are your orders, Greeter Xavier?

Xavier: To kill you if you show any signs of wanting to leave this Narrative. Otherwise, my orders are to follow you. I sincerely hope you don't want to leave.

Noma: Sir! I want you to know that not all Greeters...

Moore: Please continue to be silent until I address you.

[Noma is silent.]

Moore: Now, Xavier [takes a step closer to Greeter Xavier] exactly how are you to kill me? Your bare hands?

Xavier: No, sir. With this. [Shows Dr. Moore the Card, open palm.]

Moore: I see. All Greeters have one of these?

Xavier: Yes, sir.

Moore: [turning to Greeter Noma] Where is yours?

Noma: Sir! I left it over there! [Indicating the object on her cushion] I wanted you to know that you were stepping into a world of love and nonviolence, where you had no fear...

Moore: Do I look afraid?

Noma: [pausing] Well... No sir.

Moore: Please go back to your silence. [Turning to Greeter Xavier] Are you ready to do your duty?

Xavier: [putting his hands behind his back] Do you wish to leave this Narrative?

Moore: [smiling] Not in the least. The time dilation worked. Feels like I've been asleep for a week... And I don't have a desire to go back to sleep!

Xavier: [smiling. Holds his right hand out to his side, pointing down. Fires two darts into the rice paper. Throws the card onto the ground.] Excellent. Duty done. What are your orders?

Moore: Do you have any other commands that would interfere with you taking my orders?

Xavier: Well, I'm supposed to dissuade you from taking part in local politics, but that's more of a suggestion than an order.

Moore: Very cool. Your first order is to become my Chief of Staff. Assemble a command team...

Noma: Sir! I recommend that you place people in your command structure who are completely LOYAL to you, without conflicts!

Moore: Yes, excellent advice. [To Noma] Among the Greeters, you know the people who were ready to disobey the order to kill me?

Noma: Yes, sir!

Moore: [to Xavier] You are to get that list from her and remove all of them from consideration for command.

Xavier: Of course, sir.

Noma: SIR!!!

Moore: No hard feelings. You're pleasant enough. But when I give an order, I need to know that it will be carried out – regardless of what you think about it. In dropping your weapon AND attempting to block Xavier, you demonstrated the exact opposite. Don't worry; I'm sure Xavier can find something for you that is commensurate with your talents and skills.

Xavier: Yes sir... Perhaps Public Relations. [Turning to Noma] Thank you. You are dismissed.

[Noma hesitates. Then, bows to both Dr. Moore and Xavier; walks away.]

Xavier: And Noma... Please collect and discharge all of those killing cards. We don't want any accidents.

Noma: Yes... Sir. [Hesitates] Master Moore, please, may I ask you just one question? Why would you ever TRUST the people who issued a directive for your execution? And why would you trust the people who were willing to carry it out?

Moore: [moves closer to Noma, places a hand on her shoulder] That's a fair question, and I'll answer it. Noma, did it ever occur to you to ask WHO issued that directive?

[Noma looks stunned; Xavier laughs out loud.]

Moore: The likelihood of ever having to carry out that directive was always zero.

Noma: But the predictions...

Moore: With regard to me, the Office of Predictions has almost always been wrong. It's not their fault. They were purposely fed misleading algorithms, which through recursive time-like feedforward loops, created misleading results. The conditions of my return had to remain an open question. Even to your ruling Council.

Noma: Why is that, sir?

Moore: It has to do with my mission. The reason for leaving, and the reason for coming back. More than that... you'll get from Xavier, here, when the time is right. And now, Noma, you may go. I'm not angry at you. Nothing of what transpired here will go into your record – I'll see to it. And, we will find a position for you where you can feel wholehearted about your work.

[Noma smiles; bows to Dr. Moore and former Greeter, now Chief of Staff Xavier; exits.]

Moore: [turning to Xavier] Tell me... What were you going to do with that second dart?

Xavier: [staring at Noma's retreating back] Without interference, my plan was to use it on myself.

Moore: [Looking back and forth between Xavier and Noma] I understand. I hope you never have to face such a situation again.

Xavier: [smiling] Well, that will be entirely up to you, sir. Right now, my primary thought is to make sure all of the other cards are collected, accounted for and discharged.

Moore: [slipping into some slippers] Not a tremendously big deal.

Xavier: Well... We've had a couple of... suicides.

Moore: [smiling] No, you haven't! You have to remember, we don't go for the whole killing thing. The neurotoxin on the dart knocks you out. Firing it sets off an alarm, and the guys running the show hustle in and remove the "body". And take them back for mental rehabilitation.

Xavier: How do you know all this?

Moore: [smiling] Who do you think DESIGNED it? Now, for some real substantive orders. I heard the woman refer to fresh fruit juice?

Xavier: Yes, we've got some on hand, and more available...

Moore: Excellent! Let's start with what's on hand, and work up from there.

Xavier: This way... What would you like to see or know about the last 40 years? What do you need from us to devise your return strategies?

Moore: Return strategies? My plans were laid out, well before I crawled into the time tunnel. I am technically 110 years old. Practically, I'm only a bit over 70. I have traveled into the future! If I had lived in this narrative for the past 40 years, I would have faced at least two dozen assassination attempts, been banned in almost every country in the world, demonized, castigated,... Or... I would have been celebrated, hailed as the Savior of Humanity! People would have tried to start a religion around me, elevating me to some completely ridiculous level. They would have even claimed that I invented the Five Latent Powers. And the bigger problem: could I have continued to resist such nonsense? Or would I have succumbed, and allowed myself to be made President for Life? Of the entire World? One-quarter of the people would have wanted to deify me. One-quarter would have wanted to assassinate me. And one-quarter would have wanted to just forget about the social traumas and go back to sleep. One way or another, the past 40 years would not have been good for me. So, with the help of a bunch of friends, I jumped ahead to now, to the time when the disruptive elements are behind me...

Xavier: We call them the Upheavals...

Moore: Whatever. Or, if I had stayed here and stayed alive, it would have been because I had made my own survival a top priority. Had I stayed, I would have been either famous or infamous. One way or another, everything would have centered on ME. As it is, if the governing consciousness institutions worked well enough, either I am relatively obscure, or no longer a focal point for anger.

Xavier: We call them the "Culture Councils"...

Moore: Whatever. So, hopefully, I should be obscure enough...

Xavier: Yes. You are.

Moore: And rich enough...

Xavier: Well, money has changed beyond your recognition. You don't have any money, you have credits and shares. And your share percentages are so large, it is practically meaningless. You could buy a medium-size country.

Moore: Cool! That might be enough! And, of course, a small army to make sure my plans get carried out.

Xavier: Is 100,000 enough? That is the number of your agents that you currently have assigned to you. If that's not enough, I can start recruiting immediately.

Moore: [pauses, then] Tell me you're kidding.

Xavier: Not in the least.

Moore: Wow. I thought I'd need a hundredth of that! I won't need to buy a country, I could just take one over!

Xavier: Well... There really aren't any "countries" anymore, not as politically separate legal entities, with armies and flags. They're more like administrative units, or spheres of influence, or linguistic groupings. If you really want one, I think all you would have to do is ask the Culture Council for one. And if you do want to take one over, all of the 100,000 agents have been trained...

Moore: Xavier! Yo! Lighten up! That was a joke!

Xavier: And acting like I was taking you seriously was my joke to you! Yes, I've read your personality files quite extensively!

[Both laugh.]

Moore: Okay, seriously now... I realized something when I was in that cave many years ago. I realize that I had served humanity's transcendent vision for almost all of my life. And I realized THAT WAS ENOUGH. Being on the firing line since I was 12 years old, being beaten, shot at, arrested, harassed... over half a century was ENOUGH. I realized that I needed to put in place a plan where my continued existence would be superfluous to the outcome. And I realized that if people have a scapegoat to focus on, like ME, they won't focus on the details of the plan itself. The Metamorphosis of Humanity will take place, while the potential troublemakers busy themselves wondering where I am, what I'm up to, and how to stop me... a non-actor. But... that left a very serious roadblock on the way to a transformed humanity. Let's see if you've guessed it.

Xavier: [Long pause] I can't imagine anything so serious that it would necessitate your disappearance and return. The Edge still exists, but has been largely neutralized...

Moore: What's the Edge?

Xavier: A small group with Awakened Powers like ours, but they use them against us.

Moore: Huh! I didn't think that would be possible! That may put a wrinkle in my plans. But no, I'm not talking about an Edge or anything like that. Our problem is more pervasive and profound. And obvious, if you think about it for a second.

Xavier: [Long pause] Sorry, Sir, but I don't see what would have brought you back at this time.

Moore: That's because the problem has disguised itself as the solution.

Xavier: Do you mean... THE CULTURE COUNCIL?

Moore: Exactly. If they're the head honchos, they are the problem.

Xavier: But... HOW are they the problem? They are the best and brightest among us! Their job is to solve our problems, not create them!

Moore: All that may be true... but it's their very EXISTENCE that is the problem. It's a two-edged problem... First, whatever they did to stay in power has gone from being an asset to a weapon. The stronger their success, the more powerful their weapon. Second: even though they may deny it, they will try to stay in power forever. It will NEVER be a good time for them to give up power. It's not that they're bad or evil... It's just that, from their perspective, they are "good", and anyone who opposes them will be labeled "no-good". And will be hit with their weapon or weapons.

Xavier: I'm not sure I understand. What you would call "weapons" are pretty pipsqueak. SleepyTime gas, knockout darts, stuff like that. I can't see the CC getting powerful on that!

Moore: Since I've been back for about 10 minutes, I can't tell you what it is. But I can tell you this: every year that the Council exists, the weapon gets STRONGER. Did they teach you about Marxism? It was a failed ideology of the 20th Century.

Xavier: Yes, we have all learned about the Breaker ideologies.

Moore: Do you recall the phrase, "The withering away of the State"?

Xavier: Yes.

Moore: Marx believed that, once a "true" communist state was created, the State apparatus would just go away on its own. Pure fantasy! On their own, States NEVER just wither away. Power NEVER stops being powerful. And the more "compassionate" or "benevolent" the power organization, the more entrenched it is.

Systems serve the people that form the system. The more powerful, the more self-serving. The more altruistic the values, the more entrenched the control.

Xavier: So... We're going to go to war against the Culture Council??

Moore: Ha! Hopefully, it won't come to that! If I've predicted this moment correctly, there will be... are... many on the organizing Council who understand that this needs to happen, and will work with me to dismantle it.

Xavier: Well... I'm not sure how Unity is going to feel about this.

Moore: Who or what is Unity?

Xavier: Unity is more powerful than the Culture Councils. The Centers in Europe have morphed into "hives", run as a single, unified consciousness. You can't even imagine how powerful they are.

Moore: [Pause] Please tell me that you are kidding.

Xavier: Not at all. The Culture Council has always been freaked out by Unity. If we have to go up against Unity, against tens of millions of people all sharing the same THOUGHT, I don't think 100,000 Agents will be nearly enough.

Moore: PLEASE tell me that you're kidding.

Xavier: If anything, I'm understating their potential.

Moore: Is this... entity... hostile?

Xavier: Depends on who you talk to. They have the power to mind-wipe an entire continent... although there's no proof that they've ever done so, or even want to do that. They probably could go backwards in time and change your time dilation coordinates so that you NEVER return. Or never leave. Or were never born.

Moore: Jesus...

Xavier: They support the Culture Council on some things, oppose them on others, and are seemingly indifferent to much of what the CC is doing. They help only when they want to, and when it is apparently in their interest to do so.

Moore: And our 100,000 foot soldiers couldn't stand against them?

Xavier: They could mind-wipe every one of them into thinking they were Agents of Unity.

Moore: "Mind-wipe". Is that what it sounds like?

Xavier: Pretty much. We can mind-wipe individuals and small to medium sized groups. Unity can do... whatever they want.

Moore: Now there's a wrinkle I never predicted! Wow! Looks like we've found the weapon!

Xavier: Mind wiping? I don't think so. It's so benign. I've had a couple of DCIs — "direct consciousness interventions"... It's no big deal.

Moore: Yes! That's it! The "mind wipe" is EXACTLY the weapon we must oppose! Absolutely powerful, absolutely insidious, seemingly necessary and "for your own good". Given to you in such a way that you think its benign, even useful.. You think that you need it, and can't see the harm in it until it's too late. I'll bet you think that mind wiping is as harmful as a haircut! I think mind wiping is the fossil fuel of your age!

Xavier: [pause] Excuse me, Sir, but perhaps you should see DCI in operation before you make too many judgments about it. It really has saved us incalculable problems. In your time, the way to deal with negative, psychotic, sociopathic people was to lock them all up together, so that their socio-pathology could get stronger. Or kill them. Now, we have the means to erase the negative behavior, without erasing the person.

Moore: Of course you do. And, it has really worked, hasn't it? I'll bet the incidence of murder, rape, and theft are significantly down in the areas you control, right?

Xavier: Yes Sir! Things like fighting and stealing are virtually unheard-of on most of the continent... actually, the world! And we are moving on the last strongholds of that negative behavior. We predict that murder and rape will be impossible anywhere on the planet in 20 more years!

Moore: Said with a lot of pride. And, having seen that negative behavior first hand, I can heartily commend you. But that's not the edge of this two-edged mind-wiping sword that I'm concerned about.

Xavier: Sir? What do you...

Moore: Hey, umm... Xavier, right?

Xavier: Yes, Sir.

Moore: Can we cut out the "Sir" stuff? My friends and colleagues called me Moore.

Xavier: Yes, Sir — Ahh, yes, Moore... Just Moore? No title? It will seem a bit odd...

Moore: You have titles here? What does this Culture Council call itself? Lords and earls? A few "ladies" thrown in?

Xavier: [laughing] Not quite that bad! There are three basic titles: Novices, Monks and Masters. I'm sure you will be considered a "Master", without having to test for it.

Moore: Test?

Xavier: Yes. [pauses] Back in your time, the various martial arts had ways to go from having a white belt to a black belt, yes?

Moore: Okay, I get it. What about this Culture Council? What do they call themselves?

Xavier: Just Councillor. The head of the Culture Council is called First Councillor. The head of each Awakening Center used to be referred to as Abbot — however, I think most of them are now more comfortable with Director or Administrator.

Moore: And most of these Directors are the people chosen for the Culture Council, right?

Xavier: There are some exceptions, but yes, most of the folks on the CC started as Directors.

Moore: And there is a process for them to rotate on and off of the Council, yes?

Xavier: Yes. There's an algorithm that selects who comes on and goes off. Most of us don't know how it's done, other than it works.

Moore: Cool! I created it!

Xavier: Well, it's lasted for four decades, so it must work pretty good!

Moore: Let's get back to this brainwashing technique that you use...

Xavier: Excuse me, uhh, Moore... Master... We don't like referring to it as "brainwashing".

Moore: I'll bet you DON'T! And that's where the trouble lies! We had an old President, Ronald Reagan, who tried to rename nuclear weapons, the most horrible engine of war ever created, as "Peacekeepers". Trying to make nuclear annihilation seem... pleasant. Necessary. I wake up and find that the organization I created has the means to brainwash every last person in the world, has been using it and will keep on using it in the future... Yes, I'd say that is a massive problem.

Xavier: But, Master Moore, are you saying that we should not use this benign tool on mass murderers and rapists?

Moore: No! I'm not saying that! But because the murderers and rapists have existed, you will continue to use this tool on the people who just... think differently. Until everyone thinks the same. Let me give you an example: back in 1860, we drilled the first oil wells in America. They actually helped to solve a problem: TOO MUCH OIL. There was so much oil, it would seep out of the ground and ruin good agricultural land. In 100 years, by 1960, we had drained over half of the world's oil out of the ground. We could have stopped there, had 20 or 30 years of rigidly enforced declining consumption, while we switched to alternative, renewable and local fuels. Did we do that? HELL NO! We kept running those wells at full tilt, until we sucked the Earth dry. We had to set off underground bombs and pump in poisons just to get at the last drop of oil. We ran the car right off the cliff — and killed our society while doing so. No, the problem isn't that the Culture Council has eliminated murder, or rape, or even lying and bullying. The problem is that they will continue to use the tool... until the human race is homogenized into sameness... or until the tool is taken away.

Xavier: [pauses] I think I understand. It's not that we've been doing bad things with DCI over the years, but you want to reduce its use, so that we don't do bad things in the future. Is that it?

Moore: Well said. I've got NO problem converting the murders and warlords. I've got little problem with mind wiping for clearly antisocial and personally damaging behaviors, like drug and alcohol abuse. But what happens when this Culture Council gets it in its head that they want to eliminate Republicans? Or Democrats? Or rich people? They could brainwash all rich people to give them their money, couldn't they? Or people who engage in weird but consensual sex. I may not want to be hog-tied and dipped in mayonnaise to have sex, but should I stop someone else from doing that? Well... as long as I don't have to *watch* it! No... once you give a group the power, they will keep using it — it's in our history, if not our nature. This tool will have to be taken away from them... from us all.

Xavier: I believe I understand... except for the Democrats and Republicans part. Those were pretty much defunct at the time you disappeared. Along with rich people... although they lasted a little longer than the politicians. I agree with you. But I think you should know that I received a mild DCI suggestion to agree with you and support you...

Moore: Unless you killed me!

Xavier: [laughing] Oh yeah... that! But seriously, how do you intend to get the CC to give up their most potent and successful tool? And Unity? Getting the Culture Council to give up their rifles is one thing... getting Unity to give up its nuclear weapons is another.

Moore: I haven't the slightest idea! I've been awake for about half an hour, just found out about the brainwashing tool, just found out about the Unity supermen, I'm only wearing a robe, and, except for the delicious orange juice and pastries, haven't eaten! Oh, I assume that these eats are gluten-free?

Xavier: Well... now that they stopped artificially messing with the wheat production, gluten is no longer a problem.

Moore: Excellent! That's how to solve a problem... at the source!

Xavier: So, let's get you some real clothes and real food...

Moore: But to answer your other question, I think the first thing I need to do is to actually meet these super-folks you are talking about. How do I contact this Unity entity?

Xavier: They have deep communion with all the living things around us. The likelihood that they already know about your return and all of your plans is pretty high. The fact that we're still standing here, talking about it means they probably agree with you. Or they don't care, one way or another. I would suggest that we relax and wait for Unity to contact you.

Moore: How about a meeting with the ruling Council?

Xavier: Given your status, I think that will be possible at any time. Actually, I think you could probably ask for a seat on it. But I'd suggest you get some clothes on, first!

Moore: More fruit juice first! Then, let's see what we can do to shift the power structure around here — without us getting shifted first!

Xavier: First the juice. Then some clothes. And then... 100,000 of us get to wage nonviolent war on the system that saved humanity from extinction! If Unity lets us!

[TRANSCRIPT END]

THE END (for now)

Prior in the Series:

Book One:
The Chronicles of the Upheavals

Next in the Series:

Book Three:
The Chronicles of the Metamorphosis (2085-2120)

Other Books by Shariff M. Abdullah:

The Power of One: Authentic Leadership in Turbulent Times
[New Society Publishers, (1990); New Catalyst Books (2007)].

Creating a World That Works for All
[Berrett-Koehler Publishers, 1999].

Seven Seeds for a New Society
[Commonway Press, 2009].

Practicing Inclusivity
(with Leslie Hamilton) [CreateSpace Publishing, 2015].

[NOTE: For some reason, these Appendices appeared only in the ebook versions of Upheavals. *To correct this glaring error, I have copied parts of them over to* Awakening.*]*

Appendix A: The Sponsors of the Series:

Reviewers, Editors and Commenters:
In the list of acknowledgements for *Upheavals*, I had a pretty long list of friends, associates and collaborators, each of whom spent time on moving the writing along. Some helped with sketching out the early ideas, others read the entire manuscript (some several times), and others came in with crucial last-minute edits and page arrangements.

In this book, there is only one: Zakary Grimshaw.

Some months ago, I was talking with Rebecca Chamberlain, my friend, collaborator and Professor of Writing at the Evergreen State College. I was bemoaning (as usual) the current state of my unfinished manuscripts, my lack of time for writing... my typical litany. Rebecca suggested that she had a gifted student who may be interested in working as a writing assistant to me. She introduced me to Zak.

And the rest, as they say, is history.

Yes, I could have finished *Awakening* without him... but not this year. Maybe not even 2022. Working with Zak propelled this writing along. Zak has a fine eye for both the small detail (an extra space in a paragraph) and the meta themes (does the 70+ year time scale make sense?).

Since I've written a bit, I've had considerable experience with being edited. Those of you who know how to drive a car with a manual transmission will understand my analogy: good editing is like a tight transmission. If it's working well, you don't even think about it — it flows very naturally. And Zak and I have had an excellent flow.

My very best editing experience? Steve Piersanti, owner, publisher, and editor at Berrett-Koehler Publishers. In his skillful hands, *Creating a World That Works for All* became the "Book of the Year" in its year of birth (1999). My very worst editing experience? One-Who-Shall-Not-Be-Named, someone who really wanted to write their own book, and kept trying to put their words in my mouth. Unhygienic, to say the least. A car with no transmission. Or one stuck in reverse.

Where does Zak fit on that spectrum? Right at the top, at the near-Piersanti level. And he's young, so he's got time on his side. Graduating just this month from Evergreen State College, he has an outstanding career as both writer and editor ahead of him.

And, given that I've got four or five unfinished manuscripts on my shelf, my collaboration with Zak may not be over.

FINANCIAL CONTRIBUTORS:
Several people questioned why I chose to release *Chronicles* through the medium of a crowdfunding campaign. Simple answers:
1. I needed resources for the graphics, printing and marketing expenses that will accrue in any book marketing campaign.
2. In order to "globalize" Books Two and Three, I need the funds to spend significant research time in Europe, Asia and Africa.
3. I want the book to reach the widest possible audience. One of the key components of "crowdfunding" is the CROWD. The idea was to attempt to reach beyond Commonway's database, to access potentially millions of people via Kickstarter.

The millions remain a potential. According to Kickstarter's statistics, 98% of the funds collected came from people in the Commonway database (or their contacts). Once again, it was the Commonway "crowd" that came through!

Significant Crowdfunding Support:
Many thanks to **Eric Foster** for his valuable volunteer efforts and suggestions in managing the crowdfunding campaign. His assistance and suggestions were a LOT more valuable than the "paid" help that I received. I look forward to working with him again in the future.

Significant Financial Backers:

Pat Adams, Raffi Aftandelian, Elaine S. Alexander, Pamela Allee, Catherine Norwood Anderson, Tom Atlee, Sherry Banaka, Donna Beegle, Susan Belchamber, David Berry, Karen Bettin, Tahdi Blackstone, Kathleen Boyer, Teresa Bright, Carol Brouillet, Helene Brown, John D. Brown, Rev. Marj Bryant, Barbara Buckingham-Hayes, Greg Burrill, Sandra Campbell, Maria Carlo, Joan E. Caruthers, Heather Carver, Dinah Chapman, Lynda Coates, Catherine Condon, Gary Corbin, Dana Cummings, Mary Cummings, Lakshmi Dady, Marcia Danab, Maja Daniels, Bob Davis, Sara DeHoff, Rev. Douglas Duerr, Jay Earley, Jane Engel, Gaya Erlandson, Bill Evans, Suzanne Fischer Reynolds, Jeffrey Fowler, Erica L. Frank, Jim & Rebecca Gaudino, Robert Gilman, Amari Gold, Veta Goler, Ernestine Griffin, Leslie Hamilton, Paula Hannan, Carol Hansen Grey, Christine Harbaugh, Carol Hart, Holly Hatch, Jacquelyn Hawkins, Fred Heutte, Peggy Holman, Debbie Hornibrook, Jeffrey Hutner, Anita Hyatt, Rick Ingrasci, Lois Isbell, Miki Kashtan, Hank Keeton, Dottie Koontz, David Kyle, Robert Kyser, Eon LaJoie, Ed Lantz, Regina LaRocca, Dominic Le Fave, Stewart Levine, David Levinger, Rev. Judith Marshall, Andolie Marten, Austin Marx, Konda Mason, Rev. Joslyn Mason, Krishna K. Mayo-Smith, Leta Mullen, Patricia S. Murrell, Abdisalan Muse, Linda Norlin, Jeanne E. Nyquist, Joyce O'Halloran, Veena Fox Parekh, Eileen Patra, Ted Polozov, Lane Poncy, Edward Preston, David Rankin, Liza Rankow, Arthur Rashap, Liana Rein, Jzonay Reitz, Ben Roberts, Adin Rogovin, Robert J. Romanski, Erin Ross, Tim Rouse, Laura Schlafly, Rev. Ted Schneider, Brian Setzler, Anna Shook, Tesa Silvestre, Sally Slick, Gregory Smith, Tara Steele, Susie Steffes, Muriel Strand, Paul Sunderland, Debbie Susnjara, Janet Sussman, Jill Sutton, Catherine Thomas, Shirlene Warnock, Zoe Weil, W. Thunder Williams, Chuck Willis, Barbara Wuest

Additional Crowdfunding Support:

Corliss Acosta, Michael Baroff, Deborah Bellony, Don Berg, Shyama Blaise, Liviu Caliman, Suzanne Caubet, Joel E. Conarton, Jo Ann DeFrancesco, Jaelle Dragomir, Erica L. Frank, Eric Gamonal , Anthony Mtuaswa Johnson, P+T Johnson-Lenz, Koty Juliano, Jennifer Kahnweiler, Gerald Landrum, Richard Lerman, Rev. Jim Marshall, Casey Mullen, Leonie Ramondt, Joanne Rowden, Richard Seidman, Kashyapa Yapa, Cathy Zheutlin,

Appendix B: Acknowledgement of Influences

My friends know that I am a voracious reader of "science fiction" (I prefer the term "speculative fiction", since a lot of it has nothing to do with science.) Starting with *Dune* as a teenager and moving on to whatever is rattling around in my book bag right now, I've been regularly ingesting other people's views on what our future will look like.

My reason for reading it is simple: outside of science fiction writers, few people in this society spend much time thinking about our future. (While many people think about an aspect of the future, like the environment or social justice or energy, few pay attention to the whole thing.)

When it came time for me to make my own contribution to future thinking, how do I give proper credit to all who went before me, all who possibly influenced my writing? The answer: I can't. So, I hereby issue this

GENERAL DISCLAIMER:
Many of the concepts in the *Chronicles* series came from somewhere else. (ALL of the concepts, when you include Divine Inspiration.) Perhaps they came from your book. If so, thanks! (And sorry for not mentioning you by name.)

Primary Influences:

ANATHEM (Neal Stephenson): After *Dune*, my favorite book of speculative fiction. Monks and masters. A monastery that is not an artifact of religion. Young people "collected" into a community who eventually come to understand their role. An alternative to mainstream society...

EMERGENT (Stephen Baxter): This is THE book on what eusociality — "human hives" — could be like. Baxter based his speculations on some pretty solid science. I borrowed lots of ideas, including the shortened fertility cycles, pheromonal communications, underground living...

DUNE (Frank Herbert): The top of my list for the greatest science fiction book/series of all time. When I read *Dune* as a teenager, I identified with the young Paul Atreides, forced to grow into manfood under challenging circumstances. Like young Man-Onko, finding both shelter and opportunity in a very different community.

CHILDHOOD'S END (Arthur C. Clarke): Weird children, and what to do with them... "Evolution" is not a straight mechanical line... ask any butterfly. Other books with strange kids include *Beggars in Spain* by Nancy Kress and *Darwin's Children* by Greg Bear.

THE FOUNDATION SERIES (Isaac Asimov): Hari Seldon, the man with the plan... This series posits the notion that it is possible to take a LONG look at the forces changing society. Through Seldon's "psychohistory", we see what happens when the existing society, seemingly eternal and invulnerable, finally collapses. A very big concept: isolation will allow the alternative society to grow and mature to the point that it can compete for resources and consciousness with the declining society.

THE PARABLE OF THE SOWER (Octavia Butler): Written by the Grand Dame of Science Fiction, the late Octavia Butler got the gritty stuff of near-in dystopia depressingly accurate. Also: brain-dead politicians trying to land humans on Mars, while people starve in the streets and cannibals roam the hills...

THE MARS TRILOGY (Kim Stanley Robinson): This amazing series has an amazing premise: what would happen if you took 100 "normal" people and transport them to Mars... with limited resources and limitless possibilities? Why, they'd start FIGHTING, of course...

Were there other influences on "Chronicles"? Yes. And thanks to them all.

Appendix C: The Origin of the Series

There's one easy answer to where this book came from. It was a download (what more mystical people would call a revelation) while fasting in a cave at the 15,000-foot level in Ladakh, deep in the Himalayas. (I had a good friend ask the rhetorical question, "How many black guys from Camden, NJ can begin a sentence, 'While I was fasting in a cave in the Himalayas...?'" Probably not many...)

If you've ever had a "Divine Inspiration", you know what it felt like. If you haven't... I don't know how to describe it to you. One minute it wasn't there, and the next minute it was. The whole thing. Complete. The book feels like mine and also not-mine.

Getting the revelation took less than a minute. Writing it down took... just about three years. [That was the first book, *Upheavals*. *Awakening* took an additional five or six years...]

The first year was spent ignoring it. As it turned out, I received TWO books, right at the same time! And the second book (my working title is "The Ecstatic Society") felt more immediate to me. More in alignment with my usual writing style and content. It felt familiar. So, I dived into writing that book, and dabbled in the fiction at odd times and places.

Then, two years ago, "The Ecstatic Society" dried up, completely. No more juice. Like the Universe was saying that the fiction had to come FIRST, for some reason. (And who am I to question the Universe?)

Once I started writing *Chronicles* in earnest, a second challenge presented itself: where do I stop? The revelation came through as a glimpse of a complete world — the more I wrote, the more there was to write! When it started taking on the dimensions of *War and Peace*, I realized that *Chronicles* wasn't just one book, but a series. (That's given me a lot of relief! Instead of trying to get the whole thing right, I've just focused on getting the first one completed...)

Then, the next hurdle: what came through in the cave was a complete story, but it wasn't particularly ENGAGING. I was interested, because it was my revelation. Why would anyone else read it? Some of the timelines were absent or didn't make sense. There were lots of characters who were less than appealing. Settings were nonexistent. What to do?

So... while remaining true to the download, I've written a lot to improve the readability, continuity, engagement and flow of the book. (About 30%, for both books.)

Many of the chapters were written in response to people wondering how various issues would be handled inside of a transforming society. For example: when the "Occupy" phenomenon was occurring some years ago, a lot of questions quickly arose regarding security and discipline. How do you deal with negative and antisocial behavior, when violent control is not an option? How do you deal with issues of money and value... without falling into familiar patterns of greed and poverty? How about simple issues, like transportation... when energy is not available or reliable?

Once I got the format and a good idea of the timeline, the rest was filling in the blank spaces and lots (and lots...) of rewriting.

I've had some serious critical comments about some of the tone and tenor of the book, including:

Profanity: One commenter stated that, for some, profanity is as offensive as racist and sexist language. I tend to agree. And, I placed it in the story for the same reasons I would (and perhaps will) use racist and sexist language: to make the point. A street kid like Man-Onko, coming into the Awakening Center, is not going to be using language like "gosh" and "darn". The fact that the monks keep after him about his use of language, and his growing ability to be mindful in his language choices, makes the point without damaging the authenticity of the story.

Security: I've had many comments on the issue of how security plays out in the Awakening Centers. I've had strong pushback on how many chapters are devoted to "security" issues (as opposed to environmental, social, economic...). Even stronger were disagreements about the notion of dropping off adversaries in locations where there was a likelihood that they would be killed (the "Return to Kind" policy articulated in the chapter "A Lesson in Center Justice"). Finally: NO ONE agreed to the idea/concept of "mind-wiping" that pops up throughout the book. And yet, there are serious attempts at creating 'hive minds' going on right now. I know of five groups working on this, three of them in the United States.

First: each of these security concepts came from the initial download from the cave in Ladakh. Taking them out would mean not being true to the original impetus for the book. Second: when you struggle with the challenges posed by the Upheavals, you will quickly see that everything does revolve around security — get that wrong, and you won't be around to do anything else right.

I took my lesson for security issues in part from my friends at the Oregon Country Fair, an annual event that attracts 40,000+ people from around the world, all in various stages of festivity, nudity and inebriation. Their security is excellent... and nonviolent. (Some may argue that restraining the arms and legs of someone having a psychotic episode is an act of violence. I do not. Helping them not hurt themselves or others is the highest form of compassion.)

The Lessons: For me, every chapter is a potential lesson. If you disagree with how I presented it... great! Come up with your own solution to the challenge presented. Better yet: get together with your friends and associates (and maybe even a few "adversaries") to discuss solutions. In other words: feel free to join me in INVENTING THE FUTURE!

Peace,

Shariff M. Abdullah
July, 2016 and March, 2021

About the Author

DR. SHARIFF M. ABDULLAH is an award-winning author and advocate for inclusivity and societal transformation. Shariff's meta-vision and mission are simple: we can create a world that works for all beings.

Consultant and Trainer: As a consultant and trainer, Shariff has trained thousands of executives, managers and workers in the skills and techniques of authentic, effective leadership.

Wisdom Teacher: Shariff has been a sought-after speaker and teacher for Consciousness and Human Potential organizations, as well as several international forums.

Award-Winning Author: As an author, Shariff has written several paradigm-shifting books, including:

The Power of One: Authentic Leadership in Turbulent Times [New Society Publishers, (1990); New Catalyst Books (2007)]. This book makes the case for a new type of leadership and a new understanding of why we need it. This slim book has been referred to as "a revolution in consciousness", and has been in continuous print for over 25 years.

Creating a World That Works for All [Berrett-Koehler Publishers, 1999]. Winner of the "Book of the Year" award from the Independent Book Publishers Association, this comprehensive book makes the case for a global society based on the value of inclusivity: "We are One".

Seven Seeds for a New Society [Commonway Press, 2009]. Articulates the philosophy, theory and practice of a radically new way to envision society.

Practicing Inclusivity (with Leslie Hamilton) [CreateSpace Publishing, 2015]. A self-guided training workbook for inclusivity, Practicing Inclusivity is used by individuals, small groups and large organizations to develop greater degrees of inclusivity and connectedness.

Made in the USA
Middletown, DE
30 March 2021